I0576624

Edward Sylvester Ellis

The Camp Fires of General Lee

Edward Sylvester Ellis

The Camp Fires of General Lee

ISBN/EAN: 9783337255190

Printed in Europe, USA, Canada, Australia, Japan

Cover: Foto ©Andreas Hilbeck / pixelio.de

More available books at **www.hansebooks.com**

LEE AND JACKSON AT THE BATTLE OF COLD HARBOR.

THE

CAMP-FIRES OF GENERAL LEE,

FROM THE

Peninsula to Appomattox Court-House.

WITH REMINISCENCES OF THE MARCH, THE CAMP, THE
BIVOUAC AND OF PERSONAL ADVENTURE.

BY
EDWARD S. ELLIS,
AUTHOR OF "THE YOUNG PIONEER SERIES," "THE LOG CABIN SERIES," ETC.

PHILADELPHIA:
HENRY HARRISON & CO.

INTRODUCTION.

"THE CAMP-FIRES OF GENERAL LEE" aims to be a truthful narrative of the great part played by the Army of Northern Virginia under its illustrious commander in the most terrific campaigns of modern times. When the wounding of General Johnston, early in the war, compelled him to turn over his command to General Lee, the latter entered upon such a display of generalship that he speedily proved himself one of the foremost military leaders of the century. His campaigns represented the highest development of the science of war, and will command admiration for ages to come.

The history of those brilliant manœuvres, grand combinations and tremendous battles cannot be studied too closely by American youth. The incense wafted upward from Manassas, the Wilderness, Chancellorsville and Appomattox was the same, in truth, as that which was borne aloft from the fields of Bunker Hill, Monmouth, Trenton, Valley Forge and Yorktown, where Jerseymen and Virginians, South Carolinians and Green Mountain Boys, stood shoulder to shoulder in the struggle for liberty. The passions of the later days have departed, and those who arrayed themselves under the Stars and Bars are now among the most ardent defenders of the Union. None is quicker to give recognition of the valor of the Boy in Blue than he who wore the Gray. Brave men mutually respect each other, and no stronger ties of friendship can be formed than those that now bind together the different sections of the Union. We can, therefore, enjoy the fighting of the battles over again, each former opponent conceding the full meed of praise to the other and uttering nothing in malice. We have sought to give, so far as possible, a realistic narrative of those days by presenting pictures of the bivouac, the camp-fire and some of the numerous personal reminiscences of those engaged in the conflict.

In the preparation of these pages much assistance has been received from other histories and parties. Recognition is specially due Rev. J. William Jones, D. D., of Richmond, secretary of the Southern Historical Society, who placed many documents and papers at the author's disposal.

CONTENTS.

V.

THE CAMP-FIRE OF CHANCELLORSVILLE.

VI.

THE CAMP-FIRE OF GETTYSBURG.

VII.

THE SECOND CAMP-FIRE IN NORTHERN VIRGINIA.

VIII.

THE LAST CAMP-FIRE.

THE CAMP-FIRES OF GENERAL LEE.

THE CAMP-FIRES IN THE PENINSULA.

CHAPTER I.

ON THE CHICKAHOMINY.

"GENERAL, I am very glad to see you; I had hoped to meet you sooner."

"Yes; I was anxious to meet you, but it was impossible."

The two officers saluted each other, and the thousands of soldiers who witnessed the sight broke into tumultuous cheers.

The first speaker was Robert E. Lee, commander-in-chief of the Confederate armies. He was of striking appearance, sitting erect and graceful in his saddle, his grave, dignified countenance lighted up at the sight of his loved lieutenant. His full beard was rapidly turning gray, and the tremendous weight of the responsibility he carried on his shoulders was already seaming the handsome countenance with deep lines of care and anxiety.

General Lee wore the slouch hat which became so familiar in the years that followed, and the uniform of a major-general in the Confederate army, though its brilliancy was far less than that of many of his subordinate officers. He spoke in measured tones, with the reins of his fine steed resting idly in his left hand while he leaned over the saddle and grasped the palm of the other officer.

The latter formed a remarkable contrast to the illustrious leader of the Southern armies. He was clad in a dilapidated single-breasted coat of rusty gray, sun-scorched about the shoulders until it was almost yellow, and a faded cadet cap was tilted forward on his nose, while he bestrode a rickety sorrel horse and his stirrups were so short that his legs were drawn up in the most awkward position that can be imagined. He looked as if he was crouching behind the head of the animal and peeping at the enemy over his ears. His chief interest for the moment seemed to centre in a lemon, which he held in one hand and occasionally raised to his mouth while squeezing it with his fingers. His words, mumbled and jerked forth, sounded precisely the opposite of the measured, clearly-enunciated sentences of General Lee. His full beard swept over his breast, and the steel-blue eyes that peered out from under the flapping cap were as bright as stars. He was General T. J. Jackson, destined to be known for ever in history as " Stonewall " Jackson.

It was a very hot day in June, 1862, and while

the two men closed hands and spoke to each other the air around them throbbed with the roar of battle. Two mighty armies, those of the North and the South, were closing in the desperate grapple of infuriated giants. The officers paused and listened to the uproar. From the woods, where the divisions of Hill and Longstreet were engaged, came the long rattling roll of musketry, while from the direction of Stonewall Jackson's own troops the clamor was fiercer and more overpowering.

General Lee looked in the face of Jackson and in his measured voice remarked,

"That fire is very heavy; can your men stand it?"

The other stopped squeezing the lemon for the moment, though it was the most attractive delicacy he could raise to his lips, and, leaning his head to one side in a way peculiar to himself, listened like one who is straining to catch the sounds of music in the distance. General Lee was looking into the whiskered countenance and awaiting the reply. A moment later the bright eyes were turned toward him, and Jackson, with a nod of his head, spoke in his jerky fashion:

"My men can stand that; my men can stand almost anything."

General Lee hastily gave his instructions. Jackson saluted him, and, wheeling his ungainly steed around, galloped rapidly in the direction of his corps, which was so hotly engaged with the enemy, while the commander-in-chief remained at Cold Harbor, opposite the centre of the Federal army.

The situation early in March, 1862, was as follows: On the day succeeding the memorable fight between the Monitor and the Merrimac, General McClellan, an able officer, began a movement against the Confederates, then encamped near Manassas. Through the mud and rain the Unionists forced their way to the old Manassas battleground, only to find that the Confederates had abandoned the position the day before, taking with them all that was worth removing. General McClellan had long urged that the most feasible route to Richmond was by way of the Peninsula. President Lincoln finally yielded consent, and the Army of the Potomac was transported down the river to Fortress Monroe by a fleet of nearly four hundred vessels, and the second "On-to-Richmond" movement began. The army under the command of McClellan was a hundred thousand strong and one of the most magnificent organizations ever known. The officers and soldiers were full of enthusiasm; they had been well disciplined and trained for serious work, and all they asked was an opportunity to prove their courage and ability. McClellan made his way to Yorktown, where he found confronting him Magruder with a Confederate division of about five thousand men, exclusive of the garrisons with which he was guarding a line, thirteen miles long, extending across the Peninsula. The

Federal commander began digging, and enormous entrenchments were thrown up; ponderous guns were ordered from Washington; miles of corduroy road were built, and every preparation was made for an extended siege.

Meanwhile, General Joseph E. Johnston had reinforced the Confederates with his army from Manassas, and McClellan, having completed his most elaborate preparations, was ready to open fire. As he was about to do so he awoke to the fact that there were no Confederates in front of him, for General Johnston had withdrawn and taken position nearer Richmond. McClellan immediately started in pursuit. The Confederate rear-guard, reinforced shortly afterward by Longstreet's division, stationed themselves at Williamsburg, so as to gain time for the baggage-trains to get well in the rear of Fort Magruder, which with thirteen redoubts commanded all the roads leading northward.

Early on the morning of May 5, "Fighting Joe Hooker" arrived and began a furious attack, which lasted most of the day. The loss of the Union troops was heavy, but they remained on the ground, and prepared to renew the attack the next morning. When, however, daylight came, his adversary was invisible; for General Johnston, having accomplished his purpose, fell back, and was beyond reach. McClellan unopposed followed the Confederate army. The roads were frightful, and nearly

two weeks were consumed in marching less than
fifty miles. But the Unionists were alarmingly
close to the capital of the Confederacy. From
their camp they could look upon the spires and
steeples of Richmond, while every one within the
city plainly heard the sounds of firing in the entrenchments. Many of the inhabitants, believing
the city was doomed, fled, and the Confederate
Congress hastily adjourned.

The situation was most serious indeed. General
McDowell, who was at Fredericksburg with thirty
thousand men, was daily expected to join forces
with General Fitz-John Porter, who had captured
Hanover Court-House, and McClellan was evidently only awaiting the arrival of reinforcements
before making his final assault on Richmond.

General Joe Johnston understood the great peril
and skilfully parried it. The meteoric Stonewall
Jackson was sent out with a large force to threaten
Washington. He swept up the Shenandoah Valley
like a cyclone, captured Front Royal, sent General
Banks scurrying from Strasburg in terror toward
Washington, his panic-stricken men marching thirty-five miles in one day in order to place themselves
securely on the other side of the Potomac.

The appearance of Jackson so close to the national capital threw the Federal government into
the wildest excitement and alarm. The fear of
the capture of Washington was the incubus which
haunted the Union government for years. It was

that dread which palsied their military arm more than once and rendered harmless campaigns that otherwise would have been resistless in momentum. Whenever the Confederates found the Union army threatening Richmond, they created a diversion by threatening Washington.

The effect in this instance was all that was intended. The Union government immediately took possession of the railroads; troops were called from all quarters of the compass to protect the capital. Fremont at Franklin, Banks at Harper's Ferry and McDowell at Fredericksburg, with their sixty thousand men, were ordered to capture Jackson; but that dashing raider was as brilliant on the retreat as on the advance, and he dodged the overwhelming forces with the skill of a fox, doubling on his own trail, and without mishap rejoined General Johnston on the Peninsula.

Meanwhile, stirring events were taking place near Richmond. McClellan had pushed his left wing across the Chickahominy and taken possession of Seven Pines and Fair Oaks. The movement was hardly completed when a terrific storm came up, which overflowed the surrounding swamps and turned the stream into a roaring flood. Seizing the opportunity, General Johnston launched his army against McClellan's left wing, and would doubtless have captured it had not General Sedgwick's division of Sumner's corps crossed the Chickahominy on a tottering bridge and with a strong

2

battery of Napoleon guns plunged into the thickest of the fight and checked the Confederate advance. The Confederates were soon after driven back to Fair Oaks station, where, just at sunset, General Johnston was severely wounded by a shell, and, though the attack was renewed on the next morning, it was repulsed with little difficulty by McClellan.*

McClellan did not attempt to pursue the Confederates, and for nearly a month remained idle. During the three months which had elapsed since his arrival on the Peninsula the Confederates had improved, it may be said, every hour. They had passed their severe conscription law, enrolled their troops and gathered the largest force yet placed in the field.

* General Joseph Eccleston Johnston was one of the ablest officers of the Southern Confederacy. He was born in Virginia in 1807, graduated at West Point in 1829, and served in the Seminole war. During the Mexican war he served as captain of topographical engineers under General Scott in all the important actions, was twice wounded, and was brevetted colonel. In June, 1860, he became quartermaster-general, with the rank of brigadier-general. He commanded at Bull Run, and after recovering from his severe wound received at Seven Pines was assigned to the command of the Departments of Tennessee and Mississippi. After Bragg's defeat at Chattanooga he took command of his army, occupying a position at Dalton, Ga., which was turned by Sherman early in May, 1864; whereupon he fell back successively to Resaca, Allatoona Pass, Kenesaw Mountain and Atlanta, in turns fighting and being flanked by the much more powerful Federal army. He was superseded in July by General Hood. In February, 1865, he was assigned to the command of troops to oppose Sherman's march through the Carolinas. He fought a part of Sherman's army at Bentonville, N. C., on March 19, and surrendered the forces under his command to that general, April 26, at Durham's Station, near Greensboro', N. C. He published a *Narrative of Military Operations* in 1874.

General Robert E. Lee was assigned to the command of the Confederate army June 3, three days after General Johnston received his wound. Lee was anxious to strike the Union army a severe blow. To do so it was necessary to know the weakest and the strongest point of the enemy. This knowledge General Lee secured by means of Stuart's raid, which was one of the most brilliant exploits of the whole war.

CHAPTER II.

GENERAL STUART having secured the knowledge so important to General Lee, the latter decided to hurl his army against the Union right wing at Mechanicsville, while Jackson, who was daily expected from the Shenandoah, was to advance still farther to the left, cut off the Union base of supplies at White House, and then assail the rear. Stonewall Jackson terrified the authorities in Washington into summoning back General McDowell, who was on his way to reinforce McClellan, thus leaving the Union army in a condition to invite the attack, which was not delayed. As McClellan confidently expected McDowell, he had left his right wing comparatively unfortified, and that point, as was inevitable, was the one against which General Lee directed his assault.

McClellan knew that not only were the promised reinforcements denied him, but that the terrible Stonewall and his division were marching rapidly down the Shenandoah Valley in the direction of Richmond. Realizing his peril, he determined to abandon the York River Railroad and change

20

the base of supplies to James River, seventeen miles distant. To succeed in this important movement, it was necessary for the right wing to hold its position against all assaults until the rest of the army, with its forty miles of wagon-train, should pick its way through the White Oak Swamp; but before this movement began, General Lee had struck his blow. Generals A. P. Hill and Longstreet crossed the Chickahominy and attacked the Union right at Mechanicsville. A small Federal force behind entrenchments was soon dispersed and driven back toward Beaver Dam Creek. The Mechanicsville bridge being thus opened, General Longstreet, in obedience to Lee's orders, threw his division across the creek. Hill, who had pushed forward for a mile or two, found himself brought to a standstill by the powerful position of the Unionists on Beaver Dam Creek. Nevertheless, he advanced, but was met with such a determined resistance that he was obliged to fall back. It was beyond his power to cross the stream in the face of such a murderous discharge of musketry and cannon, and, night coming on, the attack ended for the time; but at daylight the impetuous Hill renewed the attempt to cross the stream, at a point lower down. While thus engaged the Federal troops were observed to be rapidly falling back from their almost impregnable position. This was caused by the arrival of Stonewall Jackson, who had passed around the right flank above and forced the Federals to fall back on the main army below. Hill moved steadily onward, and at noon was in front of the formidable position held by the Union army near Cold Harbor.

General McClellan had posted his army on a ridge along the southern bank of Powhite Creek, a small stream which empties into the Chicka-hominy below New Bridge. He had filled a deep ravine on his left with sharpshooters, while his right rested on elevated ground. His line of bat-tle curved backward and was protected by difficult approaches. The ground was covered with mat-ted undergrowth in 'some places, and was spongy and swampy in others. Breastworks of felled trees and of earth had been hurriedly thrown up, and behind them the vast lines of infantry, supported by artillery, confronted their assailants. Fitz-John Porter commanded the Union forces, with General Morell on his right and General Sykes on his left. Slocum's division, and afterward the brigades of French and Meagher, reinforced Por-ter, who coolly awaited the Confederate attack.

Hill opened about noon, and the battle which followed was desperate and bloody. So great was the anxiety of General Lee that in company with General Longstreet he had ridden from his head-quarters, on the Nine-Mile road, and now watched in person the behavior of his troops under fire. His coolness, his serene and majestic presence, in the swirl of the conflict were like those of the great Von Moltke, whose placid face never flushed and who felt not an additional pulse-throb when he saw the French empire crumbling into nothingness at Sedan before the advance of the Prussian eagles.

Hill assaulted the Federal lines with that dash and daring so characteristic of him, but he made no more impression than if he had charged against the side of a granite mountain. The Federal artillery did dreadful execution, and the infantry poured a merciless fire into the Confederate lines; but so impetuous was the rush of the assailants that three of Hill's regiments reached the crest of the hill, where the Union troops were stationed, and for a brief while the fight was hand to hand. But it was all in vain; mortal man could not stand the fiery sirocco that swept the earth, and the Confederates were forced to give way after two hours' hard fighting, having met with great loss and accomplished but little.

Meanwhile, General Lee was listening for the sound of Stonewall Jackson's guns; but nothing was heard, and the situation became critical. Lee, with his masterly genius, grasped every detail and fully appreciated the peril which threatened him. He saw that McClellan would probably send enough reinforcements to Fitz-John Porter to enable him to attack him in turn, or, knowing how small was the force defending Richmond, might overwhelm it and make a hurried march against the city.

Longstreet was sent to the relief of Hill, and he advanced under a fierce fire to make a feint upon the Union left. While thus engaged he caught the thunderous roar of guns and heard the tumultuous shouting on the left of Lee's line. He knew what it meant: Stonewall Jackson had arrived. Having hurled his troops into action, Jackson galloped to Cold Harbor, where General Lee was so anxiously awaiting him; and when they met, the scene took place with which our first chapter opened.

Generals Lee and Jackson having hastily formed their plans, the latter dashed back to his command, and instantly a great change took place in every part of the field. Whiting and a portion of Jackson's old division quickly moved to the right to support Longstreet and to take position between him and the remnants of A. P. Hill's division. As soon as these and a few other movements were completed General Lee ordered an attack along the whole line, and in a few minutes the long stretch between Cold Harbor and the muddy Chickahominy was aflame with fire, and the earth quivered with the shock of the contending armies. Porter's troops were worn out with their five hours of fighting, but the rattle of musketry and the roar of cannon roused them again as a giant is roused by new wine. Their artillery was reinforced, and converged wherever the Confederate battalions gleamed through the smoke and mists of battle. On the right, near McGee's farm, the cannoneers found the Confederates at the very throats of their cannon. The assailants fell in swaths, but others seemed to spring from the ground, and many cannoneers were driven from their guns; but they rushed back the next minute to recapture the pieces. Ewell was pounding away between McGee's farm and New Cold Harbor, but for a time without result. Seeing his straits, Jackson sent three brigades of his old division against the wood of New Cold Harbor. This was the weakest point of the whole Federal line, and it was assailed with the fierceness of so many tigers. The Federals made a brave defence, but were compelled to fall back. Their ammunition ran low, and they were in the last stages of exhaustion. In the narrow angle of the wood where artillery could not be used the soldiers fought singly, striking at a foe wherever found, and the conflict became blind, aimless, and, indeed, useless. At this critical moment, as the sun was sinking in the hot summer sky, Stonewall Jackson dashed up with his last reserves and ordered a general attack.

There could be but the one result. General Hood and his fiery Texans charged the Federal left with an impetuosity which carried everything before it. All in vain did the Federal artillery converge its fire upon them. As the men went down before the iron sleet the ranks closed up, and never a man faltered. Halting only long enough to fire, they rushed forward with their wild yells until the cannon were reached. The artillery-horses, wild with terror, galloped away, and the artillerymen who remained behind were trampled under the feet of the furious legions from the Lone Star State. Far over on the extreme left Longstreet had carried forward a similar movement. The Unionists fought bravely, but were compelled to give way, though they saved most of their guns and were able to check Longstreet's movement toward Alexander Bridge. But the Confederates were conquering everywhere. Two Federal regiments, while fighting like heroes in the woods near Cold Harbor, found themselves completely surrounded, and the greater number were killed or wounded. The survivors were forced to surrender. Ewell and D. H. Hill succeeded in planting their artillery on the summit of the hill held so long by Sykes's division, which was crushed by the fire.

The retreat of the Federals on the left and centre threatened to become a disastrous rout, and the situation of the Army of the Potomac was critical in the highest degree. Only a single passage remained by which they could make their way to the other side of the Chickahominy. If that were seized by the Confederates, the Army of the Potomac would be blotted out as though it had never existed. The North would receive a blow likely to prove mortal, and one which would shake every town, village and hamlet in the country to its very centre. But not yet. The terrific efforts of the

Confederates had exhausted them, and they halted to reform their lines. Night was closing in, and there came a lull in the fearful tumult, when the combatants on each side were able to halt and learn the condition of affairs.

The losses on each side were frightful. Thirty-five thousand Federals were engaged, of whom one-fifth were killed or wounded. The loss of the Confederates was fully as great, but they had gained a victory of transcendent importance. They had captured many guns and prisoners and checked the advance upon Richmond, which a short time before looked as if it were to be irresistible. The magnificent Army of the Potomac, trained to the highest point, finely disciplined, thoroughly armed and under the command of skilful officers, not only filled the hearts of the North with hope, but caused the gravest alarm throughout the South. From elevated positions in Richmond men could look off with their glasses and plainly see the Union soldiers at work in their entrenchments, and the "Stars and Bars" seemed to be intertwined, as may be said, with the Stars and Stripes which floated above the besieging forces.*

---

* Respecting the flag adopted by the Confederacy, General Joe Johnstone said a short time since:

"At the battle of Manassas—you Northerners call it Bull Run—the Stars and Bars proved a failure because they were so much like the Union colors. Indeed, both armies mistook their enemies for friends, and *vice versâ*. After the battle I had resolved to discard this flag, and called for each regiment to produce its State colors. This they were

We have alluded to the consternation in Richmond when it was found that the Unionists were hammering at the very gates of the city. The Confederate Congress hastly adjourned, President Davis sent his family farther south, and there were general preparations on the part of all to move. But all was now changed. Under the splendid leadership of Lee and his skilled and intrepid lieutenants, the army of invasion had been hurled backward; its grip upon the throat of the South had been shaken off, and it was seeking affrightedly for some path of escape from the wrath of its master. The enormous importance of the Confederate victory was moral rather than physical, for, in point of fact, the victory itself was not complete.

The severe fighting at Gaines's Mill and the inaction of the Federals on the other side of the Chickahominy led General Lee to think that he had engaged and defeated the larger part of the Army of the Potomac, and that McClellan was so environed by difficulties and dangers that he would be forced to surrender his entire command. Thus it came about that, while on the north side of the Chickahominy thirty thousand Union troops were assailed by twice as many Confederates, twenty-

not able to do, and I asked the army for new designs. Among those presented, one by General Beauregard was chosen, and I altered this only in making it square instead of oblong. This flag was afterward adopted by the Confederate armies. It was a Greek cross of blue on a red field, with white stars on the blue bars. The flag was designed by a Colonel Walton, of Louisiana, and presented to General Beauregard."

five thousand Confederates on the south side held in check more than twice as many Unionists.

While Lee was quietly preparing to capture the Army of the Potomac on the morrow, that army was making desperate efforts to gather itself together and flee from under the avalanche about to fall upon it. Generals, colonels, captains and subordinate officers were hunting up their men and putting companies and regiments in shape; privates were rushing hither and thither in the effort to find where they belonged; the sick and wounded received scant attention, but it was the best that could be given under the circumstances; the dead, who were stretched everywhere, were scarcely thought of, for what avail was it to give them any care? There was but the single overwhelming desire, "How shall we escape the crouching tiger that is gathering his muscles for the fatal leap?"

When men are intent on flight, little time is required to make preparation. The sultry summer night had no more than fairly closed in when the head of the long line of fugitives debouched from the wood and began tramping across the Alexander bridge. A squadron of cavalry had held it during the day, so as to turn back the panic-stricken Federals who might seek to escape. Hour after hour the swarming multitude tramped over the bridge, until in the small hours of the morning the last wounded man and the last cannon were safely across the stream. The regulars were the last over, and they immediately turned about and destroyed the splendid structure that had served them so well.

While this mournful procession was passing, General McClellan and his leading officers were gathered together near the south entrance to the bridge, holding a council of war. The countenance of the youthful commander was grave and he talked in guarded and serious tones. The firelight which fell on the faces of the others showed they fully appreciated the gravity of the situation. The splendid Army of the Potomac was beaten, and what should be done?

This memorable conference was marked by a most extraordinary incident: McClellan, the embodiment of caution and hesitation, suddenly astounded his officers by the proposal to capture Richmond while the main body of its defenders were too far away to offer any defence. His officers, however, had little difficulty in dissuading their leader from the project. One cannot but speculate as to what would have been the outcome of such an achievement. Unquestionably, McClellan could have taken the city, and a most remarkable complication would have followed. He, in turn, would have been besieged by the Confederates and cut off from his supplies, and, with the country around him intensely hostile, could not have sustained himself very long. But the very hour it was known that McClellan was in Richmond the Federal government would have poured forward reinforcements to his assistance; then, in all probability, Stonewall Jackson might have dashed into the national capital with his daring raiders and thrown everything into confusion. However, all this is but conjecture, and, as such a condition of affairs can never occur again, it is idle to continue the thought. It may be added that General Lee more than once seriously considered the expediency of "swapping queens," or trading capitals, and it is a most interesting question as to what would have been the result had the extraordinary trade ever been made. But McClellan was soldier enough to understand that a retreat was necessary and a change of base had become inevitable. His connections had been severed, and his only hope now was the James River, where the Union gunboats could keep the Confederates at a safe distance.

On the night following the battle Lee sent this telegram to Richmond:

"HEADQUARTERS IN THE FIELD, June 27, 1862.

"HIS EXCELLENCY, PRESIDENT DAVIS—

"MR. PRESIDENT: Profoundly grateful to Almighty God for the signal victory granted us, it is my pleasing task to announce to you the success achieved by this army to-day.

"The enemy was this morning driven from his strong position behind Beaver Dam Creek and pursued to that behind Powhite Creek, and, finally, after a severe contest of five hours, entirely repulsed from the field.

"Night put an end to the contest. I grieve to state that our loss in officers and men is great.

"We sleep on the field, and shall renew the contest in the morning.

"I have the honor to be, very respctfully,

"(Signed)   R. E. LEE, General."

It was impossible that Lee should know the intentions of McClellan. The latter might give battle with a view of preserving his communications; he might retreat down the Peninsula or down the James. The Confederate chieftain could only wait until McClellan's movements were developed. That he should be compelled to do so was a great disadvantage, but there was no help for it. He did all that was possible. Ewell's division was sent to seize the York River Railroad, and Stuart, with his cavalry, was ordered to co-operate with him. Reaching Dispatch Station, the Federals retreated across the river, and Ewell, after destroying a part of the railroad, awaited further orders.

Looking southward through the shimmering air, Lee saw vast clouds of dust rolling upward toward the sky. There could be no mistaking the meaning: the Army of the Potomac was retreating. Lee suspected that McClellan intended to escape down the Peninsula; accordingly, he sent orders to Ewell to move from Dispatch Station to Bottom's Bridge, on the road connecting Richmond and Williamsburg, with a view of checking McClellan if he attempted to cross the Chickahominy at that point. Discovering no sign that such was McClellan's intention, Ewell joined Jackson on the following day.

General Ewell, in the mean time, had pushed down the road to the White House in quest of the Federals; but they were gone, and his errand was bootless. McClellan conducted the retreat in masterly style; and when morning came, the condition of his army was infinitely improved over that of the previous evening. Lee, having satisfied himself that the Unionists were making for the James River, saw the important advantage they had gained by the skill with which McClellan had masked the movement. The Federals were so far on their way and in such good form that it was impossible to turn their retreat into the rout that had been intended. Stuart's cavalry, which could have rendered such effective service in harassing the Federals, had penetrated so far in the Peninsula that it may be said it was lost for the time, inasmuch as it did not reappear during the campaign. Ewell's soldiers, who returned during the night, were so exhausted that they were as helpless as logs until they could procure a few hours' sleep.

All through the night the vast trains of the Army of the Potomac were plodding steadily forward toward White Oak Swamp. They had gained twenty-four hours which were of inestimable importance, and they improved them to the utmost. The bridge in front of Frazier's farm had been reopened, and General Keyes, with his two divisions, had encamped at Glendale, near Nelson's farm. There he remained to cover the retreat of the army through the gloomy morass. The wagons, five thousand in number, and a drove of twenty-five hundred cattle passed safely over the single road, and in the stifling heat of the next day they pushed steadily toward the James.

It was a sad and pitiful sight. The ambulances were overcrowded with the sick and wounded, whose white bandaged faces sometimes peered out upon the moving figures or dropped back with groans of anguish when the jolting of the vehicle made the pain of their wounds greater than they could bear. Others had crawled out of the hospital and were tottering along as best they could; but many a poor fellow had overestimated his strength, and, giving out, dropped by the wayside, waiting for the Confederates to hold the canteen to his fevered lips and to gather him in with the hundreds of prisoners already taken. Unto many a boy in blue, as he lay gasping by the roadside, Death was kind enough to steal forward and close his eyes in the last, long sleep, while the thoughts of the dying soldier wandered away to his Northern home, where father and mother, brother and sister, and perhaps sweetheart, would look longingly for the form that they should never see again. It was the same with the ardent Southerner who had left his loved ones in such high spirits and with such proud hopes of the triumph that awaited the cause so dear to his heart. The terrible missiles of war know no discrimination, and the bullet crashing through the brain, the shell rending limb and body, stretched many and many a brave Confederate low. Far to the southward, in the Carolinas, in Georgia and the Gulf States, the long lists of the dead would be scanned through blinding tears and with bated breath by their friends searching for the name they dreaded to find.

Ah! how often it was found! and how again and again the roll of the fallen should grow and expand until the despairing ones should feel that Death would never be content until all were taken!

> "By fairy hands their knell is rung,
> By forms unseen their dirge is sung:
> There Honor comes, a pilgrim gray,
> To bless the turf that wraps their clay,
> And Freedom shall awhile repair
> To dwell a weeping hermit there."

CHAPTER III.

THE LINE OF BATTLE.

IT was on the morning of June 29 that Lee, having learned that McClellan was retreating toward the James, pushed forward his columns in pursuit. Magruder and Huger hurried over the Williamsburg and Charles City roads, Longstreet and A. P. Hill made for the New Bridge crossing of the Chickahominy, while Jackson, having crossed at Grapevine Bridge, aimed to strike the Federals along the south bank of the Chickahominy.

A somewhat curious complication resulted from the following situation. Sumner was not long in discovering that the Confederates were recrossing the Chickahominy and advancing upon Savage Station. Accordingly, he moved his corps from the position it had held at Allen's farm to that place, where he was joined by a portion of Franklin's corps. Heintzelman, who held position on the left of Sumner, had been directed to hold the Williamsburg road, but he fell back and crossed White Oak Swamp, while Sumner moved to Savage Station. Thus it came about that when Magruder advanced on the Williamsburg road he found no Federals to fight, while Sumner, unaware of Heintzelman's withdrawal, was astonished to discover the enemy in his front at Savage Station. Under these circumstances took place the battle of Savage Station, on the afternoon of Saturday, June 29, 1862.

The advance of the Confederates was by the Williamsburg road and along the railroad-track, preceded by an engine which drew an iron-plated car on which was mounted a heavy gun. This contrivance was more unique than effective. The engine would steam slowly along for a short distance, and then stop until the gunners within the turret of the land-monitor fired the piece. It sent the ponderous ball whirring over the country, but there is no record that it ever succeeded in striking any one.

About the middle of the afternoon the Signal Corps apprised the Federals that the Confederates were advancing. Smith had barely time to throw Hancock's brigade on Richardson's right and to extend his line to a thicket, while Brooks's brigade was sent to the extreme left. Magruder, quick to see the gap made by the withdrawal of Heintzelman, precipitated McLaws's and his own division against the most vulnerable part of the Federal line. His attack was made with his usual impetuosity and reckless bravery, when grim old Sumner arrived in the nick of time. He was able to check Magruder while Brooks re-established the battle-line on that side.

The Confederates were in high spirits, and, re-membering the splendid victory they had won at Gaines's Mill, fought with the most heroic valor, determined to deliver a telling blow upon the Federals before night could come to their relief. They saw that McClellan was conducting his re-treat with such skill that it was more than prob-able he would extricate his army, and they desired to make it cost him dear. The battle raged along the whole line until sunset. The Union lines gave way again and again under the fierce charges of their assailants, but they were reformed as often, and even the fiery courage of Magruder and his men could not effect a lasting breach in the ranks of the Federals.

And where, all this time, was Stonewall Jack-son? Ah! if he had swept down on the flank, as was his wont, with those yells that so often struck terror to the hearts of the Federals, the latter must have given way and been scattered like chaff in the hurricane. But Jackson the indomitable was still working at the bridge over which he was to cross the Chickahominy. Had that been rebuilded in time, he would have come down like a thunder-bolt; but, despite all the energy he could put forth, it was not completed until after the shades of night were closing in, when he and his soldiers hurried across. They were too late to hurl themselves on the foe, the roar of whose cannon was in their ears.

General Sumner wished to hold the ground he

had defended with such valor, but the demand for a contraction of the lines was imperative. General McClellan ordered his withdrawal, and just as it was growing light on the following morning his men resumed their march, the last brigade destroying the bridge which carried them over.

Full credit must not be denied McClellan for the masterly manner in which he conducted the retreat. If the spongy ground, matted with undergrowth and covered at intervals with trees, rendered the passage by his men difficult, it served them the inestimably good turn of making the pursuit by Lee equally hard to execute; and, on the other hand, had a general of less skill than McClellan been employed to save the immense army, he must have failed. He had succeeded in placing the White Oak Swamp between him and Lee, and he had brought off his cannon and saved his rear-guard from rout.

At daylight the approaches to White Oak Bridge and Frazier's farm were occupied by the Federals, while the Charles City road and Porter's former position beyond Glendale were covered. Keyes, with Porter close behind him, led the retreat of the army, and reached the James River early in the day; but, so far as McClellan was concerned, they were entirely lost to him. They had been detained on the way, and had sent no messenger to him. Even the topographical engineers sent out by the Federal commander had not reported, and he could only trust to the intelligence of his lieutenants to extricate themselves from the peril in which they might become involved.

General Keyes made a most fortunate discovery while retreating with his division. He came upon an old unused road leading toward the James, which was easily reopened, and which, running parallel to the one he was following, enabled him effectually to protect his long train against attack. It is difficult for one who has never witnessed such a movement to form a just idea of its magnitude. When Keyes halted on the banks of the James, the Army of the Potomac extended backward nearly ten miles. Long as was this line, and impossible as it was to defend every portion of it, yet the necessity of protecting the train forbade its shortening; for it would have been fatal to leave the passage of White Oak Swamp open to the Confederates.

The situation of the Union army may be understood from the following statement: From the passage out of the White Oak Swamp the highway runs southward to the James River, nine miles or so distant. The Union army was strung along this road on its way to Haxall's Landing, where it was seeking the protection of the gunboats. The White Oak pass, crossing a tributary of the Chickahominy, marked the termination of the famous White Oak Swamp, through which McClellan had forced his way, fighting as he went. This pass

was the only one over which the Confederates could
follow in direct pursuit of the fleeing Unionists.
The supreme importance of its being held by the
latter is therefore apparent to all, for the fate of
their army depended upon its defence.

Following the retreating Federals southward
some two or three miles, the next point from
which the Confederates could assault them was
reached. This was Glendale, where the highways
from Richmond converge. It may be said that
all the roads leading southward from Richmond
between the James and the Chickahominy draw
together at Glendale like the converging spokes
of a wheel; consequently, it required to be fortified against the Confederate assault that was certain to come. Continuing southward, the next
exposed point was Malvern Hill, just north of
Haxall's Landing, the haven of refuge to the
distressed Unionists. This was in direct communication with Richmond by the Newmarket road,
which sent off a spur to the northward to Glendale. It was sure to receive attention from Lee,
though it was the least inviting of the three points,
its natural strength being very great.

Having shown the only places where the Unionists were liable to be attacked, let us now see what
means McClellan took to protect them against his
enemy.

The Union commander visited all the threatened
points and personally directed the movements for

defence.   Keyes occupied the space between the
James at Turkey Bend on one side and Malvern
Hill on the other, Porter taking up a strong position on the same hill.   Franklin was stationed at
the pass of White Oak Swamp, near Frazier's
farm, with orders to defend it to the last, though
that officer understood its value too well to require
any urgency about the matter.   All the remaining
troops were placed in position at Glendale.

Such being the disposition of the Union troops,
let us see what was done by Lee.   None realized
more clearly than he the necessity of striking a
crushing blow with the least possible delay.   He
had confidently expected to capture the Army of
the Potomac, and now it was slipping through his
fingers.   Once on the bank of the James under
the protection of the gunboats, it would be as safe
against his utmost efforts as if lost in the woods
of Maine.   But tremendous obstacles were in the
path of the Confederate chieftain.   He and his
lieutenants had never dreamed that the scene of
the struggle would be shifted to that portion of
the Peninsula, and they were more ignorant of
the topography of the country than the Federals.
It is even stated that Lee was unable to procure
a county-map by which to guide his movements.
While the vast morass known as White Oak
Swamp offered such a secure protection to the
flank of the retreating army, it was utterly impassable for Lee except along the avenues already

pointed out; consequently, he was forced to divide his army into several divisions, which, under the peculiar character of the country, were unable to communicate with one another or to effect a junction after the defeat of the Federals. Stonewall Jackson, with four divisions, pressed eagerly forward through the White Oak Swamp with the determination of forcing the passage which Franklin had been ordered to defend to the last extremity; Hill and Longstreet were hurrying down from Richmond along the highways which debouched at Glendale into the road over which the Unionists were retreating; Magruder was immediately behind them, and was to form the right in the attack; while Wise's Legion and other troops posted on the James were directed to make all haste down the banks of that river, with the object of seizing and fortifying Malvern Hill before it could be occupied by the Federals.

Such were Lee's plans, and now let us see in what manner they were carried out.

CHAPTER IV.

THE LAST BATTLES.

STONEWALL JACKSON reached the pass of White Oak Swamp shortly before noon, and found Franklin strongly posted and awaiting him. The Federal commander had improved his time well, and had some eight or ten batteries posted to cover the passage, while the infantry, consisting of nine brigades, were drawn up in line of battle.

Jackson's force was much larger than that of the Federals—besides his four divisions, he had twenty batteries—and yet it was utterly out of his power to use his men with any advantage. There was but the single defile, the swamp on his right and left being almost as impassable as the rapids below Niagara. If he advanced, it must be along that narrow passage commanded by the guns of Franklin. Daring as was the Confederate leader, his military instinct caused him to shrink from the terrible attempt. To throw his men into that narrow defile was only to invite their slaughter, and, though the rank and file would have shrank at no risk for their beloved leader, they could not be expected do that which was impossible. But

Jackson knew the penalty of delay. His force formed the strongest half of the Confederate army, and while it stood waiting on the borders of White Oak Swamp the Unionists were making good their escape. They needed but little more time in which to place themselves beyond his reach. Stonewall Jackson was not the man to stand idle in the face of any danger, no matter how great. Several of his batteries were drawn up above the pass with the object of silencing the Union guns before the decisive charge should be made by his infantry. For a time it appeared as if Jackson was to succeed in his purpose. A couple of Union batteries were silenced and most of the guns destroyed by the projectiles. The situation was a hopeful one for the assailants, when Franklin opened with his rifled ten-pounders, which were placed so far back as to be almost beyond range of Jackson's guns. They inflicted great injury upon the Confederates.

All this time the infantry on both sides were under arms, expecting the battle to open. They were glaring across the pass at each other, chafing with fury and suffering severely from the artillery. So soon as the Union guns could be silenced the Confederate battle-yell would make the welkin ring, and they would swarm through the narrow passage as though rushing "to a festival."

But, despite the utmost efforts, the Union batteries were not silenced. The precious hours slipped by, and the boom of cannon to the south-

ward told Jackson how sorely he was needed there.
His daring soul chafed at the enforced delay, but
there was no help for it. He was not the one to
lose his head in any crisis, no matter how trying.
No temptation could induce him to make such an
assault as that of "Bob Toombs" a few days before
at Golding's farm, where the only thing accomplished was the loss of a large number of men and
a renewed proof of the fact that a man is pretty
certain to prove his ridiculous incompetency on
the very first opportunity.

Hour after hour passed; the flaming sun beat
down on the soldiers all through the sultry afternoon, and the cannon roared and boomed. Men
shrieked and many were torn to pieces, and still
the opposing forces glared at each other, awaiting
the order to leap at each other's throats. But
when darkness began creeping through the woods,
the situation was unchanged. The Confederates
remained on the borders of the swamp and had
not made a single attempt to force their way.
Thus the most formidable leader in the Confederate army, with about half the army itself, was
held at bay all day, when his presence at Glendale,
a few miles northward, would have overwhelmed
the Federals. The powerful left wing of Lee's
army was paralyzed, and no word could be sent
to or received from it.

Some two or three hours after the arrival of Jackson in front of Franklin, Longstreet and A. P. Hill

reached Glendale, the second point exposed to attack from the Confederates. They had nearly twenty thousand men, under the leadership of the foremost generals in the service. McCall's division, in the centre, was the first to receive their charge. He had arranged his soldiers in two lines, with Meade on the right, Seymour on the left, Reynolds's brigade in reserve, and his front protected by five batteries.

The Confederates, by way of introduction, dropped several scores of shells among the Unionists, and then charged with their wonted dash and vigor. McCall's division had borne the brunt of the preceding day's fighting, and they were in sore need of rest; but they fought valiantly, and repelled the first assault. Seymour and Meade were quickly assaulted in succession by the Confederates, who were searching for the weakest point in the line of defence. Hill quickly found it, in the shape of an open breach between McCall's division and Hooker's, and he immediately attempted to turn them one after the other. Hooker found himself assailed with such fury that he was forced to bring up all his reserves and a regiment from Sumner's corps to the help of Grover, commanding the First Brigade. Still farther to the right, Seymour's left wing, consisting of Seymour's brigade and a couple of German batteries from the reserve artillery, were attacked with the same impetuosity. The gunners were put to flight, and

the rest, finding themselves between two fires, ran
pell-mell back toward Hooker's brigade. The latter parted, so as to allow them to pass through their
ranks, and then, closing up, delivered a murderous fire upon the Confederates, who in the ardor
of their charge had become somewhat separated
from one another. Two of Hooker's regiments
drove Longstreet's men at the point of the bayonet upon McCall's brigades, who in return
received them with a hot fire.

Meanwhile, Sedgwick had received reinforcements from Franklin, at White Oak Swamp, who
found he had no need for so many men. They
quickly occupied the space vacated by Seymour's
disorganized troops, and the line of battle was
restored, though the Federals had lost considerable ground. But the valiant Confederates were
not dismayed, and continued the assault with their
old-time vigor. Swerving off from the line held by
Sedgwick and Hooker, they concentrated against
McCall's right and Kearny's left. The latter was
able to hold his own, but McCall gave way. Near
sunset the Fifty-fifth and Sixtieth Virginia made
a furious charge on Randol's regular battery, near
Meade. The assailants, trailing their muskets in
one hand and assuming the form of a > went
across the open space on the double quick, yelling
like so many madmen. The grape was poured
into the singular formation, and the Virginians
dropped thick and fast; but the gigantic human

wedge came with the speed of a whirlwind straight for the guns, and nothing could stay it. The gunners were killed, the cannon captured, and Meade was forced to fall back. Within less than an hour another charge captured Cooper's battery, in the centre of McCall's line, but after a furious struggle the Ninth Pennsylvania retook it, and the Confederates were forced to abandon Randol's battery.

The sun was low in the horizon, and the sounds of battle began to die out. Hill and Longstreet, with their two splendid divisions, had done some of the finest fighting ever seen, but they had attempted impossibilities. From the northward came the sullen roar of Jackson's cannon, where, as we have shown, he was held all through the day by Franklin. Magruder ought to have appeared on the field of battle long before, but remained unaccountably absent. The Confederate army was cut in twain, and there was no means of bringing the wings together. Believing the Unionists had more than sufficient reserves within call, Hill and Longstreet gave up the ground they had won, in order to extricate and gather their forces together.

Having shown the results of the Confederate demonstration against the upper and central points of the Union line, it only remains to narrate what took place on the extreme south, at Malvern Hill, on the bank of the James.

4

Wise's Legion, as we have already stated, had run a race down the James in the hope of reaching and occupying Malvern Hill ahead of the Unionists; but, having started too late, they arrived too late, and while pushing vigorously forward suddenly came against Porter's division, posted on Malvern Hill. The Confederates were at immense disadvantage, and, though they made a brave attack, it was not successful.

Several gunboats were waiting at Haxall's Landing, and General McClellan had gone on board the Galena with a view of making a reconnoissance up the river. The Galena sent a few of its Parrott hundred-pound shells into the woods in quest of the Confederate reserves. Little actual damage was done, but the terrific racket made by the awful missiles as they shattered the trees right and left produced its effect on the assailants, and, being recognized by the Unionists tramping wearily southward toward the river, filled them with the joy which comes to the shipwrecked mariner when at last he sees the friendly sail approaching.

Hour after hour the dreadful retreat continued. Every hut and cabin by the wayside was turned into a hospital, and the surgeons, with coats and vests off and sleeves rolled up, worked through the stifling heat until the perspiration streamed from them and they were scarcely able to move from exhaustion. Over the long, wearisome miles the sick, wounded and well soldiers straggled toward the James. Sometimes the drivers of the teams were thrown into a panic by the shelling and firing, and a general smash-up of everything threatened; but among the disorganized multitude there were cool heads and stern wills who kept matters in tolerably fair shape. The sight of the gleaming James as it wound peacefully southward on its way to the sea was delight unspeakable to the Federals, and never were famishing pilgrims so overjoyed at sight of the haven of refuge toward which they had been struggling so long.

The battle of Glendale was one of the fiercest of the war. It was inconclusive, though the Confederates took the most trophies. Among their prisoners was General McCall, who was captured while wandering through the woods in quest of his lost command; but before sunset on the 30th of June the last vehicle of the almost interminable wagon-train reached Malvern Hill, where vigorous preparations were under way to repel the assault sure to be made very soon.

The configuration of the James at Haxall's Landing is such that the Union forces could not remain there. The stream becomes so narrow above City Point that vessels on their way to Haxall's were exposed to batteries along the bank which were capable of sinking them. Harrison's Landing, therefore, was selected as the most favorable point for the establishment of dépôts for the army.

The wagon-train having safely reached Hax-

all's, the necessity no longer existed for holding
the positions at the outlet of White Oak Swamp
and Glendale. Franklin, at the former, began
withdrawing in the evening, and the troops at
Glendale did the same. The movement continued
through the hot, sultry night, and at daylight the
next morning the whole Federal army was concentrated around Malvern Hill, which was placed in
the best possible condition for defence.

Malvern Hill is an elevated plateau about three-
fourths of a mile wide and twice as long. McClellan's left and centre were posted on the hill, the
right curving backward through the woods toward a point on the James below Haxall's Landing.
Believing that Lee's main attack would be directed against his left, McClellan posted heavy masses
of infantry and artillery on Malvern Hill. Porter's corps held the left, the artillery, including
the reserve, amounting to sixty guns. The gunboats on the James covered the left flank.

General Lee had determined to make a most
formidable attack on the Army of the Potomac
before it got beyond the reach of his terrible forces.
He was under greater disadvantage than earlier in
the campaign, but his grim resolution was never
affected by the danger which impended. The last
battle of the Peninsula was at hand.

The concentration of the Union army had enabled Lee to unite the wings of his own army.
The powerful division under Jackson, held power-

less so long at the passage from White Oak Swamp,
was released, and at last the whole Confederate
army was gathered together for a furious onslaught.
Lee's line was formed with Jackson's divisions on
the left and those of Magruder and Huger on
the right. Longstreet and A. P. Hill formed the
reserve, on the left, and took no part in the engagement. The ground was so unfavorable for
manœuvring that the afternoon was half gone
before the line of battle was completed. Then Anderson's brigade of D. H. Hill's division attacked
Couch, but was obliged to fall back. The movement was a feeler, as may be said, the intention
of Lee being to storm the plateau of Malvern on
the left. He had massed the troops of Jackson,
Magruder and Huger, therefore, on his right.
Before making a demonstration Lee issued an
order stating that he had selected his positions so
that his artillery could silence that of the Unionists, and that as soon as it was done Armistead's
brigade of Huger's division would dash forward
with a shout and carry the battery directly in
front of them. Lee was sure the shout would be
heard by every one on his right. He therefore
announced that the outcry was to be the signal
for an advance all along the line; the instant it
was made all the troops were to rush forward
with fixed bayonets.

About six o'clock in the afternoon General D.
H. Hill was talking with his brigade command-

ers, when a thunderous shout fell upon their ears. They stopped speaking, listened and looked significantly at each other.

"That's the signal!" exclaimed General Hill, and the others expressed the same opinion.

Without an instant's delay the advance was ordered, but there was either a mistake of the signal or the other divisions failed to hear it; for when Hill advanced, he did so alone. Neither Whiting nor Magruder nor Huger stirred, while the splendid division of the gallant Hill dashed against the tier upon tier of batteries trained upon them. There could be but one result. The immense advantage was on the side of the Federals, who mowed down the Confederates in winrows. They pushed forward with the most desperate valor, only to be driven back again and again, until the plain 'was strewn with the dead and dying. Magruder and Huger afterward advanced to the support of the decimated force, but they did so in such a disjointed fashion that they contributed no support at all. To quote the report of General Hill, "instead of ordering up one or two hundred pieces to play on the Yankees, a single battery was ordered up, and knocked to pieces in a few minutes; one or two others shared the same fate of being beaten in detail. The firing from our batteries was of the most farcical character." When darkness came, the battle was still raging. The gloom was lighted up by the red flashes of the guns, and the rattle and roar was overpowering; but as the night advanced the fire slackened, and at a comparatively early hour it died out altogether.

It cannot be denied that the last battle on the Peninsula was ill-managed by the Confederates. Stuart, with his splendid cavalry, was still wandering somewhere in the Peninsula, and thus his invaluable services were lost to Lee; Hill, Magruder and Whiting had no communication with one another, and were thus unable to give that mutual support which was indispensable.

The six days' fighting had ended at last. The frightful first campaign against Richmond by way of the Peninsula had closed in rout and disaster to the Federals. The failure to capture the capital of the Confederacy was utter and complete. As we have stated, McClellan showed rare skill and brilliant military ability in extricating his enormous army from its dangerous position. Few commanders could have done so well—none, better. The last battle, at Malvern Hill, was a defeat for the Confederates, but the campaign itself was a victory of magnificent proportions.

As is generally the case, the atmospheric disturbances caused by a great battle brought on violent tempests of rain, and the armies were drenched as completely as if they had been floundering all day in the James River. The necessity for the removal to Harrison's Landing still existed, and during the night the troops were withdrawn to Harrison's Bar, on the James. Colonel Averill, with a regiment of cavalry, a brigade of regular infantry and a battery, covered the rear. General J. E. B. Stuart, having found his way back from the labyrinths of the Lower Peninsula, was sent by Lee after the retreating Federals; but he saw that McClellan had taken up too strong a position to be assailed, and he withdrew in the direction of Richmond. Finally the Army of the Potomac reached Harrison's Landing and found the rest of which they were in such imperative need.

And what was the cost of this tremendous campaign? The Army of the Potomac, June 20, when reunited before Richmond, had an effective force of one hundred and four thousand seven hundred and twenty-four men fit for duty, and eleven thousand two hundred and eighty-nine unfit for duty. On the 4th of July following, when the corps commanders made their reports, fifteen thousand two hundred and forty-nine men had been lost, of whom fifteen hundred and eighty-two had been killed, seventy-seven hundred wounded, and six thousand were missing, fully as many more having gone to the hospitals from sickness and exhaustion caused by the fearful strain to which they had been subjected. The malarial marshes of the Chickahominy were as deadly to the Unionists and Confederates as were the shell and the bullet. General Lee's losses were scarcely short of twenty thousand men, exclusive of five thousand more who were rendered unfit for service by the same causes which acted against the Unionists. Thus the Confederate chieftain sustained the loss of more than one-fourth the effective force of his entire army.

After this prolonged and terrific struggle both armies rested. McClellan carefully fortified himself at Harrison's Landing, and while he was thus engaged Lee fell back to the environs of Richmond, where he devoted himself to recruiting his army and getting ready for the next great campaign.

The North and the South were sobered by the events in the Peninsula. The self-confidence on both sides had given way to a proper appreciation of the tremendous proportions of the conflict between the two sections. Recruiting progressed rapidly on both sides, and, while the war raged in other portions of the country, intelligent and farseeing people saw that the decisive struggle was to be fought in front of Richmond, the capital of the Confederacy.

CHAPTER V.

ROBERT EDWARD LEE was born at Stratford, Westmoreland county, Virginia, January 19, 1807. He was the son of Henry Lee, who graduated at Princeton College two years before the breaking out of the Revolution, when only eighteen years of age. In 1776, he was made captain of a cavalry company, and the following year served under Washington. Lee became a major, and his legion was one of the most famous in the Revolution. In July, 1779, he captured Paulus Hook (Jersey City), for which he received the thanks of Congress and a gold medal. He was made lieutenant-colonel in 1780, and early in the following year joined General Greene in the Carolinas. The fame and exploits of "Light-Horse Harry" are a part of the history of our country.

After the war Henry Lee was a member of Congress, and in 1791 was chosen governor of Virginia. He commanded the troops sent to quell the Whiskey Insurrection, in 1794. He was appointed by Congress to pronounce the funeral oration on the death of Washington, but, unable to be present, it was delivered by Judge Marshall. He was seriously wounded in 1814 while quelling a riot in Baltimore, and never fully recovered from it. He died in 1818, in Georgia, while on his return from the West Indies.

The first wife of General Henry Lee bore him Henry Lee, celebrated for his literary ability, and a daughter, Lucy. By his second wife he had Charles Carter, Robert Edward and Sidney Smith, and two daughters, Annie and Mildred. Sidney Smith Lee became Commodore Lee of the Confederate navy, and was the father of General Fitz Lee.

Robert Edward Lee entered the Military Academy, at West Point, in 1825. He graduated second in his class, and during the entire four years never received a demerit and was never once reprimanded. On his graduation he was appointed second lieutenant in the corps of topographical engineers, to which branch, then as now, the most distinguished graduates of West Point are assigned. He was employed for several years on the coast defences of the United States. In 1832 he married Mary, daughter of George Washington Parke Custis, and granddaughter of the wife of Washington —a most estimable lady and the possessor of large estates, the most widely known being the Arlington house, in Alexandria county, opposite Washington, and the White house, on the Pamunkey, the scene of Washington's marriage.

Robert Edward Lee was the father of three sons and four daughters—George Washington Custis, William Henry Fitzhugh and Robert Edward, and Mary, Anne, Agnes and Mildred. The first two sons became major-generals, the second son being a graduate of West Point, and the third entered the war as private and was promoted to a staff appointment. In 1836 R. E. Lee was made first lieutenant, and in 1838 captain, of engineers. In 1844 he was a member of the board of visitors to the West Point Academy, and in 1845 a member of the board of engineers.

At the breaking out of the Mexican war, Captain Lee was assigned to the central army in Mexico as chief engineer under General Wool. His services were of the most important nature, and, as is well known, he won the fullest confidence of General Scott, who was quick to recognize his brilliant qualities and selected him as one of his personal staff. He was probably complimented by the commanding officer more frequently than any one else who took part in the war. He became the special favorite of the old hero, who pronounced him the greatest military genius in America.

Captain Lee was twice brevetted for his services in Mexico, and his conduct at Chapultepec led to his appointment (September 1, 1852) to the superintendency of the West Point Academy. He held this position not quite three years, and it was during that period that the course of study was extended to cover five years.

In 1855, Colonel Lee was commissioned lieutenant-colonel full rank in the Second Cavalry. This regiment unquestionably had more officers who afterward became famous than any other regiment ever in the service. Albert Sydney Johnston was colonel; R. E. Lee, lieutenant-colonel; William J. Hardee, senior major; George H. Thomas, junior major; Earl Van Dorn, senior captain, with Kirby Smith the next ranking captain, and with Hood, Fitzhugh Lee, Johnson, Palmer and Stoneman among the lieutenants.

In 1855 this regiment was sent to Texas, where for several years it was engaged in continual warfare with the fierce Indian tribes on that exposed frontier. In 1859, Colonel Lee returned to Washington, and was stationed there during the memorable John Brown raid, at Harper's Ferry. He commanded the battalion of marines which were sent to that point, Lieutenant J. E. B. Stuart acting as his aid. When they arrived, the insurgents had retreated to the fire-engine house in the armory-yard, where they had barricaded themselves, and had kept up a desultory fire on the town during the afternoon. They had captured Colonel Washington and other citizens, and were holding them as hostages. Colonel Lee immediately surrounded the engine-house with his marines, and the next morning summoned John

Brown to surrender, pledging himself to protect him and his men from the fury of the citizens. Brown refused any terms except to march out with his men and prisoners, all with their arms and with permission to leave without being followed, to the second toll-gate, where he promised to release his prisoners. After that he would "take his chances." Lee would not agree, and at his request Lieutenant Stuart remonstrated with Brown on the folly of his course. It availed nothing, and under the direction of Lee the doors of the engine-house were battered in and the inmates captured. One of the marines was killed and one wounded, while several of the insurgents were killed and wounded, Brown being among the latter. What followed is known to the world. Brown and his three surviving comrades were indicted for conspiracy with negroes to excite insurrection, for treason against the commonwealth of Virginia and for murder. They were found guilty, and hanged December 2, 1859.

Troublous times followed. The flames of civil war were kindling throughout the country. Colonel Lee saw with pain inexpressible that the fiercest and most gigantic struggle of modern times was at hand. He hoped that Virginia would remain in the Union, for he was a thorough believer in States' rights. When she seceded, therefore, he conscientiously believed his duty gave him no choice except to follow her.

No one can fully realize the pain it cost this great and good man to draw his sword in the strife. General Scott argued and plead with him, and showed him the great honors that were sure to come to him if he remained in the Union army; but it was purely a question of conscience with Lee, who would have laid down his life gladly could it have dissipated the black clouds gathering in the sky. In a letter to his beloved sister he said, "With all my devotion to the Union, and the feeling of loyalty and duty of an American citizen, I have not been able to make up my mind to raise my hand against my relatives, my children, my home. I have, therefore, resigned my commission in the army, and, save in defence of my native State, with the sincere hope that my poor services may never be needed, I hope I may never be called upon to draw my sword."

Respecting Lee's resignation J. William Jones, D. D., contributes a most interesting statement. He says that in obedience to orders to report to the commander-in-chief, in Washington, Lee reached there on the 1st of March, 1861, just three days before the inauguration of President Lincoln. "His hopes for the averting of civil war were doomed to a sad disappointment, and events followed so rapidly that by the middle of April he was compelled to decide whether he would go with the North or with Virginia in the great struggle—

whether he would accept the command of the United States armies in the field or 'share the miseries of his people,' while he gave up place, fortune and his beautiful home at Arlington to serve his native Virginia. If any influence could have swerved Lee from his purpose, it was his friendship for his commander and his high respect for his opinions. General Scott used all of his powers of persuasion to induce him to adhere to the Union and serve under the 'old flag,' and finally Francis Preston Blair (at General Scott's suggestion) was sent by Mr. Lincoln to offer him the supreme command of the United States armies in the field. This statement has been questioned, but the proof is conclusive. Besides the positive testimony of Montgomery Blair, who got it from his father, and of Reverdy Johnson and other gentlemen, who received it from General Scott, I found soon after his death, in General Lee's private letter-book, in his own well-known handwriting, and was permitted to copy, the following letter, which settles the whole question beyond peradventure. Senator Cameron had stated on the floor of the Senate that Lee had sought to obtain the chief command of the army, and, being disappointed, had then 'gone to Richmond and joined the Confederates.' Reverdy Johnson of Maryland—himself an ardent Union man—repelled the charge, and thereupon General Lee wrote him as follows:

"'LEXINGTON, VA., February 25, 1868.

"'HON. REVERDY JOHNSON, UNITED STATES SENATE, WASHINGTON, D. C.—

"'MY DEAR SIR: My attention has been called to the official report of the debate in the Senate of the United States of the 19th instant, in which you did me the kindness to doubt the correctness of the statement made by the Hon. Simon Cameron in regard to myself.

"'I desire that you may feel certain of my conduct on the occasion referred to so far as my individual statement can make you. I never intimated to any one that I desired the command of the United States army, nor did I ever have a conversation with but one gentleman, Mr. Francis Preston Blair, on the subject, which was at his invitation, and, as I understood, at the instance of President Lincoln.

"'After listening to his remarks I declined the offer he made to me to take command of the army that was to be brought into the field, stating as candidly and as courteously as I could that, though opposed to secession and deprecating war, I could take no part in an invasion of the Southern States.

"'I went directly from the interview with Mr. Blair to the office of General Scott, and told him of the proposition that had been made to me, and my decision.

"'Upon reflection after returning to my home, I concluded that I ought no longer to retain any

5

commission I held in the United States army, and on the second morning thereafter I forwarded my resignation to General Scott.

"'At the time I hoped that peace would have been preserved, that some way would have been found to save the country from the calamities of war, and I then had no other intention than to pass the remainder of my days as a private citizen.

"'Two days afterward, upon the invitation of the governor of Virginia, I repaired to Richmond, found that the convention, then in session, had passed the ordinance withdrawing the State from the Union, and accepted the commission of commander of its forces, which was tendered me. These are the simple facts of the case, and they show that Mr. Cameron has been misinformed.

"'I am, with great respect, your obedient servant,

"'R. E. LEE.'

"It will be seen from this letter that no sooner had Colonel Lee received and rejected this proposition, which tendered him rank far beyond what he could hope for by siding with the Confederates, he went immediately to his friend General Scott and told him all about it. The last interview between Scott and Lee was a very affecting one. The veteran begged Lee to accept the offer of Mr. Lincoln, and not to 'throw away such brilliant prospects' and 'make the great mistake of his life.' Lee expressed the highest respect for General Scott and for his opinions, repeated what he had said to Mr. Blair—that, while he recognized no necessity for the state of things then existing, and would gladly liberate the slaves of the South, if they were his, to avert the war, yet he could not take up arms against his native State, his home, his kindred, his children. They parted with expressions of warmest mutual friendship, and General Lee returned to Arlington.

"The night before his letter of resignation was written he asked to be alone, and while his noble wife watched and prayed below he was heard pacing the floor of the chamber above or pouring forth his soul in prayer for divine guidance. About three o'clock in the morning he came down calm and composed and said to his wife,

"'Well, Mary, the path of duty is now plain before me. I have decided on my course. I will at once send my resignation to General Scott.'

"Accordingly, he penned the following letter:

"'ARLINGTON, VA., April 20, 1861.

"'GENERAL: Since my interview with you on the 18th instant I have felt that I ought not longer to retain my commission in the army. I therefore tender my resignation, which I request you will recommend for acceptance. It would have been presented at once but for the struggle it has cost me to separate myself from a service to which I have devoted the best years of my life and all the ability I possessed.

" ' During the whole of that time—more than a quarter of a century—I have experienced nothing but kindness from my superiors and the most cordial friendship from my comrades. To no one, general, have I been much indebted as to yourself for uniform kindness and consideration, and it has always been my desire to merit your approbation. I shall carry to the grave the most grateful recollections of your kind consideration, and your name and fame will always be dear to me.

" ' Save in defence of my native State, I never again desire to draw my sword. Be pleased to accept my most earnest wishes for the continuance of your happiness and prosperity, and believe me most truly yours,

" ' R. E. LEE.

" ' LIEUTENANT-GENERAL WINFIELD SCOTT,
    " ' Commanding United States Army.'

" The newspapers of the South, and especially of Richmond, were very bitter against General Scott for not siding with Virginia, his native State, in the contest; but General Lee always spoke of his old friend in terms of high respect, while regretting that he did not see it to be his duty to come with his State. Soon after he took command of the Virginia forces a friend called to see him one day, accompanied by his five-year-old boy, a sprightly little fellow, whom the general soon had dandling on his knee. Soon the father asked Henry,

"'What is General Lee going to do with General Scott?'

"The little fellow, who had caught the slang of the times, at once replied,

"'He is going to whip him out of his boots.'

"General Lee's voice and manner instantaneously changed, and, lifting Henry down, he stood him between his knees, and, looking him full in the face, said with great gravity,

"'My dear little boy, you should not use such expressions. War is a serious matter, and General Scott is a great and good soldier. None of us can tell what the result of this contest will be.'

"All through the war he was accustomed to speak of General Scott in the kindest terms, and a short time before his own death I heard him in a company of gentlemen at Lexington, Va., pay a warm tribute to the memory of his old friend ·and esteemed commander. General Scott was even more demonstrative in his expressions of admiration and friendship for Lee. His despatches and official reports from Mexico were filled with the warmest commendations of his favorite engineer officer. Of his services during the siege of Vera Cruz, General Scott wrote:

"'I am compelled to make special mention of Captain R. E. Lee, engineer. This officer greatly distinguished himself at the siege of Vera Cruz.'

"In his report of Cerro Gordo he mentions several times the efficient service which Captain Lee performed, and says,

"'This officer was again indefatigable during these operations in reconnoissances as daring as laborious and of the utmost value. Nor was he less conspicuous in planning batteries and in conducting columns to their stations under the heavy fire of the enemy.'

"In his official report of the final operations which captured the City of Mexico, General Scott declares Captain Lee to have been 'as distinguished for felicitous execution as for science and daring,' and says again, 'Captain Lee, so constantly distinguished, also bore important orders from me (September 13) until he fainted from a wound and the loss of two nights' sleep at the batteries.' When, soon after General Scott's return from Mexico, a committee from Richmond waited on him to tender· him a public reception in the capitol of his native State, he said, 'You seek to honor the wrong man. Captain R. E. Lee is the Virginian who deserves the credit of that brilliant campaign.'

"General William Preston of Kentucky says that General Scott told him that he regarded Lee 'as the greatest living soldier in America,' and that in a conversation not long before the breaking out of the war General Scott said with emphasis,

"'I tell you that if I were on my death-bed to-morrow, and the President of the United States should tell me that a great battle was to be fought for the liberty or slavery of the country, and asked my judgment as to the ability of a commander, I would say with my dying breath, Let it be Robert E. Lee.'

"I have been allowed to copy the following autograph letter of General Scott, which illustrates this point:

"'HEADQUARTERS OF THE ARMY, May 8, 1857.

"'HON. J. B. FLOYD, SECRETARY OF WAR—

"'SIR: I beg to ask that one of the vacant second lieutenancies may be given to W. H. F. Lee, son of Brevet Colonel R. E. Lee, at present on duty against the Comanches.

"'I make this application mainly on the extraordinary merits of the father, the very best soldier I ever saw in the field; but the son is himself a very remarkable youth, now about twenty, of a fine stature and constitution, a good linguist, a good mathematician and about to graduate at Harvard University. He is also honorable and amiable, like his father, and dying to enter the army. I do not ask the commission as a favor, though if I had influence I should be happy to exert it in this case. My application is in the name of national justice, in part payment (and but a small part) of the debt due to the invaluable services of Colonel Lee.

"'I have the honor to be, with high respect,

"'Your obedient servant,

"'WINFIELD SCOTT.'

"In a public address delivered in Baltimore soon after the death of General Lee, Hon. Reverdy Johnson said that he 'had been intimate with General Scott, and had heard him say more than once that his success in Mexico was largely due to the skill, valor and undaunted energy of Lee. It was a theme upon which he (General Scott) liked to converse, and he stated his purpose to recommend him as his successor in the chief command of the army. I was with General Scott in April, 1861, when he received the resignation of General Lee, and witnessed the pain it caused him. It was a sad blow to the success of that war in which his own sword had as yet been unsheathed. Much as General Scott regretted it, he never failed to say that he was convinced that Lee had taken that step from an imperative sense of duty. General Scott was consoled in a great measure by the reflection that he would have as his opponent a soldier worthy of every man's esteem, and one who would conduct the war upon the strictest rules of civilized warfare. There would be no outrages committed upon private persons or private property which he could prevent.'

"A prominent banker of New York who was very intimate with General Scott has given me a number of incidents illustrating Scott's high opinion of Lee. On one occasion a short time before the war this gentleman asked him in the course of a confidential interview,

"'General, whom do you regard as the greatest living soldier?'

"General Scott at once replied,

"'Colonel Robert E. Lee is not only the greatest soldier of America, but the greatest soldier now living in the world. This is my deliberate conviction from a full knowledge of his extraordinary abilities; and if the occasion ever arises, Lee will win this place in the estimation of the whole world.'

"The general then went into a detailed sketch of Lee's services and a statement of his ability as an engineer, and his capacity not only to plan campaigns, but also to command large armies in the field, and concluded by saying,

"'I tell you, sir, that Robert E. Lee is the greatest soldier now living; and if he ever gets the opportunity, he will prove himself the greatest captain of history.'

"In May, 1861, this gentleman and another obtained a passport from General Scott to go to Richmond to see if they could do anything to promote pacification. In the course of the interview General Scott spoke in the highest terms of Lee as a soldier and a man, stated that he had rejected the supreme command of the United States army, and expressed his confidence that Lee would do everything in his power to avert war, and would, if a conflict came, conduct it on the highest principles of Christian civilization. He cheerfully granted the passport, and said,

"'Yes, go and see Robert Lee. Tell him for me that we must have no war, but that we must avert a conflict of arms until the sober second thought of the people can stop the mad schemes of the politicians.'

"In the interview which these gentlemen had with General Lee he most cordially reciprocated the kindly feelings of General Scott, and expressed his ardent desire to avert war and his willingness to do anything in his power to bring about a settlement of the difficulties. But he expressed the fear that the passions of the people, North and South, had been too much aroused to yield to pacific measures, and that every effort at a peaceful solution would prove futile. Alluding to Mr. Seward's boast that he would conquer the South in 'ninety days,' and to the confident assertions of some of the Southern politicians that the war would be a very short one, General Lee said with a good deal of feeling,

"'They do not know what they say. If it comes to a conflict of arms, the war will last at least four years. Northern politicians do not appreciate the determination and pluck of the South, and Southern politicians do not appreciate the numbers, resources and patient perseverance of the North. Both sides forget that we are all Americans, and that it must be a terrible struggle if it comes to war. Tell General Scott that we must do all we can to avert war; and if it comes to the worst, we must then do everything in our power to mitigate its evils.'

"Alas that the wishes and aspirations of these two great soldiers could not have been realized! Men will differ as to whether Scott or Lee was right in the course which each thought proper to pursue on the only great question which ever divided them, but all must admire that pure friendship which neither time nor circumstances could break."

Colonel Lee resigned his commission April 20, 1861, and proceeded at once to Richmond, where he offered his services to Virginia. Governor Letcher immediately conferred on him the rank of major-general, and he was given charge of the force that the Legislature authorized for the defence of the State.

General Lee began without delay the task of organizing this force and of preparing for the invasion that was certain to come. This was a most difficult work, but it was accomplished with consummate skill and success.

Virginia seceded April 17, and joined the Confederacy May 8. General Lee was ordered to retain command of the Army of Virginia until the military organization of the Confederacy was completed. He was made a general in the regular army, ranking next to Sidney Johnston. The Federal forces at Fortress Monroe were heavily reinforced, Alexandria was occupied in the latter part of May, and, soon after, General McClellan with a strong column entered West Virginia. The first conflict of any moment was at Great Bethel, between Yorktown and Hampton, on the 10th of June, where a column of Federals numbering five thousand men, with artillery, was defeated by a force of eighteen hundred infantry and six pieces of artillery. Other engagements followed, and finally, July 21, took place the battle of Bull Run, ending in the utter rout and overthrow of the Union army and their turbulent flight to the entrenchments of Washington. But everything went wrong for the Confederates in West Virginia. The people were strongly Union in sentiment, and McClellan pushed matters with such vigor and ability that he became the most popular general in the Federal army, and soon after succeeded to the supreme command.

General Garnet, the Confederate commander, having been killed, General Lee was ordered to West Virginia to assume command of the army in that region. This was his first service in the field during the civil war. He displayed caution, skill and true generalship; but the operations in West Virginia had little effect on the progress of the war, and therefore it is not necessary to follow them in detail.

In the fall of 1861 the efforts of the Federal government were directed chiefly against the Southern coast, and General Lee was ordered to Charleston and to take command of the coast department. The repeated failures of the Union attempts to make any real impression in that section during the years that followed attest the skill and thoroughness with which Lee performed this duty.

General Lee was made commander-in-chief of the Confederate armies March 13, 1862. He retained the position, however, but a few months. General McClellan, with his enormous and admirably-disciplined army, landed on the Peninsula in May and began his campaign against Richmond. During the terrible struggle at Seven Pines, as has already been told, General Johnston was severely wounded. Naturally enough, General Lee succeeded him, and thenceforward directed all the movements of the Confederate army in Virginia to the close of the war.

The history of the campaign in the Peninsula has already been told.

II.

THE CAMP-FIRES IN NORTHERN VIRGINIA.

CHAPTER VI.

ON THE RAPPAHANNOCK.

On the 7th of July a steamer on its way from Fortress Monroe stopped at Harrison's Landing, and a single passenger stepped ashore. He was tall, angular and of uncouth figure, with strongly-marked features; the eyes and countenance which were wont to light up with original and quaint humor were serious and grave to the last degree. Those who looked at the visitor recognized President Lincoln, who had come to Harrison's Landing to consult with the commander of the Union army about the measures to be adopted in the alarming crisis. General McClellan believed that all the resources of the government should be used to forward him men and munitions of war. The James River was now open to him as a line of supplies, and he favored the bold design of transferring the Army of the Potomac to the south bank of that stream and destroying the commu-

73

nications of Richmond by way of Petersburg. The wisdom of this plan cannot be questioned in face of the fact that two years later General Grant adopted it, captured Richmond and destroyed the Southern Confederacy.

President Lincoln was much impressed by the views of McClellan; but when he returned to Washington, he was dissuaded by General Halleck, commander-in-chief of the army, from allowing McClellan to execute his plans. McClellan was shortly afterward removed from the command of the Army of the Potomac, which was placed in charge of Major-General John Pope. Pope came from the West with a reputation for vigorous aggressive warfare that promised great results in the East.

General Pope was not afflicted with undue modesty, and was no way backward in proclaiming the mighty things he proposed to do. He dated his "Headquarters in the Saddle"—evident reversal of facts as concerned himself—and announced that he came from a region where they hunted the enemy and when they found him beat him.

A month passed after the visit of President Lincoln to Harrison's Landing, and the army was still there. Some desultory firing and a few skirmishes broke the idle stillness now and then, but it needed no very observant eye to note beneath all this calm the preparations for a most important movement. Transports were continually coming and going laden with cavalry, war-material and the sick and wounded, and everywhere was the bustle of activity and preparation. The truth was that in spite of McClellan's protest it had been decided to transfer the army to Fortress Monroe, and the government had decided to take charge of the conduct of the war with a view of teaching the West Pointers that some things could be done as well as others.

General Lee remained before Richmond, watching every movement of McClellan at Harrison's Landing. It was not long before he learned that another army was advancing from the Upper Rappahannock and had already occupied Culpeper county. There could be no doubt that it intended to capture Gordonsville, the point of junction of the Orange and Alexandria and Virginia Central Railroads, with the purpose of advancing upon Richmond. It was this "Army of Virginia," numbering fifty thousand men that had formerly served under Banks, McDowell and Fremont, which was placed under the immediate command of Pope. He assured the President and other parties who were interested in the question that they need feel no further concern for the safety of the national capital. He would attend to that; and if Lee presumed to make any demonstration, he would be taught a lesson that he would remember a long time.

General Pope's next proceeding was the issuance of orders so oppressive and tyrannous to the

citizens around him that General Lee, by direction
of the Confederate authorities, sent an indignant
protest to General Halleck, commander-in-chief
of the Union armies. The result was a modifica-
tion of Pope's orders so as to bring him within
the pale of civilized warfare.

Pope's army lay at Culpeper, the right extending toward the Blue Ridge and the left almost
reaching the Rapidan River. He thus threatened
to destroy Lee's communications with South-western Virginia. The movement of Pope was a wise
one, for at the time it was made the main Federal
army was at Harrison's Landing, and Lee could
not assure himself as to what part it was intended
to play in the great campaign about to open. He
therefore determined to remain for the time in
front of Richmond; for should he withdraw, the
temptation to march in would be too great for the
Union army to resist.

On the 13th of July, Lee sent Jackson in the
direction of Gordonsville; he led his old division
and the fire-tried one of Ewell. They went by
railroad to Gordonsville, where they arrived on
the 19th of July, and Jackson at once set himself
to work to penetrate the design of the Union commander. He found that, as we have stated, General Pope had advanced to the Rapidan and was
threatening the railroad connections; furthermore,
he quickly learned that the Federal force was so
much larger than his own that it would have been

6

folly to attack it.   He sent to General Lee for
reinforcements, and the Confederate leader immediately forwarded A. P. Hill's division.   General
D. H. Hill, who commanded a moderate force on
the south bank of the James River, was ordered
to create a diversion by opening fire on McClellan's transports.   It was now brain against brain.
This state of indecision lasted until nearly the
middle of August, when the secret was discovered.
It was known that General Burnside had reached
Hampton Roads from the southern coast with a
large force.   The direction taken by his flotilla
would settle the question; for if the new advance
was intended to be by way of the James, the
flotilla would ascend that river; if General Pope
was to make the real movement, General Burnside would move in that direction.

One evening early in August a small steamer
bearing a flag of truce ascended the James, and,
passing the Confederate outpost, halted at Aiken's
Landing, a place designated for the exchange of
prisoners.   One of the passengers was noticeable
for the extreme anxiety he showed to land.   As
soon as he touched the shore he made for General
Lee's headquarters, scarcely taking breath until he
had made known the important news he carried.
He was the famous partisan John S. Mosby, and he
had penetrated the secret which General Lee was
so anxious to learn.   Mosby told the commander
that at the very moment he was leaving Hampton

Roads that morning the whole of Burnside's corps was embarking, and he knew beyond all question that its destination was Acquia Creek. This solved the perplexing problem, and Lee's anxiety now was to strike Pope before Burnside could join him. Jackson was apprised of the important news, and with his usual promptness he started on the 7th of August to attack Pope at Culpeper. Ewell led, followed by Winder and A. P. Hill, forming all together an army of upward of twenty-five thousand men.

So soon as Pope learned of the crossing of the Rapidan he put his troops in motion with a view of concentrating them in front of Culpeper. On the morning of the 8th the Federal cavalry on the north bank were driven back by General Robertson in the direction of Culpeper Court-House. They threatened the train of Jackson's division, and Lawton's brigade of Ewell's division was detached to protect it. As a consequence, it took no part in the conflict which followed. The infantry and artillery, having followed the cavalry across the Rapidan, continued toward Culpeper. The next day they were near Cedar Run, within eight miles of Culpeper Court-House, where the Federals were discovered in strong force.

The Unionists consisted of Banks's corps, which had been sent forward to meet Jackson's advance. His command was a powerful one, and was strongly posted. Jackson began at once to form his line.

Ewell's division, the first to arrive, was pushed in
advance, so as to secure a position on Slaughter
Mountain where he would be able to bring his
artillery to bear on the Federal line. Early's
brigade was in the advance, and, forming on the
right of the road and charging across an open
field, he drove the Federal cavalry to the crest of
an adjoining hill. While climbing this hill the
Federal artillery opened on him, and many of
their cavalry appeared in the fields on the left.
Protecting his troops as best he could, Early hurried forward three guns to the crest of Slaughter
Mountain and replied with spirit to the Federal
artillery. Jackson's division appearing, a portion
of it was sent to Early's assistance, the rest being
held in reserve. While forming in line its leader,
General Charles S. Winder, was mortally wounded
by a shell, and the command passed to General
William B. Taliaferro. During this manœuvre
General Ewell occupied the position assigned him,
on the north-west termination of Slaughter Mountain, a couple of hundred feet above the valley
below. Posting Latimer's battery in the most
available spot, he opened on the Federal guns,
and the artillery duel continued for some time
between the two armies. Two hours later General Banks advanced his skirmishers, and then
his infantry, from the woods to the rear and left
of the batteries. A second body of infantry appeared almost at the same moment from a valley

where they were unobserved, and moved against Early's right. Banks's attack was an impetuous one, and the flame of battle quickly extended along the whole line.

Finding himself sorely pressed, Early called for reinforcements. Banks pressed him still harder, and, massing his infantry on his right, dashed at the Confederate left. Bearing down the forces by his superior numbers, he turned the flank and gained the Confederate rear. Taliaferro's brigade was rolled back, followed by Early's disorganized left, and it looked as though the whole line would give way before the cheering and enthusiastic Unionists. But the keen eye of "Stonewall" had detected the peril, and at the critical moment A. P. Hill's division arrived. The Stonewall brigade, held in reserve, had been called up, and Branch's brigade from Hill's division was attached to it. Jackson placed himself at their head, and then the thunderbolt was hurled against the victorious Federals.

"Stonewall Jackson! Stonewall Jackson!" yelled the Confederates, as the well-known figure galloped back and forth through the smoke amid the flying bullets, cheering the men, who were nerved to their utmost by the mere knowledge that he commanded. "This was one of the few occasions when he is reported to have been mastered by excitement. He had forgotten, apparently, that he commanded the whole field, and imagined himself a simple colonel leading his regiment. Everywhere, in the thickest of the fire, his form was seen and his voice heard, and his exertions to rally the men were crowned with success. The repulsed troops reformed"* and the advance of the Federals was checked, and they were forced into the woods, the battle continuing with great fierceness until the arrival of Pender's and Archer's brigades, when a general charge was made on the left and in the centre. The Unionists were driven steadily backward over the valley and into the woods beyond. General Ewell joined the impetuous charge, pressing the Federals, who fell back all along the line, until at dark the original position of the Confederates was reoccupied by them.

Jackson was eager to reach Culpeper Court-House before daylight, and he hurried on in pursuit; but the utmost circumspection was necessary, and he had not gone far when he discovered the Federals in his front in large numbers, General Pope having despatched heavy reinforcements to Banks. Jackson sent Field's brigade and Pegram's battery forward, which opened an effective fire; but the Federals replied with such success that the assailants were silenced and the battery withdrawn. A careful reconnoissance on the morrow convinced Jackson that the Unionists were too strong to be assailed, and he posted his army so as to resist any attack likely to be made, after which

* Cooke's *Life of Stonewall Jackson.*

his wounded were sent to Gordonsville, the dead buried, and a general preparation was made for effective operations. The rain fell in torrents all day, and on the morrow the request of General Pope, sent under a flag of truce, for permission to bury such of their dead as had not been interred by the Confederates, was granted. On the night succeeding (August 11), General Jackson retreated to Gordonsville to avoid being attacked by a much larger force than his own, and there awaited reinforcements. Little advantage could be claimed by either side, though two of the Federal generals were wounded and General Prince was made prisoner.

But the vigorous demonstration of Jackson excited the gravest alarm of Halleck, the Federal commander-in-chief, for the safety of the Union army in Virginia. It required no extraordinary sagacity to see that so soon as General Lee could relieve himself of McClellan's threatening presence he would hurry to the assistance of Jackson, or, rather, would assume personal charge of the campaign in Northern Virginia. Well might the Northern heart tremble for the result! The grisly phantom of the capture of Washington again caused many anxious conferences in that city. Pope was so far advanced on the Rapidan that a sudden assault by Lee would be likely to crush him before any reforcements could go to his assistance. McClellan was urged to hasten the embarkation of his troops at Harrison's Landing, with a view of giving Pope all the help and reinforcements possible.

General Lee saw that his opportunity had come, and he grasped it with his usual promptness and vigor. General Longstreet with his division and two brigades under General Hood were sent to Gordonsville from Richmond. General Stuart was ordered to leave enough cavalry to menace the Federals at Fredericksburg and to guard the Central Railroad, then to report to General Jackson with the remainder. R. H. Anderson was recalled from the James and despatched after Longstreet. D. H. Hill's and McLaw's divisions, a couple of brigades under General Walker and Hampton's cavalry brigade remained on the James to resist any demonstration from that quarter. On the 15th of August, 1862, Longstreet reached Gordonsville, and General Lee was directly behind him.

Monday morning, August 25, was one of the hottest days of the season. Scarcely a breath of air was stirring and the cool shade of the trees was never more inviting; but great interests were at stake, and it was the time for work. Jackson marched up the south bank of the Rappahannock, dragging his cannon with much labor and difficulty, and crossed at Hinston's Ford. Close under the shadow of the Blue Ridge, along roads infrequently travelled, the grim hero led his men, aim-

ing in the most direct line possible for Thoroughfare Gap, by which the Manassas Gap Railroad
makes its way through the Bull Run Mountains.
It was all-essential that this pass should be occupied in advance of the Federals. Passing through
Orleans, in Fauquier county, Salem was reached at
midnight, after a march of thirty-five miles. The
people along the route gazed at the Confederates in
amazement and delight. It was a long time since
they had seen any of them, and they wondered
what it all could mean. Their eager queries, it
need hardly be said, were not answered in a very
satisfactory manner.

Throughout the day General Stuart had kept
his cavalry in motion on the right of Jackson
with a view of concealing his movement from the
Federals. The exhausted, hungry soldiers threw
themselves on the ground and slept soundly until
roused at daylight, when they were again in motion. Heading straight for Thoroughfare Gap,
Jackson found on his arrival that not a solitary
Federal was in sight. Pushing on through Gainesville, Bristoe Station, on the Orange and Alexandria Railroad, was reached late in the afternoon.
Shortly after, General Stuart and his cavalry
arrived, and took position on the right flank of
Jackson. This was scarcely done when the rumble of cars was heard approaching from the direction of Warrenton Junction. General Ewell disposed of his forces to take possession of the train,

for the capture was likely to be a valuable one. The rumble and roar rapidly increased, and suddenly a heavily-loaded train under full speed thundered around the curve. The engineer caught sight of the Confederates, and he knew what was up. He gave his engine full steam and ducked his head when the Second Virginia Cavalry raised their weapons and fired. The bullets whistled around and through the cars, but the track was clear, and the terrified fugitives were speedily beyond reach of the Confederates. The train reached Manassas in safety, but it was hardly out of sight when the increasing rumble and roar down the track announced that other trains were coming. Determined that no more should run the gauntlet, Ewell's soldiers hastily piled a lot of logs on the track. A minute later the second engine burst into sight around the curve, and the vigilant engineer instantly saw that something was amiss. He whistled for brakes and reversed, but his momentum carried him forward into the obstructions, which threw the engine off the track and over on its side—fortunately, without injury to him or the fireman. Immediately behind the train came a third, which was also captured. The noise of still others was heard, but from some cause or other the drivers seemed to suspect that everything was not right. The approaching engineer, having halted his train, sent out several ringing blasts from the whistle, which, being interpreted into English, were addressed to the other engineer in advance and asked the question,

"*Is it all right ahead?*"

Among Ewell's forces were several railroad-men, who recognized the signal. One of them ran to the prostrate engine, which seemed to be oozing steam from from every pore, and, jerking the whistle-cord several times, sent back the signal by way of reply.

"*All is right! Come on!*"

But there may have been something in the "touch" of the strange hand at the whistle which failed to quiet the fears of the cautious engineer who was seeking information. He did not approach, as he had been signalled to do, but prudently reversed his engine and lost no time in getting back to Warrenton.

It will thus be seen that the first step in Lee's plan of the campaign was successful. Jackson had flanked Pope and was now in his rear, where his own situation was far from being secure.

Arriving at Bristoe Station, Jackson ascertained that the Federals had stored an immense amount of supplies at Manassas Junction, only eight miles distant. Appreciating the necessity of capturing these, General Trimble was sent in that direction to make the capture. It was late in the day when he started, and, to make sure of its success, General Stuart was despatched after Trimble with orders to take command of the expedition. A

smart engagement took place in the early darkness, when the place was captured with several
hundred prisoners and its enormous supplies.   Besides the horses, negroes and prisoners, there were
hundreds of tents, about a dozen locomotives, two
railroad-trains, tons of bacon, hundreds of barrels of beef, thousands of barrels of flour, wine,
delicacies of every description and a vast supply
of forage.

The scene which followed was of so ludicrous a
nature that even Jackson smiled when he looked
on.   There were probably no hungrier men between Maine and Texas than were his soldiers
when they arrived the next day.   They had been
living on roast corn, and their appetites were fierce
enough to make a pair of calfskin boots tempting.
They snuffed the victuals before they were within
reach, and as they marched up were told to help
themselves.   It is a waste of words to say they
accepted the invitation.   The splendid bakery, capable of turning out fifteen thousand loaves daily,
was instantly put on "double time" and made
to do more work than was ever done by it before.
Men with rapacious appetites were not particular
about a proper degree of baking, and, waiting only
until the bread was half done, it was hauled from
the oven smoking, but tossed among the famishing
Confederates.   Whoever caught the prize instantly
tore it apart, and his jaws closed in it like those
of a steel trap.   Ragged, frowsy, barefooted, with

spiky hair shooting through the crown of the torn hat, the eyes of the Confederate glowed with delight over the top of the loaf as he endeavored to force half of it at one time between his jaws. Sometimes the tears which filled those projecting eyes were not tears of joy: they were caused by the. bread in the mouth, which seemed red hot and fairly sent the steam hissing through ears, nostrils and eyes; but the soldier hung on, for he could not afford to lose a single morsel. Many a bottle of choice wine, jar of canned fruit and jelly which had been sent by mothers, sisters and sweethearts in the North to the boys at the front failed to reach their destination. It would have shocked the heart of the maiden over-much could she have seen the bottle of delicious currant-wine which she had despatched to her own darling Harry grasped by the grimy hand of a shaggy Confederate, who, placing the mouth between his lips, elevated the bottom until it pointed toward the blue sky, and held it there until the contents had gurgled down his capacious throat. Then, after he had clapped his other hand several times against the bottom, to make sure that no stray drop escaped, he reluctantly removed it from between his teeth, smacked his lips, rubbed his stomach, smiled almost to his ears and absolutely groaned with bliss.

How many of the boys who were at Manassas that day and took part in the wild feast, and who are now living, would dare attempt what then was done with impunity? One fellow made a splendid meal from a raw mackerel and a pint of molasses; another washed down some uncooked pork with wine, which, giving out too soon, was supplemented with a gill or so of vinegar; still another smothered a huge chunk of cheese with lard and lobster-salad, and then asked his comrades to hold him down, inasmuch as he felt so good that he was sure the wings were sprouting out of his back. In the division of the spoils the scene could not have been more ludicrous. A participant told Cooke that his share was a toothbrush, a box of candles, a quantity of lobster-salad, a barrel of coffee, and other articles of diversified nature. As one of the happy fellows remarked, it was worth starving half to death for the enjoyment that such a feast gave.

CHAPTER VII.

MANŒUVRING FOR POSITION.

GENERAL LEE took with him about seventy-five thousand men, divided into two army corps. His expectation of surprising Pope failed through an intercepted letter which had fallen into Pope's hands a few days before, and which made known the intended movement. But the Federal commander, when he could almost hear the tramp of the terrible legions, found himself with an effective force of only fifty thousand men. Convinced that certain defeat awaited him if he remained on the Rapidan, he had withdrawn to the Rappahannock. This course was a wise one, but it did not harmonize with the high-sounding proclamations which he issued on assuming command of the army. The Federal movement, when completed, placed Reno at Kelly's Ford; Banks, at Rappahannock Station; McDowell, at Rappahannock Ford; with Sigel on the extreme right, farther up the river. It was in front of this formidable array that General Lee presented himself on the morning of the 21st of August. He was at the head of the Confederate army, with Longstreet on his right and Jackson on his left.

The position of the Federal army completely commanded the south bank of the Rappahannock, held by Lee; every crossing was so closely guarded that the Confederate leader did not run the risk of an attempt to force a passage. The two armies spent the day in cannonading each other, and Lee determined to cross at a more favorable place. General Longstreet was ordered into position near the railroad-bridge and Beverly's Ford, so as to mask the movements of General Jackson, who had been selected to make the crossing at a point farther up stream. Jackson with his three divisions, preceded by Stuart's cavalry, advanced with his usual celerity; but he was discovered when near Hazel River, which lay on his route. Two Federal brigades hastily crossed and attacked his rear —not with the expectation of defeating, but with the hope of delaying, him. The Confederate leader beat them off, and reached Freeman's Ford before dark. Sigel, however, was strongly guarding the pass, and, going still farther up, Jackson took possession of Warrenton Springs, which was guarded by only a small outpost. He had scarcely done so when it began raining hard, and the river rapidly rose. Early's brigade, which had been thrown across the river, found itself cut off from the southern bank by the submergence of the fords. The situation was very dangerous, for, the high water having destroyed the fords in front of Longstreet, the Federals withdrew from his front to concentrate upon Early. General Pope's preparations for this attack looked as if he thought the whole Confederate army was on the southern shore. While the complicated and elaborate preparations were under way, Stuart and his cavalry appeared in the rear of the Federal forces and created consternation. Stuart captured all the staff-papers of General Pope, including his despatch-book, which contained copies of the general's correspondence with the government. Among the trophies taken was a new and gorgeous uniform of General Pope. Some days later a burly negro was decked out in this, and as he strutted back and forth with his chest thrust out like a pouter-pigeon the exhibition was one of the most ridiculous that can be conceived. It was as dark as Egypt and raining furiously. Thus it was that Stuart failed to discover a rich convoy parked near him and with a weak guard protecting it. Having demoralized the wagon and railway service, Stuart dodged the forces that were hastily gathering to intercept him.

While these lively proceedings were under way Rosser's and Brien's regiments were sent to attack another camp and to destroy the railroad. Before anything could be accomplished all the lights in the camps were put out, and the men scrambled into the wagons. The rain was still pouring in torrents, and the darkness was absolutely impene-

7

trable. The Confederates, under the circumstances, concluded not to attack, but to give their attention to the railroad. When an attempt was made to destroy the bridge, the task was found more difficult than was anticipated. It was so thoroughly saturated that it was impossible to set fire to it. Then, when axes were brought, the high water placed the men at such disadvantage that little could be done. The structure was so strongly built that many hours would be required to cut it down. Meanwhile, the Federals were gathering on the other side the stream and dropping shots among the eager Confederates. Every hour of delay increased the danger, and Stuart withdrew with the same celerity that he had made his advance to the point.

The contrast between the executive ability of Lee and Pope was never more vividly shown than in the movements and manœuvring preceding the general engagement. Early remained in his exposed position at Warrenton Springs all day, and was never molested. Jackson spent the time in erecting a temporary structure, by which communications were reopened, and at daybreak Early rejoined his chief without receiving a hostile shot. Some hours later Buford's cavalry galloped up to the spot, looked around, and, finding the bird had flown, turned about and galloped back. For three days and nights the Federals were kept marching toward the different points of the compass, here, there, everywhere, through the drenching rain, the frightful mud and water, with insufficient rations, discouraged, disgusted and worn to the last stages of exhaustion. Stragglers lined the roads, and a more miserable set of wretches the mind cannot picture. And during this terrible ordeal the Confederate army for fully one-half the time remained tranquil and at rest, husbanding its strength and making preparations for the impending struggle.

General Stuart sent Pope's captured despatch-book to General Lee, who sat down at his ease to enjoy its contents. The first interesting item on which the Confederate leader stumbled was the correspondence wherein Pope admitted his inability to hold the Rappahannock and begged for reinforcements. Among the other "tidings of comfort and joy" was an accurate (because "official") account of the strength and disposition of the Federal army, the views of General Pope, the fact that McClellan had left Westover, that a part of his army was on the way to join General Pope, that the rest were following hard after, and that the army of Cox was withdrawing from the Kanawha Valley for the same purpose. When all these reinforcements should join Pope, he would be at the head of an army of two hundred thousand men. It need not be said that General Lee found this despatch-book "mighty interesting reading," and that he fully digested all the contents, turning over and scrutinizing the covers to make sure he missed nothing. The conclusion followed as a matter of course that if ever there was a call for promptness on the part of the Confederates, that time had come. It being clear that nothing was to be feared from McClellan, the rest of the force on the James was ordered up to take part in the campaign in Northern Virginia. This force consisted of a portion of D. H. Hill's command, McLaw's division, Walker's two brigades and Hampton's cavalry.

The tactics adopted by Lee were as brilliant as they were daring. Conscious of the great stakes at risk, he acted on the principle that the more audacious his course, the greater were the results to be attained. Jackson was directed to cross the river above Pope's right, pass around his flank, gain his rear and cut his communications with Washington; while the movement was under way Longstreet was to occupy Pope's attention by threatening démonstrations in front; so soon as Jackson had advanced far enough Longstreet was to follow him with all haste. By this strategy Lee hoped to throw his whole army on Pope's line of communications, and to compel him to fight before reinforcements could reach him. It can readily be perceived that the situation of Jackson would be a most critical one, for he too would be cut off from immediate help and was liable to be overwhelmed before reinforcements could go to his assistance. But the terrible fighter leaped to the performance of his duty with the eagerness which characterized him on every occasion.

General Jackson on the morning of the 27th moved with all his troops except Ewell's division to Manassas. Ewell remained at Bristoe's Station, with orders to delay the advance of the Federals as much as was possible should they withdraw from the Rappahannock, and, if too hard pressed himself, to fall back and rejoin the main body at Manassas.

And what was General Pope doing all this time?

CHAPTER VIII.

LEE retained Longstreet's command in front to divert Pope's attention while Jackson was executing his flank movement. Stealthy as was the latter, it did not escape the knowledge of Pope, who, however, was unable to make certain of its precise purpose. His position, it may be said, was that of a man watching a body whirling about his head with inconceivable celerity. He became bewildered and began sending orders hither and thither, marching his men up and down and here and there until the wonder became whether he ever would be able to extricate the army from its labyrinth of danger. Fitz-John Porter telegraphed to Burnside, "I suspect the Confederates know what they are doing, which is more than any one here or anywhere knows." Finally, as the best course, Pope decided to fall back nearer Washington. Shortly after reaching this decision he awoke to the fact that Jackson was in his rear, at Manassas.

Now was the opportunity for Pope to deliver a most effective blow; for when Jackson was at Manassas, Longstreet was two marches off. What was to prevent Pope from placing himself between the two columns and overwhelming each in detail? He had received large reinforcements from the Army of the Potomac and other sources, and was amply able to carry out this plan, which required only promptness and ordinary generalship. Pope exhibited intermittent flashes of perception, and he now appeared to grasp the situation; but he could not hold fast long enough to make his movements effective.

The only thing for Pope to do was to push forward his left and occupy the road by which Longstreet must advance to join Jackson. With this end in view, he ordered General McDowell, with his own and Sigel's corps and Reynolds's division, to march to Gainesville. This would place forty thousand men directly in the road by which the Confederate main column must march to join Jackson. Reno's corps and Kearny's division of Heitzelman's corps were directed to support this force, which marched for Greenwich, while Pope, with Hooker's division, advanced along the Orange and Alexandria Railroad toward Manassas Junction. Banks was to remain at Warrenton, relieving Porter's corps, which was also ordered to Gainesville. To quote Swinton, "These dispositions were not only correct: they were brilliant. The lame and impotent sequel is now to be seen."

The main column, under McDowell, was to reach

its position at Gainesville and Greenwich on the night of the 27th. It succeeded in doing so, and at the same time Pope, with Hooker's command, advanced along the railroad in pursuit of Jackson at Bristoe Station. During the afternoon, when near the place, Pope came upon General Ewell, who, it will be remembered, Jackson had left at that point for the very purpose of obstructing the Federal march. A sharp engagement instantly opened, and Ewell, finding himself hard pressed, fell back, as he had been directed to do, and joined Jackson at Manassas Junction. Under the belief that the battle would be renewed in the morning at Bristoe Station, General Porter was ordered up from Warrenton Junction; but the intense darkness and the difficulties of the road prevented his reaching Bristoe until about nine o'clock the next day, yet nothing was lost by the delay, inasmuch as Ewell had already joined Jackson. It now looked as if Jackson was inextricably entangled and was sure to be entrapped. In his order to McDowell, Pope exultingly added, "If you will march promptly and rapidly at the earliest dawn upon Manassas Junction, we shall bag the whole crowd." McDowell with his forty thousand men was at Gainesville, between Jackson and Lee, the latter being a full day's march distant, west of Bull Run Mountains.

"When, on the night of the 27th, Pope learned that Jackson was in the vicinity of Manasses, he directed McDowell, with all his force, to take up the march early on the morning of the 28th and move eastward from Gainesville and Greenwich upon Manassas Junction, following the line of the Manassas Gap Railroad, while he ordered Hooker and Kearny and Porter to advance northward from Bristoe Station upon the same place. From Gainesville to Manassas Junction the distance is fifteen miles; from Bristoe Station, it is eight miles; and from Manassas Junction west to Thoroughfare Gap, where Lee must debouch through the Bull Run Mountains to unite with Jackson, is twenty miles.

"This move was a great error. Pope's left (McDowell's column) was his strategic flank, and should have been thrown forward rather than retired; for in withdrawing from the line of the Warrenton turnpike to Manassas Junction he permitted Jackson, by a move from Manassas Junction to the north of the turnpike, to do precisely what he should at all hazards have been prevented from doing—namely, to put himself in the way of a junction with the main body of Lee's army. Could Jackson, indeed, have been induced to remain at Manassas Junction for the convenience of Pope, that general's strategy would have worked to a charm; but Jackson was fully alive to the peril of his situation, and while Pope thought he was in the act of "bagging" Jackson, Jackson was giving Pope the slip. The details are as follows: During the night of the 27th and morning of the 28th, Jackson moved his force from Manassas, by the Sudley Springs road, across to the Warrenton turnpike; crossing which, he gained the high timberland north and west of Groveton, in the vicinity of the battlefield of the 21st of July, 1861. When, therefore, Pope, with the divisions of Hooker and Kearny and Reno, reached Manassas Junction, about noon of the 28th, he found that Jackson had already gone!

"Pope then tried to correct his error by calling back McDowell's column from its march toward Manassas Junction and directing it on Centreville, to which point he also ordered forward Hooker, Kearny and Reno, and afterward Porter. But much time had been lost; the columns on the march toward Manassas had been forced to take other roads than those indicated for them, and it was late in the afternoon when McDowell, with one division of his whole command (King's), regained the Warrenton turnpike and headed toward Centreville. Now, Jackson, as already seen, had taken position on the north side of the turnpike, near Groveton; so that on the approach of King's column it unwittingly presented a flank to Jackson, who assailed it furiously. Jackson attacked with two divisions (the Stonewall division, then under General Taliaferro, and Ewell's division), while the fight on the Union side was sustained by King's division alone. The behavior of the troops was exceedingly creditable, and they maintained their ground with what Jackson styles "obstinate determination." The loss on both sides was severe, and on the part of the Confederates included Generals Ewell and Taliaferro, both of whom were severely wounded, the former losing a leg. Unfortunately for Pope, during the night King withdrew his command to Manassas, leaving the Warrenton turnpike available for Jackson's withdrawal or Longstreet's advance. That same night, too, General Ricketts (whom McDowell had detached with his division to dispute the passage of Thoroughfare Gap with Longstreet) also withdrew to Manassas. Thus affairs went from bad to worse."[*]

[*] Swinton.

CHAPTER IX.

THE MARCH OF THE CONQUEROR.

"They've cut the wires! The Confederates are between Pope and Washington!"

It was an anxious group that were gathered about the electrical instrument at headquarters in Washington. The telegraph-wires throbbed with the messages flashing back and forth, and the party listened to the continuous clicking of the instrument as though it was delivering the verdict of their own doom.

All at once it stopped; the chattering tongue had become mute. Men looked inquiringly at each other and then at the telegraphist. He smiled grimly:

"*They've cut the wires! The Confederates are between Pope and Washington!*"

The explanation, as we learned long ago, was the true one. General Stuart had just reached Bristoe Station, where he seized the two railroad-trains and cut the wires.

The authorities were at their wits' end; the old terror of the capture of Washington caused them to quake once more. Was it some daring raiders that had cut the wires, or was Lee and his army between the Union commander and Washington? Ought a regiment or powerful reinforcements be sent out to the rescue of Pope? Finally a brigade of New Jersey troops under General Taylor took the cars to Bull Run Bridge, where they disembarked, crossed the stream and set out to learn what they could about Manassas. The Confederates ambushed the entire brigade, killing one-third of them and wounding their leader. The rest scampered to Centreville, where a few troops rallied around the remnants of the command.

It was not until the morning of the 29th that General Pope learned the real position of his adversary, and by that time he had scattered his own troops all over the country by his contradictory orders; so that their great strength was practically unavailable. Sigel and Reynolds were near Groveton, and they were ordered to engage the Confederates, while Pope endeavored to shape up matters elsewhere. Reno's corps and Heintzelman, with Hooker and Kearny's divisions, were directed to countermarch from Centreville, and Porter with his corps and King's division of McDowell's command was pushed forward to regain the position at Gainesville, which had been abandoned the day before.

Meanwhile, the redoubtable Jackson maintained his position on the elevated land near Groveton. He thus secured complete command of the Warrenton road, over which Lee was advancing to join him, and even then was close at hand. The gray-coated Cromwell could afford to feel little alarm about what his bombastic adversary was doing; nevertheless, like the true general he was, he disposed of his troops in an admirable order, his right resting on the Warrenton turnpike and his left near Sudley mill. Most of the troops were sheltered in the thick woods in the rear of the railroad cut and embankment. In obedience to orders General Sigel attacked this force, and suffered severely from the hot fire he received. Near noon Reno's command and the divisions of Hooker and Kearny joined him, and Porter had advanced from Manassas Junction with a view of flanking Jackson's right by marching to Gainesville; but before he could do this Lee's van arrived at Thoroughfare Gap, Longstreet reaching the ground before noon. Assuming position on Jackson's right, he drew an extension of the Confederate line across the turnpike and the Manassas Gap Railroad. By this means every point by which Porter could have advanced on Gainesville was covered.

The Union general, however, was about to form his line when General McDowell appeared. McDowell says he ordered Porter to advance and attack the Confederates, while Porter is equally emphatic in declaring that McDowell told him to stay where he was; the reader is welcome to believe whoever he chooses. McDowell took King's division from Porter, and, joining it to Ricketts's division (both of which belonged to McDowell's corps), moved toward the battlefield of Groveton, which was reached toward evening. Porter remained in his former position the rest of the day.

Matters went from bad to worse so far as the Federals were concerned. Pope's opportunity for engaging Jackson's corps alone was gone, and, with his own forces out of position, the Union leader was compelled to face the whole Confederate army under the eye of the masterful Lee himself. Pope not only did not know where McDowell and Porter were, but he was unaware of the alarming fact that Longstreet had joined Jackson.

No general of ability could find justifiable grounds for assailing Jackson in his entrenched position, but about the middle of the afternoon Pope ordered Hooker to make the attack. The indignant Hooker remonstrated, but Pope insisted, and the general who well deserved his title obeyed with great spirit. So well, indeed, did Grover's brigade do its work that it penetrated between the Confederate brigades of Gregg and Thomas, on the extreme left. They secured possession of the railroad embankment, and by the most furious kind of hand-to-hand fighting held it for some time; but Jackson then sent reinforcements forward, and the Unionists were driven out. When the time had passed for helping Hooker, Kearny was sent to his assistance, but the Confederates quickly drove him out after the others.

Having learned the location of Porter's command, Pope sent him orders to assail the enemy's right, flank and rear, Pope believing that the right flank of Jackson, near Groveton, was the right of the Confederate line. Near sunset, when Pope supposed Porter was about to make the attack, Heintzelman and Reno were ordered to assault the Confederate left. The order was obeyed with great dash and vigor. Kearny struck the demoralized division of Hill, on the left of Jackson, when their ammunition was nearly exhausted. Hill's flank was doubled up on his centre and the railroad embankment seized, but the Confederates had a fashion of throwing reinforcements to the right point at the right time, and Kearny was driven back.

All was silent on the left, where Porter was expected to join in the battle. The order which Pope forwarded to Porter was sent at half-past four, and reached him just at dusk, when he deemed it too late to do as directed. The night was intensely dark, and no attempt to advance was made.*

---

* This failure of Porter to obey the orders of Pope was the cause of an acrimonious discussion for years. Porter was court-martialled and dismissed from the army; many heated partisans contended that he ought to be shot. When time had allowed the passions on both sides to cool, Porter secured a reopening of the case. The testimony of Longstreet and other ex-Confederate commanders was secured, and it may be said that for the first time the full truth became public. Without entering into the discussion, it is enough to say that Porter did the best thing possible. By remaining where he was he held Long-

It had been a day of disaster to the Union army. Pope had thrown away the most tempting chances. He had blundered right and left, while Lee and his lieutenants had been successful in every direction. Thousands of men were killed and wounded, and there was little promise of hope for the Federals on the morrow. Bitter must have been the reflections of their commander when he recalled his bombastic proclamations on taking command of the army, and then saw how completely he had been outgeneralled by his adversaries. In the desperate plight in which he was placed he ought to have turned over the command of his forces to some other leader or retreated to Washington; but he did neither.

The condition of the Union army was pitiable. The men had scarcely a mouthful to eat for two days; they were worn almost to death from continual marching and fighting; stragglers were

street's corps inactive in his front during the terrible battle. It was utterly beyond his power to make the attack which the commanding general ordered, inasmuch as Longstreet's' corps was directly in his path. No doubt Porter was impatient with Pope and gave him little sympathy, but it was a fortunate thing for the Union army that he did not obey the orders of its commander. Porter continually knocked at the doors of Congress for relief; he obtained many friends who were anxious to see justice done him. Among these the most noted was General Grant, who at first had denounced him in the severest terms. Finally a bill was introduced reinstating Porter in the army without back-pay. It passed both Houses of Congress with little opposition, but was vetoed on technical grounds by President Arthur. The moral purpose of Porter's persistent battle for justice, however, has been accomplished.

S

everywhere; the horses had been in harness or under the saddle for more than a week; there was uncertainty in all directions, except the single one as to the incompetency of the general commanding. Pope decided to hold his position, and make another attack on the morrow. Before doing so it was natural that he should send a despatch to Washington announcing that Lee was in full retreat and fleeing to the mountains. The next day Pope revised this opinion.

Saturday, August 30, dawned bright and clear, and at the earliest streakings of light the confronting armies began assuming position for the tremendous conflict. General Lee's position was the same as on the previous day—his left near Sudley Ford, his centre at Groveton and his right on the Manassas Gap Railroad. Colonel S. D. Lee held the centre with thirty-two pieces of artillery; Longstreet's command stretched away obliquely from Jackson's, forming with it an angle of nearly forty-five degrees. The cavalry covered both flanks, the entire army being present, with the exception of Anderson's division, which was held in reserve.

"Now, by one of those curious conjunctures which sometimes occur in battle, it so was that the opposing commanders had that day formed each the same resolution: Pope had determined to attack Lee's left flank, and Lee had determined to attack Pope's left flank. And thus it came about that when Heintzelman pushed forward to feel the enemy's left the refusal of that flank by Lee, and his withdrawal of troops to his right for the purpose of making his contemplated attack on Pope's left, gave the impression that the Confederates were retreating up the Warrenton turnpike toward Gainesville. To take advantage of the supposed retreat of Lee, Pope ordered McDowell with three corps—Porter's in the advance—to follow up rapidly on the Warrenton turnpike and 'press the enemy vigorously during the whole day.' But no sooner were the troops put in motion to make this pursuit of a supposed flying foe than the Confederates, hitherto concealed in the forest in front of Porter, uncovered and opened a heavy fire from their numerous batteries, and while King's division was being formed on Porter's right in order to press an attack clouds of dust on the extreme right showed that the enemy was moving to turn the Union line in that direction, and that, instead of retiring, he was in the full tide of an offensive movement. To meet this manœuvre, General McDowell detached Reynolds's command from the left of Porter's force, north of the Warrenton turnpike, and directed it on a position south of that road to check this menace. The Warrenton turnpike, which intersects the Manassas battlefield, runs westward up the valley of the little rivulet of Young's Branch. From the stream the ground rises on both sides—in some places quite into the hills.

The Sudley Springs road, on crossing the stream at right angles, passes directly over one of these hills, just south of the Warrenton turnpike, and this hill has on it a detached road with fields stretching away from it some hundreds of yards to the forest. This is the hill whereon what is known as the 'Henry house' stood. To the west of it is another hill—the Bald Hill, so called—which is, in fact, a rise lying between the roads and making about the same angle with each and running back to the forest. Between the two hills is a brook, a tributary of Young's Branch. Upon the latter hill General McDowell directed Reynolds's division and a portion of Ricketts's command, so as to check the flank manœuvre that menaced the seizure of the Warrenton turnpike, which was the line of retreat of the whole army."*

The disastrous blunder of these movements lay in the fact that when Reynolds's division was detached from Porter's left it uncovered the very key to Porter's line. Colonel Warren, who commanded one of Porter's brigades, saw the danger, and without waiting for orders rushed forward his brigade of a thousand men and assumed the place vacated by Reynolds's division. Porter then made his attack on the Confederate position, but he accomplished nothing substantial, and finally, after suffering great slaughter from the artillery and infantry fire, he was driven back from the field. The truth

* Swinton.

was that, in making the attack on Jackson, Porter exposed himself to Longstreet's batteries. "It gave me an advantage I had not expected to have," said Longstreet, "and I made haste to use it. Two batteries were ordered for the purpose, and one placed in position immediately and opened. Just as this fire began I received a message from the commanding general informing me of General Jackson's condition and his wants. As it was evident that the attack against General Jackson could not be continued ten minutes under the fire of these batteries, I made no movement with my troops." Before the second battery could be placed in position the enemy began to retire, and in less than ten minutes the ranks were broken and that portion of his army put to flight. Colonel Warren with his thousand men maintained his position against great odds, fighting with splendid valor till all of Porter's troops had retreated, and then he fell back only when the Confederate bayonets were pressing the very faces of his men.

Night was at hand, and the Federal troops not only had suffered fearfully, but were in a demoralized condition. Jackson was quick to perceive this, and started in pursuit. Longstreet, sure that he would be ordered to join, threw his troops against the Federal centre and left. In a brief while the whole Confederate army was advancing upon the conquered Unionists. Pope was compelled at last to see that he was thoroughly and most ingloriously whipped. Like McClellan in the Peninsula, he could attempt but one thing—to extricate and save his army. While engaged in the effort, Longstreet carried Bald Hill, held by Ricketts and Reynolds, and menaced the Henry house hill. Had this been taken, Pope and his army would have been destroyed; but a battalion of regulars—who are ready to die at any time rather than acknowledge themselves beaten by volunteers—maintained the ground until relieved by the brigades of Meade and Seymour. When the gasping troops had fled across Bull Run and scrambled into position on the heights of Centreville, they retired. The impenetrable darkness and the uncertainty of the fords decided Lee to cease pursuit on the banks of the stream; otherwise, to retort with Pope's words, he would have "bagged the whole crowd."

Pope drew a sigh of relief when he reached Centreville, for there he united with the corps of Franklin and Sumner, and there he remained during the entire day. But General Lee was not yet through with him. He sent Jackson to Pope's right, while Longstreet was directed to stay on the battlefield and engage the attention of the enemy. There was still hope of cutting off Pope's retreat to Washington.

As is nearly always the case, the cannonading had caused such elemental disturbances that a heavy rain set in, and Jackson's march was very difficult and rendered tardy, while his men suffered much from exhaustion. At night he bivouacked near Chantilly, pushing on the next morning in the same direction.

· Pope meanwhile had fallen back so as to cover Fairfax Court-House and Germantown. There, on the evening of September 1, Jackson struck his right, at Ox Hill, near Germantown. It was raining in torrents, which beat directly in their faces as they made the assault, which fell on Reno, Hooker, a part of McDowell and Kearny. The Confederates were held at bay until Reno was killed, the ammunition exhausted, when the Union right fell back in disorder. Kearny instantly forwarded Birney's brigade from his own division, following it with a battery, which he placed in position. A gap still remained on Birney's right, which was pointed out to Kearny. The dashing one-armed hero—one of the bravest men on either side—rode forward to make a reconnoissance, and before he was aware entered the Confederate lines. He was in the act of wheeling his horse to escape, when he was shot dead. The next day the Federals withdrew within the lines of Washington, and the disastrous campaign was ended.

Pope seized the first opportunity to vacate his command. The Army of Virginia went out of existence and its corps were united with the Army of the Potomac, who clamored so loudly, " Give us back our old commander!" that McClellan was again made its leader.

The precise losses on both sides during Lee's campaign in Northern Virginia cannot be known with certainty. The Confederate authorities give the following figures as indicating their losses between August 23 and September 2: Longstreet's corps, four thousand seven hundred and twenty-five men; Jackson's corps, four thousand three hundred and eighty-seven; total, nine thousand one hundred and twelve. The confusion in the Federal army and its quick reorganization under McClellan precluded anything like an accurate estimate, but their loss was appalling. The Confederates captured nine thousand prisoners, thirty pieces of artillery and more than twenty thousand stands of arms in the engagement on the plains of Manassas alone. They have set down the Union losses at thirty thousand, and it is probable that they are not far out of the way.

Lee's campaign in Northern Virginia had been a wonderful success, and was a fit introduction to the Confederate invasion of the North.

III.

THE CAMP-FIRE OF ANTIETAM.

CHAPTER X.

FACING NORTHWARD.

IT is not to be supposed that when General Lee marched from Richmond to prosecute his campaign in Upper Virginia he had any thought of making an invasion of the Northern States. This, it may be said, is self-evident, for no one could have contemplated such colossal incompetency in the leadership of the Federal armies, and consequently the overwhelming success of the Confederates was beyond the expectation of any one. The Federal army in Northern Virginia had been sent skurrying into the entrenchments of Washington, and the excitement and consternation throughout the North was beyond description. Months before, the defeat of Banks had caused a general fear of the fall of the national capital, and now the whole Confederate army was almost within sight of the city.

"Is there to be no end of this? Must we be defeated over and over again? Are there no lead-

ers who can gain the semblance of a victory with
the army in Virginia? While our soldiers are
fighting so well in the West, it is nothing but
defeat, defeat, defeat, in the East."

These were the questions and remarks on the
lips of the millions of angered and impatient
Northerners. They did not despair, but became
the more exasperated with the gross mismanagement of affairs in Washington. The feeling was
common that, while they felt little admiration or
sympathy for Pope personally, yet he had been
"sold out" by Fitz-John Porter, and perhaps
others. The recall of McClellan to command the
reorganized Army of the Potomac was one of the
most satisfactory steps that the Federal government
could have taken. With that extravagant impul-
siveness which is characteristic of the American
people, he had been christened the "Young Napoleon," and all sorts of wild prophecies of his
success were uttered everywhere. Beyond question he was popular with the army, and the cry
which we have quoted, "Give us back our old
commander!" was literally a thunderous demand
from the Federal soldiers which could not be disregarded. McClellan assumed command and began reorganizing the army with the same vigor
and ability he had shown from the first. No one
could surpass him in that respect, and the univer-
sal confidence felt in his generalship added incal-
culably to the *élan* of the soldiers.

The all-absorbing question that every one asked
was, " What does General Lee mean to do ?" The
majority believed that he could walk unopposed
into Washington and make his own terms with
the national government, but at no time was there
danger of such a catastrophe to the Federal cause.
Lee's men had suffered frightfully ; they were ragged, barefooted, exhausted and famishing; they
had been forced to their utmost capacity, and imperatively needed rest. Washington had been put
in the best condition possible for defence, and had
a vast force of brave and tried soldiers to man her
entrenchments. Twice Lee's army could not have
taken it, so long as the garrison was there. If one
thing could be set down as certain, it was that the
Confederate chieftain, after such a magnificent success, would not turn about and march to his own
desolated valleys and stricken plains without leading his powerful legions farther North.

Many explanations have been given of the Confederate invasion of the North, and even Lee's own
words are not clear; but it may be ascribed to
several causes. The opportunity to do so with a
triumphant issue was too tempting to be resisted.
Thus far, despite the success of the Confederacy,
the battle had been fought on her own soil, and
her sufferings had been great; consequently, there
was a natural desire to press the bitter cup to the
lips of the invaders. Then, the Confederacy had
many friends in England and France, especially in

the latter country, where Louis Napoleon was willing to intervene if England would only join him. But the wily "nephew of his uncle" was waiting for the Confederates to strike some tremendous blow against the North which would justify him in stepping between the combatants and ordering the warfare to stop. Great as were the victories already gained by the Confederates, they were hardly enough to warrant this momentous step. If Lee could capture Baltimore or Philadelphia and cut off Washington, he would compel a peace on the basis of the independence of the Confederacy. The gates to Maryland were carried off their hinges by the turbulent flight of the Federal army, and the broad highway to that beauteous country

"Fair as a garden of the Lord"

was invitingly open. Food, clothing and abundant *matériel* were within the grasp of those who so sorely needed them. The famishing nostrils caught the odor of smoking viands, and the thin muscular fingers twitched with eagerness to clutch the boundless riches upon which their eager eyes rested.

General Lee saw that the most effective way of diverting the demonstration of the Union arms from Richmond was by an advance movement which, if prosecuted with the success that seemed very probable, would prevent any offensive movements by his enemies until the following year, and such delay was of inestimable importance in securing the mediation of foreign powers.

And lastly a natural error prevailed among the Confederates respecting the sentiments of the Marylanders: the State, being slave, was considered as rightly belonging to the Confederacy. The Union troops had been assailed when going through Baltimore on their way to the relief of Washington, and it was believed that if a safe opportunity was given the citizens they would gladly declare their allegiance to the Confederacy, furnish a large number of recruits in addition to those already in its army, and yield an enormous amount of supplies of which the Confederacy stood in extreme need. These causes, when united, were enough to justify General Lee in his determination to transfer the war to Northern soil, and he set out on the campaign with masterly skill. Instead of assailing Washington or Baltimore, he began manœuvring so as to induce McClellan to uncover them. As the first step in the important campaign, his plan was to enter Western Maryland and establish his communications with Richmond through the Shenandoah Valley. Then, by threatening Pennsylvania by the Cumberland Valley, he hoped to draw the Union army far enough into the State to afford his army the chance to seize Washington or Baltimore or to compel McClellan to fight when removed far beyond his base of supplies.

D. H. Hill's command had arrived on the 2d

of September, and the Confederate army was a
compact whole, held well in hand by the mighty
genius of Lee.   Hill's division was assigned to the
advance, and marched to the Potomac at a point
nearly opposite the Monocacy.   The Federals
guarding the river were scattered, and the division crossed into Maryland.   The rest of the day
and the following night were employed in destroying the locks and embankments of the Chesapeake
and Ohio Canal, one of the principal means by
which Washington was supplied with fuel.   Jackson, after allowing his soldiers a single day's rest,
had marched from Ox Hill on the 3d of September.   Two days later he crossed the Potomac at
White's Ford, near Leesburg, and the bands struck
up the popular air, "Maryland, my Maryland,"
while the thousands of throats thundered the cho-
rus with the same enthusiasm shown by the Federal legions in singing "John Brown's body lies
mouldering in the grave."   Even the grim, silent
Jackson was thrilled; his gray eyes kindled, and
a great joy overflowed his soul.   His fervency of
belief in the righteousness of the Confederate cause,
his profound piety and faith, saw in the scene the
fulfilment of God's pleasure and design.   He was
almost overcome with the delight which suffused
his whole being.

On the 6th of September the march was resumed, General D. H. Hill conducting the advance, in the temporary absence of Jackson, who

had been hurt by a fall from his horse. In a few hours Frederick City was reached, and on the 8th the whole army was drawn up on the left bank of the Potomac. Lee had arrived and established his headquarters at Frederick. The best of order was preserved, and the people were astonished at the considerate treatment they received when the temptation to violence was so great.

But a grievous disappointment awaited the Confederates. Instead of being received with open arms, they were viewed with distrust and disfavor. They were anything but welcome, for, no matter how strongly they might sympathize with the invaders, self-interest forbade the people to go farther. The ragged and grimy soldiers were not calculated to rouse the enthusiasm of the sentimental secessionist, and the officers in charge of the recruiting-offices which were opened found plenty of leisure-time on their hands, for scarcely a recruit came forward. Under these dispiriting circumstances, General Lee issued the following address to the people of Maryland:

"HEADQUARTERS ARMY OF NORTHERN VIRGINIA,
Near Frederickton, September 8, 1862.

"TO THE PEOPLE OF MARYLAND:

"It is right that you should know the purpose that has brought the army under my command within the limits of your State, so far as that purpose concerns yourselves.

" The people of the Confederate States have long watched with the deepest sympathy the wrongs and outrages that have been inflicted on the citizens of a commonwealth allied to the States of the South by the strongest social, political and commercial ties.

" They have seen with profound indignation their sister deprived of every right and reduced to the condition of a conquered province.

" Under the pretence of supporting the Constitution, but in violation of its most valuable provisions, your citizens have been arrested and imprisoned upon no charge and contrary to all forms of law. The faithful and manly protest against this outrage made by the venerable and illustrious Marylander to whom in better days no citizen appealed for right in vain was treated with scorn and contempt. The government of your chief city has been usurped by armed strangers; your Legislature has been dissolved by the unlawful arrest of its members; freedom of the press and of speech have been suppressed; words have been declared offences by an arbitrary decree of the Federal executive and citizens ordered to be tried by a military commission for what they may dare to speak.

" Believing that the people of Maryland possessed a spirit too lofty to submit to such a government, the people of the South have long wished to aid you in throwing off this foreign yoke, to enable you again to enjoy the inalienable rights of freemen and restore independence and sovereignty to your State.

"In obedience to this wish, our army has come among you, and is prepared to assist you with the power of its arms in regaining the rights of which you have been despoiled. This, citizens of Maryland, is our mission, so far as you are concerned. No constraint upon your free will is intended; no intimidation will be allowed. We know no enemies among you, and will protect all, of every opinion. It is for you to decide your destiny freely and without constraint. This army will respect your choice, whatever it may be; and, while the Southern people will rejoice to welcome you to your natural position amongst them, they will only welcome you when you come of your own free will.

"R. E. LEE,

"*Gen. Commanding.*"

This proclamation was perused with general interest by the people of Maryland, but they did not flock to the Confederate standard: it was impossible to "enthuse" them.

An illustrated paper hit off the situation in a cartoon which represented a wealthy Marylander, a day or two before the arrival of General Lee, watching his last load of goods as they were about to start Northward. He addressed the driver:

9

"Jim, have you got everything?"

"Yes, sir."

"Sure you haven't left anything?"

"Yes, sir; nothing is left."

"Not so much as a horse, cow, pig or chicken?"

"Not a living creature. There isn't even a hen's egg on the place, nor enough to afford a meal for a mosquito."

"All right, then. Drive on, and I'll stay behind to welcome General Lee and his brave boys."

CHAPTER XI.

GENERAL LEE rested his line upon the Shenandoah Valley. During the battle of Manassas the northern end of this valley was occupied by twelve thousand Federals, four thousand of whom, under General White, were at Winchester, and the rest at Harper's Ferry, under Colonel Miles. So soon as White learned of Lee's advance upon the Potomac, he withdrew from Winchester and occupied Martinsburg, while Miles was cut off from Washington by Stonewall Jackson, who, it will be remembered, had crossed the river near Leesburg. However, it was an easy matter for the Federals to cross in turn into Maryland, and, falling back, join the troops that were organizing for the resistance to the Confederate advance. When the latter passed the Potomac, Harper's Ferry and Martinsburg became of no account; for the railroad passing through those places was of no value to the Confederates, because it took a different direction from the one they were following. As a consequence, the Federals who stayed on the Virginia shore simply invited the Confederates to make them prisoners.

131

General Halleck was still commanding Harper's Ferry and Martinsburg from his headquarters in Washington, and he sent peremptory orders that the former should be defended to the last. Why he gave such a ridiculous order is hard to understand. It is said he claimed that Harper's Ferry was the key to Maryland, but, as we have shown, the sweep of the Federals had carried the gates with them; so the keys were useless. When Lee, at Frederick, learned that the Federals were still at Harper's Ferry, he decided to accept the invitation and go out and "bag the whole crowd." With this purpose he suspended for several days his advance Northward.

On the 10th of September the Confederate army turned its back on Washington and took up the line of march toward the Upper Potomac, entering the mountainous section of Maryland. For the purpose of capturing Harper's Ferry, Jackson, with his three divisions, the two divisions of McLaws and the division of Walker, was detached. Jackson was to go by way of Sharpsburg, crossing the Potomac above Harper's Ferry and advancing by the rear; McLaws was to proceed by way of Middleton, on the direct route to the ferry, and occupy the hills known as the Maryland Heights; Walker was to cross below Harper's Ferry and seize Loudon Heights. The movement was begun on the 10th, and it was intended the surrender should be forced by the 13th, after which the captors would immediately rejoin Lee on the march to Boonsboro' or Hagerstown.

It must not be forgotten that McClellan all this time was following Lee, though he did it from afar, and was obliged to keep so near Washington that he could whirl about and run back to its protection should the invaders turn in that direction. So guarded and slow were his movements that Lee was warranted in believing he could detach enough of his army to capture Harper's Ferry and to return before the Union commander could strike him.

It is one of the remarkable facts connected with the history of the late war that whereas General Halleck did a most foolish thing in ordering Harper's Ferry to be held, and that General Lee did what only ordinary generalship required him to do in capturing it, yet the Federal blunder proved in the end disastrous to the Confederate cause.

On the morning of September 12, Jackson entered Martinsburg and captured a large amount of stores abandoned by the Federals, who had withdrawn in great haste. Pushing on, he reached the Federal outer line, on Bolivar Heights, in the rear of Harper's Ferry, the next morning. General Hill, still leading the advance, encamped near Halltown, a couple of miles from Bolivar Heights. The rest of the force was near by, and General Jackson now set out to learn whether McLaws and Walker had arrived. His signals were answered

from the mountains opposite, and he instantly despatched couriers to Maryland and Loudon Heights
to see whether the two divisions were in position
for the attack.

General Walker had crossed the Potomac on
the night of the 10th, at Point of Rocks, and
marched hurriedly to Loudon Heights, which were
occupied three nights later. The courier sent by
Jackson dashed up shortly after, and, having com-
municated with Walker, galloped back to Jackson
with the news that Walker had arrived. The day
was so far gone, however, that the attack was deferred until the next morning. McLaws at that
time was steadily working his way up Maryland
Heights, which, once reached, placed Harper's
Ferry at his mercy, as will readily be perceived
from the following description.

The Elk Ridge Mountains, extending north and
south across portions of Maryland and Virginia,
seem to have split in two to allow the clamoring
waters of the Potomac to pass through. This naturally leaves a high rocky wall on each side. The
one on the north bank is called Maryland Heights,
and the one on the south is known as Loudon
Heights. Directly between the latter and Harper's Ferry the Shenandoah sweeps into the Potomac, and behind this river is a smaller ridge,
known as Bolivar Heights, which slopes off southward into the Shenandoah Valley. In the little
basin formed by this trio of mountain-peaks nestles

Harper's Ferry, the scene of the opening drama of the great civil war, in 1859, when John Brown made his memorable raid. Harper's Ferry is one of the most picturesque little towns in America, the mountain-peaks being about two miles from each other, with the town itself slumbering in the valley below. It will thus be seen that a strong force on any one of these ridges could bombard Harper's Ferry with the greatest ease.

Colonel Miles, in distributing his command for defence, posted a strong force on Maryland Heights, the highest of the three mountain-peaks, but, unfortunately for him, the larger part was down in the valley below. The commonest prudence would have saved him from leaving a single soldier in the death-trap, into which the Confederates could pour a resistless fire not only of cannon, but of musketry. Had he kept his entire command on Maryland Heights, he could have held it with ease until the arrival of McClellan, who even then was hurrying to his relief. Had the Federals strained their ears, they might have caught the boom of Franklin's signal-guns. He was hastening to their assistance and firing at intervals to apprise Colonel Miles of the fact, that he might be encouraged to hold out, as he had promised he would do. But the monumental blundering which was the distinctive feature of the Federal campaigns in the East during the early years of the war showed itself again at Harper's Ferry. It was folly to attempt to hold it, but Colonel Ford, when he awoke to the fact that Stonewall Jackson had turned his eye toward him, made only a feeble show of resistance, then spiked his guns, tumbled them down the rocks and hurriedly retreated to Harper's Ferry. Thus it was that Maryland Heights, towering far above the others, was vacated by the Federals. McLaws laboriously dragged some of his cannon to the top, and, looking across and down upon the other mountain-peaks, he saw both swarming with his comrades; the Stars and Bars fluttered in the wind, and on Loudon and Bolivar the cheers of the Confederates swept back and forth through the autumn air far above the doomed army below. Looking down on the quaint little town, nestling in the basin like one of the Alpine villages, every private in the Confederate forces felt that their game was as good as bagged already. The Federals had placed themselves between the upper and nether millstones, and they would be ground to powder.

The investment of Harper's Ferry was complete, and at daylight on the morning of September 15 a terrific plunging fire was opened on the garrison. It had lasted but an hour, when Colonel Miles called his officers together and told them it was useless to fight longer: they were at the mercy of their assailants, and he felt the best thing to do was to surrender. All assented, and the Confederate artillerymen, who were pouring their fire into the one common receptacle below, suddenly caught sight of a white flag fluttering through the smoke. Those who observed the token ceased firing, but several shots followed before the signal was fully recognized. The last one of these struck and mortally wounded Colonel Miles. It was fortunate for him that it did so; for had he survived, a disgrace awaited him far worse than death. Harper's Ferry was taken, and Colonel White surrendered more than eleven thousand men, seventy-three pieces of artillery, thirteen thousand small arms and an immense amount of military stores.

It is said that when the surrender was made General Jackson was leaning against a tree, sound asleep. Placing his hand on his shoulder, A. P. Hill introduced Colonel White, who had come to arrange the terms of capitulation. The eyelids parted just long enough for the leader to recognize his visitors, when he spoke one word: "Unconditional!" Then the drowsy eyelids drooped again, and he resumed his slumber, which was destined to be of short duration.

The terms were not such as Colonel White expected, but he had no choice; his command was completely disorganized, and it was utterly beyond his power to make any further defence. The surrender took place, as has been stated, and stirring events in other quarters immediately demanded the attention of Jackson.

CHAPTER XII.

THE surrender of Harper's Ferry was not completed when a courier, his horse covered with foam, arrived from General Lee with orders for Stonewall Jackson to join him at once. Leaving A. P. Hill to receive the surrender and superintend the removal of the captured property, and directing McLaws and Walker to follow without a moment's unnecessary delay, Jackson hurried to rejoin his chief. It was a time when no exertion could be spared, and the tired leader and equally tired men pushed forward all night with grim resolution, and reached Lee the next morning at Sharpsburg.

To understand the important events which immediately followed, it is necessary to go back a few days in the order of events; for the investment, assault and capture of Harper's Ferry were simultaneous with momentous proceedings in other quarters.

It has already been shown that Lee never meditated a direct attack on Baltimore or Washington, but his manœuvres were made for the purpose of drawing McClellan away from those cities, with a

138

view of falling upon them before "Little Mac" could return to their defence, or of compelling him to accept battle when removed from his base of supplies. General Lee left Frederick on the 10th, after Jackson had gone, and, moving by South Mountain, headed toward Boonsboro'. General Stuart with his cavalry was left east of the mountains to watch McClellan, who was known to be cautiously advancing. Word having reached Lee that the Federals were approaching from the direction of Chambersburg, Pennsylvania, General Longstreet was sent to Hagerstown to keep an eye on their movements and to hold them in check, while D. H. Hill halted near Boonsboro' with the purpose of shutting off the flight of the garrison at Harper's Ferry through Pleasant Valley, and to render such support to the cavalry as might be needed.

General Lee was making some exceedingly close calculations and predicating enormous risks on their success. The first fact which he accepted as already demonstrated was that Harper's Ferry would be compelled to capitulate on the 13th. McClellan was advancing so tardily that he would give Jackson time to return and rejoin Lee before the Federals could make an attack; but Harper's Ferry was not captured until the 15th, and McClellan did not allow the grass to grow under his feet, though it must be admitted that it sprouted. So soon as it was known that General Lee had crossed into Maryland, General McClellan moved to Frederick City to meet him. He reached that point on the 12th, and drove out the cavalry left there by General Stuart to watch him.

The Federal army, it will be remembered, was composed of the remnants of the Army of Virginia and the Army of the Potomac, and it had been placed in charge of McClellan in obedience to the demands of the country and of the army itself. Hooker commanded the First Corps (McDowell's old corps); General Reno, the Ninth Corps, formerly of Burnside's old force; and the Twelfth Corps, formerly commanded by Banks, was under General Mansfield. Besides these, Burnside's corps was brought up from Fredericksburg and attached to McClellan's forces. The effective strength of this army was eighty-seven thousand one hundred and sixty-four men of all arms.

On the march to Frederick City, General McClellan advanced by five parallel roads, with the purpose of covering Washington and Baltimore. The left flank rested on the Potomac, and the right on the Baltimore and Ohio Railroad.

All this time, as will be remembered, General McClellan was in utter ignorance of Lee's plan of campaign; hence the extreme caution with which he advanced. But at this juncture a most extraordinary piece of good-fortune befell the Union commander. When he reached Frederick, on the

morning of the 13th, an officer picked up a piece
of paper from a small table in the house which had
served as the headquarters of General D. H. Hill.
He observed the printed heading, *"Headquarters
Army of Northern Virginia,"* and, naturally enough,
unfolded and read the paper, whose great importance requires that it should be given in full:

"HEADQUARTERS ARMY OF NORTHERN VIRGINIA,
September 9, 1862.

"Special Orders
  No. 191.

"The army will resume its march to-morrow,
taking the Hagerstown road. General Jackson's command will form the advance, and after
passing Middleton, with such portion as he may
select, will take the route toward Sharpsburg, cross
the Potomac at the most convenient point, and
by Friday night take possession of the Baltimore
and Ohio Railroad, capture such of the enemy
as may be at Martinsburg and intercept such
as may attempt to escape from Harper's Ferry.

"General Longstreet's command will pursue the
same road as far as Boonsboro', where it will halt
with the reserve, supply and baggage trains of
the army.

"General McLaws, with his own division and
that of General R. H. Anderson, will follow General Longstreet. On reaching Middleton he will
take the route to Harper's Ferry, and by Friday
morning possess himself of the Maryland Heights

and endeavor to capture the enemy at Harper's Ferry and vicinity.

"General Walker with his division, after accomplishing the object in which he is now engaged, will cross the Potomac at Cheek's Ford and ascend its right bank to Lovettsville, take possession of Loudon Heights if practicable by Friday morning, Key's Ford on his left, and the road between the end of the mountain and the Potomac on his right. He will, as far as practicable, co-operate with General McLaws and General Jackson in intercepting the retreat of the enemy.

"General D. H. Hill's division will form the rear-guard of the army, pursuing the road taken by the main body. The reserve, artillery, ordnance and supply trains, etc., will precede General Hill.

"General Stuart will detach a squadron of cavalry to accompany the commands of Generals Longstreet, Jackson and McLaws, and with the main body of the cavalry will cover the route of the army and bring up all stragglers that may have been left behind.

"The commands of Generals Jackson, McLaws and Walker, after accomplishing the objects for which they were detached, will join the main body of the army at Boonsboro' or Hagerstown."

It is easy to imagine how the eye of McClellan kindled when this paper was placed in his hands and he read it through from beginning to end. It gave him the very knowledge for which he was seeking, and for which his government could have. afforded to pay millions of dollars. There, on the white paper before him, was a full revelation of Lee's plans, heretofore an impenetrable mystery to the Union commander, and the prosecution of which had thrown the North into consternation.

No doubt General Lee smiled in his dignified way when he sat down a few days before to examine the contents of General Pope's despatch-book, but it is safe to conclude that McClellan smiled almost to his ears when he perused a copy of "Special Orders No. 191."

The possession of this document was of the greatest value to General McClellan. It furnished him with an accurate description of General Lee's designs, showed him the disposition of his forces, and gave him an advantage over the Southern army which the reader will readily appreciate, and which should have resulted in the destruction of the Army of Northern Virginia. In short, that army was by the discovery of this order placed at the mercy of General McClellan.*

The Union leader saw the inestimable value of the hours, and instantly set to work to use to the utmost the knowledge which had come to him in such an extraordinary manner. Naturally, he decided to take advantage of the division of Lee's

---

* McCabe's *Life and Campaigns of General Lee.*

army by securing the passes of South Mountain, occupying Pleasant Valley, beating the Confederate army in detail and rescuing Colonel Miles at Harper's Ferry from Stonewall Jackson, who was on the point of griping the garrison by the throat. McClellan advanced swiftly, and on the afternoon of the 13th was in front of the passes of South Mountain. At that very hour McLaws and Anderson were placing their forces in position at Harper's Ferry.

After leaving the Potomac, beginning at the northern shore of that river and extending through Pennsylvania, the great range of the Blue Ridge is called the South Mountain. Two miles farther westward is the range known as Maryland Heights. The country lying between these two ranges is named Pleasant Valley, and is from two to three miles in width; it is very rugged, and almost Alpine in its character. There are two roads leading from Frederick City to the western part of the State—the main, or Hagerstown, road, which passes the South Mountain at Turner's Gap, near the village of Boonsboro'; and another, which passes the mountain at Crampton's Gap, about five or six miles farther to the south. These passes are very strong, and are impregnable against direct attack if properly defended. They may be turned, however, by mountain-roads leading to positions commanding them, high upon the sides of the mountain.*

* McCabe.

The Confederate cavalry in front of the passes of South Mountain exerted themselves to check McClellan, but he drove them back without difficulty. He then determined to throw his centre and right against the pass leading to Boonsboro', while Franklin's corps was to force the passage of Crampton's Gap, assail McLaws in the rear, drive him away and rescue the garrison at Harper's Ferry.

On the afternoon of the 13th, shortly after McClellan's arrival at South Mountain, Lee learned of his presence there; he saw at once that the Union commander, by some means unknown to him, had penetrated his designs. General D. H. Hill was ordered to occupy Turner's Gap and prevent McClellan from forcing his way through. Lee was still ignorant of what was going on at Harper's Ferry, though confident it would fall that day, which was the date fixed for its capture. He had counted on being joined by Jackson and his forces before McClellan could strike him, and but for the discovery of the orders sent to D. H. Hill the junction would have been effected as originally intended. This hope was frustrated, and it now became necessary to hold McClellan east of the mountains until the fall of Harper's Ferry, and until Jackson could reunite with the main body of the Confederate army.

General D. H. Hill understood the danger that threatened the army. He sent back the brigades

10

of Garland and Colquitt, and shortly after moved his whole division to the Gap. McClellan, as usual, was tardy in his movements. Had he displayed the vim and dash of Jackson, he would have possessed himself of the passes before the Confederates had time to take such precautions. At the time the Federals appeared in front the Confederates numbered scarcely two thousand, but they made such a bold stand that McClellan hesitated until General Hill had placed his whole division in position. But this division was only five thousand strong, and could not hold the entire line against such an attack as the Federals were capable of making. Hill could occupy the pass itself, but could not defend the two mountain roads by either of which the position might be turned.

Early in the forenoon Reno opened a sharp artillery-fire on the Confederate right, forgetting the high precipitous peak which overlooked and commanded the ridge to the right of the pass. Garland's brigade at first checked the Federal advance, but, their commanding officer being killed, his men were demoralized and driven back, and Reno established himself on the first ridge on the mountain-side. A vigorous continuance of the charge, and the Federals would have gained the road; but they had suffered severely, General Reno himself being killed. General Hill ordered up Anderson's brigade to replace that of Garland.

They were directed to hold the road, and Colonel Rosser, with his cavalry regiment dismounted as sharpshooters, and a battery of artillery were ordered to hold a mountain-path farther to the right. Colquitt's brigade and two batteries were sent to the support of Anderson, and several guns were placed in position to command the approach to the precipitous peak, which the Federals might have seized long before.

The vital importance of this peak was so clear to all that the Unionists determined to secure possession of it. When Hooker arrived with his corps, in the middle of the afternoon, he was ordered to carry the position, and he made the attempt with great spirit and bravery. The ground is very difficult, but the Federals ran nimbly forward, leaping over the obstructions like so many deer. The Confederate artillery did little damage, owing to the precipitous character of the ground, but the riflemen, behind trees, rocks and everything that would afford shelter, poured a murderous fire into their assailants. They fought bravely, however, and before it was dark had carried the crest.

Longstreet's main column had reached the pass about the middle of the afternoon, and his troops were stationed on both sides of the turnpike, near the centre of Hill's line. They were speedily engaged, and, though just in from a severe march, they fought with great spirit and repulsed the

Federal attack on the centre; but when darkness ended the conflict, the advantage was on the side of the Union forces. Though they had lost many men, including General Reno, the Confederate loss was still greater. They had repulsed every attempt against their centre, but on the left the peak held by Rodes's brigade had been carried, and the whole Confederate line was commanded by the guns of the Federals. Their position was no longer tenable, and Lee decided to retire from South Mountain and take position at Sharpsburg.

Lee had heard from Jackson that Harper's Ferry was certain to be captured the next day, and there was no special reason, therefore, for holding the mountain any longer. When stationed at Sharpsburg, he would be on the flank of any Federal force moving through Pleasant Valley upon the Confederates on Maryland Heights. Furthermore, he would hold the fords of the Potomac, thus preserving his line of retreat to Virginia should he meet with a reverse.

CHAPTER XIII.

AT BAY.

MEANWHILE, stirring events were taking place six miles to the southward, at Crampton's Gap. Franklin had reached there in the middle of the forenoon of the 14th, and immediately threw forward both of his divisions, Slocum on the right and Smith on the left. The pass was defended by a part of McLaws's force, who himself was engaged in the investment of Harper's Ferry. The Confederates were driven back from the base of the mountain, where they were sheltered by a stone wall, and forced up its precipitous sides. General Howell Cobb had been directed by McLaws to hold the pass if he had to lose every man while doing so, but he believed the attacking force was much less than it was. Such also was the opinion of General Stuart, who had been attentively watching the battle. It required three hours for the Federals to carry the pass, but they finally succeeded, capturing several hundred prisoners and stand of arms, including one piece of artillery.

When General McLaws learned that the Unionists had taken Crampton's Pass, he saw he was placed in a dangerous situation. Harper's Ferry had not

149

yet fallen, and his retreat up Pleasant Valley was cut off. If he withdrew along the river-shore at the base of Maryland Heights, his force would be decimated by the fire of the garrison at Harper's Ferry and Franklin would fall upon his rear. To attempt to retreat in any other direction would be equally certain to bring disaster. There seemed but the one thing to do—fight it out on that line if it took all the autumn. General McLaws, therefore, left only one regiment to hold Maryland Heights, while the major portion of his force took position in Pleasant Valley, less than two miles from Crampton's Gap, from which Franklin's soldiers were issuing into the valley. The bold front of the Confederates deceived Franklin, and, darkness coming on shortly after, no further demonstration was made that evening.

McLaws expected that as a matter of course he would be attacked early the next morning, but Franklin began cautiously manœuvring to obtain a position from which his artillery could command the Confederate line. McLaws was silently awaiting the attack, when news reached him that Harper's Ferry had surrendered and he was ordered to withdraw to the south side of the Potomac, and to lose not an hour in hastening to the assistance of Lee. McLaws did his duty well. He crossed over to Harper's Ferry early in the afternoon, and on the following morning went into camp at Halltown, where his men were given a little rest, which they sorely needed. The march was taken up again the next day, and just as the sun was rising on the 17th he joined Lee at Sharpsburg.

When the Confederates withdrew, on the morning of the 15th, McClellan pushed forward with all his army in pursuit; but he had not advanced far when the heads of his columns were checked at Antietam Creek, a small stream which, running toward the Potomac, empties into it six miles above Harper's Ferry. On the hills west of this brook General Lee had turned at bay, and was waiting with his army to give the Federals battle. McClellan had interfered a great deal with the plans of the Confederate leader, although he had not been able to prevent his carrying out the main object of his campaign. The cowardice of the garrison at Harper's Ferry and the resistance received at South Mountain had enabled Jackson not only to capture the former, but had given him the opportunity to rejoin his chief and afford his priceless assistance in the general engagement that was at hand.

But many things had gone amiss with Lee. The unexplainable occupancy of Harper's Ferry by the Federals had caused him to modify his original plan far enough to lead him to turn aside and capture that point. Though this capture was unexpectedly easy, it necessarily occupied several days which were of the utmost account. Worst of all was the discovery of "Special Orders No. 191," by which the whole minutiæ of the Confederate campaign was laid bare to General McClellan, who, as McCabe remarks, was given such an advantage that he ought to have destroyed the Confederate army.

The Confederate army well-nigh went to pieces from straggling; the enfeebled, the sick, the footsore, the barefooted and the lame dropped out of the ranks and were strung all along the weary march. So great, indeed, was this straggling that at one time General Lee lost heart and declared that his army was ruined. It had become imperatively necessary, therefore, that he should turn at bay and not only deliver battle, but allow many of the stragglers who were laboring painfully forward to join him. The army which had faced about on the west bank of Antietam Creek when the battle opened numbered less than forty thousand muskets.

The position chosen by Lee was admirable. At his back was the Potomac, which by a series of most extraordinary curves offered the best possible protection to his flanks. In the centre of the small peninsula was the little town of Sharpsburg, from which start four principal roads. The upper one runs almost due north, toward Hagerstown; the second follows a south-west course, toward Shepherdstown; the third runs south-east, to Rohrersville, and crosses Antietam Creek a short distance from Sharpsburg; away to the north-east stretches the fourth road, through Keedysville, on the Antietam, to Boonsboro'. Thus from Sharpsburg as a centre extended four great arms almost at right angles to one another. It was by the road to the north-east that the advance divisions of the Army of the Potomac debouched on the evening of September 15, in front of the Confederate position on the west side of Antietam Creek. General Lee had posted his men so as to guard two of the stone bridges across the creek, the other two which span the stream being so far removed that they were considered of no importance; besides, his lines would have been too attenuated had he attempted to guard those bridges. But above the upper bridge were a number of fords easily accessible. Instead of coming down to the edge of the stream to defend these, Lee drew his army back in the direction of the Potomac, so as to close the peninsula and rest the end of his line on that river.

On the evening of the 15th, when the Federal army emerged to view, Lee had not yet consolidated his forces, as we have stated; in fact, his halt had for one of its main purposes this very junction of his scattered soldiers, to save them from being destroyed by McClellan in detail. He had twenty thousand men with him when he turned at bay, and he had succeeded in posting only two brigades of Longstreet's corps, under Hood, to the north of the town, where it confronted the advance of the

Federals by the upper fords. The principal part of his force remained in front of the positions which McClellan began to take with his main army. Longstreet had deployed on the right of the Boonsboro' road, and Hill on the left. The ground was elevated, and could not have been better chosen: the surface was so rough and uneven, as it sloped away to the creek, that it rendered manœuvring by an attacking force very difficult.

Strange fact that the centre of the Confederate line should have been marked by a church which seemed to shrink from the dreadful havoc that impended! That house of God, where the words of peace and good-will toward men had been so often proclaimed, was to tremble with the roar of cannon, and the ground was to run red with the blood of brothers arrayed against brothers. The structure, known as "Dunker Church," stands just west of the Hagerstown turnpike, about equally distant from Sharpsburg, the Potomac and Antietam Creek. It is close to the intersection of a cross-road running north-east, and a dense wood skirts the road at that point. Farther on toward Hagerstown was an extensive clearing almost enclosed by woods; it sometimes bordered the road and at intervals drew away from it. It extended, also, a considerable distance to the east of the highway just above the church.

In the direction of the Antietam the ground was likewise difficult and rocky, and Lee had

drawn up his army in such position that if Mc-
Clellan threatened his extended left he could mass
his troops at that point, so as to resist an attack,
while, with the two bridges on his right and the
narrow neck of the peninsula on his left to defend, he was able, in case of reverse, to retreat
over the Potomac by the Shepherdstown ford.

The Federal army began arriving on the banks
of the Antietam toward the close of the 15th, and
by dawn on the next morning all had reached the
place, with the exception of the two divisions of
the Sixth Corps and those of Morell and Couch,
while more than one-third of Lee's army was yet
on the right bank of the Potomac. McClellan,
therefore, still held the opportunity for an overwhelming assault, and a fog overhung the field of
operations; so that his movements could have been
screened from the Confederates. But the Federal
commander was not that kind of a general: he
did not propose to exhaust his men by hurrying
them into position. He waited until the sun dissipated the mists, in order that he might see where
they were going; this took until the middle of
the day, and the most precious hours were irrecoverably lost to the Federal commander.

CHAPTER XIV.

By two o'clock in the afternoon McClellan had fixed upon his plan of battle. His several corps had deployed along the hills on the east of Antietam Creek, and opened with artillery on the Confederates. Burnside, with the Ninth Corps, was posted among the hills south of the Rohrersville road, in front of the Confederate right, from which he was separated by the stone bridge that spanned the creek. On the hills over which ran the Keedysville road were posted the first line of Sykes's division on the left of the road, and Richardson on the right. They thus held the positions taken the day before. The remaining two divisions of Sumner's corps were posted in the rear of Richardson. Toward the right Hooker was stationed, on the heights whence the road slopes toward Antietam Creek. Directly behind him was Mansfield's scant corps, while Pleasanton with his cavalry occupied the fords and the upper bridge of the creek. This force of McClellan numbered over sixty thousand men, fifty thousand of whom were prepared for battle. Many of them, however, were new recruits who had never been under fire

156

before, while the Confederates had been baptized in the flame of battle.

But Lee, as we have shown, had less than one-half as many men with which to oppose this powerful army. He arranged his line of battle, however, and made his dispositions as calmly and with as much confidence as though he was assured of capturing the entire Federal army. Longstreet was on his right, D. H. Hill in the centre, both holding the hills which overlook the Keedysville and Rohrersville roads, while most of the artillery was concentrated in front, so as to guard the passes of the little stream. Far over to the extreme left, by Dunker Church, Hood was stationed with two brigades, while Jackson with his decimated divisions strove to cover the extensive opening between Hood's right and Hill's left, on the Antietam, with a view of linking them together, so far as such a thing was possible.

The fog slowly lifted now and then; and when the armies could catch sight of each other, they saluted with their murderous artillery. This continued until two o'clock, when Hooker began the advance, with the view of crossing the Antietam at the upper bridge and fords, held by the Federal cavalry, and of attacking the Confederate left. McClellan proposed by this means to turn the position of Lee, for it promised to be far less difficult than a direct attack in front. Burnside was to maintain his original position, on the Rohrersville road, while the rest of the Federals were ordered to hold themselves in readiness to follow Hooker across the creek and to support him in his attack. Hooker obeyed with his usual promptness, and came at once in collision with Jackson's outposts, which were supported by Hood, who hastened forward from Dunker Church. The battle, therefore, opened in the extensive clearing already referred to, which extended to the north and east of this church. What promised to be a most sanguinary struggle was terminated by darkness, and both armies slept on their arms.

During the night Mansfield's corps crossed the Antietam and took position behind Hooker, while Sumner was instructed to follow at daybreak with the Second Corps. Franklin, with the divisions of Slocum and Smith, was to advance from Pleasant Valley, so as to reach the scene of battle by ten o'clock; Porter, with his second division, was to arrive near the same time. Thus, with the single exception of Couch's division, the whole Army of the Potomac would be concentrated for the purpose of crushing the Confederate army, which had not been able as yet to consolidate its different wings, though they were hurrying toward the one central point. Lee was quick to detect the plan of McClellan, and he strengthened his left wing by sending Jackson to Hood's brigades, in the woods, which they had held with such bravery the evening before, and where they had suffered severely. D. H. Hill, in the centre, was to support Jackson whenever it became necessary.

Hooker was not the man to hesitate after receiving his orders, and he renewed the attack at daylight on the 17th with his accustomed spirit and dash. It was the purpose of McClellan to compel Lee to send most of his forces to the neighborhood of Dunker Church, and thus open the way for an onslaught by Burnside at the lower bridge. This would fall upon Longstreet, on the Confederate centre and right; and if successful, the Federals, who were threatening Sharpsburg and the Williamsport ford, would compel Lee to retreat. McClellan was warranted in believing that his preponderating numbers would enable him to carry out this plan, though it will be seen that it could succeed only by the prompt and unfaltering co-operation of his lieutenants.

The morning of the 17th, unlike that of the previous day, was clear. Hooker advanced his three divisions, Doubleday on the right, Meade in the centre and Ricketts on the left. Meade quickly found his men the targets for Starke's division, which had relieved Hood, and, sheltered behind rocks, stumps, trees and all kinds of *débris*, poured a deadly fire upon the advancing Federals. The struggle for the possession of the wood was of the most desperate and bloody nature. The losses were numerous; men dropped rapidly, and the deaths among the officers were frightful. Vet-

erans who had fought in the war from the opening
battle found the fight in the wood the most sanguinary that had yet taken place. How the Confederates held their ground so long against such
overwhelming odds and after such appalling losses
is amazing, and was another proof that the world
has never produced better fighters.

All three of Hooker's divisions were speedily
engaged, and were supported by the fire of the
Federal batteries on the left bank of the Antietam, which raked the scant soldiers of Jackson,
though it inflicted less loss than the incessant discharge of musketry; still, the Confederates remained firm for more than an hour, when they
began falling slowly back, until the large clearing
already described was reached. Across this they
ran into the woods on the east, beyond the Hagerstown turnpike, in search of shelter. Hooker
pressed close behind them, evidently believing that
he had the Confederates on the run and could keep
them running; but he committed a costly error.
Stuart's horse-artillery had occupied the hills fring-
ing the woods to the west of Dunker Church, and
which commanded the patch of forest where the
Confederates had taken refuge. This artillery held
Doubleday in check, while Ricketts, on the left, was
hotly engaged with three brigades under D. H. Hill,
that had been drawn from the Confederate centre for the support of Jackson. Meade was in bad
shape on account of his great losses, and he received

a murderous volley of musketry while approaching the Hagerstown pike. Lawton, who was held in reserve with his division near Dunker Church, was now sent forward by Jackson to the support of Starke. They supported him with such vigor, and from the edge of the woods rained such a destructive fire upon the Federals, that they broke and skurried for cover. Quick to perceive his opportunity, Lawton ordered a charge. He was supported by some of Starke's men, and they were sweeping everything before them, when at this most critical moment the Federal general Mansfield, who had been summoned by Hooker in great haste, arrived, and but for this timely aid Hooker would have been destroyed.

Exasperated by his bloody repulse, Hooker would not admit that his opportunity was gone. He reformed his broken line with the best brigade in the centre, and returned to the assault. He succeeded in reaching the edge of the woods, but there he was again hurled back, with the same dreadful losses as before.

The veteran Mansfield now hurried his men into the battle. His two divisions were deployed in the shape of a crescent in the clearing, while in the woods to the east Greene, with one of the divisions, attacked Hill, who was fighting Ricketts. The Federal Williams, on the right, rushed across the Hagerstown pike with his men, and tried desperately to drive out the Confederates from the

11

woods and hills to the west, so as to flank those who were defending the position near Dunker Church. General Starke was killed, and Lawton, who succeeded him, was wounded, while officers as well as privates were literally mowed down. Jackson's troops fell back before this concentrated attack, which threatened to be irresistible.

But on the Federal side the losses were more terrible. Mansfield was dead, and so were hundreds of his men. Indeed, the ground in both the woods and the clearing was strewn with lifeless bodies. Those who kept their feet and were able to fight had to leap over the prostrate forms, and sometimes they were so close that they lay on top of one another. The living trampled the dead and dying, whose cries of anguish, joining the crash of musketry, the thunder of cannon and the shouts of the combatants, made a din whose overpowering horror was beyond imagination.

Lee saw that the fate of his army was at stake, and he sent all the reinforcements he could spare to the support of his left. In fact, he called his entire centre to the help of the sorely-pressed Jackson, while Hood, who was held in reserve, joined him. Hooker was still fighting as best he could, but he could not withstand this impetuous charge, which swept him and his men from the open ground to the shelter of the wood from which a short time before they had dislodged Starke's division. In this furious struggle Hooker himself was severely wounded, and carried off the battlefield, while Hart-suff and Crawford had also been stricken down. Finding themselves deprived of leaders, the soldiers fought with blind ferocity. Crouching behind trees, and, indeed, anything that promised the slightest protection, they fired in the direction of the Confederates as fast as they could load and discharge their hot, smoking pieces. The artillery lent them great assistance, or they could not have been able to make any stand at all. Greene, however, still maintained his grip in the woods, which reached over to Dunker Church. It was evident that the battle itself was to be fought on and around the clearing to which we have already several times referred.

But Federals and Confederates were so exhausted that they could only pant and glare at each other while waiting for reinforcements. Indeed, the latter were already rushing thitherward from both sides. Sumner had crossed the river, and was marching rapidly in the direction of Hooker's cannon. Lee found himself with only two divisions of Longstreet with which to protect the entire line of the Antietam, but McLaws outran Franklin in the race from Harper's Ferry, and, crossing the Potomac twice, joined his chief just in time to hasten to the defence of Dunker Church. But, prompt as he was, Sumner was ahead of him with his Second Corps, and the outlook was most serious for the Confederates. It was yet early in the forenoon, and most important results were to be attained before the sun went down in the West.

With Lee's attention almost entirely occupied with his left, McClellan saw that the time had come to assault the Confederate right. McClellan from a commanding position was intently watching the battle, and fully an hour previous he had sent an order to Burnside (who, it will be remembered, was stationed on the right bank of the Antietam, confronting with thirteen thousand men the right of Lee's army, with the stone bridge between them) to capture the bridge and attack Longstreet. Instead of making a general assault, Burnside sent Crook's weak brigade against those who were defending the bridge, supporting the assailants by two regiments only from the division of Sturgis. The Confederates waited until the Federals were within a few rods, when they drove them back with great loss; a brigade which attempted to cross the stream some distance below was repulsed in the same rattling fashion. Two more regiments were sent to renew the charge at the bridge, but they met with no better success than before, and at the end of two hours not the least impression had been made on Lee's right.

McClellan could not comprehend the inactivity of Burnside, and sent order after order to him to make a general attack. With such a powerful force at hand, Burnside continued to send driblets —as they may be called—to the assault, with the result that the Confederates defeated them every time with little difficulty, inflicting great loss upon the assailants.

Sumner and his Second Corps were again fighting on the right, Sedgwick in the advance, with French close behind him. Forming his division in column by deployed brigades, Sedgwick debouched into the clearing, on the east side, and, charging diagonally across it, drove back Hood's two brigades, who were making such a gallant fight. Sedgwick pressed steadily forward until he reached the Hagerstown pike, across which he passed until he entered the woods, from which Hooker and Mansfield had been repeatedly driven. Dunker Church was occupied, and the Confederates were driven across the open fields beyond. Thus the Federals had secured the key to the battlefield, and it looked as if the struggle was decided irretrievably against the Southerners; but the bravery and impetuosity of Sedgwick proved his weakness.* He had been carried by the momentum of his own assault too far, and his flanks were exposed. True, General Doubleday and the woods afforded some protection to his right, but the left invited attack by the Confederates, and two of his divis-

* One of the remarkable facts connected with this battle was that a considerable time elapsed before either the Federal or the Confederate leaders perceived the immense value of this position.

ions were beyond supporting distance. Now was the time when he needed reinforcements.

The Confederates were equally in need, and were fortunate enough to receive them first. McLaws, with five thousand men, arrived from Sharpsburg by the Hagerstown pike, and without a moment's delay hurled them against Sedgwick's left. Sedgwick faced his third brigade about, but it was too late. The charge of the Confederates bore down everything before them. The brave General Sedgwick, who had been wounded three times and refused to relinquish his post, exerted himself to the utmost to rally his troops. He shouted and besought them to stand firm, dashing hither and thither and swinging his sword over the heads of the terrified soldiers; but all in vain. The panic was complete, and the Federals were driven pell-mell out of the woods they had so recently secured at such a terrible cost. A charge was made by Williams's second brigade, under Gordon, but the most it could do was to withdraw again with enough haste to prevent its capture. McLaws was on its heels, and would have inflicted sad havoc had he not been checked by the Federal artillery-fire.

Previous to this, Sumner, with a view of saving Sedgwick, had ordered his two other divisions to attack, but the divisions were widely separated. The three columns of the first, on reaching the cross-road leading to Dunker Church, were wheeled in line of battle, and marched around the end of the wood to attack the right of McLaws; but an enfilading fire threw the second line into confusion. The rest of the two divisions held their ground more firmly, and speedily came into collision with Hill's soldiers near the Roulette farm, which lies to the north-east of Dunker Church. This was at the very moment that Sedgwick was hotly repelling the attack of McLaws at Dunker Church. The whole right, therefore, were fighting furiously. It was the golden opportunity for Burnside, but he stirred not. Sumner and Sedgwick listened, so far as they could amid the crash and swirl of battle, for the sounds of his attack, which would divert the unbearable pressure upon them; but a tomblike silence prevailed in that direction. Messengers were continually galloping from McClellan to Burnside with positive orders for him to attack at once and with all his force, but a wooden man might as well have occupied his place; he continued immovable.*

Lee was not the leader to allow such an opportunity to pass unimproved. He detached another division from Longstreet's corps and sent R. H. Anderson to check the Federals, who were beginning to make progress on the Confederate left. Thus it was that Longstreet was charged with the

---

* It is hard to understand this inactivity of Burnside. Porter disliked Pope, but the commander of the Ninth Corps and McClellan were warm personal friends, and Burnside could not have failed to see the urgent need of such an advance, which he had been repeatedly ordered to make.

defence of the whole line of the Antietam, when his force amounted only to about four thousand men.

And still Burnside, with three times as large a force, gave no sign of moving.

CHAPTER XV.

McLAWS, finding his soldiers exposed to a most destructive fire, assailed the right flank of the first division that had been sent to the help of Sedgwick. He failed, however, to break it, while farther along the Federal left General Meagher's Irish brigade held their own against the most determined Confederate assaults. Meagher himself was wounded, but the lads from the Emerald Isle rallied under Colonel Burke and fought with a bravery worthy of all praise.

The Confederates, as was their favorite custom during the war, repeatedly massed their soldiers and made impetuous assaults upon what appeared to be the weakest portion of the Federal line; but for a time little was accomplished by this course. The Roulette farm was taken and the hills near by were reoccupied, but the Confederates made such a determined stand at the sunken road near by that for a time they could not be dislodged. Finally they were flanked by a couple of regiments, driven out, and after another furious conflict the Federals gained possession of the Piper house.

It was now high noon, and matters looked bad for the Confederates. Dunker Church had been turned, and a little farther advance would yield to Sedgwick not only the clearing, but the woods through which the tide of battle had swept so often during the forenoon. Pleasanton covered the movement with three batteries of horse-artillery and protected his flank; he drove out the detachments left by Lee to guard the bridge of the Keedysville road. Thus the way was opened for Porter to cross the Antietam with his two divisions. But insurmountable obstacles interposed. The Federal division which had turned Dunker Church could not advance unassisted. Hooker and Mansfield's men were mixed up with Sedgwick's, and the Confederate batteries near Dunker Church enfiladed the Federals every time they attempted to advance. Porter continued in reserve, and still General Burnside slept.

During the last hour, however, the Federals had received the powerful reinforcement of Franklin with the two divisions of the Sixth Corps. Between twelve and one o'clock they swung into line to the support of the right, but the loss on each side had been so fearful, and the exhaustion so great, that neither could assume the offensive. Lee had not a man in reserve, while only about half of the Federal army had been engaged. The Confederate leader contracted his lines by withdrawing his left wing from Dunker Church, which was immediately taken possession of by the Federals, who also sent a brigade to rescue a battery in imminent danger of capture on the Hagerstown pike, while another brigade had been sent to the relief of French, who was short of ammunition. McLaws's soldiers were encountered in the woods, near Dunker Church, and they repulsed the Federal attack; but Franklin massed all of Slocum's division behind the church and prepared to assault the Confederate left wing. The divisions of French and Richardson, which had been doing a large share of the fighting on the Union side, opened a lively fire upon the Confederates, during which General Richardson was mortally wounded. Under the protection of Pleasanton's cavalry Porter had secured possession of the Keedysville road, and hurried six battalions of infantry across to the support of the mounted batteries of the cavalry division.

It was one o'clock, and Burnside still slept. Determined to wake him up at all hazards, McClellan sent a superior officer with instructions to see that his orders were executed. This awoke Burnside, and he prepared to make a resolute effort to carry the passes of the Antietam. The fire of Longstreet's artillery converged upon this bridge with such deadly effect that the partial attempts, as they may be called, were easily repulsed, and the stern necessities of the case caused Lee to withdraw most of his men to defend the tremendous assaults on his left. As a consequence, when Burnside threw forward the four regiments of General Ferrero, supported by a powerful force, Toombs and his weak brigade were unable to stem the rush. The Federals lost nearly three hundred men, but they carried the bridge. Simultaneously, Rodman's division availed themselves of a newly-discovered ford lower down-stream and rushed across the Antietam to the western side, while Burnside with the Ninth Corps occupied the hills between Sharpsburg and the stream adjoining the Rohrersville road.

It looked now as if a general advance by the Federals would carry every position of the Confederates. With more than double their number, McClellan ought to have forced his mighty but exhausted adversary into Sharpsburg; but it was not attempted, and therefore was not done. Burnside spent a couple of hours in reforming his line and waiting for the rest of his corps to join him; Sumner, on reaching Dunker Church, was so impressed by the disorganization of Sedgwick's corps that he assumed the responsibility of forbidding the general attack which Franklin was about to begin; McClellan, in the centre, held Porter's corps in reserve, to be prepared for any demonstration on the part of the Confederates. Thus more than twenty thousand men stood idle, when Lee had had every one of his engaged for hours.

When the afternoon was half gone, Burnside was forcing Toombs's attenuated and exhausted brigades before him, and had almost secured the Confederate artillery, when A. P. Hill, arriving from Harper's Ferry with his powerful division, assailed Burnside's left flank with a furious impetuosity which carried everything before it. The Federals were checked, and then compelled to fly. They fought desperately, and several diversions were made in their favor; but there was no stopping the Confederates, and finally Burnside was driven to the shelter of the bluff overlooking the Antietam. This ended the fighting on the Federal left, and, as that on the right had ceased some time before, hostilities for the day were over. The battle of Antietam, the fiercest and bloodiest of the war thus far, was ended. The Federal loss was one thousand and forty-three prisoners, nine thousand four hundred and sixteen wounded, and two thousand and ten killed. This appalling loss included three division commanders, two corps commanders and eight generals. Lee had more than fifteen hundred killed, including Generals Starke and French, while his wounded and prisoners swelled the total to fully eight thousand. No such bloody battle had been fought since the opening of the war, and it carried sorrow and grief to thousands of homes through the North and the South. The scene on the Antietam battleground on the evening of September 17, 1862, was one of the most awful that imagination can conceive, and yet Death was to garner more terrible harvests before the strife should cease. After consulting with his lieutenants on the morning of the 18th, McClellan decided to defer assailing Lee until the next day, the attack at that time being based on the expected arrival of promised reinforcements from Washington; but on the night of the 18th, Lee withdrew across the Potomac, and on the morning of the 19th he and his army stood on the soil of Virginia.

The Federals claimed Antietam as a great victory, and the Confederates did the same. The former vaunted themselves much on the fact that Lee was forced to turn back from his contemplated invasion of the North and to withdraw once more to his old fighting-ground, but the Confederates claimed that the withdrawal of Lee was not in consequence of the battle of Antietam—or Sharpsburg, as they call it—but had been decided upon before the conflict took place. Lee was disappointed in obtaining recruits in Maryland and he was far removed from his base of supplies, while he knew that immense reinforcements were on their way to McClellan. Common prudence, therefore, dictated that he should fall back nearer his base, where he could easily sustain himself, as he proved more than once. There can be no question that Lee handled his troops with far more ability than did McClellan. The very fact that with half as many soldiers, poorly supplied, he was able to repel assault after assault and to inflict such frightful losses upon his assailants, leaves no ground for argument on this point. General Lee was one of the greatest generals of modern times.

General Longstreet was the first to withdraw on the night of the 18th, recrossing the river near Shepherdstown. The rest of the army followed, the cavalry bringing up the rear, and the next morning the troops were in position to receive any attack which the Federals might choose to make. Finding his wily adversary had gone, McClellan began to think about pursuit. Porter was pushed forward and crossed the river at a safe distance from the main body, but, falling upon Pendleton and his six hundred infantry, drove him off and captured four of his guns. A considerable force was established on the south shore when General Lee, who was some distance away, learned what had taken place; he sent A. P. Hill back with orders to force Porter over the river. The scene which followed was frightful. The Federals were attacked with such fury that they were driven headlong into the Potomac. Hundreds were taken prisoners, and hundreds more were drowned or shot.

When General Lee was in the neighborhood of Winchester, he issued the following general order to his gallant army, which had endured so many hardships:

"HEADQUARTERS ARMY OF NORTHERN VIRGINIA,
October 2, 1862.

"General Order
No. 116.

"In reviewing the achievements of the army during the present campaign, the commanding general cannot withhold the expression of his admiration of the indomitable courage it has displayed in battle and its cheerful endurance of privation and hardship on the march.

"Since your great victories around Richmond you have defeated the enemy at Cedar Mountain, expelled him from the Rappahannock, and after a conflict of three days utterly repulsed him on the plains of Manassas and forced him to take shelter within the fortifications around his capital.

"Without halting for repose you crossed the Potomac, stormed the heights of Harper's Ferry, made prisoners of more than eleven thousand men, and captured upward of seventy pieces of artillery, all their small arms and other munitions of war.

"While one corps of the army was thus engaged, the other ensured its success by arresting, at Boonsboro', the combined armies of the enemy advancing under their favorite general to the relief of their beleaguered comrades.

"On the field of Sharpsburg, with less than one-third his numbers, you resisted from daylight until dark the whole army of the enemy, and repulsed every attack along his entire front, of more than four miles in extent.

"The whole of the following day you stood prepared to resume the conflict on the same ground, and retired next morning, without molestation, across the Potomac.

"Two attempts subsequently made by the enemy to follow you across the river have resulted in his complete discomfiture, each being driven back with loss.

"Achievements such as these demanded much valor and patriotism. History records few examples of greater fortitude and endurance than this army has exhibited, and I am commissioned by the President to thank you in the name of the Confederate States for the undying fame you have won for their arms.

"Much as you have done, much more remains to be accomplished. The enemy again threatens us with invasion, and to your tried valor and patriotism the country looks with confidence for deliverance and safety. Your past exploits give assurance that this confidence is not misplaced.

"R. E. LEE,
"<i>Commanding General.</i>"</div>

The battle of Antietam ended McClellan's military career. The North had manifested great impatience with his long delay the previous year in marching against Richmond: his popularity, however, was very great, especially with his soldiers and subordinates; and the impatience became exasperation when he shrank from vigorously pursuing Lee after the battle of Antietam, but he was engaged in organizing just such a pursuit when he received an order relieving him from the command of the Army of the Potomac, which was turned over to General Burnside.

GENERAL LEE AT THE BATTLE OF FREDERICKSBURG.

IV.

THE CAMP-FIRES OF FREDERICKSBURG AND CHANCELLORSVILLE.

CHAPTER XVI.

RESTING ON THEIR ARMS.

THE Confederate army was in a deplorable condition. Cold weather was at hand, and the majority were in rags and without shoes. Still more, they were half starved and subjected to suffering which would have rendered desperate, men with half their courage. General Lee was urgent in his demands that the government should do something at once for the fire-tried veterans who had fought so hard for their country, but the government seemed unable to rise to the occasion, and the citizens of Richmond and Petersburg became so indignant that they forwarded a large supply of shoes to the army. This stirred the authorities to do something.

Meanwhile, the stragglers were rapidly gathered in, and their "vacation" had placed them in the best possible condition. The army rapidly aug-

mented, and in less than a month was in better
condition than before. Those were jolly and en-
joyable days, and the Confederates were a happy
lot, overflowing with rugged health and exuberant
spirits, dearly loving a frolic and continually sky-
larking. Their sport may have been rude and
boisterous, but it was honest and gave them the
vitality they needed to carry them through the
tremendous campaigns yet before them.

"The only useful occupation of this brigade,"
wrote one of Jackson's soldiers, "has been to destroy all the railroads in reach—apparently, too,
for no better reason than the fellow had for killing the splendid anaconda in the museum : because
it was his 'rule to kill snakes wherever found.'

"It is when idle in camp that the soldier is a
great institution, yet one that must be seen to be
appreciated. Pen cannot fully paint the air of
cheerful content, hilarity, irresponsible loungings
and practical spirit of jesting that obtains, ready to
seize on any odd circumstance in its licensed levity.
A 'cavalryman' comes rejoicing in immense top-
boots, for which, in fond pride, he has invested full
forty dollars of pay; at once the cry of a hundred
voices follows him along the line: 'Come up out
o' them boots! Come out! Too soon to go into
winter-quarters! Boots, where be you going with
that fellow?' A bumpkin rides by in an uncom-
monly big hat, and is frightened by the shout,
'Come down out of that hat! 'Tain't any use to

say you ain't there, for we see your legs sticking out.' A fancy staff-officer was horrified at the irreverent reception of his nicely-twisted moustache as he heard from behind innumerable trees, 'Take them mice out o' your mouth! We see their tails hangin' out.' Another, sporting immense whiskers, was urged to 'Come out of that bunch of har! I know you're in thar: I see your ears working.'

"Whenever there was great cheering along the line, it used to be said, 'It's either Jackson or a rabbit.' The meaning of this was that whenever a rabbit was started in the bivouac of a brigade the entire complement of officers and men would turn out to pursue Bunny, and, by heading him off here and turning him there, poor Bunny, who in the end would become bewildered by the diabolical yells and cheers which met him at every turn, was generally captured. General Jackson shunned, if he could, the demonstrations which greeted him whenever he passed a camp of his own corps or of Longstreet's. The men would gather on the roadside waving their hats and yelling like demons, the yells being taken up from camp to camp as 'Old Jack' went skurrying along on his old sorrel as fast he could lay feet to the ground. There was a spice of mischievousness in this, for soldiers are like schoolboys, and they knew how badly Jackson hated notoriety; but their admiration and enthusiasm for him were such that they would have charged the

very gates of Hades at his bidding. Never were
more genuinely sorrowful tears shed than those
that fell from the eyes of his army on Jackson's
bier.

"Just before the battle of Fredericksburg (Burnside's), General J. E. B. Stuart presented Jackson
with a brand-new uniform covered with gold lace
and stars and as gaudy as a peacock's train. Jackson had never worn it, but on the morning of the
grand assault Stuart had persuaded him to put it
on. Accompanied by Stuart and some of his staff,
he rode slowly in front of the Confederate lines from
right to left; but he was not recognized until he
reached Pickett's division, then placed in the centre
of the line. Stuart mischievously pointed out the
gorgeous-looking individual to some officer of the
division, and it ran down the line like wildfire:
'Old Jack's got a new uniform!' Instantly the men
leaped upon the breastworks, yelling wildly and
swinging their hats, until Jackson could bear it no
longer; but, turning a reproachful look upon Stuart, he clapped spurs to his old sorrel and galloped
off to his own command. Suffice it to say he pulled
his new duds off as soon as he had an opportunity.

"Now, who can explain the philosophy of it?
Neither Johnston nor Beauregard nor Longstreet
nor Hill nor Early, nor even Jeb Stuart, was ever
looked upon by the army in the same light as Lee
and Jackson, and yet all these officers were worthy of enthusiastic admiration and unflinching

support. It is one of the mysteries that make us believe that actions and events are largely beyond the ken of the pure reasoning faculties."

In the month of October, in accordance with an act of the Confederate Congress, the Army of Northern Virginia was divided into two corps, and the command of the First assigned to Major-General Longstreet and that of the Second to Major-General Jackson. Longstreet's corps included the divisions of McLaws, Hood, Pickett and Walker; Jackson's, the divisions of A. P. Hill, Ewell and Jackson's old division, under General Taliaferro. General D. H. Hill commanded the reserve, General Stuart the cavalry and General Pendleton the artillery. At that time the Army of Northern Virginia numbered about sixty thousand men.

President Davis's extreme partiality was a great injury to the Confederacy. It was said that any man for whom he had formed a friendship years before was certain of a "soft" position under the new order of things, and the President shut his ears against every complaint made by aggrieved parties, no matter what their rank. He was unjust and severe to those for whom he formed a dislike, and could see no good in them. J. D. McCabe, Jr., as illustrative of this weakness on the part of the President, mentions the case of Colonel Northrop, commissary-general under the Confederate government. More than twenty years before, he and Mr. Davis had been friends in the Black Hawk war;

part of the interval had been spent by Northrop as a patient in an insane asylum. His appointment to the important post named caused much surprise and indignation, but the President could not be dissuaded, and he sustained that officer against the whole country. General Lee joined the list of remonstrants and more than once urged the President to remove him for incompetency, but without avail.

The wonder is how the Confederacy stood Northrop. He not only knew nothing of the duties of his office, but he insulted those who came in contact with him, and acknowledged the right of no one besides the President to presume to make a suggestion to him. His mismanagement and brutality starved the army in the midst of plenty, robbed the people and in the end caused all classes to distrust and dislike the government; yet when Senator Orr, on the 18th of January, 1864, when the cause was on the verge of the destruction to which Colonel Northrop had contributed so greatly, waited on Mr. Davis to ask the removal of the commissary-general, the President declared to him that Colonel Northrop was one of the greatest geniuses in the South, and that if he had the physical capacity he would put him at the head of an army. When, finally, he did resign, a general shout of thankfulness went up from the whole South.[*]

The army, as a matter of course, was paid in

* *A Rebel War-Clerk's Diary.*

Confederate money, which rapidly deteriorated in value; even their pittances reached them only at long intervals. Secretary Memminger showed an incompetency on a par with that of Northrop. Great wars and revolutions are the occasions when bad men flourish and sleek hypocrisy rolls up its ill-gotten gains. In the North men made fortunes in the bounty business, and millions were accumulated by the "trooly loyal" out of their contracts with the government, which were so fat that they fairly exuded oil. They were present in the South. Some of them strutted about in uniform, pretending that trifling wounds were too severe to permit them to join the brave boys at the front; some of them clamored for more vigorous measures on the part of the government, but took care that they received their wages in yellow gold; some of them held back their corn for higher prices and calmly swore that the Federals had ruined their crops, and then looked upon the starving soldiers with assumed pity; some of them locked up thousands of shoes and clothing, while there was nothing between the bare feet of the gray-jackets and the frozen ground. These wretches, in fact, were everywhere, and managed to cast an anchor to windward by sending a good quantity of gold to Europe to await their flight when the "cruel war was over." It seems inevitable that such shameful accompaniments should mark every revolutionary movement, and no surprise, therefore, should be felt that there was so much of it both north and south of Mason and Dixon's line during the war.

The Confederate government became uneasy over the preparations of the Federal authorities for a more vigorous prosecution of the war. They asked Lee to fall back to the valley, but he replied he was strong enough to beat McClellan, and said that if he withdrew it would be to yield his means of subsistence to the Federals, because he had not any way of carrying it with him. Instead of retreating before the enemy showed himself, he ordered the cavalry in the neighborhood of Culpeper and Manassas to make more offensive operations.

General Lee organized a diversion with a view of inducing the Federals to draw off some of the troops from McClellan's army or to cause him to delay his advance into Virginia. General Loring was directed to march from Western Virginia with some eight thousand men, threaten Wheeling, and afterward join the Army of Northern Virginia by way of the Monongahela. Loring concluded that Lee didn't understand his business, and he therefore declined to make the movement. As a consequence, Loring was removed; but the Confederate government refused to allow Lee to draw any troops from Western Virginia to reinforce his own. Indeed, this policy of scattering was carried to a dangerous point by the government, despite the protests of the leading journals, and of Lee himself. It was utterly beyond the power of the Confederacy to defend its immense line of seacoast or one-half the extended points which were threatened. Its true course was to contract its lines and to concentrate its troops.

The Baltimore and Ohio Railroad was most unfortunately located—that is, for its own welfare. It had been used by both Federals and Confederates, and played an important part in the war. At the beginning of hostilities, Sharp, the superintendent of transportation, whose sympathies were strongly with the South, performed a most remarkable exploit. He ran about a dozen locomotives out to Martinsburg, had them taken from the rails, and under a strong military escort they were dragged by mules across the country over the turnpike to the nearest railroad-line, whence they were taken to Richmond. They did effective service during the war, and after the close of hostilities most of the engines were recovered by the Baltimore and Ohio road. Some of them were found as far south as New Orleans.

Many strange experiences took place along the line of this railway. An engineer told the writer that one night he was running at a high rate of speed, only a short distance out of Baltimore. He had behind him some valuable supplies belonging to the Federal government, and a strong guard was on board. There was little fear of trouble, but of course he kept a vigilant lookout. He was intently watching the rails as the gleam of his headlight struck them, when all at once, to his unspeakable dismay, one of them leaped aside and bounded out of sight. There was no person near it, nor was there any evidence that it had been touched; yet it not only bounded from its position on the ties, but went skipping and plunging down the bank into the woods, where it disappeared. The engineer reversed and applied his brakes, but he was so close to the gap that there was no saving the engine, which the next moment was bumping over the gravel and ties. The engine didn't upset, but it was badly damaged, and a long delay followed. Investigation showed that the missing rail had been unfastened and then carefully put back in place. Around each end was wound a telegraph-wire, which reached downward into the woods at the side of the track; several men held the concealed ends and waited for the train. At the right instant the unfastened rail was snapped down the bank out of sight, after which those who did it ran back in among the trees and concealed themselves.

As the war progressed this railroad-line became more useful to the Federals than to the Confederates, and Lee determined to damage it to the utmost. Accordingly, some forty miles of it between Sir John's Run and Harper's Ferry were destroyed and all the bridges and culverts blown up.

CHAPTER XVII.

ABOUT this time General Stuart performed an exploit of such a daring nature that it won the admiration of the Federals as well as of the Confederates.

General Lee knew of the vigorous preparations on foot by his adversaries for the prosecution of the war, and he decided to learn something more definite; he therefore ordered "Jeb" (J. E. B.) Stuart to make an excursion into Pennsylvania in quest of this knowledge. General Stuart immediately organized a force of eighteen hundred men and four pieces of artillery, under the command of General Hampton and Colonels W. H. F. Lee (son of General Lee) and Jones. The men were enjoined to exercise propriety and to confine themselves strictly to the objects of the expedition. On the morning of October 9, the command started on its perilous mission, and the following day crossed the Potomac between Hancock and Williamsport, driving off a Federal picket stationed there. A short distance out, on the National road, a dozen men in charge of a signal station were captured

189

with their flags and apparatus. By this means the interesting information was gained that a large Federal force had gone by, scarcely an hour before, in the direction of Cumberland. Stuart was strongly tempted to dash into Hagerstown and secure the immense lot of Federal stores there, but the main object of his expedition would thereby be imperilled, and he kept straight ahead, fully alive to the value of every hour.

Just as it was growing dark the galloping horsemen reined up in sight of Chambersburg. Having no knowledge of the force that might be in the place, Stuart felt that it would not do to wait till morning; but he wished to give the women and children time to take themselves to a place of safety. He therefore sent a summons into the city demanding its surrender under a threat of almost immediate shelling in case of resistance. The officer who rode into the place with the summons hunted high and low for some official to whom to deliver it, but not one could be found. It looked as if all the frightened authorities had "resigned," but there were plenty of people in the streets, and to a number of these the order was read. Shortly after, the command rode into town and occupied it.

The inhabitants, naturally enough, were in a state of excitement at sight of the Confederate cavalry among them, and for a time general consternation reigned everywhere; but General Stuart assured all that if they would remain in their homes they would not be disturbed. This pledge was kept in spirit and letter. The people at first peeped timidly out from their houses upon the bronzed troopers, but, finding them harmless so long as undisturbed, they viewed them more at leisure, and even ventured to enter into conversation with them. The troopers were models of courtesy and politeness, never intruding into a house without asking permission and returning profuse thanks for the attentions received. Indeed, the Confederates were so scrupulously careful in this respect that they were bitterly denounced by the fiery Daniel in the *Richmond Examiner* for playing the part of milksops. "Treat them as they treat us!" he insisted. Nearly three hundred sick soldiers were found in the hospital in Chambersburg; they were paroled and left where they were. A large lot of arms were destroyed, the railroad and telegraph wire cut, and the railroad-station, machine-shops and several trains of loaded cars were burned.

By this time the Army of the Potomac, and, indeed, the whole North, knew of the startling raid on which Stuart was engaged. The call to capture the daring troopers came from every quarter, and McClellan resolved that not one of the party should escape him again. He quickly made preparations intended to render it impossible for them to recross the Potomac.

General Pleasanton, at the head of his fine cavalry, was despatched in pursuit of Stuart, under

orders to spare neither men nor horses and never
to rest until the whole party were destroyed or
captured. General Averill, on the Upper Potomac, was also directed to join in the pursuit,
while General Crook, who was at Hancock, on his
way to Western Virginia, was ordered to place his
division on the cars, and to be ready to move to
any point above Hancock in the event of Stuart
attempting to return in that direction. The commander at Harper's Ferry was instructed to keep
a sharp eye on every ford in his vicinity; General
Burnside was to send two brigades on the cars to
Monocacy Junction, and to wait there, with steam
up, ready to hasten to any point on the line which
Stuart might threaten; Colonel Rush, at Frederick, was to keep his lancers ranging through
the neighborhood of Chambersburg, so as to warn
Burnside of Stuart's arrival; while General Stoneman, at Poolesville, guarding the fords below the
mouth of the Monocacy, was to prevent Stuart
from crossing the river.

With all these precautions, it would seem beyond
the power of Stuart to extricate himself and his
command from the labyrinth of danger in which
they were involved. The situation was exciting;
for while the cavalry leader knew that everything
possible had been done and was under way to bag
him, yet he was without definite knowledge of the
nature of the measures taken by the Federals. It
was not at all impossible, therefore, that he might

run into the very trap set for him. He was convinced, however, that General Crook, whom he had so narrowly missed on his entrance into Federal territory, would do everything to head him off from the Upper Potomac. Carefully looking over the ground, the Confederate leader decided to take the most direct route, which led through Leesburg. It was necessary that the Federals should be deceived ·as to his intentions. When, therefore, Stuart left Chambersburg, on the morning of October 11, he headed for Gettysburg, but after passing the Blue Ridge wheeled about, galloped a half dozen miles in the direction of Hagerstown, and then passed through Emmettsburg, where he was loudly cheered by the inhabitants, who informed him that he was directly behind a party of Rush's lancers. Scarcely reining up, Stuart galloped in the direction of Frederick, and speedily captured a messenger bearing a despatch from Colonel Rush. An examination of this despatch made known that while the Federals were uncertain of the precise locality of Stuart, yet they were making thorough preparations to secure him. The value of this despatch lay in the fact that it gave him a pretty clear idea of the nature of the arrangements for his capture.

Stuart felt that it was no time to let the grass grow under his feet, and he certainly was in imminent danger of being taken by the enemy. He followed a bee-line toward the Potomac and crossed

13

the Monocacy a short distance from Frederick, pressing onward through Liberty, New Market and Monrovia, on the Baltimore and Ohio Railroad, and at break of day on the 13th he was in Hyattstown, which was on McClellan's line of wagon-communication with Washington. Several wagons were captured, and the troops galloped into Barnesville, out of which a squadron of Federal cavalry had ridden but a short time before.

By this time Stuart had a clear idea of the plans of McClellan. He was aware that a division of five thousand men were vigilantly guarding the fords in front of him. Every passing hour increased his peril, and, believing that the boldest course was the safest, he continued straight for the Potomac, prepared to cut his way through whatever troops might oppose. The point at which he aimed was Poolesville; but when he came in sight of it, he wheeled aside and took to the woods, speedily debouching into the highway leading from Poolesville to the mouth of the Monocacy.

The troopers were no more than fairly in the road when they found themselves confronted by the head of the column of General Pleasanton's cavalry, who were on their way to Poolesville. Stuart instantly charged and drove them back on their infantry, which boldly advanced to recover the lost ground. The Confederates leaped from their horses and hotly engaged the Federal skirmishers. The latter were held in check until the artillery could be brought up, when Pelham promptly opened with his single piece, which did most effective service. Aided by this "bombardment" and the concealment of the ridge on which Pelham was firing, Stuart hurried his command to White's Ford, scattering with the rest of his artillery some two hundred Federal infantry on the Virginia shore. As good fortune would have it, the interposing canal was dry, and the Confederates crossed to the south side of the Potomac without the least difficulty.

Stuart was no more than fairly on the Virginia shore when the cavalry and infantry of General Stoneman came forward on the rush. Pelham received them with his guns, favorably located on the proper side of the stream, and held back Stoneman from crossing the stream in pursuit. General Stuart leisurely retired from the river during the day, and on the 14th rejoined the army at Winchester. On the march not a man was killed, though two of them lost their way and two or three others were wounded. An unexpected result from this brilliant raid was the ruin of many Federal horses. Those belonging to Pleasanton and Averill were so completely used up that they were worthless, and the advance of the Army of the Potomac was delayed until they could be replaced.

As evidence of the extraordinary vigor of this raid, it may be stated that Stuart marched between eighty and ninety miles in twenty-four hours, while Pleasanton did almost as well.

The following is the despatch which General Lee sent to Richmond:

"WINCHESTER, VA., October 14, 1862.

" HON. G. W. RANDOLPH:

" The cavalry expedition to Pennsylvania has returned safe. They passed through Mercersburg, Chambersburg, Emmettsburg, Liberty, New Market, Hyattstown and Burnsville. The expedition crossed the Potomac above Williamsport, and recrossed at White's Ford, making the entire circuit, cutting the enemy's communications, destroying arms, etc., and obtaining many recruits.

"R. E. LEE, General."

Late on the night of November 7, General Mc-Clellan was sitting in his tent at Rectortown talking with General Burnside. A violent snow-storm was raging, and the particles sifted against the tent like so much fine sand. By and by, when there was a lull in the conversation, General Buckingham was presented as the bearer of despatches from Washington. He handed a letter to Mc-Clellan, who opened and read the following:

"WAR DEPARTMENT, ADJUTANT-GENERAL'S OFFICE,
Washington, November 5, 1862.

" General Orders,
No. 182.

" By direction of the President of the United States, it is ordered that Major-General McClellan be relieved from the command of the Army of the Potomac, and that Major-General Burnside take the command of that army.

"By Order of the Secretary of War.

"E. D. TOWNSEND,
"Assistant Adjutant-General."

McClellan read the despatch through carefully, and then, without the least agitation, passed it over to Burnside with the remark,

"Well, general, you are to command the army now."

CHAPTER XVIII.

THE UNION ADVANCE.

At the time McClellan was relieved from the command of the Army of the Potomac he was well advanced on his new campaign against the Army of Northern Virginia. The Federal forces numbered one hundred and ten thousand men fit for duty. McClellan's plan contemplated an advance up the Shenandoah Valley, directly against Lee, but President Lincoln was strongly in favor of entering Virginia east of the Blue Ridge, in the attempt to cut off the Confederate army from Richmond; he promised McClellan thirty thousand more men if this plan was followed. The advance, however, was deferred until bad weather set in and the roads became almost impassable, but the route east of the Blue Ridge was finally agreed upon.

McClellan's plan, as stated by himself, was as follows: "To move the army well in hand parallel to the Blue Ridge, taking Warrenton as the point of direction for the main body, seizing each pass in the Blue Ridge by detachments as we approached it, and guarding them after we had passed so long as they would enable the enemy to trouble our communications with the Potomac. We depended upon Harper's Ferry and Berlin for supplies until the Manassas Gap Railway was reached; when that occurred, the passes in our rear were to be abandoned and the army massed, ready for action or movement in any direction. It was my intention, if, upon reaching Ashby's or any other pass, I found that the enemy were in force between it and the Potomac, in the Valley of the Shenandoah, to move into the valley and endeavor to gain his rear. I hardly hoped to accomplish this, but did expect that by striking in between Culpeper Court-House and Little Washington I could either separate their army and beat them in detail or force them to concentrate as far back as Gordonsville, and thus place the Army of the Potomac in position to adopt the Fredericksburg line of advance upon Richmond, or to be removed to the Peninsula if, as I apprehended, it was found impossible to supply it .by the Orange and Alexandria Railroad beyond Culpeper."

But the days went by, and still McClellan did not move. Finally the impatient President sent him peremptory orders to advance, and the movement was begun at Berlin, five miles below Harper's Ferry. On the 2d of November the entire army was across the river.

The very hour that Lee learned of McClellan's advance he put his own army in motion. He comprehended the Federal plan of campaign, despite the efforts made to mask it, and sent one division

of Longstreet's corps to the neighborhood of Up-
perville to watch the movements of the Federals.
Jackson was ordered to take position on the road
between Berryville and Charlestown, to prevent
any advance from Harper's Ferry and to check
any movement through the passes of the Blue
Ridge into the valley. The cavalry was directed
to co-operate with him.

In the latter part of October the Union army
began withdrawing from the mountains and moved
toward Warrenton. Longstreet's corps immediately
passed the Blue Ridge and posted itself at Culpeper
Court-House. In order to delay the Federal army
by exciting the fears of General McClellan for the
safety of his rear, General Jackson was ordered to
remain for some time near Millwood. He advanced
one of his divisions to the east side of the Blue
Ridge, and remained west of it with his main body.
As soon as Longstreet moved to Culpeper the cavalry were withdrawn from the valley and sent after
him. The danger to which this separation of the
two portions of the Confederate army exposed General Lee was very great, and would have been rash-
ness on the part of any commander had it not been
required by the necessities of the case. It is said
that both Generals Lee and Jackson were convinced
of their ability to foil the designs of General Mc-
Clellan, in spite of the risk attending a division of
the army.*

* Cooke's *Life of Stonewall Jackson.*

General Burnside was without the ability to command the Army of the Potomac, and he knew it. He had declined twice before to become its leader, and gladly would he have evaded the great responsibility a third time. He shrank from taking the mantle from McClellan's shoulders, and it was a bright day for the Confederate cause when he consented to do so. Assuming command of the fine army, he remained quiet at Warrenton for ten days, while he familiarized himself with his new duties. An important step was taken by consolidating the six corps of his army into three grand divisions of two corps each, the right grand division being under General Sumner, the centre grand division under General Hooker and the left grand division under General Franklin.

At this time the Confederate army was divided by two marches, and Burnside was presented with a most inviting opportunity for striking a blow; but he had made "other arrangements," and did not propose to be diverted from them. His plan was to march direct to Fredericksburg and establish himself on the south side of the Rappahannock before his design could be detected and interfered with. There is good authority for saying that at that time the Federal leader had no fixed campaign in his mind, but he hoped to be able to spend the winter with his army in Fredericksburg, within easy reach of his base of supplies. He did not favor the overland route to Richmond, but hoped, when spring should come, to embark his entire army and repeat McClellan's attempt to reach the Confederate capital by way of the Peninsula.

When the Union commander explained his plan of operations, it aroused no enthusiasm in Washington; but assent was given, and on the 15th of November the movement in front of Warrenton began. The scheme was that the army should move along the northern side of the Rappahannock to Falmouth, where it would cross by means of a ponton-bridge (the boats of which were to be forwarded from Washington) and take possession of the bluffs on the other shore. He had scarcely begun the movement when General Lee detected his purpose, but he made no attempt to interfere with his adversary. As the army of Lee was only about half that of Burnside, his intention was to avoid a battle unless his opponent tempted it by some great blunder on his part, or unless Lee was forced to deliver battle in self-defence; in which event, he meant it should be from his own chosen position. His ultimate intention was to hold the Federal army at bay by a series of manœuvres and counter-movements until the season was too far advanced for it to attempt anything before spring. Burnside's purpose being apparent, Lee at once instituted a counter-movement, passing the Rapidan and hurrying in the same direction. A reconnoissance by Stuart left no doubt of the Federal plan, and Lee moved with his accustomed vigor and promptness.

General Sumner with the advance of the Federal army arrived opposite Fredericksburg on the afternoon of November 17. The little town at that time was occupied by a regiment of Virginia cavalry, four companies of Mississippi infantry and a single light battery. It would have been a very easy matter for Sumner to cross and seize the heights back of the place, and he was anxious to do so, but Burnside forbade him. The other two grand divisions speedily followed, and on the evening of the 20th the entire Army of the Potomac was concentrated opposite Fredericksburg; but when Burnside looked across the narrow river to the heights beyond, he saw the crimson flags and the multitudinous gray-coats grimly awaiting him. At that time, too, Stonewall Jackson was hastening thither; so that Lee was confident of having his whole army in hand in time to repel the Federal assault.

Finding himself confronted by the Army of Northern Virginia, under the matchless Lee himself, Burnside could only proceed to establish his communications by way of Aquia Creek and complete his preparations for the tremendous assault upon the Confederate lines. His troops were posted along the northern shore from opposite Port Royal to a point above Falmouth. Aquia Creek was made his base of supplies, and the railroad

from that point to the Rappahannock was completed. Burnside had thrown away a golden
opportunity that could never come again when
he forbade Sumner to cross the river and seize
the heights on the other side, but now, having
resolved on an advance movement, he delayed no
longer than was absolutely necessary.

Lee employed himself in strengthening his new
position. A strong battery was posted on the bank
four miles below Fredericksburg, so as to prevent
any Federal gunboats from ascending the Rappahannock. The fords above were also closely
guarded by the cavalry, and W. H. F. Lee and
his brigade were at Port Royal sharply watching
their adversary.

When Burnside felt ready to make the attempt
to cross, there were no ponton-trains, and they
did not arrive until a week later—a period which,
it need not be said, was improved to the utmost
by the Confederate leader. Rash and reckless as
Burnside sometimes showed himself to be, he did
not dare to throw his army against the tiers of
cannon which frowned upon him from the commanding heights behind Fredericksburg. A flank
movement seemed indispensable, and preparations
for making it at Skenker's Neck, twelve miles
below Falmouth, were set on foot; but before
anything could be done the Confederates discovered the project, and met it with such effective
means that it was abandoned.

The Confederate left seemed vulnerable to a movement up the Rappahannock, but none was attempted. Why it was not cannot be fully understood; but one discovery had much weight with Burnside: he learned that his threatened advance across the river at Skenker's Neck had caused Lee to station a large force at that point to prevent the turning movement. The Federal commander, therefore, was of the belief that by making a sudden advance Lee and his army would be taken at great disadvantage and driven from their entrenchments before the force at Skenker's Neck could be summoned to their assistance. Could Burnside have forced this plan to the conclusion, he hoped it would have been a triumph indeed; but there were the gravest reasons for fearing a disastrous repulse. The most skilful leader might well shrink from taking such a risk against an army of proven courage under such a chieftain as Lee, but Burnside did not hesitate, and on the 10th of December, 1862, the preparations were complete for opening the battle of Fredericksburg.

CHAPTER XIX.

LET us look over the scene of conflict before the bloody drama opens.

Fredericksburg lies on the south bank of the Rappahannock, and directly opposite extends a range of hills which completely command the city. On the southern shore the land is lower, but the depth of the channel is such that a line of bluffs is formed, which serve as excellent entrenchments for a force after crossing to attack the troops beyond. The only offset to this advantage is a range of hills enclosing the level ground. Beginning on the west of Fredericksburg—where it is called "Marye's Hill"—it curves around back of it, gradually sloping away from the city, until about a mile from the river it becomes a level plain. It is thus seen that it is easy for a strong force to cross the Rappahannock from the northern shore, because the bluffs command the opposite city and banks, while on the southern side the opponents must necessarily post themselves so far back that little resistance can be offered. It was not difficult for the Federal army to reach the other shore, but the all-important question was, What was to be done after it got there?

On the night of December 10, General Hunt, chief of artillery of Burnside's army, posted one hundred and forty-seven cannon on the Stafford Heights, designed to command the city, to protect the crossing of the river and to occupy the attention of the Confederate batteries beyond. Burnside's plan was to cross at five different points by means of ponton-bridges, three of which were to span the river opposite the city and two a couple of miles below. The grand divisions of Sumner and Hooker were to use the upper, and Franklin's grand division the lower, bridge.

Lee could not prevent the Federals from coming over, and his dispositions were made with that fact in view, and with the purpose of opening on his adversary after he should plant himself on his side of the Rappahannock. With a view of annoying the Federals as much as possible while attempting the crossing, the Seventeenth and Eighteenth Mississippi regiments, of Barksdale's brigade, were posted along the southern shore. They were able to secure good shelter, and were very successful in their work.

Burnside made his preparations with great secrecy, and at two o'clock on the morning of December 11 the working-parties cautiously moved down to the edge of the stream and began launching the boats and constructing the bridges. A heavy fog overhung the Rappahannock, which gave ground for the hope that the bridges might be finished without discovery; but the Confederates were on the alert, and the Federals were no more than fairly at work when the boom of two cannon in quick succession announced that the movement was discovered.

The Mississippians in Fredericksburg were wide awake. In the stillness of the night they could hear the bridge-builders, and as the wintry morning slowly broke they caught the outlines of the spectral forms through the mist. The riflemen instantly opened with such effective aim that the toilers were driven from their work. The attempt was several times repeated, but the Mississippians commanded the situation until they were dislodged by a furious bombardment from the one hundred and forty-seven Federal cannon.

This bombardment was frightfully disastrous to Fredericksburg. Many of the citizens who had fled on the first alarm had returned with their families, believing they were in no danger. Burnside gave no notice of his intention, but opened with such fury that consternation, terror and widespread death followed. In the bleak morning the women and children fled to the open fields, half clothed and terrified, while others crouched in the cellars of their houses and tremblingly prayed for the awful storm to subside. The bombardment lasted an hour, during which tons of death-dealing missiles were hurled into the city, and it was set on fire in several places. Little else, however, was accomplished, for the guns could not be depressed enough to reach the sharpshooters along-shore, while the Confederate army was too far removed to receive any material injury.

At noon another attempt was made to lay the ponton-bridge, but the workmen were again driven off. Then Burnside hastily crossed three regiments in boats, who drove the Mississippians into the upper part of the town; after which, but a few minutes sufficed to complete the structure. Later in the afternoon Howard's division of Couch's corps passed over and entered the town, the Mississippians keeping up the fight until dark, when they were withdrawn. Franklin found no such difficulty when he attempted to lay his bridges, two miles below. The sharpshooters were without protection, and were easily driven off; so that by noon he had completed the means for transporting his division across the river.

The sheltering mist and fog still brooded over the river and served the Federals well. All through the raw and chilly night of December 11, during the following day and part of the following night their legions were hurrying over the ponton-bridges which spanned the stream. The Confederates crouched among the hills above, grimly awaiting the hour for opening the death-struggle. By dawn of the 13th the entire Army

14

of the Potomac was on the southern shore of the Rappahannock, and at the same hour the whole Army of Northern Virginia was concentrated on the heights behind Fredericksburg.

General Lee's position was as follows: Longstreet's corps constituted the left, with Anderson's division resting on the river, and those of McLaws, Pickett and Hood extending to the right in the order named. Ransom's division supported the batteries on Marye's and Willis's hills, at the foot of which Cobb's brigade, of McLaws's division, and the Twenty-fourth North Carolina, of Ransom's brigade, were stationed, protected by a stone wall. The immediate care of that point was given to General Ransom. The Washington Artillery occupied the redoubts on the crest of Marye's Hill, and those on the height to the right and left were held by part of the reserve artillery, Colonel E. P. Alexander's battalion and the division batteries of Anderson, Ransom and McLaws. A. P. Hill, of Jackson's corps, was posted between Hood's right and Hamilton's Crossing, on the railroad; his front line, consisting of the brigades of Pender, Lane and Archer, occupied the edge of a wood. Lieutenant-Colonel Walker, with fourteen pieces of artillery, was posted near the right, supported by the Fortieth and Thirty-fifth Virginia regiments, of Field's brigade, commanded by Colonel Brockenborough. Lane's brigade, thrown forward in advance of the general line, held the woods, which here projected into the open ground. Thomas's brigade was stationed behind the interval, between Lane and Pender, and Gregg's in rear of that, between Lane and Archer. These two brigades, with the Forty-seventh Virginia regiment and the Twenty-second Virginia battalion, of Field's brigade, constituted General Hill's reserve. Early's and Taliaferro's divisions composed Jackson's second line, D. H. Hill's division his reserve. His artillery was distributed along his line in the most eligible positions so as to command the open ground in front. General Stuart, with two brigades of cavalry and his horse-artillery, occupied the plain on Jackson's right, extending to Massaponax Creek.*

This position of Lee was one of unusual strength, and fully justified his confidence that he could successfully resist every attempt of the Federals to carry it. Burnside, having failed to surprise Lee, determined to storm the Confederate position. His plan contemplated the assault of Jackson at Hamilton's Crossing by Franklin's grand division, which composed the Union left, strengthened by one of Hooker's corps, the force including about one-half the Federal army. The point aimed at was the weakest part of the Confederate line. After carrying it Franklin was to seize the railroad and the wagon-road leading to Richmond, while Sumner with the rest of the army was to storm the formidable heights on Lee's left.

* General Lee's report.

Early on the morning of the 13th, General Lee mounted his horse at his headquarters, in the rear of his centre, and galloped along his line of battle toward his right, where he expected the main assault would be made; Generals Jackson and Stuart rode with him. The cavalry leader was, as usual, in full uniform; but Lee was in his suit of plain gray, with slouch hat, high cavalry-boots, short cape, without sword and with little to denote his exalted rank. Jackson amazed every one by his appearance; he was clothed in a uniform so gorgeous that it fairly dazzled the eyes of the beholders. The fact was, as we have stated in another place, the uniform was a present to him from Stuart, who mischievously enjoyed the fun it caused among the soldiers and the disgust of Jackson himself over the attention he excited.

The Confederate army was in high spirits, and cheered the leaders as they rode along the lines. The officers continued until they reached the river-road approaching Fredericksburg parallel to the line of battle; there they paused and endeavored to find out whether the Federal line was moving. The fog would not permit them to see clearly, but from the gray mist came the hum and muffled roar which told of the number in motion. General Lee was still intently peering into the obscurity, when the near crack of rifles fell upon his ears: the Federal sharpshooters had caught sight of the famous leaders and were firing at them. Lee remained sev-

eral minutes as though unconscious that he was the
target for so many bullets, and then rode back in
his dignified fashion until he reached the eminence
in his centre, near the telegraph-road; there he
stationed himself, so as to overlook and direct the
battle.

It was near ten o'clock when the fog lifted and
the combatants gained a clear view of each other.
The column of General Franklin was seen moving
to attack the Confederate right, near Hamilton's
Crossing. The force was Meade's division, which
was checked for a time by an extraordinary ob-
struction in the form of a single section of a battery of Stuart's horse-artillery, under the command
of the daring youth Major Pelham; he was on the
Port Royal road, and opened a destructive enfilading fire upon the Federal left. Four of their batteries hotly replied, but he held his ground until
ordered to withdraw by Stuart. Thereupon Franklin extended his left down the Port Royal road, and
opened his batteries upon Jackson's lines. Receiving no reply, the Federal infantry were pushed forward toward the position held by Walker's guns.
When but little more than two thousand feet separated them, Walker's fourteen guns converged on
the advancing line with such fury that for a few
minutes it was thrown into confusion. The men
soon rallied, however, and rushed forward, assailing Jackson's front line, under A. P. Hill. Before
an open space between the brigades of Archer and

Lane could be closed Meade's two divisions swarmed through, and forced back Hill's men upon Jackson's second line.   Jackson immediately brought up this line, which included the divisions of Early, Trimble and Taliaferro.   Attacking the Federals in front and on both flanks, they were driven over the railroad upon the plain beyond.   Taliaferro's division routed the Federals from the woods in front and drove them into the railroad-cut, from which they were dislodged by Hoke and Atkinson's batteries and forced across the plain to the shelter of their own batteries.   The assault on Jackson's extreme left was repulsed by his artillery, while Early drove back his assailants until checked by the guns on Stafford Heights.   Thus the attack of Franklin had failed, and for the rest of the day he occupied himself in shelling the Confederate line and in skirmishing with Jackson's advanced infantry.

CHAPTER XX.

THE DECISIVE STRUGGLE.

THE withdrawal of the Federal attack on the Confederate right was accompanied by the thunder of Sumner's assault upon Lee's left. In obedience to Burnside's order, this attack was made by a single division, supported by another division. General French led the former, and Hancock supported it.

It was about noon when the Federals debouched from Fredericksburg and made the desperate attempt to seize Marye's Hill. From the moment they emerged from the town and came into fair range they were exposed to a severe fire, which rapidly assumed the most murderous character. The Federals were mowed down and gaps opened in their ranks which Longstreet declared could be seen a mile distant. Still the brave men pressed steadily forward with a courage worthy of a better leader, until the discharge of musketry became a literal torrent of flame, as if from the mouth of hell itself. No living creature could stand such a concentrated tempest, and the shattered columns broke and fled, leaving the ground covered with dead and dying to the number of one-half the

215

attacking force. This repulse was one of the bloodiest of the war.

Right behind French came Hancock, who was joined by the fragments of the first line, which still preserved its formation, and with the same dauntless courage as before they swept into the maelstrom of death. For five—ten—fifteen minutes they held their ground with the men melting like snowflakes in the sun, until of the five thousand whom Hancock led into the charge more than two thousand were dead or helpless on the ground. But the carnage was not yet complete, and Howard's division now rushed into the crater, Sturgis's and Gettys's divisions of the Ninth Corps advancing to the help of the survivors of the Second Corps, who could go no farther, and yet would not retire. They succeeded in holding for a time their position, though they were subjected to a fire so destructive that the wonder is they maintained the ground at all.

It is hardly to be supposed that General Burnside had contemplated the bloody sequence to which he was committing himself when first he ordered a division to assail the heights of Fredericksburg, but, having failed in the first assault, and then in the second and third, there grew up in his mind something which those around him saw to be akin to desperation. Riding down from his headquarters, at the Phillips house, about a mile back from the river, to the bank of the Rappahannock, he walked restlessly up and down, and, gazing over to the heights across the river, exclaimed vehemently, "That crest must be carried to-night!" Already, however, everything had been thrown in except Hooker, and he was now ordered over the river.[*]

But Hooker had not parted with his brains, even though Burnside had done so. He crossed with his three divisions, carefully reconnoitred the ground, and saw that he had been directed to do that which was absolutely impossible: it was only taking his men forward and placing them where they were certain to be slaughtered without the power to do anything against their enemy. Hooker went to Burnside and begged him to withdraw his order, but the commander refused. Couch had already pushed his men forward, and was striving to open a breach large enough to permit the rush of the Federals. Nothing, however, was accomplished, and Humphrey's division was formed in column of assault and ordered to charge. They dashed forward with unloaded muskets, and succeeded in advancing as far as Hancock's men had done a short time before, when they nearly reached the stone wall. Four thousand were in the column of assault: in a few minutes seventeen hundred were stretched on the ground, and the rest broke and fled. The slaughter was appalling, and the generalship inconceivable in its stupidity. And yet, bloody as was the repulse, there is reason to

[*] Swinton.

believe that another "charge" would have been ordered by the commander had not the gathering darkness compelled a cessation of hostilities.

The night which closed in upon the scene was dreadful beyond conception. The Army of the Potomac had · suffered the most terrible repulse in its history. Of the brave soldiers who had marched resolutely forward in obedience to the blundering orders, eleven hundred and eighty were dead, nine thousand and twenty-eight wounded and twenty-one hundred and forty-five were prisoners. They had stormed the impregnable heights of Marye with an unfaltering courage which commanded the admiration of the Confederates themselves; and when at last forced to flee, they left more than six thousand of their number either dead or wounded at the base of the hill. And the blindest private among the wounded and survivors knew that it never ought to have been !

When the different leaders met the commander in the gloom of the evening, they were unanimous in urging that the army should recross the Rappahannock without delay; but Burnside shook his head. He had determined upon another assault on the morrow, and had, indeed, issued orders to that end. There can be no doubt that his brain was overweighted by the enormous load of responsibility, and he was in no condition to command such an army. He announced his intention of leading his old Ninth Corps; fortunately, however, the counsels of his wise and intrepid lieutenants prevailed, and at the last moment he gave over the wild project.

The loss of Lee, including those of the 11th, were five hundred and ninety-five killed, three thousand nine hundred and sixty-one wounded and six hundred and fifty-three prisoners. This was less than one-half the Federal loss, and the moral effect of the achievement on the Army of Northern Virginia amounted almost to inspiration. It was anxious that the fight should be renewed on the morrow, and Lee expected that such would be the case.

But the Army of the Potomac had received a well-nigh fatal blow. The soldiers lay on their arms all the next day—which was Sunday—dispirited beyond expression and expecting an attack from Lee, who, had he known their demoralized condition, could have destroyed or captured them all. Indeed, he had the cannon-balls heated with which to bombard Fredericksburg, where the Federals were huddled together; but the Confederate leader wished to save his ammunition for the expected attack.

For two days the dead and wounded lay stretched on the frozen ground between the lines of the combatants. No more horrible picture of war can be imagined than that of the writhing and dying soldiers vainly begging for the help which could not

be given them.   Burnside finally asked for a few
hours in which to carry off his wounded.

The night of the 15th was marked by a violent tempest of wind and rain; in the unspeakable
gloom and utter darkness the Federal army made
its way back to the northern shore.   On the following morning General Lee discovered what had
taken place, though even then he suspected another
attack upon him was intended.   But the battle of
Fredericksburg was over, and its result was a woeful
disaster for the Union cause and a corresponding
triumph for the Southern Confederacy.   A few days
were sufficient to show that no further demonstration would be attempted by the Federal army before
the following spring.   The Confederates established
themselves in winter quarters along the Rappahannock, from Fredericksburg to Port Royal, and were
as comfortable as possible in their rude huts.

On the last day of the " year of battles " General Lee issued the following:

"HEADQUARTERS ARMY OF NORTHERN VIRGINIA,
December 31, 1862.

"General Order
     No. 132.

" The general commanding takes this occasion to
express to the officers and soldiers of the army his
high appreciation of the fortitude, valor and devotion displayed by them, which, under the blessing
of almighty God, have added the victory of Fredericksburg to the long list of their triumphs.

"An arduous march performed with celerity under many disadvantages exhibited the discipline and spirit of the troops and their eagerness to confront the foe.

"The immense army of the enemy completed its preparations for the attack without interruption, and gave battle in its own time and on the ground of its own selection.

"It was encountered by less than twenty thousand of this brave army, and its columns, crushed and broken, hurled back at every point with such fearful slaughter that escape from entire destruction became the boast of those who had advanced in full confidence of victory.

"That this great result was achieved with a loss small in point of numbers only augments the admiration with which the commanding general regards the prowess of the troops, and increases his gratitude to Him who hath given us the victory.

"The war is not yet ended. The enemy is still numerous and strong, and the country demands of the army a renewal of its heroic efforts in its behalf. Nobly has it responded to her call in the past, and she will never appeal in vain to its courage and patriotism.

"The signal manifestations of divine mercy that have distinguished the eventful and glorious campaign of the year just closing give assurance of hope that, under the guidance of the same almighty Hand, the coming year will be no less fruitful of events that will ensure the safety, peace and happiness of our beloved country and add new lustre to the already imperishable name of the Army of Northern Virginia.

"R. E. LEE, General."

RICHARD KIRKLAND, THE HUMANE HERO OF FREDERICKSBURG.

"'CAMDEN, S. C., January 29, 1880.

"'To THE EDITOR OF THE "NEWS AND COURIER:"

"'Your Columbia correspondent referred to the incident narrated here, telling the story as 'twas told to him, and inviting corrections. As such a deed should be recorded in the rigid simplicity of actual truth, I take the liberty of sending you for publication an accurate account of a transaction every feature of which is indelibly impressed upon my memory.

"'Very truly yours,

"'J. B. KERSHAW.'

"Richard Kirkland was the son of John Kirkland, an estimable citizen of Kershaw county, a plain, substantial farmer of the olden time. In 1861 he entered as a private Captain J. D. Kennedy's company (E) of the Second South Carolina volunteers, in which company he was a sergeant in December, 1862.

"The day after the sanguinary battle of Fredericksburg, Kershaw's brigade occupied the road at the foot of Marye's Hill and the ground about Marye's house, the scene of their desperate defence of the day before. One hundred and fifty yards in front of the road, the stone facing of which constituted the famous stone wall, lay Syke's division of regulars, United States army, between whom and our troops a murderous skirmish occupied the whole day, fatal to many who heedlessly exposed themselves even for a moment. The ground between the lines was bridged with the wounded, dead and dying Federals, victims of the many desperate and gallant assaults of that column of thirty thousand brave men hurled vainly against that impregnable position. All that day those wounded men rent the air with their groans and their agonizing cries of 'Water! water!'

"In the afternoon the general sat in the north room, up stairs, of Mrs. Stevens's house, in front of the road, surveying the field, when Kirkland came up. With an expression of indignant remonstrance pervading his person, his manner and the tone of his voice, he said,

"'General, I can't stand this.'

"'What is the matter, sergeant?' asked the general.

"He replied,

"'All night and all day I have heard those poor people crying for water, and I can stand it no longer. I come to ask permission to go and give them water.'

"The general regarded him for a moment with feelings of profound admiration, and said,

"'Kirkland, don't you know that you would get a bullet through your head the moment you stepped over the wall?'

"'Yes, sir,' he said, 'I know that; but if you will let me, I am willing to try it.'

"After a pause the general said,

"'Kirkland, I ought not to allow you to run a risk, but the sentiment which actuates you is so noble that I will not refuse your request. Trusting that God may protect you, you may go.'

"The sergeant's eye lighted up with pleasure. He said, 'Thank you, sir,' and ran rapidly down stairs. The general heard him pause for a moment, and then return, bounding two steps at a time. He thought the sergeant's heart had failed him. He was mistaken. The sergeant stopped at the door and said,

"'General, can I show a white handkerchief?'

"The general slowly shook his head, saying emphatically,

"'No, Kirkland, you can't do that.'

"'All right,' he said; 'I'll take the chances,' and ran down with a bright smile on his handsome countenance.

"With profound anxiety he was watched as he stepped over the wall on his errand of mercy—Christlike mercy. Unharmed he reached the nearest sufferer. He knelt beside him, tenderly raised the drooping head, rested it gently upon his own noble breast, and poured the precious life-giving fluid down the fever-scorched throat. This done, he laid him tenderly down, placed his knapsack under his head, straightened out his broken limb, spread his overcoat over him, replaced his empty canteen with a full one, and turned to another sufferer. By this time his purpose was well understood on both sides, and all danger was over. From all parts of the field arose fresh cries of 'Water! water! For God's sake, water!' More piteous still the mute appeal of some who could only feebly lift a hand to say, 'Here, too, is life and suffering.'

"For an hour and a half did this ministering angel pursue his labor of mercy, nor ceased to go and return until he relieved all the wounded on that part of the field. He returned to his post wholly unhurt. Who shall say how sweet his rest that winter's night beneath the cold stars?

"Little remains to be told. Sergeant Kirkland distinguished himself in battle at Gettysburg and was promoted lieutenant. At Chickamauga he fell on the field of battle in the hour of victory. He was but a youth when called away, and had never formed those ties from which might have resulted a posterity to enjoy his fame and bless his country, but he has bequeathed to the American youth—yea, to the world—an example which dignifies our common humanity."

CHAPTER XXI.

GENERAL BURNSIDE was a valiant and able corps commander, but he demonstrated his utter unfitness to handle an army. Such a disastrous repulse as the Army of the Potomac had suffered could be due only to the incompetency of its leader, for braver and more heroic soldiers never shouldered the musket. We have shown how he disregarded the protests of Hooker when the latter was ordered to make a charge certain to end in frightful disaster, and how he was barely dissuaded by the united voice of all his commanders to withdraw an order for a general movement which would have resulted in another sanguinary defeat. The North was exasperated, and the *morale* of the army itself was seriously impaired. It was impossible that it should be otherwise: Burnside's officers had no confidence in his military judgment, and the soldiers themselves looked upon him as incompetent. He keenly felt all this, and, stung to the quick, determined on one more effort to recover his waning, if not lost, prestige.

The first of these movements was undertaken

15

toward the close of December. His intention was to cross the Rappahannock seven miles below Fredericksburg, so as to turn the Confederate position, and at the same time to send a cavalry expedition to cut Lee's communications with Richmond. All the preparations were complete, and the raiding column had actually started when the commander received a despatch from Washington forbidding him to enter upon active operations without first consulting the President. Naturally enough, Burnside was angered. The cavalry expedition was recalled, and he proceeded to Washington to obtain an explanation of the reason why he was checked on the eve of an important demonstration. The explanation was promptly given him, and it was not calculated to salve his wounded feelings. President Lincoln said that certain general officers of the army had been to see him with the information that another movement was contemplated, and they earnestly urged the President to forbid it, for they were morally certain it could end only in disaster. While the President did not prohibit General Burnside from active operations, yet he gave him to understand that nothing of the kind was to be undertaken until after full consultation with the government.

The general found himself in a humiliating position. The North was clamoring for him to "do something," and yet his own officers and soldiers had lost faith in his ability, and the comman-

der-in-chief of the army and the navy held him
motionless. He saw but the single way out of his
galling situation : that was to organize a campaign
whose promise of success would win the consent
of the President, push it to triumph, and thus
reinstate himself in the confidence of the army;
but, as Swinton tersely says, "unfortunately, success was already too necessary to him, and he made
too much contingent upon it; for if success was
needful as the means of recovering the confidence
of the army, this very confidence was itself indispensable as a condition of success."

Burnside's second plan was to cross the Rappahannock six miles above Fredericksburg, at a point
which was fordable in summer, but impassable in
winter. He explained his purpose to President
Lincoln, and requested him to approve of it or
to accept his resignation. The President listened
carefully until all the details were made clear, when
he told Burnside to go ahead and he hoped better
fortune would attend him that time. The general
thereupon proceeded to "go ahead."

As Lee had a force in observation at each point
where a crossing was likely to be attempted, it was
decided to make several feints both above and
below the place selected, so as to conceal the real
purpose from the Confederate commander. Sigel's corps, which had lately joined the Army of the
Potomac, was stationed so as to guard the communications with Falmouth, while that of Couch was

to draw attention to the lower part of the river. New roads were cut through the forest, to facilitate the movements of the forces, batteries planted, rifle-trenches formed and numerous demonstrations made at different points.

The roads were in excellent condition and the weather was favorable. January 19 the columns were put in motion, and the next night the grand divisions of Franklin and Hooker bivouacked near the proposed crossing. The preparations were speedily completed. The ponton-bridges, which had already more than once done duty, were placed a short distance back of the river, positions for the artillery were selected, and it was decided that the passage should be made the following morning. But the elements mercifully intervened. A fierce tempest of rain swept over the men, who painfully toiled in sleet and darkness, drawing the pontons nearer the river and dragging the guns into position. The weather became biting cold, and all through the long hours of inky gloom the brave men struggled and floundered in the mud, which in that section of the Union assumes a character that renders it the worst on the face of the earth. When the dismal morning light forced its way through the chilling rain, the preparations were not completed; and, besides, the watchful Confederates had discovered what was going on, and were massed ready to repulse the intended crossing. Such being the case and the rain still pouring, it would be supposed that

Burnside would be quick to see the utter hopelessness of the enterprise; but not so: he kept his poor fellows at the wretched business. When the mules were hitched to the pontons, they sank to their bellies in the sticky paste, floundered, and gave up exhausted without stirring the boats; then long ropes were attached, and hundreds of men tugged and pulled and tumbled about in the rain and mud, and gave up, panting and exhausted.

While the Federals were thus employed the Confederates called across the river with such unnecessary expressions as "How are you making out, Yanks?"—"All together, now!"—"Here we go!"—"Stop and rest, boys, and we'll go over in the morning and help you!"

Burnside persisted in keeping his men at the utterly useless toil until the morning of the 22d; the rain was still descending, and he was compelled to see that it was not only impossible to make any advance, but that it would be a herculean task for his army to extricate itself from the fathomless sea of mud in which it was struggling. Not only that, but the three days' rations with which they set out were nearly gone. Even the commander was compelled to face the hard facts, and the order to withdraw was given. Corduroy-roads were constructed, and by superhuman exertions the cannon and vehicles were dragged away from the river, which, fortunately, was so swollen that the Confederates could not interfere seriously with the retreat, though their stinging taunts accompanied the disheartened Federals until they were beyond hearing.

Burnside was bowed down over the failure of his last undertaking. No doubt he felt that the stars in their courses were fighting against him; but when the elements intervened and prevented the crossing in the depth of winter, it was a merciful intervention indeed. No intelligent person can study the situation without reaching the conclusion that the Union army, under the circumstances, had not the slightest prospect of success, and, with the Rappahannock behind it, it is hard to conceive how it could have been extricated from its exceedingly perilous situation. In writing to the Richmond government, Lee said, "It was fortunate for the Federals that they failed to get over the river." Knowing how careful and modest Lee was in expressing his views, it is impossible not to grasp the tremendous height and breadth and depth of those few words.

The dismal collapse of the "mud-march," as it was called, threatened for a time to destroy the *morale* of the Union army. What little confidence the leading officers possessed at one time in their commander was irrecoverably gone, and the rank and file sought not to conceal their disgust.

It was natural that General Burnside should feel embittered toward the leaders who distrusted his ability; it was natural, also, that he should attribute his failure to their lack of sympathy and co-operation. Feeling that such a state of affairs could not continue, he determined on heroic measures. He therefore made an official request of President Lincoln that he would dismiss Generals Hooker, Brooks, Newton and Cochrane from the service of the United States, and would deprive Generals Franklin, Smith, Sturgis, Ferrero and Colonel Taylor of their respective commands. The only charge that could be brought against these men—known to be among the most competent in the army—was that they lacked confidence in their chief. Had the President done as requested, the Army of the Potomac would have been hopelessly disorganized. When Burnside presented as the alternative the acceptance of his resignation, the President did not hesitate: Burnside was relieved January 25, and the name of his successor was the very first which appeared on the list of those who he demanded should be dismissed from the service of the United States.

The winter of 1862–63 was a very severe one. As early as December a number of the Federal pickets were frozen to death while standing guard on the Rappahannock, and the condition of the Confederate army was deplorable. They were miserably clothed, and Lee himself notified the War Department that several thousand of his men were barefooted. He asked the government to seize all the shoes in the hands of speculators, pay an equitable price and distribute them among the soldiers. The suggestion, however, was not adopted.

Like the illustrious Father of his Country, Lee shared the privations and sufferings of his men. He declined the proffer of a house in which to establish his headquarters, but used what is known as a "house-tent," scarcely differing from those in which the privates slept. It was pitched in a small opening in the wood, close to the narrow road leading to Hamilton's Crossing, while the tents of the officers of his staff were grouped near. The only evidence that this was the headquarters of the army was the presence of an orderly, who was there to summon couriers to carry despatches.

"Within, no article of luxury was to be seen; a few plain and indispensable objects were all which the tent contained. The covering of the commander-in-chief was an ordinary army-blanket, and his fare was plainer, perhaps, than that of the majority of his officers and men. This was the result of an utter indifference in Lee to personal convenience or indulgence. Citizens frequently sent him delicacies, boxes filled with turkeys, hams, wines, cordials and other things peculiarly tempting to one leading the hard life of a soldier, but these were almost uniformly sent to the sick in some neighboring hospital. Lee's principle in so acting seems to have been to set the good example to his officers of not faring better than his men, but he was undoubtedly indifferent naturally to luxury of all descriptions. In his habits and feelings he was not the self-indulgent man of peace, but the thorough soldier, willing to live hard, to sleep upon the ground and to disregard all sensual indulgence. In his other habits he was equally abstinent. He cared nothing for wine, whiskey or other stimulant, and never used tobacco in any form. He rarely relaxed his energies in anything calculated to amuse him, but when not riding along his lines or among the camps to see in person that the troops were properly cared for, generally passed his time in close attention to official duties connected with the well-being of his army or in correspondence with the authorities at Richmond. When he relaxed from this continuous toil, it was to indulge in some quiet and simple diversion, social converse with ladies in houses at which he chanced to stop, caresses bestowed upon children —with whom he was a great favorite—and frequently in informal conversation with his officers. At 'Hayfield' and 'Moss Neck,' two hospitable houses below Fredericksburg, he at this time often stopped, and spent some time in the society of the ladies and children there. One of the latter, a little curly-headed girl, would come up to him always to receive her accustomed kiss, and one day confided to him, as a personal friend, her desire to kiss General Jackson, who blushed like a girl when Lee, with a quiet laugh, told him of the child's wish. On another occasion, when his small friend came to receive his caress, he said, laughing, that she would show more taste in selecting a younger gentleman than himself, and, pointing to a youthful officer in a corner of the room, added, 'There is the handsome Major Pelham;' which caused that modest young soldier to blush with confusion. The bearing of General Lee in these hours of relaxation was quite charming and made him warm friends. His own pleasure and gratification were plain and gratified others, who in the simple and kindly gentleman in the plain gray uniform found it difficult to recognize the commander-in-chief of the Southern army.

"No one doubted during the war that General Lee was a sincere Christian in conviction, and his exemplary moral character and life were beyond criticism; beyond this it is doubtful whether any save his intimate associates understood the depth of his feeling on the greatest of all subjects. Jackson's strong religious fervor was known and often alluded to, but it is doubtful if Lee was regarded as a person of equally fervent convictions and feelings. And yet the fact is certain that faith in God's providence and reliance upon the Almighty were the foundation of all his actions and the secret of his supreme composure under all trials. He was naturally of such reserve that it is not singular that the extent of this sentiment was not understood. Even then, however, good men who frequently visited him and conversed with him upon religious subjects came away with their hearts burning within them. When the Rev. J. William Jones, with another person, went, in 1863, to consult him in reference to the better observance of the Sabbath in the army, his eye brightened and 'his whole countenance glowed with pleasure, and as in his simple, feeling words he expressed his delight we forgot the great warrior, and only remembered that we were communing with an humble, earnest Christian.' When he was informed that the chaplains prayed for him, tears started to his eyes, and he replied, 'I sincerely thank you for that, and I can only say that I am a poor sinner trusting in Christ alone, and that I need all the prayers you can offer for me.'"*

One of the several remedies which Lee proposed to his government was adopted. He had suffered much inconvenience in the previous campaigns on account of his inferior artillery and poor fixed ammunition. As he possessed a number of superior guns which had been captured from the Federal army, he replaced his old ones with them, so far as they went, while all his twelve-pounder howitzers and smooth-bore six-pounders were recast into twelve-pounder Napoleon, ten-pounder Parrott and three-inch rifle-guns. As a consequence, the army was soon better supplied in that respect than ever before.

Meanwhile, the Army of the Potomac was buck-

* J. E. Cooke's *Life of Lee.*

ling on its armor for the spring campaign. Beaten though it had been again and again, demoralized and shattered by its repeated change of leaders, abused by those who stayed at home and found their principal employment in criticising the operations in the field, it still retained its vitality to an amazing degree, and was the nucleus around which soon gathered another host, sufficient, it would seem, under capable leadership, of sweeping all resistance from its path.

When General Burnside was relieved of its command, it was necessary to find another, and, as we have intimated, the choice fell upon Joseph Hooker, or "Fighting Joe," as he had come to be known. He was a soldier of unquestioned ability and courage, as he had proved on more than one bloody field, and, what was of equal importance, he possessed the unbounded confidence of his fellow-officers and the soldiers who were to serve under him. He at once instituted a number of wise reforms in the army. He checked the wholesale desertion by removing the causes for it; he abolished the "grand divisions" and infused his own warm vitality into the different corps, to each of which was given a distinctive badge; to those who were homesick— and, indeed, to all who desired it—he granted furloughs; he united the cavalry under one leader and rendered it what it should have been—one of the most effective arms of the service. He had the good sense to see that no important movement could be made during the tempestuous season, when the atrocious roads were impassable, and the time, therefore, which must elapse before the setting in of spring was wisely occupied in preparing for the momentous campaign which was then to open.

And so it was that when spring came the Army of the Potomac numbered one hundred and twenty thousand men, with twelve thousand finely-equipped cavalry and an artillery force of more than four hundred guns. It was composed of the First Corps, under General Reynolds; the Second, under General Couch; the Third, under General Sickles; the Fifth, under General Meade; the Sixth, under General Sedgwick; the Eleventh, under General Howard; and the Twelfth, under General Slocum.

The Confederate army was much weaker in point of numbers, for General Lee had detached two divisions, under Longstreet, for operations south of the James River, and those which were left showed an effective force of about fifty thousand men.

V.

THE CAMP-FIRE OF CHANCELLORSVILLE.

CHAPTER XXII.

PRELIMINARY MOVEMENTS.

WHEN the next bloody drama opened, General Lee and his army occupied the heights to the south of the Rappahannock, from Skenker's Creek to United States Ford—a distance of twenty-five miles. He had closely guarded all the available crossings of the river, and had so disposed his troops that they could readily be concentrated upon any threatened point.

On the morning of March 16, General Stuart received a despatch from his chief informing him that a column of Federal cavalry was in motion and urging him to be on the watch for it along the Upper Rappahannock. A small force was stationed at Kelley's Ford and General Fitz Lee's brigade was placed in readiness to repel any demonstration. Nevertheless, the pickets were lax, and General Averill and his cavalry easily forced the passage of the river on the following morning and captured the picket-guard. Pushing rapidly forward, they collided with Fitz Lee's brigade, and a rattling fight opened, and lasted several hours. The losses were severe on both sides, those of the Confederates including the gallant young Major Pelham, who had won such remarkable fame as an artillerist. The Federals were finally compelled to withdraw, and a period of inactivity lasted until about the middle of April. Then, when the roads were in good condition, Hooker put in operation his formidable scheme for the capture of Richmond and the crushing of the "rebellion."

Briefly stated, the Federal campaign was as follows: Hooker proposed to launch his main army against Lee's left by crossing it at Kelley's Ford, twenty-seven miles above Fredericksburg, and passing around his flank to Chancellorsville. The Confederate right was so strongly posted that it was secure. This was to be Hooker's main movement, he thinking, with the best of reason, that if it succeeded Lee would be compelled to abandon his almost impregnable entrenchments and accept battle on ground chosen by his enemy. With a view of masking his real purpose, Hooker's plan was to cross the Rappahannock directly opposite Fredericksburg with much flourish, as though his real attack was to be made there. The main column was composed of the Fifth Corps, under Meade; the Eleventh Corps, under Howard; and the Twelfth Corps, under Slocum. They arrived at Kelley's Ford on the 28th of April, and crossed that night with slight opposition, reaching the Rapidan on the afternoon of the same day. The points were Ely's and Germanna's fords, where the water was quite deep and swift. Time was all-important for the Federals, and the men were ordered to strip and wade the stream. They did so, supporting their clothes and cartridge-boxes on their bayonets. The crossing was picturesque and ludicrous in the highest degree. The men were in fine spirits, and they frolicked like so many schoolboys. Many a bundle carefully held aloft received a mischievous jolt which brought it into the water, and all sorts of pranks were played upon one another. In the deepest portion the current reached the armpits of the soldiers, numbers of whom were carried off their feet, but they were "speared" by a cavalry picket below, and the following morning saw the entire force safely over. The artillery and trains crossed by means of the ponton-bridges. This force, it will be borne in mind, was under the immediate charge of Hooker himself. Couch's Second Corps remained at United States Ford to guard the Rappahannock at that point until Hooker had marched far enough down-stream to uncover it, when it was to cross the river and rejoin him at Chancellorsville. This programme was carried out without break or hindrance, and the four corps bivouacked at Chancellorsville that night, Thursday, April 30, after a long and tedious march. At the same time, Hooker established his headquarters in the hamlet, which consisted of a single large brick house and several outbuildings.

The Federal commander had done excellently well so far: he had placed himself in a position which took in reverse Lee's entire line, and he had fifty thousand well-equipped and disciplined men under his immediate command, all eager for the fray.

While Hooker was prosecuting this movement Sedgwick was equally busy. Early on the morning of the 29th he threw three bridges across the Rappahannock three miles below Fredericksburg. A strong column passed over during that and the succeeding day and made formidable demonstrations, as though it was the intention to attack the Confederate position in the rear of the town. Lee did not penetrate the meaning of Hooker's movements until after the crossing of the Rappahannock, on the 29th, though the Confederate leader strongly suspected that an attack was intended on his left.

On the afternoon of April 30, Hooker's troops reached Chancellorsville. Posey and Mahone's commands had been withdrawn from Banks's and Ely's fords by General Anderson and concentrated at Chancellorsville; General Wright's brigade also reinforced the Confederate forces shortly after. Then General Anderson fell back from Chancellorsville to Tabernacle Church and awaited Lee, who was calmly studying the development of Hooker's

16

intentions.   Though, as we have said, he suspected
the meaning of Sedgwick's demonstrations, he was
too prudent to act upon his suspicion until it became certainty ; that certainty was reached on the
evening of the 30th, when he learned that Sedgwick was sending troops to Hooker at Chancellorsville.   Thereupon, General Jackson was ordered
to march at once to Anderson's support with his
entire command, excepting Early's division, which
remained to confront Sedgwick.   The order to
General Jackson was handed him in the evening,
and he set out to obey it about midnight, taking
A. P. Hill's, Rodes's and Colston's divisions.   He
marched steadily until the next morning, when he
reached Tabernacle Church.

The single brick house honored with the name
of " Chancellorsville " is about ten miles from
Fredericksburg, and is in the centre of an almost
unbroken expanse of thicket and stunted wood,
known by the name of the " Wilderness."   One
who is familiar with it says, " There all is wild,
desolate and lugubrious.   Thicket, undergrowth
and jungle stretch for miles, impenetrable and un-
touched.   Narrow roads wind on for ever between
melancholy masses of stunted and gnarled oak.
Little sunlight shines there ; the face of Nature
is dreary and sad.   It was so before the battle ; it
is not more cheerful to-day, when, as you ride
along, you see fragments of shell, rotting knap-
sacks, rusty gun-barrels, bleached bones and grin-

ning skulls. Into this jungle General Hooker penetrated. It was the wolf in his den, ready to tear any one who approached. A battle there seemed impossible; neither side could see its antagonist. Artillery could not move; cavalry could not operate; the very infantry had to flatten their bodies to glide between the stunted trees. That an army of one hundred and twenty thousand men should have chosen that spot to fight forty thousand, and not only chosen it, but made it a hundred times more impenetrable by felling trees, erecting breastworks, disposing artillery *en masse* to sweep every road and bridle-path which led to Chancellorsville,—this fact seems incredible."

But it was no part of Hooker's scheme that he should be imprisoned in the Wilderness. He followed the retiring Confederate force in the direction of Fredericksburg until clear through the Wilderness, and, reaching the open country beyond, made his preparations for battle on ground admirably fitted for the handling of a large body of men. Besides, the distance separating Hooker from Sedgwick was shortened one-half and communication between the two rendered easy.

A brief way beyond Chancellorsville, toward Fredericksburg, is an elevated ridge which commands the former as well as the region known as the Wilderness, and from which the Federal army could advance into the open country behind Fredericksburg. Hooker could not fail to perceive the priceless value of this elevation to whomsoever could secure it.   On the morning of the 1st of May he pushed on from Chancellorsville, forcing back Anderson's command, and thus gaining the ridge.   While in the act of doing so Jackson arrived.   He instantly hurried the brigades of Ramseur, McGowan, Heth and Lane to Anderson's assistance, holding the rest in reserve.

Jackson appeared at a most critical moment, but Hooker scarcely waited to identify the Confederate force, when, to the amazement of the other officers, he gave orders to withdraw from the elevation and to take position in the Wilderness.   The leaders protested against the movement, impressing upon him the enormous value of the ridge just secured; but all the fight seemed to have been knocked out of Hooker.   He had decided to fall back to Chancellorsville, assume the strongest position possible, and there await the attack of Lee.   The unquestionably brave Federal leader seemed to have been suddenly stricken with an absolute collapse of all the qualities which had won for him the complimentary *sobriquet* of "Fighting Joe."   His army withdrew as ordered, and took form in the jungle, which was one of the very worst fighting-grounds that could have been chosen.   Jackson, as was to have been expected, immediately occupied the ridge which had been turned over to him very much as a gentleman rises from his chair and bows a lady to it.   Jackson followed the Federals until under the fire of their works at Chancellorsville. He was too wise with his small force to attack his enemies in their strong position, and he fell back a short distance and awaited the arrival of Lee, who joined him at nightfall with the rest of McLaws's and Anderson's divisions.

Hooker's line of battle ran east and west along the Fredericksburg and Orange Court-House plankroad, with Chancellorsville placed in the middle of a clearing. The line was some five miles in length, reaching from a short distance east of Chancellorsville westward in front of the Orange plank-road for three miles, when the right flank bent sharply back in a defensive crotchet. Meade's corps (Fifth), with one division of Couch's (Second), formed the left; Slocum's corps (Twelfth) and one division of Sickles's (Third), the centre; and Howard's (Eleventh), the right. The other divisions were held in reserve. As General Hooker had concluded to fight a defensive battle, trees were felled in front of the line to form abatis and rifle-pits were thrown up, and during the whole night the woods resounded with the strokes of a thousand Confederate axe-men engaged at the same work.*

Bad as was the position in which the Federal commander had placed his army, General Lee himself was in a situation so perilous that all his masterly genius was required to avert disaster and to lead it to another of its many triumphant victories.

* Swinton.

He had an army of forty thousand men at Chancellorsville, and General Early, with eight thousand more, held the heights of Fredericksburg. It will be observed, therefore, that the Confederate army was in a very critical position; for should General Hooker and his eighty thousand men at Chancellorsville, and Sedgwick with his thirty thousand men at Fredericksburg, seek to come together, the Confederate army would be crushed between them. Again, if Sedgwick should assail Early at Fredericksburg and drive him from his position (as undoubtedly he could do), it would then be an easy matter for Sedgwick to fall upon Lee's rear, while Hooker could advance from Chancellorsville, and, between the two Federal columns, the Confederate army was in great danger of being ground to atoms.

What should be done?

CHAPTER XXIII.

JACKSON'S FLANK MOVEMENT.

In this desperate situation of the Confederate army Stonewall Jackson submitted a plan to his chief, which the latter accepted and acted upon at once. The proposal was worthy of the great and daring brain which conceived it, and stamped Stonewall Jackson as one of the most brilliant soldiers of his time. It was this: General Lee with the divisions of McLaws and Anderson was to keep Hooker engaged all the next day by threatening demonstrations, while Jackson moved with his corps around the Federal right wing and by a sudden resistless attack doubled it up upon Hooker's centre, took his line in reverse and shut him off from his line of retreat by way of United States Ford. In accordance with this admirable scheme, General Lee commenced a series of demonstrations the following morning (Saturday, May 2) against the Federal left. He first attacked Couch's corps, on the left, then Slocum's, in the centre, slowly and steadily moving to the right until Hooker was fully convinced that he intended to play into his hands by assailing his powerful army in its entrenched position. But all this time Stonewall Jackson and his battle-tried veterans, twenty-two thousand altogether, were executing their splendid flank movement. A requisite to success was that it should be concealed from the Federal army. Jackson had started at an early hour, and a little more than a mile from Chancellorsville he left the plank-road and took the Old Mine road, in the direction of the Furnace, a group of old buildings used for smelting iron, and lying between two and three miles to the right of Chancellorsville.

Just as Jackson and his men reached this point General Sickles discovered the rapidly-moving soldiers, but, as the road dips to the southward near the hill, Sickles made the natural mistake of supposing the Confederates were retreating toward Richmond. He hastily sent forward two divisions to reconnoitre, and, suddenly surrounding the Twenty-fourth Georgia after the passage of the main column, nearly the whole regiment was captured. General Sickles was so certain the Confederates were withdrawing that he telegraphed the result to Hooker, who, equally positive, sent word to Sedgwick: "We know the enemy is flying, trying to save his trains; two of Sickles's divisions are among them."

Pleasanton's cavalry and two brigades of infantry were sent to the help of Sickles, while Jackson was doing his utmost to reach a position from which to deliver his terrible blow. It was difficult to force

their way through the broken country, and the
road was very narrow for the passage of artillery.
Striking the Brock road, Jackson turned into and
followed it until he reached the point where it
crosses the Orange plank-road, quite near the
Federal flank. A moment later General Fitz
Lee pointed out a hill from the top of which could
be seen the entire Federal position; acting on this
suggestion, Jackson quickly grasped the situation.
One of his aids was sent to order the column to
cross the plank-road, thus gaining the turnpike.
This was effected late in the afternoon, and the
Federal line was thus completely turned. Without losing a minute, the troops were made ready
for action. Rodes's division was deployed in line
of battle to the left of the turnpike, A. P. Hill
and Colston following close after with artillery and
advancing along the road in column. Jackson had
not only determined to strike the Federal flank,
but he was resolved on executing a much more
important movement, and one of amazing daring:
it was to extend his lines to the left, swing round
the left wing, and thus interpose himself between
Hooker and the Rapidan. The Federal line, against
which Jackson made ready to launch his men like
so many thunderbolts, reached across the old turnpike, and behind it was a second line, covered by
artillery in the earthworks at Chancellorsville. It
was Howard's Eleventh Corps, that was all unconscious of what was coming.

The Federal troops were mostly at supper, when their blood was curdled by the fierce yells which suddenly rent the air, and Jackson and his brave men burst upon them with the resistless fury of a cyclone. The rout was complete and the demoralization indescribable. Rodes and his men with their frightful outcries stormed the works, swarmed like a mountain-torrent over them, and, pressing on, followed by the division in the rear, captured or killed everybody that came within reach. The Federal artillery dashed off, the horses lashed to a dead run, and the guns, bounding against tree-trunks and stumps, were quickly overturned. No such wild panic had been seen during the war, and it was pushed with resistless impetuosity. Colston's division overtook Rodes's line, and the two leaped into the Federal works together. Colonel Crutchfield, Jackson's chief of artillery, lost no time in hurrying his batteries to the front and opening a hot fire on the Federal works at Chancellorsville. The infantry pressed steadily onward until the whole Eleventh Corps were flying like chaff in a whirlwind.

Stonewall Jackson was at the head of his men; those who saw him declare that he seemed carried away by the excitement of the moment. He leaned forward on his horse, extending his arm far in front, as though he wished "to push the men forward," and his voice was heard exclaiming, "Press forward! press forward!" every few minutes during the entire attack. When not thus mastered by

the ardor of battle, his right hand was raised
aloft with that gesture now familiar to his men,
as though he were praying to the God of battles
for victory.*

It was near six o'clock in the evening when the
assault was made, and it lasted for two hours, during which the Eleventh Corps was forced back on
the Twelfth, which held the centre, and Jackson's
advance was within a half mile of Hooker's headquarters. By this time it had become dark, and the
Confederates suddenly found themselves entangled
in the abatis of felled trees with which Hooker had
bordered his works around Chancellorsville. The
confusion became so great that the troops were
halted, and Rodes was ordered to fall back and
reform his men, while A. P. Hill's division was
stationed in their front. The scene which followed surpassed the wildest flights of delirium.
Soldiers, horses, wagons, cannon and ambulances
dashed pell-mell across the clearing around Chancellorsville, men and beasts crazed with terror and
aiming straight for the Rappahannock, as though
intent on plunging in to escape the yelling demons
at their heels. Officers shouted, swore, begged,
entreated and showered blows upon the frantic
fugitives without producing the slightest effect.
A person when thoroughly panic-stricken is a rav-
ing lunatic, and therefore beyond control. But for
the intervening abatis which entangled the pursu-

* Cooke's *Life of Stonewall Jackson.*

ing Confederates, the history of Hooker's army would have ended then and there.

A momentary flash of genius came to the Federal leader. Quick to note the check in the pursuit, he was equally quick to take advantage of it. He opened with his twenty-two guns upon the woods held by the Confederates, and, placing himself at the head of his old division, became the splendid soldier he had shown himself on many a battle-field. The fire of his daring stayed the disorganized masses, and he posted them on the clearing, directly in front of Jackson, and coolly awaited his charge. Fresh artillery were hurried forward, and were soon driving their fiery missiles into the woods which held the Confederates. It was a storm against which it was idle to beat, and the hurricane-like charge of Jackson was stayed.

It was ten o'clock, and the moon was climbing the sky. The dense gloom of the forest was lit up by flashes of fire, and the missiles described flaming curves high in the air overhead, while the crash of musketry, the scream of shells, the boom of cannon, the shrieks of the dying, the frenzied prayers and yells of those who still grappled in the death-combat, made a scene which belongs not to earth, but to Hades.

Soon it was reported that the Federal line was advancing, and A. P. Hill ordered his men forward to check it. They were in motion, when in the uncertain moonlight they saw two officers walking slowly to the rear, supporting between them another, who was wounded. It was evident he was badly hurt, for he leaned heavily upon his friends and was moving slowly and with great pain.

"Who is he? Who is he?" asked the troops as they hurried by, suspecting that he was some distinguished leader who was thus escorted.

"A Confederate officer," was the invariable reply to these questions, which were repeated every few seconds.

Suddenly an old veteran thought he saw something familiar in the limp, bareheaded figure staggering like a drunken man between the officers. He took two or three steps forward, stopped short, and, peering intently for a moment, exclaimed,

"Great God! that is Stonewall Jackson!"

CHAPTER XXIV.

THE FALL OF STONEWALL JACKSON.

WHEN the lull in the terrific fighting came, it was near ten o'clock in the evening; the stillness which succeeded was oppressive from its contrast with the infernal uproar that shook the earth and air but a brief while before. A few ragged clouds drifted in front of the moon, which looked down on one of the saddest scenes that had greeted it during all the long ages it had swung round this planet.

Stonewall Jackson was intent on completing the movement which we have already explained. He was burning with eagerness to swing his troops around, so as to cut off the Federals from United States Ford, and thus capture the entire army. So anxious was he to learn the precise position of his enemy that while his troops were forming for the assault he rode forward to reconnoitre, instructing his men not to fire unless cavalry approached from the direction of the enemy. He was accompanied by a few officers, and advanced quite close to the Federal lines. When the little group dare go no farther, they reined up and listened intently for sounds from the direction of Chancellorsville.

GENERAL LEE AT THE BATTLE OF CHANCELLORSVILLE.

Suddenly a volley was fired at them by the Confederate infantry, who took them to be Federals on a reconnoissance. Several of the party were struck, and fell from their horses; and Jackson, seeing the danger, wheeled to the left and galloped into the woods to escape a renewal of the fire. A minute later the men fired again, when less than a hundred feet distant. Jackson was struck three times—twice in the left arm, and once in the right hand. He dropped the bridle-reins with his left hand, but caught them again with the bleeding, tremulous fingers of the right. His startled horse wheeled and dashed toward Chancellorsville, and an interposing limb struck Jackson in the face, brushed off his cap and came near sweeping him from his horse. By a great effort, however, he retained his seat until he reached the road, where Captain Wilbourn, one of his staff-officers, tenderly helped him from his steed and laid him at the foot of a tree. All was still again, and only Captain Wilbourn and a courier were with the stricken chief, whose wounds were more severe than was supposed.

On the edge of the wood, a short distance off, were seen the dark outlines of a horse and rider as silent and motionless as if carved in stone. Captain Wilbourn called to this horseman to ride back and learn what troops had fired on them. Without speaking, the stranger rode away, and was seen no more. The identity of this mysterious person was unknown for a long time, and caused much speculation and wonder; but after the war, when the matter was discussed, Captain Revere, of the Federal army, stated that it was himself. He was on a reconnoissance, when he came upon the group at the foot of the tree, and was not long in learning they were Confederates. When ordered to find out who had fired the destructive volley, he rode off, and took good care not to return.

General Jackson was supported by his officers, but speedily became so weak that he was unable to walk even when leaning on the shoulders of his friends; he was therefore placed on a litter and carried toward the rear. A short distance only was passed when the artillery-fire from the direction of Chancellorsville became so fierce that the bearers were forced to lower the litter and lie down beside it. In a few minutes the fire slackened, and the bearers resumed their work. They walked slowly and with great care, but in the darkness they sometimes stumbled, and Jackson suffered dreadfully. When the moonlight fell upon his ghastly face, his friends were shocked, believing he was dying; but he rallied, and when borne to a place of safety sent a note to General Lee informing him of his misfortune. The note did not reach Lee until near daylight the next morning.

When Jackson fell, the command naturally devolved upon General A. P. Hill; but almost the next moment he was wounded, and it then went to

General Rodes, but, brave and capable as he was, he was so unacquainted with Jackson's command and his plans that he sent for General Stuart, to whom the command was formally relinquished. In consequence of the confusion and darkness, Stuart was unable to do anything, and deferred all operations until morning. As it was necessary that General Lee should know the particulars of Jackson's misfortune, Captain Wilbourn was sent to give him the sad information. The following is Captain Wilbourn's interesting statement, as furnished by J. E. Cooke:

Lee was found lying asleep in a little clump of pines near his front, covered with an oilcloth, to protect him from the dews of the night, and surrounded by the officers of his staff, also asleep. It was not yet daybreak, and the darkness prevented the messenger from distinguishing the commander-in-chief from the rest. He accordingly called for Major Taylor, Lee's adjutant-general, and that officer promptly awoke, when he was informed of what had taken place. As the conversation continued the sound aroused General Lee, who asked,

"Who is there?"

Major Taylor informed him, and, rising upon his elbow, Lee pointed to his blankets and said,

"Sit down here by me, captain, and tell us all about the fight last evening."

He listened without comment during the recital, but when it was finished said with great feeling,

"Ah, captain, any victory is dearly bought which deprives us of the services of General Jackson even for a short time."

From this reply it was evident that he did not regard the wounds received by Jackson as of a serious character—as was natural, from the fact that they were only flesh-wounds in the arm and hand—and believed that the only result would be a temporary absence of his lieutenant from command. As Captain Wilbourn continued to speak of the incident, Lee added with greater emotion than at first,

"Ah! don't talk about it. Thank God it is no worse!"

He then remained silent, but, seeing Captain Wilbourn rise as if to go, he requested him to remain, as he wished to "talk with him some more," and proceeded to ask a number of questions in reference to the position of the troops, who was in command, etc. When informed that Rodes was in temporary command, but that Stuart had been sent for, he exclaimed, "Rodes is a gallant, courageous and energetic officer," and asked where Jackson and Stuart could be found, calling for pencil and paper to write to them. Captain Wilbourn added that, from what he had heard Jackson say, he thought he intended to get possession, if possible, of the road to United States Ford, in the Federal rear, and so cut them off from the river that night or early in the morning. At these words Lee rose quickly and said with animation,

"These people must be pressed to-day!"

About this time a messenger arrived from Wilderness Tavern with a note from the wounded general. Lee read it with much feeling, and dictated the following reply:

"GENERAL: I have just received your note informing me that you were wounded. I cannot express my regret at the occurrence. Could I have directed events, I should have chosen, for the good of the country, to have been disabled in your stead.

"I congratulate you upon the victory, which is due to your skill and energy.

"R. E. LEE, General."

General Jackson's wound soon assumed a grave character. His arm was amputated, but the relief was only temporary. Pneumonia set in, and he died on the following Sunday, May 10. In the delirium of his last moments he called out,

"A. P. Hill, prepare for action!"

When Stonewall Jackson breathed his last, Lee exclaimed, "I have lost my right arm!" and he spoke the truth. He was the ablest of the many brilliant lieutenants that gathered around the illustrious leader of the Southern armies. No man aroused such enthusiasm among his troops, nor was ever a commander more idolized by his men than

was the fiery Virginian, whose sweep was as resistless as that of the Alpine avalanche. He was not
a great general like Lee, with the power to plan and
combine immense campaigns, but as an executive
officer the world has never seen his superior. His
intense piety resembled at times the fanaticism of
Cromwell. He believed in the righteousness of
the Southern cause with all his heart, body, mind
and soul. He felt no more doubt of its triumph
than he had of the rising of the sun. Next to
his God and the Confederacy, he rested his faith
in General Lee. No man was ever more warmly
loved than was the commander of the Confederate armies by Stonewall Jackson. He ardently
believed that a better man or an abler military
leader than Lee had never lived, and Jackson
was thrilled by an exalted joy in carrying out
in his own resistless fashion the plans and orders
of his superior.

"General Lee is not slow," said Jackson, in dis-
cussing the military question with a friend; "no
one knows the weight upon his heart, his great
responsibilities. He is commander-in-chief, and
knows that if an army is lost it cannot be replaced.
No! There may be some persons whose good opinion of me will make them attach some weight to
my views; and if ever you hear that said of General Lee, I beg you will contradict it in my name.
I have known General Lee for five and twenty
years. He is cautious—he ought to be—but he

is not 'slow.' Lee is a *phenomenon.* He is the only man whom I would follow blindfold."

WHY "STONEWALL" JACKSON DID NOT DRINK.

Colonel A. R. Boteler, in the Philadelphia *Weekly Times*, tells the following story concerning General Jackson:

"Having lingered to the last allowable moment with the members of my family 'hereinbefore mentioned'—as the legal documents would term them—it was after ten o'clock at night when I returned to headquarters for final instruction, and before going to the general's room I ordered two whiskey-toddies to be brought up after me. When they appeared, I offered one of the glasses to Jackson; but he drew back, saying,

"'No, colonel, you must excuse me: I never drink intoxicating liquors.'

"'I know that, general,' said I; 'but, though you habitually abstain, as I do myself, from everything of the sort, there are occasions—and this is one of them—when a stimulant will do us both good. Otherwise, I would neither take it myself nor offer it to you. So you must make an exception to your general rule, and join me in a toddy to-night.'

"He again shook his head, but, nevertheless, took the tumbler and began to sip its contents. Presently putting it on the table, after having but partially emptied it, he said,

"'Colonel, do you know why I habitually abstain from intoxicating drinks?' and, on my replying in the negative, he continued: 'Why, sir, because I like the taste of them; and when I discovered that to be the case, I made up my mind at once to do without them altogether.'"

CHAPTER XXV.

THE LAST STRUGGLE AT CHANCELLORSVILLE.

GENERAL JACKSON had fallen in battle, as may be said, but the hurrying rush of the furious strife could not be checked or stayed therefor. Stuart, his successor, made his dispositions to renew the battle at daylight, forming the corps in three lines, Hill's division being the first, Colston's the second and Rodes's the third.

On the Federal side the savage doubling up of Hooker's right by Jackson rendered necessary several important changes in the line. Accordingly, a new front was formed on that flank with Sickles and Berry. Reynolds's corps had arrived from below Fredericksburg, and greatly added to the spirit of the army. There was no talk of retreating, and the struggle on the morrow, therefore, was certain to assume a tremendous and decisive character. Sedgwick was below Fredericksburg with the Sixth Corps, numbering twenty-two thousand men. General Hooker sent orders to him to occupy the town, seize the heights, move to the plank-road connecting that place with Chancellorsville and join the main body by daylight the following morning.

At early dawn General Stuart opened his attack on the Federal lines, scarcely a half mile distant. Their war-cry was "Charge, and remember Jackson!" Sweeping resistlessly forward, they quickly occupied the ridge of which mention has been made, and, bringing up thirty pieces of cannon, turned them upon their adversaries. The Federals resisted bravely and assailed Stuart's left with great vigor. For a time it looked as if they could not be checked, but at last they fell back. Meanwhile, General Lee was pressing the Federal left and centre with the divisions of Anderson and McLaws, slowly forging to the right to unite with the Second Corps. Anderson's division was on his left, and, pushing forward, it gradually formed a connection with Stuart at the moment the latter had repulsed the attack on his left. The Confederate army was now reunited, and General Lee gave the command to storm the Federal works around Chancellorsville. The assault was made with fiery energy, and after a savage struggle the works were captured; but the Federals rallied, and with the same splendid valor drove out the Confederates. Again was the position taken, and again lost. The flame of battle surged back and forth, until, on the fourth charge, when the dead bodies were so thick that the feet of the combatants could not touch the ground, the works were secured, and at ten o'clock the Confederate flag floated over Chancellorsville.

The scene at that time was horrible beyond description. The woods, which were full of wounded, had been set on fire by the shells and the blazing building, and hundreds of poor fellows were burning to death; many more than is suspected perished in this awful manner. The shouts of combatants, the shrieks of those caught in the roaring flames, the heavy discharge of artillery and the crash and rattle of musketry gave to the picture a terrible grandeur such as must haunt all the participants therein to their last hour.

It is hard to find a satisfactory explanation of Hooker's course at Chancellorsville, where, it is said, he went in with the stride of a giant and came out with the step of a dwarf. His combinations and plans were excellent, in a military sense; and ought to have ensured success even against such a masterly leader as Lee, whose army numbered less than one-half as many as that of the Federals, while at the beginning of the battle he was placed at great disadvantage as respects position. We are inclined to believe that the true explanation was given by a Federal soldier, which is to the effect that when Hooker was awakened from his exultant dream that Lee would not dare give him battle the Federal commander was scared into a perfect collapse of terror. The knowledge that Lee meant fight, and the fiery disruption of Jackson on his flank, drove all courage from him, and his only thought and hope was to get beyond reach of the impetuous Confederates and their fearless leaders.

As if convinced that defeat awaited him, General Hooker had caused a strongly-entrenched line to be constructed in the rear of his first position, so as to cover the United States Ford. It had the form of a redan thrown forward in the angle between the Rapidan and the Rappahannock, and was very strong. The corps of Meade and Reynolds, incredible as it may seem, had been held idle during the struggle of the morning, and they were now formed within it; there for the time the disorganized fragments of the rest of the army found temporary shelter. But, strong as it was, General Lee resolved to attack it; the fire of battle possessed him and his men, and they meant that the Federal army should not escape them again. But at the moment the mailed hand was raised to smite, an alarming sound from the direction of Fredericksburg caught his ear. With his hand still aloft, the warrior listened: the ominous rumble was the tramp of Sedgwick's legions, who, having vanquished Early at Fredericksburg, were advancing to assail him in the rear.

It will be recalled that Hooker had ordered Sedgwick to attack Early at Fredericksburg Heights, and then to hasten to his assistance. These orders reached Sedgwick about midnight, and he immediately put his column in motion. The town was occupied before daylight Sunday morning, a small Confederate force being driven back. It was not yet light when a detachment was sent to seize the heights occupied by Early. The assault was repulsed, when Gibbons's division of Couch's corps, which was opposite Falmouth, was ordered to join the assailants. Early had under him his own division and Barksdale's brigade of Mississippians, of McLaws's division. This force was attacked by more than three times its number. Before the overwhelming onslaught, the defenders could not sustain themselves: they were driven back, and ere noon the entire Confederate force was killed, captured or dispersed. Unable to stay the resistless torrent, the Confederates retreated over the Telegraph road southward, and General Sedgwick, as instructed by his chief, immediately advanced up the turnpike toward Chancellorsville for the purpose of attacking Lee in the rear. It was this intelligence which arrested Lee when on the very point of storming the Federal works at Chancellorsville.

With that intuitive grasp of all the possibilities which often flashed upon Lee like an inspiration, he determined not to await the arrival of Sedgwick, but to send a force large enough to defeat him. Nine times out of ten such a division of his army in front of an enemy much his superior numerically would have resulted in disaster, but this occasion may be called the " tenth." Sedgwick was a skilful and brave general with more than twenty thousand men flushed with victory; Hooker was cowed, beaten and paralyzed. Nothing was to be feared from him: everything was to be dreaded from the detachment hurrying along the plank-road. And then and there, in front of the Federal host, General Lee detached five brigades from his little army and sent them back to give battle to Sedgwick. To this force it was expected that Early's troops would be added, while General Wilcox, who had been sent to guard Banks's Ford, was already in motion to dispute the Federal advance. When the brigades sent by Lee had united with General Wilcox, they immediately formed in line of battle, which opened at four o'clock and lasted until dark. Sedgwick was effectually checked, and made no effort to advance farther that day.

When he left Fredericksburg, Early returned and took possession of the heights, thus placing himself in the rear of Sedgwick and enabling him to prevent him recrossing the Rappahannock at Fredericksburg. Lee resolved to crush Sedgwick and then to turn and assail Hooker, in accordance with his original plan. With this purpose, he assumed personal command of three brigades of Anderson's division and on Monday morning marched to Salem Church, where he proceeded to form his line of battle. Unexpected delays prevented the attack until late in the afternoon, when a general advance was made upon Sedgwick with the purpose of cutting off his retreat by way of the river. But the Federals resisted with such stubbornness and bravery that Lee was foiled. They held their ground until dark, when they were so hard pressed that they began slowly falling back. They retreated in good order to Banks's Ford, where a ponton-bridge had been laid, and over which in the gathering gloom of night the Federals effected a safe passage to the other shore.

Having disposed in this decisive fashion of Sedgwick, Lee returned to finish Hooker, but that leader had improved the hours of grace unexpectedly given him; and when, on Wednesday morning, everything was ready for the grand assault, the Federal works were found deserted. General Hooker and his army had recrossed the river, covering the ponton-bridge with pine-boughs, so as to muffle the sound of the artillery-wheels.

The Confederate loss at Chancellorsville aggregated ten thousand two hundred and eighty-one; the Union loss was seventeen thousand one hundred and ninety-seven killed, wounded and missing. Besides the killed and wounded left behind, fourteen pieces of artillery and twenty thousand stand of arms fell into the hands of the Confederates. For them the victory was the grandest of the war. They had disastrously beaten an army of more than double their numbers, and the generalship displayed by General Lee was of the most remarkable character. It was fitting that the noontide of Stonewall Jackson's life should be crowned by one of the most daring, brilliant and decisive exploits recorded in history.

VI.

THE CAMP-FIRE OF GETTYSBURG.

CHAPTER XXVI.

PRELIMINARY MOVEMENTS.

THE magnificent achievements of the Army of Northern Virginia were not duplicated by the other armed forces of the Confederacy: there was but one Lee, and the Federals had made substantial progress in the West. General Bragg had been discomfited so often that the people clamored for his removal, but President Davis clung all the closer to him. General Pemberton was shut in at Vicksburg, with General Grant grimly waiting till starvation should compel him to succumb, and matters in the Trans-Mississippi Department were in anything but an encouraging shape for the Southern cause.

Profoundly sensible of the gravity of the situation, General Lee visited Richmond and held a long conference with the authorities. At the consultation it was determined to invade the North a second time. There were the best of reasons for such a course. The Army of Northern Virginia was nearly seventy thousand strong, and there were no better soldiers in the world. The splendid triumph at Chancellorsville had roused them to the highest pitch of enthusiasm, and their *morale* was perfect. They were in the finest state of discipline, were excellently armed, and, as Longstreet expressed it, were in a condition to undertake anything. It was known, at the same time, that the Federal army was in worse form than it had been for many months. The best tribute to its discipline and cohesiveness was the fact that after such blundering leadership it still remained an army; but the terms of enlistment of many of the troops were expiring, and the desertions were so numerous that General Hooker notified President Lincoln that his infantry was reduced to an effective strength of eighty thousand men.

Vigorous preparations were instantly set on foot for the invasion of the teeming fields of Pennsylvania, where the Confederate legions saw corn, wine and oil in abundance. General Longstreet's corps had rejoined the army immediately after Chancellorsville, and General Ewell succeeded Jackson in the command of the Second Corps. A third corps was organized and placed under A. P. Hill, and both he and Ewell were raised to the grade of lieutenant-general. Longstreet's corps included the divisions of McLaws, Hood and Pickett; Ewell's corps, the divisions of Early, Rodes and Johnson; and Hill's corps, the divisions of Anderson, Pender and Heth. Besides these, there were ten thousand cavalry under Stuart. These preparations were not unknown to Hooker nor to the North, whose system of gathering news through the papers made it impossible for such a great movement to be kept secret for any length of time. There were intimations in the journals of a mighty campaign in process of organization south of the Potomac, and something "in the air" prepared every one for the startling tidings which speedily flashed across the border.

By the first day of summer everything was in readiness for the advance, and General Lee began manœuvring to draw General Hooker from his position on the Rappahannock. On the 3d of June, Longstreet's corps marched from its encampments at Fredericksburg and on the Rapidan toward Culpeper Court-House, followed the next day and the succeeding day by Ewell's corps. A. P. Hill stayed at Fredericksburg with a view of deceiving Hooker into the belief that the entire Confederate army still confronted him.

Though well aware that something unusual was going on, General Hooker had no means as yet of learning the truth. In hope of gaining light, he sent, June 6, Sedgwick's corps across the Rappahannock at Deep Run. General Hill notified Lee of the movement, but, knowing its meaning, Lee permitted Ewell and Longstreet to continue their march to Culpeper Court-House, where they arrived on the 8th. General Stuart and his cavalry were there awaiting them.

THE CAVALRY-FIGHT AT FLEETWOOD, OR BRANDY STATION.

Caution, skill, energy and fine generalship marked the movements of General Lee in marshaling his hosts for the terrific struggle at Gettysburg. His purpose was to manœuvre so as to withdraw the Federal army from Virginia without bringing on a collision between the armies. The first step was to send forward one division of Longstreet's corps toward Culpeper; this was followed by another, and then all of Ewell's corps was sent in the same direction. A. P. Hill stayed on the south bank of the Rappahannock, near Fredericksburg, to confront the Federal advance upon Richmond.

It was at this juncture that one of the most impressive scenes of the war took place. On the 8th of June, Lee's head of column reached Culpeper, and a review of Stuart's cavalry took place in a broad open space east of the court-house. Above a little knoll rose a tall pole from which floated the Confederate flag, while directly below sat General Lee on his charger; his short cavalry cape fell from his shoulders, and the old slouch-hat half concealed the grave, handsome face beneath. His bright, clear eyes looked out on the long column of eight thousand cavalry, first drawn up in line, and then passing in front of the. commander at a gallop, Stuart and his staff at the head, with sabres at tierce-point. Such a display always delighted the chivalrous Stuart, who bounded into battle with the overflowing spirits of a boy let loose from school. A sham-conflict followed—a proceeding so puzzling to the Federals that the next morning they sent two divisions of cavalry, supported by two brigades of picked infantry, to learn what it meant. This force crossed at Kelley's and Beverley's fords, and the result was the most remarkable cavalry-fight of the war. It is conceded by both sides that it surpassed any combat of its kind ever fought on this continent. The forces engaged were numerous, the soldiers were veterans toughened in battle, and they fought like heroes from the very opening to the close.

The Federal general Buford launched his division against one of Stuart's brigades near Beverley's Ford. It was just as day was breaking, and the assault was made with such fierceness that the Confederates were forced back toward Fleetwood Hill. Stuart had established his headquarters on the crest of this hill, and, seeing how the battle was going, he spurred to the front on a swift gallop, opening with a destructive fire from his artillery and sharpshooters, while Hampton's division was sent to attack the Federal left. But, at the same time, the Federals were making a most dangerous movement against Stuart's rear. General Gregg, with

18

the second division of Federal cavalry, crossed at Kelley's Ford, below, and, ignoring the force there, attacked the rear, behind Fleetwood Hill. At this time the great sabre-fight was at its height, when Stuart was aroused by the assault upon his rear. Falling rapidly back, he met the Federals coming up the hill, repulsed them and charged in turn. Back and forth swung the combatants, as if clinging to the opposite edges of a great pendulum. The Federal artillery was captured and recaptured three times, finally remaining in the hands of Stuart. At this juncture General Gregg made a fierce charge along the eastern slope of the hill, but Stuart had anticipated the movement, and checked it by a furious fire of shell; and the gallant Georgian general P. M. B. Young charged the Federals. This was done with the sabre, and carbine and pistol played no part in the fight. After a determined resistance, the Federals were routed and driven in disorder toward the river.

General W. H. F. Lee bravely met the attack on the left, near the river, and repulsed it. In the fight General Lee, who was the son of the commanding general, was severely wounded, but he drove the Federals back to the river, while Hampton, on the right, did the same, under the fire of Stuart's guns on Fleetwood Hill. By sunset the whole Federal force had retreated to the other side of the Rappahannock, leaving behind several hundred dead and wounded. Besides General Lee, General Butler lost a foot, Colonel Williams was killed, Captain Farley was slain, Captain White wounded and Lieutenant Goldsborough captured. The Federal loss was severe, among it being the brave Colonel Davis of the Eighth New York Cavalry.

Many thousand cavalry fought each other in a hand-to-hand encounter from morning till night. It was "give and take" from the beginning to the end, and there were personal encounters, individual exploits and wonderful escapes which, if all told, would fill this volume.

What a significant proof of the prodigious character of the civil war that this tremendous cavalry-contest—the most remarkable, as has been said, that was ever fought in this country—was in reality only a preliminary skirmish, as may be said, of the stupendous shock of arms that was to shake the continent! It had no perceptible effect on the great contest, and more than one history of those eventful times makes no mention of it.

CHAPTER XXVII.

MANŒUVRING FOR BATTLE.

THE most important result of the cavalry-fight at Brandy Station was the discovery by Hooker of Lee's presence at Culpeper and his plan of invasion. These facts were learned through captured correspondence.

Hooker saw that no time was to be lost. He immediately pushed up the river to Rappahannock Station and Beverley, while the cavalry guarded the fords above. Suspicious as he was of the intention of the Confederate leader, he could not be certain of the form it would take. He supposed he was attempting to repeat the campaign of the previous year in which Pope figured so discreditably; he therefore gave his full attention to protecting his communications and to guarding against a sudden march by the Confederates upon Washington.

Lee was advancing with the greatest secrecy and skill, his eye fixed upon Hooker like the scrutiny of a tiger when stealing upon his prey. He saw that his opponent was completely deceived, and he therefore ventured on another daring move. Ewell's corps marched swiftly toward Chester Gap, hurried through that defile, and reached Winchester at the close of the afternoon of the 13th, having marched more than seventy miles in three days. By this audacious manœuvre Lee's line of battle was expanded to a length of one hundred miles, for his right (Hill's corps) was at Fredericksburg, his centre (Longstreet's corps) was at Culpeper, and his left (Ewell's corps) was at the head of Shenandoah Valley. The mere statement of the fact would condemn the military judgment of Lee were it not supplemented by the fact that he *knew his man.* They had met before, and it was an encounter of a giant and a dwarf.

The wisdom of striking the Confederate army while drawn out in this attenuated fashion could not fail to present itself to Hooker, who suggested it to President Lincoln and General Halleck; but they disapproved of it. The opinion of the President was expressed in his characteristic fashion : " In case you find Lee coming to the north of the Rappahannock, I would by no means cross to the south of it. I would not take any risk of being entangled on the river, like an ox jumped half over a fence and liable to be torn by dogs front and rear without a fair chance to gore one way or kick the other." Some days later the President wrote: " I think Lee's army, and not Richmond, is your true objective-point. If he comes toward the Upper Potomac, fight him when opportunity offers ; if he stays where he is, fret him and fret him." Still later, when the Confederate advance became definitely known, the President wrote to General Hooker: "If the head of Lee's army is at Martinsburg and the tail of it on the plank-road between Fredericksburg and Chancellorsville, the animal must be very slim somewhere. Could you not break him?"

Hooker broke up his camps along the Rappahannock as soon as he learned that Lee had entered the Shenandoah Valley, and headed for Washington, following the line of the Orange and Alexandria Railroad. Lee did not hesitate, but pushed his grand campaign with his accustomed brilliancy, boldness and skill.

Hill waited at Fredericksburg until the Union army withdrew, when, his purpose accomplished, he marched for Culpeper, where Longstreet's corps were still in position, while Ewell, remembering that he was at the head of Stonewall Jackson's old division, was dashing into the Shenandoah Valley. General Jenkins with his cavalry brigade had been directed to push toward Winchester, and Imboden and his troopers had approached Romney to shut off any reinforcements that might be sent by way of the Baltimore and Ohio Railroad. They were in position and ready to co-operate with Ewell when he entered the valley.

When Ewell crossed the Shenandoah River near Front Royal, he sent Rodes's division to Berryville to cut off communication between Winchester and the Potomac, while with the divisions of Early and Johnson he advanced straight upon Milroy in Winchester. This town, from its peculiar position, had a most extraordinary experience during the war. The contending hosts swept back and forth through it time and again, until the inhabitants had to be alert to keep informed as to which authority was over them. It had changed hands as often as four times in one day, and during the war was captured and recaptured more than sixty times.

When Ewell thundered at the gates, General Milroy and about six thousand men were within. Ewell was eager to make a closer acquaintance with this individual, whose outrages in the valley were of such character that the Confederate government had ordered its forces to refuse him the rights of a prisoner of war if captured. When Milroy found who was after him, his chief solicitude was to get away. He had the means of making a splendid defence, but the following night he crept out of Winchester with his command. In their tumultuous flight, however, they were intercepted and most of them captured. Milroy managed to save himself and a handful of men by outrunning their pursuers to the Potomac.* Berryville having been

---

* "Milroy's defence of the post entrusted to his care was infamously feeble, and the worst of that long train of misconduct that made the Valley of the Shenandoah to be called the Valley of Humiliation."— *Swinton.*

"In my opinion, Milroy's men will fight better under a soldier."— *General Hooker's letter to President Lincoln.*

taken, with several hundred prisoners, and the garrison at Harper's Ferry having withdrawn to Maryland Heights, the valley was entirely cleared of all Federal forces.

Stonewall Jackson's old corps sustained its reputation for dash, vim and rapidity of movement, for it had captured more than four thousand prisoners, twenty-nine pieces of artillery, two hundred and seventy wagons and ambulances and a large quantity of valuable stores. The loss in the corps was slight, and as a consequence the enthusiasm was unbounded.

When Hill advanced from Fredericksburg to Culpeper, Longstreet left the latter place, marched northward along the eastern side of the Blue Ridge and took position at Ashby's and Snicker's gaps. Behind this screen Hill dodged into the Shenandoah Valley, and posted himself at Winchester.

Lee's consummate strategy improved his situation at every move, until within a couple of weeks from the opening of the campaign he had everything in the shape desired. He was so strongly posted in the valley that he was ready to welcome the attack of his enemy, no matter how great his numbers, while he was at liberty to send a powerful raiding-column into Maryland or Pennsylvania without serious danger of being molested.

But Hooker was in a state of nervous fear, and resolved that he would not be drawn into the trap which Lee had evidently set for him. The spectre of the colossal soldier in the dreaded gray coat still haunted the authorities in Washington, and the Federal commander clung to his position in the neighborhood of Manassas and Fairfax, so as to guard the approach to the capital, while Pleasanton and his cavalry cautiously felt the ground in the direction of the Blue Ridge, where Longstreet was powerfully posted, with Stuart's troopers on his front. On the 17th of June a brisk collision took place between Pleasanton and two brigades of Stuart near Aldie, and General Pleasanton was driven back. Feeling quite sure of Lee's position, Hooker now sent forward the Twelfth Corps to Leesburg, the Fifth to Aldie, and the Second to Thoroughfare Gap. While engaged in manœuvring, it suddenly occurred to Hooker that he was wandering about the country precisely as Lee wished him to do; he therefore once more devoted his attention to the protection of the capital and awaited the further development of Lee's purposes. He was not kept long in waiting.

Hill and Longstreet having relieved Ewell in the Shenandoah Valley, the latter, on the 22d of June, marched into Maryland. At the same time, Imboden's cavalry, galloping westward, destroyed the Baltimore and Ohio Railroad and the Chesapeake and Ohio Canal. Having done this damage, Imboden captured the city of Cumberland, Maryland.

A week previous, when Ewell invested Winches-

ter, Jenkins's cavalry were ordered into Pennsylvania in quest of supplies. They were directly on
the heels of Milroy's fleeing wagon-train. The
terrified teamsters, with their perspiring horses
lashed to a dead run, tore through the streets of
Chambersburg, shouting that the whole rebel army
would be in town before night. That sort of business was not calculated to exert a soothing effect
on the inhabitants, for, allowing for some natural
exaggeration, they knew there was a strong substra-
tum of truth in the announcement. Sure enough,
the Confederate troopers arrived that evening. The
inhabitants were treated with much consideration,
and, having gathered a large number of horses and
cattle, Jenkins sent them toward the Potomac, while
he and his cavalry set out to join Ewell's force,
which, it will be remembered, had entered Maryland on the 22d of June. Ewell advanced by two
columns on Hagerstown, and, crossing the border
into Pennsylvania, moved up the Cumberland Valley, reaching Chambersburg the next day.

By this time, as may well be supposed, the North
was in a state of unprecedented excitement. The
Confederates were advancing toward the polar
star, and who should say where they would stop?
Many believed they would " water their horses in
the Delaware," and that Philadelphia was doomed
to fall. The State records and treasures were hastily sent forward to New York, and consternation
prevailed such as was never known since the open-

ing of the war. President Lincoln issued a proclamation, calling upon the States of Maryland,
Pennsylvania, Ohio and West Virginia to furnish one hundred thousand militia, to serve for
six months unless sooner discharged, to repel the
invasion. Even in New York the people listened
tremblingly for the tramp of the armed legions
from the South. Major-General Couch had been
detached from the command of the Second Corps
of the Army of the Potomac and assigned to the
command of the Department of the Susquehanna,
with his headquarters at Harrisburg. He issued
a stirring appeal to the Pennsylvanians to rally
to the defence of their State, and Governor Cur-
tin called on the militia to come forward. The
response was so feeble that it was not until several regiments arrived from other States that
General Couch was able to make the least pretence of defence. Even then he was compelled to
confine his attempts to fortifying the line of the
Susquehanna.

On the 27th of June the entire Confederate
army was concentrated at Chambersburg. General Lee issued a complimentary address to his
soldiers, and strict orders were enforced against
the sale of liquors or molestation of persons and
private property. Lee felt himself greatly handi-
capped by the absence of Stuart and his cavalry,
for without them he had been unable, since crossing the Potomac, to gain any reliable news of the

Army of the Potomac. With the purpose of keeping the Federal army east of the Blue Ridge, so that Lee might preserve his own communications with the Valley of Virginia through Hagerstown and Williamsport, Ewell was sent with a division east of South Mountain. It halted at York, while the rest of the corps proceeded to Carlisle. Lee had his forces well in hand and was about to advance upon Harrisburg, when he was checked by the first authentic tidings of the Army of the Potomac.

Hooker did not dare move to the northern side of the Potomac until Lee fully disclosed his purpose; when he learned that the rear of the Confederate army was entering Maryland, he ventured to move. The Federal army made the crossing of the Potomac at Edwards's Ferry on the 25th and 26th of June and began concentrating at Frederick. This position was of vast importance, for, as will be seen, it enabled Hooker either to pass South Mountain and intercept Lee's communications or to move toward the Susquehanna in the event of Lee marching upon Harrisburg. Hooker inclined to the former plan, and accordingly advanced his left wing to Middleton and sent General Slocum with the Twelfth Corps to Harper's Ferry. At that point was a garrison of eleven thousand men, which it was intended should unite with Slocum and by moving upon Chambersburg threaten the Confederate rear. This proposal, however, was vetoed by General Halleck, whose affection for Harper's Ferry would not countenance its abandonment. Hooker insisted, and showed the great results promised by his plan. Halleck would not yield, and, exasperated by the stupidity of his superior officer, Hooker resigned. His resignation was accepted, and on the next day, June 28, Major-General G. G. Meade, commanding the Fifth Army Corps, became commander of the Army of the Potomac. Though General Meade never rose to the height of a great soldier, he was a man who understood his profession too thoroughly to fail to do it honor, and his appointment was one of the wisest ever made by his government, which also had the good sense to refrain from trammelling him with instructions to pursue any definite policy, leaving him to be guided by the necessities of the situation.*

When General Meade assumed command, the army was lying near Frederick City, with its left thrown out to Middleton. On the 29th, Lee learned that its advanced force was beyond Middleton, as if it meant to pass over the mountains and assail his rear. Ewell's troops were at York and Carlisle, while Stuart's whereabouts were still unknown. Seeking to draw Meade away from the Potomac, Lee began concentrating his army east of the mountains. Longstreet and Hill were ordered to advance from Chambersburg to Get-

* J. D. McCabe, Jr.

tysburg, while Ewell was directed to march from York and Carlisle to the same point. Feeling keenly the loss of Stuart, Lee proceeded at a leisurely pace, and thus, not knowing the movements of Meade, the latter was enabled to reach Gettysburg first, and to fortify it against the Confederate advance. Stuart had harassed the flanks of the Federal army while it was in Virginia, but he was not able to delay its progress. He crossed the Potomac at Seneca Falls, and, passing east of Meade's army, arrived at Carlisle just after Ewell had left for Gettysburg.

On the night of June 30, Meade learned that Lee was concentrating his forces east of the South Mountain to meet him. It was beyond Meade's power to determine where the shock of battle would take place, as that must depend largely on circumstances which could not be foreseen. The general line of Pipe Creek, on the dividing-ridge between the Monocacy and the waters running into Chesapeake Bay, was selected as a favorable position, though its ultimate adoption was held contingent on developments that might arise. Accordingly, orders were issued on the night of the 30th for the movement of the different corps on the following day. The Sixth Corps, forming the right wing of the army, was ordered to Manchester, in rear of Pipe Creek, headquarters and the Second Corps to Taneytown; the Twelfth and Fifth Corps, forming the centre, were directed on Two Taverns and

Hanover, somewhat in advance of Pipe Creek; while the left wing, formed of the First, Third and Eleventh Corps, under General Reynolds, as it was closest to the line of march of the enemy, was thrown forward to Gettysburg, toward which, as it happened, Lee was then heading. Strategetically, the position at Gettysburg was of supreme importance to Lee, for it was the first point in his eastward march across the South Mountain that gave command of direct lines of retreat toward the Potomac; but it was not of the same moment to Meade, especially if a defensive rather than an offensive battle was to be fought, and the topographical features of Gettysburg, that make it so advantageous for the defence, were then wholly unknown to him. While, therefore, the left wing, under Reynolds, was thus thrown forward in advance of the rest of the army as far as Gettysburg, it was not with any predetermined purpose of taking up position there, but rather to serve as a mask while the line of Pipe Creek was assumed.

But, while in war commanders propose, fate or accident (so called) often disposes; and at the time these movements were in execution events were occurring that were to lift the obscure and insignificant hamlet of Gettysburg into historic immortality as the scene of the mightiest encounter of modern days.*

On the 29th of June the Federal general

* Swinton.

Buford and his cavalry occupied Gettysburg, to which point General Reynolds had been ordered. On the following night two divisions of Hill's corps bivouacked within half a dozen miles of Gettysburg, on the Baltimore and Chambersburg road, while Ewell paused at Heidlersburg, nine miles distant from the little town. General Reynolds with the left wing of the Federal army was on Marsh Creek, four miles south of Gettysburg, his purpose being to occupy the town the next morning. Longstreet's corps was west of the mountains, and only the two divisions of Hill were east. Such was the situation at dawn of the fateful 1st of July, 1863.

CHAPTER XXVIII.

GETTYSBURG: FIRST DAY.

In the warm sunshine of the morning of July 1, A. P. Hill and Ewell continued their advance toward Gettysburg, destined to be the scene of one of the most terrific battles of modern times. A mile from the town Hill's advanced division came in collision with Buford's cavalry, posted on the Chambersburg road, along which the Confederate divisions were approaching. Buford served his artillery with such skill that he held the Confederate force in check until the arrival of Reynolds, who, hearing the sound of his guns, hurried forward with his own First Corps and the Eleventh Corps, under General Howard. An hour later Reynolds came upon the field with the division of the First Corps under General Wadsworth. Reynolds's instructions were to avoid bringing on an engagement at Gettysburg, but, in case the Confederates appeared in force, to fall back to Pipe Creek. He found Buford so hard pressed, however, that he was compelled to throw forward his main body to save him. While advancing, he was assailed with such suddenness that the line of battle was formed under fire. This attack was made

19   289

by the division of General Heth, of Hill's corps, which was in the advance. They forced the Unionists backward, but while following up their success they were in turn repulsed by an attack on their right flank led by General Reynolds in person. In the charge the Confederates had several hundred men captured, including Brigadier-General Archer, while General Reynolds was shot dead by a rifle-ball. His loss was a severe one to the Federal army. "He was a brave and skilful soldier, an honest-hearted gentleman, and had conducted himself so humanely and generously to the people of Fredericksburg that they mourned his death almost as though he had been one of their own leaders."* The Federals rallied, and speedily recovered the ground from which they had been driven on the right, manœuvring so well that they surrounded two regiments of Davis's brigade of Mississippians in the railroad-cut and compelled them to surrender, with their battle-flags. The battle of Gettysburg having opened, events hurried on with tremendous speed. The two remaining divisions of the First Corps of the Federal army arriving on the ground, one of them was immediately thrown forward to support the left, which was hard pressed by Hill. The fight became fierce and sanguinary.

It will be remembered that Ewell encamped the night before at Heidlersburg, nine miles from

* J. D. McCabe, Jr.

Gettysburg. While on the march to the latter point the thunder of cannon announced the opening of the great battle, and he made all haste. Rodes, with the advance, reached the field just as Hill was crowding the left so hard. Without delay he secured a commanding position on the Federal right and opened briskly upon it. The Federals responded by throwing forward a division of infantry, who speedily captured several hundred members of Iverson's North Carolina brigade. Thus, contrary to the intentions of both Meade and Lee, a severe conflict was brought on when both commanders were manœuvring for position in which to receive instead of to make an attack. When the boom of the cannon fell upon Lee's ears, he was at the headquarters in the rear of his troops which Hill had left a short time before. He supposed it was an accidental collision with a body of Federal cavalry; when he learned that Hill was engaged in a desperate fight with the Union infantry, he was astonished, and by no means pleased, for his army was not in shape to deliver battle. But it was upon him, and could not be avoided. He ordered Hill's corps to be closed up, and sent forward reinforcements as rapidly as he could; then, mounting his horse, he rode in the direction of the firing.

Meanwhile, the line of battle rapidly widened, the two armies having gradually extended, in the form of a crescent, for a distance of several miles,

Gettysburg being in the rear of the curve. The Eleventh Corps of the Federals came upon the field, General Howard taking command after the fall of Reynolds. Almost at the same time Pender's division of Hill's corps arrived opposite, and directly afterward Early's division of Ewell's corps came up and took position to the north of the town, across the Harrisburg road. This caused the Federals to extend their lines still farther to the right, thereby weakening them to a fatal degree.

At three o'clock in the afternoon Early made a fierce assault upon the Union right, under General Barlow, who was severely wounded, and his men were driven back. Rodes charged the Federal centre, which was the key-point to the field, and, breaking through, swept away the right of the First Corps and the left of the Eleventh. The break was a disastrous one, and the Federals fled tumultuously into Gettysburg, the right of the First Corps swarming among the streets in such a disorganized state that Early captured more than five thousand prisoners and several pieces of artillery. The Confederates were still in close pursuit when they were recalled by their commander.

General Meade, having learned of the fall of Reynolds, sent General Hancock, who arrived at the hour the terrified Federals were pouring through Gettysburg. Hancock had been instructed to examine the ground with a view of determining whether it was best to make a stand there or retire to Pipe Creek, as was the first intention; but on his arrival the Federal general found a more serious duty on hand. He saw at once that unless the panic of the First and Eleventh Corps was stayed a great disaster was likely to overtake the Union army. That able soldier by the magnetism and power of his presence did that which Howard could not do. The panic was checked, and the contending hosts paused to take breath and concentrate their strength for the next leap at each other's throats.

General Hancock formed his line along Cemetery Hill, to the south and west of the town. This position was one of immense strength, and after carefully examining it from a distance General Lee decided to make no attack upon it until the arrival of Longstreet and the remainder of Ewell's corps. These troops were ordered to hurry forward, while the Confederate leader did everything possible to learn the exact strength and disposition of the Federal army. In his failure to storm and carry the heights before Hancock seized them General Lee let slip an opportunity which rarely presents itself during a campaign. He has been sharply criticised by his own friends for his inaction on that important occasion, but such criticism cannot be justified. No man, no matter how great his intelligence and ability, ought deliberately to pronounce judgment against the military genius of General Lee; the very fact that he refrained from carrying the heights is proof that he had the best of reasons for this course. At this remote day no one can have sufficient grounds upon which to base a judgment contrary to that of the Southern leader. It was as Stonewall Jackson once remarked: Lee never for one moment forgot the enormous responsibility which rested upon his shoulders. There were doubtless many instances in which he might have accomplished almost miraculous results by launching his hosts where opportunity presented, but in doing so he inevitably ran the risk of failure—failure disastrous, overwhelming and irremediable. He showed his wisdom by declining such "extra-hazardous" risks. In the instance under discussion he was without definite knowledge of the movements, strength and disposition of Meade's army; his own had not yet arrived on the ground (though he had more than enough to capture the heights), and doubtless he had reasons which have never been clearly set forth for refraining from the assault. Nevertheless, the truth remains that the failure to occupy the heights was disastrous beyond calculation in its consequences to the Confederate army.

Now that Destiny had ordered that the supreme life-and-death struggle between the Southern hosts and the Northern legions should take place around this insignificant hamlet, and that consequences momentous to mankind for ages to come should flow therefrom, let us try to understand the battle-ground and the complex movements which took place thereon during those fateful days in July, 1863.

Gettysburg lies in the centre of a small valley formed by several ranges of hills; north of the town the country is not so rugged, but south, east and west the hills are high and steep. To the westward, distant about a mile, is a ridge bordering the east bank of Willoughby's Run; a quarter of a mile from the town, in the same direction, is another elevation, called Seminary Ridge. It was in the valley between these ridges that the battle of July 1 was fought. South of the town, and a quarter of a mile away, is Cemetery Ridge, running due south. Just beyond the limits of Gettysburg this ridge makes a curve to the eastward, and then, turning to the right again, falls off toward the south, forming a hook whose convexity is turned toward Gettysburg, and is called Cemetery Hill. Farther to the eastward, where it slopes to the south, it is named Culp's Hill. Returning now to the main ridge, which recedes with almost arrowy directness straight away from Gettysburg toward the south, the ridge is found to terminate three miles distant in a sort of flourish known as Round Top, which is a high wooded peak. Just north of this peak is a smaller one, called Little Round Top, or Weed's Hill. Crossing over to Culp's Hill, on the right, a small stream, known as Rock Creek, flows along the base and empties into the Monocacy, while

Plum Run, another creek, runs in front of Cemetery Ridge from near Cemetery Hill to Round Top and beyond. To the west of this ridge the country is commanded by it, and is of a broken character. The Taneytown road, running due south along Cemetery Ridge, crosses the elevation at the cemetery; the Baltimore turnpike crosses the ridge a short distance to the east and trends to the right, passing over Rock Creek about a mile eastward from the Taneytown road. The Emmettsburg road turns off from the Baltimore turnpike just out of Gettysburg, and, bearing to the westward, intersects the Taneytown road in front of the cemetery and continues to the south-west, the highways named spreading out from the southern outskirts of the town like the three spokes of a wheel. Beginning at Round Top, the terminus of the ridge, and passing directly northward around the curve called the Cemetery and on to the other terminus, Culp's Hill, the distance is about four miles. From the eastern side of Gettysburg put out the Bonnaughtown road and the York turnpike; to the north-east, the Harrisburg road; to the north, the Carlisle road; to the north-west, the Mummasburg road; and south of this, the Chambersburg turnpike and Millerstown road.

A careful study of the map is necessary to understand the battle of Gettysburg.

CHAPTER XXIX.

GETTYSBURG: SECOND DAY.

THE struggle on the afternoon of July 1 had been severe, but it was only the prelude of what was to come.

On the night following this grand opening General Meade brought up the remainder of his army (excepting the Sixth Corps, which was on its way from Manchester) and posted it on Cemetery Ridge. The right, consisting of Slocum's corps the (Twelfth) and Wadsworth's division of the First Corps, held Culp's Hill; the centre, composed of Howard's Eleventh Corps and Robinson's and Doubleday's division of the First Corps, were on Cemetery Hill; the left, including Hancock's Second Corps and Sickles's Third Corps, were posted along Cemetery Ridge; while Sykes's Fifth Corps was in reserve on the right, and Sedgwick had not yet arrived. This line of battle, as will be perceived, following the line of the ridge, partook of the form of a horseshoe facing northward toward Gettysburg. It was a grand position, and was held by one hundred thousand men and two hundred guns.

On the same evening that the Federals assumed this line the Confederates occupied Gettysburg and the country to the east and west. Ewell was on the left, and held the town; Hill's corps took possession of Seminary Ridge, thus confronting the centre and left of the Federal line on Cemetery Ridge; while Pickett's division, which did not arrive until the morning of the 3d, were posted on the right of Hill, in front of Round Top.

Here, again, we reach a point where General Lee has been severely criticised for his course of action. It is plain to all that the Federal position was almost, if not quite, impregnable in its strength; it certainly was as strong as was Fredericksburg when Burnside launched the brave Army of the Potomac against it. Why, then, when Lee was far removed from his base of supplies, did he attack his powerful and strongly-entrenched adversary. Lee himself refers to the question as follows: "It had not been intended to fight a general battle at such a distance from our base unless attacked by the enemy, but, finding ourselves unexpectedly confronted by the Federal army, it became a matter of great difficulty to withdraw through the mountains with our large trains. At the same time, the country was unfavorable for collecting supplies while in the presence of the enemy's main body, as he was occupying the passes of the mountains with regular and local troops. A battle thus became, in a measure, unavoidable. Encouraged by the successful issue of the engagement of the first day, and, in view of the valuable results that would ensue from the defeat of the army of General Meade, it was thought advisable to renew the attack." There is more in the foregoing words than appears at first sight. A strong factor in the arguments which led Lee to renew the attack was the unbounded confidence of his soldiers. When they recalled Manassas, Fredericksburg, Chancellorsville and the Wilderness, they could not be blamed for their faith in their own superiority over their adversaries—a faith which doubtless amounted to a contempt for them; and it is not at all unlikely that Lee himself felt it to a less degree, though it cannot be said he despised his enemy. The courage and self-confidence of the Confederate army were so strong that battle could not be denied them.

The 2d of July dawned bright and clear and with the armies confronting each other in their new positions. Most of the day was spent in adjusting the troops, so that it was not until quarter to five in the afternoon that Lee opened the attack. The result of his careful reconnoissances was the decision that the left and left centre of the Federal line was the proper point of attack. This was held by Sickles's corps, and was opposite Longstreet. It was at this point that General Sickles committed a serious indiscretion which threatened grave consequences. Directly in front of him the ridge was not clearly defined, but several hundred yards far-

ther on the elevation becomes considerable. Fearing the consequences of the seizure of this ridge
by the Confederates, he seized it himself. He
meant well enough, but he was mistaken in judgment. "Though to a superficial examination the
aspect of this advanced position seems advantageous, it is not really so, and, prolonged to the
left, it is seen to be positively disadvantageous. It
affords no resting-place for the left flank, which
can be protected only by refusing that wing and
throwing it back through low ground toward
Round Top; but this, in turn, presents the danger of exposing a salient in a position which, if
carried, would give the enemy the key-point to
the whole advanced line."*

General Lee was quick to detect the blunder
of Sickles, and he directed Longstreet to attack
at once; for he understood the value of the position in the main struggle to follow. It was a quarter to five, therefore, when Longstreet opened a
heavy cannonade upon Sickles, in which Ewell,
on the left, speedily joined. Under cover of this
cannonade Hood's division charged against Sickles's left, which curved back from a peach-orchard
along the Emmettsburg road toward Round Top.
Attacking sharply, Hood swung around to the
right, and, unperceived by Sickles, shoved his
right wing in between his extreme left and Round
Top. And there and then took place one of

* Swinton.

those incidents which no human prescience can foresee, and which, apparently unimportant in themselves, are the source of tremendous results.

At the time Hood was assailing Sickles, Little Round Top was comparatively undefended, and yet it was the key-point to the whole Federal line. Had Hood suspected the truth, he would have taken possession of it with a rush. Still, seeing the importance of the position, he cautiously worked his way toward it with a part of his division, and was certain to secure it unless some extraordinary obstacle presented itself. That obstacle appeared at the most critical moment. At the time of the attack, General Warren, chief-engineer, and his officers were using Little Round Top for signalling-purposes, when, seeing that the quarters were likely to become very warm, they began gathering up their flags to leave; but Warren, understanding the imperative necessity of holding the hill, told them to make a show of occupancy by waving their flags while he cast about him for some force to bring to the spot. It happened just then that Barnes's division was passing on its way to reinforce Sickles. Warren assumed the responsibility of detaching a brigade, with which he hurried back to position, dragging, with great labor, a battery up the hill. All this was done while Hood's men were advancing, and they now charged gallantly. The fight was hand to hand and of the most desperate character, but the Texans were repulsed; they

clung, however, to the rocky glen at the base of
the hill, and, resolutely pushing their way up the
ravine between the Round Tops, turned the left
Federal flank, but only to be driven out by a fierce
charge with the bayonet, Meanwhile, Hood had
hurled his left against Sickles's centre, and Mc-
Laws's division was sent to his support. Sickles
speedily found himself so hard pressed that he
called for reinforcements, and three brigades were
sent him; but even with their help he was unable
to hold his position. Longstreet, concentrating
upon his exact centre, near the peach-orchard,
succeeded in breaking through, drove back the
Federals and secured the key-points to Sickles's
advanced line, thus proving the error committed
by that officer in making the movement before
the battle. The Federals tried again and again
to regain the orchard, but Longstreet repulsed
them each time with great slaughter. As Longstreet continued pushing forward, another division was brought up, and assailed him just as he
reached a wheatfield and fringe of woods on the
west side of Plum Run. The Federals, in turn,
were gaining, when Hood, having carried Sickles's
left, appeared on the right of the peach-orchard.
Ayres's division of regulars was advanced to meet
him, but he forced his way through an opening between Caldwell's left and Ayres's right, and doubled
both divisions back on their main line, at Cemetery
Ridge. Sickles's left had fared ill, and his centre

now became the target of the Confederates. A. P. Hill suddenly assailed Humphreys's division (constituting Sickles's right wing) with Anderson's division. Humphreys was speedily driven back, and the whole advanced position of Sickles fell into the possession of the Confederates, Sickles himself being disabled and losing a leg. But, despite the brilliant work of the Confederates, the main line of the enemy had not been broken. There was scarcely any hope for Longstreet, though his exuberant men pushed on and soon reached Cemetery Ridge, where General Hancock repulsed their attack. Night was now close at hand, and Longstreet withdrew his men to the western verge of the wheatfield, where they remained till morning.

Ewell, as ordered by Lee, had made an assault on the Federal right centre, at Cemetery and Culp's Hill. The design was to prevent his enemy sending reinforcements to the left, where Longstreet was pounding with such vigor; but Ewell was so delayed that he did not attack until sunset. With Early's division on his right and Johnson's on his left, Ewell dashed forward in the face of a heavy artillery-fire, charged up the slope, and in a short fierce struggle drove out the Federal artillerists and infantry, whose works at nightfall remained in the hands of the Confederates. If he could retain his grip throughout the next day, it would enable General Lee to take Meade's entire line in reverse.

Thus closed the second day with matters in an unsatisfactory shape for both sides. Lee had not succeeded, nor had he failed; he had gained some important advantages, but the Federal main line remained substantially intact. Longstreet had not accomplished what was intended, though he occupied strong ground and had forced Sickles from his advanced position. Lee had sought to drive the Federals from Cemetery Ridge, but found himself unable to do so, though he had pushed back the right and left and gained considerable advantage. It was the hairbreadth mischance by which the Confederates failed to seize Round Top Hill which prevented the complete success of Lee's movement in that direction.

The losses during the first two days in July were appalling, amounting to more than twenty thousand men on each side; among these were many of the best officers, either killed or wounded. General Barksdale was in the hands of the Federals, mortally wounded, while the tidings from the sanguinary field threw hundreds of homes in both North and South into mourning.

While this terrible fighting was going on, General Lee, it need scarcely be said, attentively watched every part of the field. "In company with General Hill, he occupied during the battle his former position on Seminary Ridge, near the centre of his line, quietly seated, for the greater portion of the time, upon the stump of a tree and looking thoughtfully toward the opposite heights, which Longstreet was endeavoring to storm. His demeanor was entirely calm and composed; an observer would not have concluded that he was the commander-in-chief. From time to time he raised his field-glass to his eyes, and, rising, said a few words to General Hill or General Long of his staff. After this brief colloquy he would return to his seat on the stump and continue to direct his glass toward the wooded heights held by the enemy. 'A notable circumstance, and one often observed on other occasions, was that during the entire action he scarcely sent an order. During the time Longstreet was engaged—from a little before five until night—he sent but one message and received but one report. Having given full directions to his able lieutenants and informed them of the objects which he wished to attain, he, on this occasion as upon others, left the execution of his orders to them, relying upon their judgment and ability." *

On the night succeeding the second day's battle Lee held a council of war with his leading officers; the great question discussed was whether the attack should be renewed on the morrow or whether they should fall back toward the Potomac. Weighty reasons could be adduced for either course. The Confederate supplies, including ammunition, were running low and the army had lost severely. All seemed to feel that the fate of the Southern Con-

* J. E. Cooke.

20

federacy rested on the bayonets of the Army of
Northern Virginia, and the defeat of one was the
doom of the other.   On the other hand, the success
of Lee, while not decisive, was encouraging, and the
splendid army of veterans was unshaken in spirit
and determination.   In the words of J. E. Cooke,
"the issue of the second day had stirred up in Lee
himself all the martial ardor of his nature, and
there never lived a more thorough *soldier*, when
he was fully aroused, than the Virginian.   All this
soldiership of the man revolted at the thought of
retreating and abandoning his great enterprise.   He
looked, on the one hand, at his brave army, ready
at the word to advance again upon the enemy—at
that enemy, scarce able on the previous day to hold
his position—and, weighing every circumstance in
his comprehensive mind, which 'looked before and
after,' Lee determined on the next morning to try
a decisive assault upon the Federal troops, to storm,
if possible, the Cemetery Ridge, and at one great
blow terminate the campaign and the war."

GENERAL LEE AT THE BATTLE OF GETTYSBURG.

CHAPTER XXX.

GETTYSBURG: THIRD AND LAST DAY.

IT will be remembered that at the close of the second day Lee had accomplished nothing in the way of piercing the Federal lines except on their right, where Ewell had effected a lodgment within the breastworks on Culp's Hill. This fact led Lee to strengthen Johnson, who was close to the elevation, with the intention of making his main assault at that point; but before the preparations could be completed, Meade during the night posted a strong force of artillery so as to bear upon Johnson, and at the earliest streakings of light on July 3, he opened a heavy fire, and a powerful force of infantry moved against the Confederates. A fierce conflict was instantly precipitated, and, though Johnson was outnumbered, he held his ground for four hours, when he was driven out and the Federal line re-established.

This disaster compelled Lee to change his plan of battle, and he now determined to make the Federal centre his objective point, hoping to break apart the two wings. These preparations consumed several hours, during which an impressive silence reigned over the embattled hosts, though the Federals saw their foe busily employed in massing his artillery. When the sun was directly overhead, Lee had one hundred and forty-five pieces of cannon on Seminary Ridge, opposite to Meade's centre. Divining Lee's purpose, the Federal commander lined the crest of Cemetery Hill with eighty pieces of artillery.

At one o'clock the Confederate batteries suddenly opened, and, a short time after, the Federal battery replied from the opposite heights. The thunder and flame and smoke of more than two hundred pieces of artillery made up the most terrific cannonade that can be conceived. For two hours the tremendous outburst continued, the earth quivering from the shock, while the whole valley fairly rocked with a thunderous outroar such as was never before heard on the American continent. The terrible enginery of war combined to give the scene a grandeur that was awful in its very sublimity and caused strong men leagues away to turn pale with terror.

Gradually the Federal fire slackened, and the crouching troops grasped their muskets with a tighter grip, compressed their lips and braced themselves for the more deadly shock that they knew was coming. From Seminary Ridge, a mile away, as the heavy bank of vapor lifted, debouched a column of five thousand men clad in Confederate gray, their red battle-flags flying and the gun-barrels and bayonets gleaming in the sunlight. They marched with the beautiful even tread of a dress-parade, but the fire of deadly determination was in their eyes, and they meant that no mortal power should check their advance upon the Federal position. This was Major-General Pickett's division, formed in double line of battle, supported by Heth's division, of Hill's corps, under General Pettigrew. Pickett had only arrived that morning, but his command was the very flower of the Confederate army, every man a hero and all under the leadership of heroes seasoned in the flame of many battles. Heth's division was composed principally of new troops from North Carolina. General Wilcox's brigade was also designed to cover Pickett's right flank during the advance, the assaulting column numbering about thirteen thousand, all under the command of General Pickett. Kemper's and Garnett's brigades were in front, with Armistead close behind; Pettigrew marched on the left, and Wilcox with his troops in columns of battalions following on the right. The two armies were silent, all eyes fixed upon the impressive scene. The splendor of that advance compelled murmurs of admiration from tens of thousands of enemies. It was magnificent and thrilling beyond description. It was like a vast machine working with absolute precision and perfection.

With the same even, unvarying, beautiful step the line swept forward until the Emmettsburg road was reached, when the Confederate batteries stopped their thunder, for the infantry was coming within their range. When they were about halfway between the two armies, the Federal artillery opened and mowed down scores; but the gaps were immediately closed up, and the line advanced still faster and without a tremor until within musketry-range, when the crest of the hill outblazed with the fire of the Federal infantry, and the deadly sleet was driven in the very faces of the assailants. Pettigrew's division, despite the efforts of its commander, was hurled backward, leaving two thousand prisoners and fifteen standards in the hands of the Union army.

As Wilcox had fallen behind, Pickett and his heroes were left alone to breast the awful tempest. With the same marvellous precision they delivered a volley at the breastworks in their front, and then with their resounding yells rushed up the crest of Cemetery Ridge and took possession of the works at the point of the bayonet. But at what fearful cost! Garnett was dead; Armistead lunged forward, mortally wounded while cheering on the breastworks; Kemper was helpless; the dead and dying were everywhere, and the triumph was of only a few minutes' duration. The Federals rallied on their second line, against which Pickett's men dashed in vain, and a converging fire was poured upon them against which nothing with the breath of life could stand. Looking around for his support, Pickett saw that he was alone, and it was death to every one of his command to attempt to hold his works. The order was given to fall back, and sullenly and reluctantly the survivors withdrew from a charge that was as sublime in its true heroism and daring as that of the immortal Six Hundred at Balaklava.

Of the five thousand men who advanced with such proud bearing under Pickett, thirty-five hundred were killed, wounded or prisoners in the hands of the Union army. Of his three brigade commanders, Garnett was killed, Armistead dying and Kemper frightfully wounded. Of the fourteen field-officers who were in the advance, only one came back. The Federals paid dearly in killed and wounded for their victory, among the latter being Generals Gibbon and Hancock, though the latter remained on the field until the issue was decided.

Standing on Seminary Ridge, General Lee, with his glass to his eyes, watched the wonderful charge, fight and repulse of Pickett. When he saw the broken masses reeling back, he rode among them and by his cheerful words and manner did his utmost to comfort the brave fellows. They cheered him in turn, and showed their faith in his prowess was unshaken. But Lee realized that it was impossible to break through the Union lines. There was some apprehension that Pickett's repulse would be followed by a general attack on the part of Meade, but he was too wise to incur such a risk, and quiet reigned for the rest of the day.

That night the corps of General Ewell was withdrawn from the town and posted on Seminary Ridge, where the entire Confederate army entrenched itself. The Federals occupied Gettysburg the next morning. Finding he was in no danger of attack, General Lee began removing his wounded and his arms from a portion of the field. The retreat was begun at night by the Chambersburg and Fairfield roads, which lead through the South Mountain range into the Cumberland Valley. As usual, a severe storm came up in the afternoon and lasted through the night, making the retreat laborious, slow and painful.

The second Confederate invasion of the North was ended.

The Union loss at Gettysburg was two thousand eight hundred and thirty-four killed, thirteen thousand seven hundred and thirty-three wounded, and six thousand six hundred and forty-three missing, making the dreadful total of twenty-three thousand one hundred and ninety. The Confederate losses cannot be given with accuracy, but, owing to the circumstances of the battle, they must have been considerably greater. General Lee left most of his wounded in the hands of his enemy, who claimed a capture of thirteen thousand six hundred and twenty-one prisoners.

CHAPTER XXXI.

So soon as General Meade learned of the retreat of General Lee he made haste to pursue him. Sedgwick's corps was despatched along the Fairfield road, and his cavalry galloped over the Harrisburg highway. The Confederate rear-guard was overtaken late in the day at the point where the Fairfield road runs along the South Mountain. Before any attack could be made Sedgwick was recalled by an order from Meade, who had determined on another route: that was to take the one east of the mountains, which was almost twice as long as the road by which Lee was retreating. Hoping to intercept Lee, General French, who was at Frederick with the garrison of Harper's Ferry, was ordered to seize the lower passes of the South Mountain before they could be occupied by Lee. French was also to occupy Harper's Ferry. These orders were promptly carried out by French, who sent out a cavalry force as far as Williamsport and destroyed a Confederate ponton-bridge across the Potomac. Meade carefully felt his way, being joined on the march by French's division and other reinforcements sent from Washington, until

313

his army was nearly, if not quite, as strong as before the battle. On the 7th of July the Federal headquarters were at Frederick, and three days later were at Antietam Creek.

General Lee had from the first a work of extreme difficulty before him, but he went at it with that calm self-confidence which he never failed to display under the most adverse circumstances. One part of his train followed the Fairfield road and the rest went through Cashtown, General Imboden's cavalry guarding the advance. The immense length of the wagon-trains exposed them to Federal forays, and as they defiled from the mountain-passes they lost a few wagons and ambulances from this cause.

July 6 the Federal cavalry made an attack at Williamsport, but were driven off by Imboden before any substantial injury was inflicted. General Stuart and his cavalry arrived soon after, and not only repelled another assault, but pursued their assailants several miles. The violent rain-storm which had lasted so many hours rendered the roads passable only by great labor, and the army plodded slowly after the wagon-trains. The pursuit by Meade was "from afar," and was conducted with such extreme circumspection that Lee would not have had the slightest difficulty in getting away but for the fact that on reaching the Potomac it was found so swollen by the recent rain as to be no longer fordable, and the single ponton-bridge he possessed had been destroyed by the enemy. The only thing, therefore, to do was to wait till the river's volume should subside. Accordingly, he selected a secure position, and the three days which passed before his pursuers appeared were spent in strengthening it against attack. A portion of the old ponton-bridge was recovered, and after great labor a new bridge was finished on the 13th.

The situation of the Confederate army during those days was very critical. Ammunition and supplies were low, and none could be obtained from any source. The river was impassable, and the Federal army, reinforced and exultant, was approaching. It came in sight on the 12th, and Lee gathered his forces for the assault which he was confident would be speedily made; but it was Meade who seemed to think himself in danger, for he began to fortify his line. But at high noon on the 13th those who examined the subsiding Potomac reported that it was fordable, and, everything being in readiness, General Lee ordered the passage to be begun that night. The frightful condition of the roads, however, delayed everything; so that the troops did not arrive until after daylight on the 14th. Ewell's corps had forded the river at Williamsport, while those of Longstreet crossed on the bridge at Falling Waters.

On the night of the 13th, General Meade determined to attack the Confederate army the following morning. His preparations were elaborated with the care and skill which he always displayed. When, at last, these were completed, the Federal commander awoke to the fact that Lee and all his army were on the other side of the Potomac. They had withdrawn with complete success. Two guns so mired that their horses could not drag them off and several disabled wagons were left, including a number of men, who, throwing themselves in the mud alongside the road and sinking into heavy sleep, were missed in the darkness by the officers sent to arouse them, and thus fell into the hands of the pursuers. On the 15th of July, General Lee withdrew from the Potomac to the neighborhood of Winchester. Two days later a detachment of Federal cavalry which had crossed at Harper's Ferry were attacked by General Fitz Lee at Kearnysville and driven back with considerable loss.

General Meade, unwilling to relinquish the great prize almost in his grasp, as it seemed, determined to cut off Lee from Richmond or compel him to fight before he could move east of the Blue Ridge. Crossing his army at Harper's Ferry on the 17th and 18th of July, he sought to occupy the passes before they could be reached by the Confederates. Thereupon, Lee turned up the Shenandoah Valley, his progress hindered by the high water in the Shenandoah River. Longstreet was ordered on the 19th of July to proceed to Culpeper Court-House by way of Front Royal. He succeeded in moving part of his command over the Shenandoah in time to prevent the occupation of Manassas and Chester Gaps by the Federals. A ponton-bridge was laid; the rest of the corps crossed, and marched through Chester Gap to Culpeper, where they arrived on the 24th. Hill's corps followed, Ewell reaching Front Royal on the 23d and encamping near Madison Court-House on the 29th. A portion of the Federal army entered the valley during this march of Lee, and a capital opening was presented for a flank attack; but it failed through the mismanagement of General French, who was buffeted hither and thither and held back by the Confederates as they willed until the opportunity had passed. Finding, at last, that the Confederate army had successfully eluded him, Meade marched at a leisurely pace toward the Rappahannock, while Lee withdrew to the vicinity of Culpeper.

The failure of the second Confederate invasion of the North was a tremendous blow to the South, accompanied as it was by the fall of Vicksburg and the loss of the Mississippi River; but the Confederacy only buckled on its armor and prepared again for the fiercer conflict that was to come. It was the general belief throughout the South that had a great victory been won at Gettysburg the South and the North would have formed a treaty of peace on terms acceptable to both. The South was none the less determined to win those terms, but the disasters caused her to realize that the struggle would be harder, longer and more sanguinary than before. July 15, President Davis issued his proclamation calling into the military service all persons residing in the Confederacy, and not legally exempt, between the ages of eighteen and forty-five years. The 21st of August was appointed a day of fasting, humiliation and prayer. It was observed throughout the South, and nowhere more impressively· than in the army.*

---

* General Lee's order respecting the observance of this day is worthy of preservation:

"HEADQUARTERS ARMY OF NORTHERN VIRGINIA.
August 13, 1863.

"General Order,
    No. 83.

"The President of the Confederate States has in the name of the people appointed the 21st day of August as a day of fasting, humiliation and prayer. A strict observance of the day is enjoined upon the officers and soldiers of the army. All military duties except such as are absolutely necessary will be suspended. The commanding officers of brigades and regiments are requested to cause divine services suitable to the occasion to be performed in their respective commands.

"Soldiers! we have sinned against almighty God. We have forgotten his signal mercies, and have cultivated a revengeful, haughty and boastful spirit. We have not remembered that the defenders of a just cause should be pure in his eyes, that 'our times are in his hands,' and we have relied too much on our own arms for the achievement of our independence. God is our only refuge and our strength. Let us humble ourselves before him. Let us confess our many sins and beseech him to give us a higher courage, a purer patriotism and more determined will, that he will convert the hearts of our enemies, that he will hasten the time when war, with its sorrows and sufferings, shall cease, and that he will give us a name and place among the nations of the earth.

"R. E. LEE, General."

VII.

THE SECOND CAMP-FIRE IN NORTHERN VIRGINIA.

CHAPTER XXXII.

A SERIES OF MANŒUVRES.

A PERIOD of rest and inactivity now followed in Northern Virginia. The vast conflict was pushed in other quarters, and tremendous campaigns were lost and won in the South and South-west. In September, Longstreet's corps was sent to Tennessee to help Bragg against Rosecrans. The veterans acquitted themselves with the same courage and skill they had shown in the East.

General Meade's army was also weakened by the withdrawal of a large portion, which was forwarded to North Carolina, while another force was sent to New York to assist in quelling the riots that had broken out there from the attempt to enforce the Conscription act. But, deeming himself strong enough to make a demonstration against the Confederate army when weakened by the withdrawal of Longstreet's corps, Meade sent his cavalry across the Rappahannock, and General Lee, believing that a general attack was contemplated, retired to a strong position behind the Rapidan. Meade was afraid to assail him, and prepared for a flank movement; but before he could put it in execution he was notified from Washington that it was necessary to detach two more corps from his army and send them to Tennessee, where matters were in a critical state on account of the defeat of Rosecrans at Chickamauga—an achievement with which the fire-tried veterans of Longstreet had much to do.

The Eleventh and Twelfth Corps were transferred, with Hooker as their commander, to the West. This left Meade in such a weakened condition that he was obliged to remain strictly on the defensive. When his absent men were returned to him and he was about to assume the offensive, Lee himself initiated a series of important operations. His purpose was to deliver a blow which would seriously disable the Army of the Potomac or compel it to keep beyond the Rappahannock until the season was so far advanced that it could attempt nothing until spring. His first move was intended to take the Confederate army around the right flank of Meade and lodge it between him and Washington. The Rapidan was crossed on the 9th of October, and, advancing with great care and secrecy, he passed by way of Madison Court-House well to the right of Meade. Hampton's cavalry division, under Stuart, moved on the right of the column, while that of Fitzhugh Lee remained to guard the southern line of the Rapidan and to mask the general movement.

The first definite tidings reached Meade on the 10th in the shape of an attack on his outpost at James City, consisting of a detachment of Kilpatrick's cavalry and an infantry force belonging to the Third Corps. They were pushed back to Culpeper Court-House, where the Federal army lay.

Meade saw that his right flank had been turned, and without delay he started his trains toward the Rappahannock, following with his army the same night. When Lee, therefore, approached Culpeper, on the 11th, he discovered that the Federal army had passed beyond the Rappahannock. He halted for the rest of the day. Stuart bore hard upon the rear of Meade's column, covered by Pleasanton's cavalry. General Fitz Lee's division, which had repulsed Buford, rejoined General Stuart. In the afternoon the Federal cavalry near Brandy Station was driven across the river by Stuart. The next morning, October 12, Lee resumed his advance with the purpose of reaching the Orange and Alexandria Railroad north of the city and checking the retreat of the Federal army. A force of their cavalry was encountered and defeated at Jeffersonton, and late in the afternoon Lee reached the Rappahannock opposite Warrenton Springs. Cavalry and artillery were drawn up on the opposite bank, but they were driven away and the river was crossed. Pushing on, Stuart speedily reached War-

21

renton, where the Confederate army was concentrated on the 13th. Uncertain of the whereabouts of Meade, Lee believed he had halted between Warrenton Junction and Catlett's Station, on the railroad. To settle the question, General Stuart with two thousand cavalry was sent in the direction of Catlett's.

A curious complication was brought about by Meade's change of mind and subsequent course. Believing he had been too hasty in retreating across the Rapidan, he turned back toward Culpeper to meet Lee and give him battle. This movement was begun on the afternoon of the 12th, so that it came about that, while the Confederate army was hurrying to interpose itself between the Federal army and Washington, the Federal army was groping southward in search of its opponent. The scattering of the cavalry at the crossing of the Rappahannock speedily became known to Meade, who saw at once the compromising situation in which he was placing himself by his false move. He immediately recalled the troops on the way to Culpeper Court-House; and on the day that Lee concentrated at Warrenton, Meade returned to the north side of the Rappahannock. The unexpected movement of Lee had "disjointed" French's corps, and Meade was therefore compelled to await his arrival. General Warren, with the Second Corps, was ordered to halt until French could be brought into his right place, and to cover the retreat " of the army with his own corps, moving through Fayetteville and Auburn to Catlett's Station, after which he was to follow the line of the railroad northward." This movement was under way when Stuart set out on his reconnoissance to Catlett's Station. Observing French's column in the act of withdrawing from the river, he fell back toward Warrenton. On entering the road leading from Warrenton to Manassas, Stuart suddenly found himself confronted by the corps of General Warren, and the still more alarming discovery was made that he was hemmed in between the Federal columns and in imminent danger of being captured or destroyed. The cavalry were in the most perilous situation that can be conceived. Their immunity for the time depended on not being seen by the Federals, who, it may be said, surrounded them; but it looked as if discovery must come every minute. The cavalry were in a strip of woods, in which they hid themselves on seeing their danger; but their enemies were so close that the neigh of a horse, the clank of a sabre or an incautious word would betray them.

Stuart called his officers around him to consider what should be done. By way of introducing the subject, he stated that the question of surrender was not before them: under no circumstances would he consider that. The conclusion was that the only course was to abandon their nine pieces of horse-artillery and cut their way out under cover of the darkness. But Stuart was not satisfied with this decision, which compelled him to lose his guns, and he decided on another course. Several of his men were dismounted, and each was given a musket and an infantry knapsack. Trusting the night to conceal their uniforms, they were directed to make their way through the Federal lines to Warrenton, tell General Lee that Stuart was surrounded and ask him to send some friends to help him out. A couple of these men succeeded in stealing through the Federal lines, and lost no time in hastening to Lee and apprising him of the perilous situation of Stuart. It would have been an irreparable loss to the Confederate army should the dashing officer be captured or slain, and Lee was quick to respond to the appeal of his lieutenant. But the hours were most anxious ones to Stuart and his command as they crouched among the trees, expecting every moment to be discovered. During the night two of Meade's officers wandered among the troopers with no suspicion of their danger until each felt the cold muzzle of a pistol against his nose, lit up, as it seemed, by the gleam of the soldier's eyes behind it, and the whole endorsed by the whispered threat that the least move or outcry would bring instant death. The prisoners submitted quietly, and caused no trouble. Early the next morning, Caldwell's division, posted on the heights of Cedar Run to protect General Warren's rear, stirred up their camp-fires and began preparing breakfast. It was not long before they were alarmed by the sharp firing of musketry from the advance of General Ewell's column, approaching over the Warrenton road. The sounds thrilled the anxious troopers with delight, for it was the announcement that their friends were at hand and danger was past. Immediately, Stuart opened with his artillery on the Federal line, causing great confusion and the loss of a number of lives; then, limbering up his guns, he dashed off and joined General Ewell.

General Lee intended, after crossing the Rappahannock, to leave Warrenton in two columns. His left, under Hill, was to march along the turnpike to New Baltimore, there to move to the right and hasten to Bristoe Station. The right, under Ewell, was to proceed through Auburn and Greenwich to the same point, where the two wings would unite. When General Warren found himself attacked by Ewell and Stuart, he believed he was surrounded, and hastily prepared to make a good fight to save himself; but Stuart, having sent his compliments, was only too glad to extricate himself from his dangerous position, and the Confederate advance was checked until Ewell arrived with his main body. Then the pressure became too great, and Warren retreated across Cedar Run.

In the mean time, General Meade was advancing along the railroad toward Centreville, with Warren bringing up the rear. It was at Centreville that the Federal commander had determined to give battle. Lee bent all his energies to intercept his opponent before he could reach that point, but Meade was hurrying over the interior and shorter line, and easily maintained the lead. The whole force was beyond Bristoe Station when General Hill and two of his brigades came panting to the spot. Hill quickly formed his line for the purpose of attacking the rear, when, to his astonishment, Warren and his troops appeared, coming toward Bristoe. They had been delayed by the causes explained, and, hurrying along the railroad, reached Bristoe just in time to find themselves confronted by Hill's corps. The situation again became critical for Warren, who was in danger of being overwhelmed by the whole army of Lee; but the Federal commander disentangled himself with highly creditable vigor and skill. Warren was thoroughly acquainted with the ground, and he posted his men along the railroad, where most of them were protected by a steep embankment. The attack of Hill was repulsed with heavy loss, including four hundred and fifty prisoners, five pieces of artillery and two standards. It may be said that Warren's situation in a brief while became more dangerous than before, for the battle was hardly over when Ewell's corps appeared. Before the dispositions for attack, however, could be made, night set in, and under its protection Warren withdrew and joined Meade at Centreville.

The position of the Federal commander was admirable. He was not only strongly entrenched, but in the event of defeat he could fall back on Washington, the effort of Lee to cut him off from the national capital having been foiled. Lee saw that nothing was to be gained by assault, and he therefore withdrew in the direction of the Rappahannock. With a view of hindering as much as possible Meade's return to Culpeper, he destroyed the Orange and Alexandria Railroad between Bull Run and Warrenton Junction.

The withdrawal of the Confederate army was covered, as usual, by Stuart, who was continually skirmishing with the Federal cavalry. On the 19th he was at Buckland with Hampton's division. A brisk interchange of shots took place with the Federals, and he retreated slowly toward Warrenton, with a view of drawing his enemies after him, so as to give Fitzhugh Lee, who was approaching by the Auburn road with his division, a chance to assail Kilpatrick, who commanded the Federal cavalry, in front and rear. The programme was carried out without halt or hitch. A few miles from Warrenton, Fitzhugh Lee made his attack, and Stuart wheeled about and assailed Kilpatrick in front. The latter retreated in confusion, followed by Stuart to the vicinity of Haymarket, and by Fitzhugh Lee to Gainesville.* At the latter

---

* "I pursued them from within three miles of Warrenton to Buckland, the horses at full speed the whole distance, the enemy retreating in great confusion."—*Stuart's Report.*

point the Federal infantry rallied to the support of the cavalry. Having secured a number of prisoners, Stuart fell back toward Buckland.

The Army of the Potomac advanced to Warrenton, where it was forced to wait until the Orange and Alexandria Railroad could be repaired. This was soon accomplished, and it resumed its advance in two columns toward the Rappahannock, behind which Lee had taken position near Culpeper, with Ewell on his right, Hill on the left and his cavalry on each flank. The major part of the army was well back from the river, but outposts were established at Kelley's Ford down stream and at Rappahannock Station above, and on the north bank of the Rappahannock. The Federal army was divided into two columns, the left under General French, consisting of the First, Second and Third Corps, and the right under General Sedgwick, consisting of the Fifth and Sixth Corps. The latter was ordered to cross the river at Rappahannock Station, while French was to force the passage at Kelley's Ford. This ford was guarded only by Rodes's division of Ewell's corps, and they were easily driven away by French, who secured a number of prisoners.

At Rappahannock Station, General Early threw Hoke's and Hays's brigades into the strong works which had been erected some time before by the Federals on the northern bank. The force numbered about two thousand men, and it was believed that if defeated they would be able to recross the stream under fire of the guns. It was a foolish and costly mistake to the Confederates. The column of Sedgwick came up late in the afternoon, and as quickly as they could make ready stormed the works, killing and wounding a hundred, capturing fifteen hundred prisoners and four guns. The few men who escaped did so by swimming the river. Not wishing to be drawn into a general engagement, Lee withdrew behind the Rapidan, while Meade resumed the position he held before his retreat to Centreville.

The campaign was without substantial result to either side. It consisted mainly of manœuvres accompanied by little fighting, and the relative position of the two armies at its close was the same in effect as at its opening.

CHAPTER XXXIII

THE CAMP-FIRE OF MINE RUN.

HAVING withdrawn behind the Rapidán, Lee placed his army in winter-quarters. His position was so strong that he had no fear of successful molestation from the enemy, against whom was opposed only the single corps of Ewell. Hill's corps was stationed in detached divisions at different points on the Orange and the Virginia Central Railroads, with a view of making it more convenient to subsist it through the winter. Hill's cantonments stretched almost to Charlottesville, while the artillery was still farther back, but so situated that it could be concentrated at any menaced point. The lower fords of the Rapidan—Ely's, Culpeper Mine, Germanna and Jacob's Mill—were left unguarded.

This fact becoming known to Meade, he allowed the clamor throughout the North to tempt him to another effort to deliver an effective blow against the Army of Northern Virginia. His plan was simple enough: he trusted that by crossing the Rapidan at the lower fords he could wedge his army between the corps of Ewell and Hill and overwhelm them in detail. His troops, supplied with ten days' rations, were to move as follows: "The First Corps was to cross the Rapidan at Culpeper Mine Ford and proceed to Parker's Store, on the plank-road to Orange Court-House. The Second Corps was to cross at Germanna Ford and proceed out on the turnpike (which runs parallel with the plank-road) to Robertson's Tavern. To this point, also, the Third Corps, crossing at Jacob's Mill Ford, and followed by the Sixth Corps, was to march by other routes, and there to form a junction with the Second Corps. With the left at Parker's Store and the right at Robertson's Tavern, the army would be in close communication on parallel roads, and by advancing westward toward Orange Court-House would turn the line of Mine Run defences, which, it was known, did not extend as far south as to cross the turnpike and plank-roads."* The Federal columns started promptly, as intended, on the morning of November 26, and, as the point of concentration was barely twenty miles distant, Meade was confident of having his army in position by noon the next day. The river, however, was not crossed until the following morning, when, in obedience to orders, the army pushed on with all possible haste.

No matter how secret the precautions of such a great movement, it could not be concealed from Lee, who noted the "signs" a couple of days before. All the fords were put under the closest

* Swinton.

surveillance, and it soon became known where Meade intended to cross. Lee suspected he was making for Chancellorsville, so as to gain his rear, and he vigilantly watched for the first indication of Meade's purpose. It came in an altogether unexpected manner.

The Second Corps of the Federal army, under General Warren, reached Robertson's Tavern shortly after noon, and immediately became involved in a brisk skirmish with Ewell, but, under orders to refrain from battle until the arrival of French, no attack was made, But French began with a stumble and kept it up all the way. After crossing the Rapidan at Jacob's Mill, he took the wrong road to Robertson's Tavern, and, passing far to the right, suddenly ran against Johnson's division of Ewell's corps. Johnson attacked at once, and a brisk fight followed, which lasted until sunset. By the time French was able to extricate himself and open communication with Robertson's Tavern it was night.

It was this occurrence which gave Lee the knowledge he wanted, and he made his dispositions with his accustomed promptness and skill. Hill's corps, scattered here and there south of Orange Court-House, was ordered up, and reached the ground during the night. Thereupon, Ewell was withdrawn to the west side of Mine Run, where preparations were immediately perfected to shut off the Federal advance in that direction. The southern line was of exceptional strength. It followed a range of hills some seven or eight miles in length, extending due north and south, with the Mine Run Creek flowing along its base. Lee superintended most of the engineering operations in person; which statement is all that is required to show they were beyond improvement. He and his officers and men were in the highest spirits, for no one had a doubt of their ability to defend themselves against any assault that could be made.

It was this formidable line of fortifications which barred Meade's advance on the wintry morning of the 28th of November. Still, the Federal commander had no thought of retiring, and, placing his army in position, he spent the day in hunting the most favorable point of attack. The result of these careful reconnoissances and the council that followed was the decision that General Warren, with some twenty-six thousand men, was to seek to turn the Confederate left, while Sedgwick, with the Fifth and Sixth Corps, was to attempt to turn the right. French, with three divisions, was to take no part, but to hold the line between Sedgwick and Warren. The next day was spent in perfecting preparations. It was agreed that on the morning of the 30th the attack should open. Sedgwick was to deliver a heavy artillery-fire, after which Warren would advance, and an hour later Sedgwick was to make his effort to turn the right. Everything was in readiness at daylight, and the army impatiently awaited the signal. Soon the boom of Sedgwick's cannon awoke the oppressive stillness, and the thunder rolled along the line, but in the direction of Warren, on the left, the silence continued like that of the tomb. Meade and the rest of the army were astounded, unable to understand the cause of this extraordinary inaction; but the explanation was speedily brought to the leader by an aide from Warren.

General Warren, when he came to inspect the Confederate right, just before attacking, found that Lee had made it absolutely impregnable. He might launch his command against it, but it would be Fredericksburg over again. His men were ready to attempt whatever was required of them, but, with a moral heroism which did him credit, Warren declined to order the assault, preferring to sacrifice himself rather than his men. General Meade immediately rode over to the line and carefully inspected it; he was compelled to acknowledge that Warren was right and it would be a crime to order men to make the assault. It was a bitter disappointment to the Federal commander, but he was too good a soldier not to see the truth as it was. He had advanced in order to satisfy the impatient demands of the North, and now, having marched his army up the hill, it only remained to march it down again. He might move far over to the left in the hope of manœuvring Lee out of his position, but the issue would be very doubtful, as his trains were beyond the Rapidan and supplies were low. Besides, they were on the edge of winter, and the weather was already so severe that a number of soldiers had frozen to death. On the night of December 1, therefore, Meade returned to his old position on the Rapidan. As soon as his flight was discovered Lee started in pursuit, but the Federal army was too active, and crossed over the river before he could overtake it.

Both armies now went into winter-quarters, Lee holding the south bank of the Rapidan, his cantonments extending from the river along the railroad to Orange Court-House and Gordonsville. Meade's troops were distributed along the Orange and Alexandria Railroad all the way from the Rapidan to the Rappahannock. The feeling was general that the final conflict was approaching, and both governments put forth their utmost efforts to prepare for the life-and-death struggle.

"WE were on the Rapidan River where it was a little stream hardly one hundred feet wide. General Lee sent me word I must go out and break up the communication between our pickets and the enemy's. They had got to trading with each other in newspapers, tobacco, and whatever would vary the monotony of picket-life. They would not shoot at each other, and so it was not military-like; so I started out one morning on my horse and rode the whole length of the picket-line, and just as I came to a certain point I saw that there was confusion and surprise, as if I had not been expected.

"'What is the matter, men, here?' I asked.

"'Nothing, general; nothing is here.'

"'You must tell me the truth,' said I. 'I am not welcome, I see, and there must be some reason for it. Now, what is the matter?'

"'There has been nobody here, general. We were not expecting you, that is all.'

"I turned to two or three of the soldiers and said,

"'Beat down these bushes here.'

"They had to obey, and there suddenly rose up out of the weeds a man as stark naked as he had come into the world.

"'Who are you?' asked I.

"'I am from over yonder, general.

"'Over yonder? Where?'

"He pointed to the other side of the river.

"'What regiment do you belong to?'

"'The One Hundred and Fourth Pennsylvania, general.'

"'What are you doing in my camp?'

"'Why, I thought I would just come over and see the boys.'

"'See the boys! What boys? Do you mean to say you have entered my camp except as a prisoner? Now, I am going to do this with you: I am going to have you marched to Libby prison just as you are, without a rag of clothes on you.'

"'Why, general, you wouldn't do that just because I came over to see the boys? I didn't mean any harm. I felt lonesome over there and wanted to talk to the boys a little, that's all.'

"'Never mind, sir; you march from this spot, clothed as you are, to Libby prison.'

"'General,' said the man, 'I had rather you would order me to be shot right here.'

"'No, sir; you go to Libby.'

"Then several of my soldiers spoke up:

"'General, don't be too hard on him; he's a pretty good fellow. He didn't mean any harm; he just wanted to talk with us.'

"'This business must be broken up,' said I—'mixing on the picket-line.'

"It had not been in my heart, however, to arrest the man, from the beginning. I only wanted to scare him, and he did beg hard.

"'I'll tell you what I will do with you this time,' for I saw he was a brave, good-humored fellow: 'if you will promise me that neither you nor any of your men shall ever come into my lines again except as prisoners, I'll let you go.'

"'God bless you, general!' said the man; and without any more ado he just leaped into that stream, and came up on the other side and took to the woods."—*General Gordon.*

VIII.

THE LAST CAMP-FIRE.

CHAPTER XXXIV.

THE WILDERNESS.

LATE in the tempestuous winter of 1864 a heavy-set, grim-featured man clad in the uniform of a major-general in the United States army sat in his tent in the South-west intently studying the most momentous question of the century : " How shall the Federal Union be restored ?" He was a born fighter ; he had led his blue-coated legions to triumph on more than one crimson battle-field. He believed in "pounding" his adversary—in "never letting go," and in winning by hard knocks and the momentum of superior numbers. Contemplating the mighty resources of the North and the fast-waning strength of the South, he felt that the problem was solved. With an army practically limitless in numbers, in a superb state of discipline, with able lieutenants and the command of boundless wealth and material, he had but to keep hammering away, and, though the mallet was wood, yet under the multitudious blows the rock at last must be split to fragments. The man was Ulysses S. Grant, who on the 2d of March, 1864, was confirmed by the Senate lieutenant-general, and on the 10th of the same month, by special order of President Lincoln, assigned to the command of the armies of the United States.

In his ragged tent on Clarke's Mountain, in Virginia, sat, at the same time, a man of handsome features, erect form, clear eye, silvered beard and august presence wrestling with the problem of his life: "How shall the Southern Confederacy conquer a peace and secure its independence?" For three years he had led his army to victory after victory. While the leaders of his opposing forces had been weighed in the balance and found wanting, this man had grown steadily in the confidence and love of the Southern people until he was now their idol. He had won the fear and respect of his foes; he had proven to the world that he was master of the science of war. While disaster had overtaken the gray-coated hosts in other sections, he had never been overthrown; he still rode his white horse a conqueror, and the army under him was still defiant and eager for the fray. But, while the Federal power must increase, the Confederate power must decrease. There were no more resources upon which to draw; the currency was fast becoming worthless; many brilliant officers had fallen, and brave men had been stricken down by tens of thousands; the ranks were decimated, and the long, thin, gray battle-line of ragged and gaunt veterans was daily growing thinner and weaker. The South itself was in the field, and the Southern Confederacy was upborne on the bayonets of the Army of Northern Virginia. If that was conquered, then was the end. But not yet. In the face of discouragement and defeat elsewhere, Robert E. Lee contemplated the future with the serene assurance of the Christian warrior and the high resolve to do his whole duty and to leave the issue with the God of battles.

In the month of April, 1864, the Army of Northern Virginia and the Army of the Potomac awoke from their winter's sleep, and, springing to their feet, confronted each other, as they had done so many times in the terrible years that were gone. They glared fiercely, compressed their lips, knit their muscles and entered upon the most terrific struggle of modern times. It was the last campaign, and soon the last camp-fire would be extinguished.

When General Grant came to Virginia, the Army of the Potomac was reorganized into three corps, Major-General W. S. Hancock commanding the Second; Major-General G. K. Warren, the Fifth; and Major-General John Sedgwick, the Sixth. The command of the army continued with General Meade, and Major-General P. H. Sheridan was made the leader of the cavalry corps. Before active operations were begun, the Ninth Corps, under Burnside, returned East from its campaign in Tennessee and united with the Army of the Potomac, which as it marched southward numbered one hundred and forty thousand men of all arms.

Months before the opening of the last campaign the "dead point" of the Army of Northern Virginia had been reached: no more reinforcements could be obtained. The corps of Longstreet, which had been doing such effective work in Tennessee, rejoined Lee the 1st of May, but it brought only two divisions. As nearly as can be ascertained, the effective force of Lee's army was slightly more than fifty thousand men. The line defended by the Confederate army was naturally strong, and had been fortified to such an extent that no fear was felt of a direct attack. The line of the Rapidan was held by small detachments, mainly for the purposes of observation. The army itself was distributed from the vicinity of Somerville Ford, on the Rapidan, to Gordonsville. Hill was at Orange Court-House; Ewell, on the Rapidan; and Longstreet, at Gordonsville. It was necessary for Lee to keep vigilant watch and be ready to concentrate at any threatened point. The plan of General Grant was to cross the Rapidan, attack Lee's right, cut his communications, and, forcing him out of his position, compel him to fight between his line and Richmond. If Lee should be beaten, then

Grant intended to pursue him to Richmond and capture both the army and the city. Simultaneous with this movement, Major-General B. F. Butler was to ascend the James River from Fortress Monroe, seize City Point, and, advancing up the south bank of the river, cut the Confederate communications south of the James, and, if possible, capture Petersburg. General Grant intended, in case of his own failure to defeat Lee before reaching Richmond, to move his whole army to the south side of the James and attack from that direction. In such an event Butler's column would be used to cover the transfer. While these important movements were in progress in Eastern Virginia the army of General Sigel was to be organized into two expeditions, one in the Kanawha Valley, under General Crook, and the other in the Shenandoah Valley, under Sigel in person. The latter was to cut the Central Railroad, one of the great channels of supplies for Lee, while the former, seizing the Virginia and Tennessee road, would shut out the other source, in South-western Virginia. If this grand scheme could be pushed to a successful conclusion, then, beyond all question, the days of the Confederacy were numbered.

The Army of the Potomac began moving at midnight on the 3d of May. The advance was in two columns. The right, consisting of Warren and Sedgwick's corps, crossed the Rapidan at Germanna Ford, and the left, which was Hancock's corps, made the passage six miles below, at Ely's Ford. The army bivouacked on the night of the 4th between the Rapidan and Chancellorsville. Early the next morning the march was resumed. Having turned Lee's right flank, Grant intended to push quickly through the Wilderness to Gordonsville, thus planting his army between that of Lee and Richmond. But Lee, watching every act of his adversary, was quick to fathom his plan and to form a brilliant and audacious scheme. He decided to allow Grant to cross the Rapidan without molestation, and then to assail him while marching through the Wilderness.· Amid the thicket and ooze, where the Federal commander could not use his artillery, the Southern leader believed he could destroy his army. Accordingly, while it was crossing the Rapidan, he sent forward Ewell's and Hill's corps, the former by the old turnpike, the latter by the plank-road, and directed Longstreet to march without delay from Gordonsville and move down on the right of Ewell, so as to assail the Federal· advance while it was in motion. Curiously enough, while Warren's corps, constituting this advance, bivouacked that night at Old Wilderness Tavern, at the intersection of the road from Germanna Ford with the Orange and Fredericksburg turnpike, the camp-fires of Johnson's division of Ewell's corps were kindled along the latter highway. Only three miles separated the hostile forces, and neither suspected the fact.

Each column resumed the march early the next morning, the Federal army still unsuspicious of any assault from Lee, who was supposed to be hurrying in the direction of Richmond, on the hunt for some suitable place where he could make a stand against the host almost three times as numerous as his own. Sedgwick's corps followed Warren, and, to protect against any demonstration from Lee by way of the Orange Turnpike, Griffin's division was thrown out on that road, while Crawford's division was advanced by way of a wood road to Parker's Store. As we have stated, Johnson's division, of Ewell's corps, encamped May 4 within three miles of Old Wilderness Tavern, where Warren lay with the Federal advance. Rodes was in the rear of Johnson, while Early followed, coming to a halt at Locust Grove. Johnson learned of the presence of his enemy the next morning, and, hastening forward, secured some high ground, where he began forming his line.

General Grant, who had reached the field, was still unsuspicious of the scheme of General Lee. Believing the force in advance was insignificant in numbers, he made his dispositions to brush it from his path. About noon three divisions of Warren's corps made a furious assault on Johnson's division. A hot fire was poured into them, but they pushed on unflinchingly, and broke the line where it crossed the turnpike and was held by the brigade of General J. M. Jones. With exultant cheers the Federals swept forward, the Confederate leader being killed while vainly trying to rally his men. The whole division was in imminent danger of being routed, when General Stewart at the critical moment. brought his brigade from its position in line of battle and launched it upon the head of the victorious column. The shock checked the exultant Federals, who were tumbled back in such headlong haste that two pieces of artillery were left behind and captured. The stillness was scarcely broken by the sound of firing when General Ewell sent Rodes's division to Johnson's assistance, and ordered General Gordon to take his own and Daniels's brigades and repel the foe on the right. Gordon obeyed orders in his usual vigorous fashion, driving back the Federals for more than a mile and capturing an entire regiment. The attack on the left was a little later, and was repulsed by the brigades of Pegram and Hays. The original position was taken, and Ewell awaited the arrival of Hill and Longstreet.

The severity of the opening struggle showed Grant his mistake. He saw that Lee intended to force him to battle in the Wilderness, and he therefore made his dispositions to accept the conflict in that most unfavorable spot.

The Sixth Corps, under General Sedgwick, was brought up, and Hancock was directed to hurry forward with the Second. He was approaching by the Brock road, which crosses the Orange plank-

road between two and three miles south-west of
Old Wilderness Tavern and four miles south-east
of Parker's Store. A. P. Hill's corps, which had
left Verdiersville early that morning, was moving
along the plank-road toward the Brock road crossing, which, if reached in time, would enable him
to cut off the Second Corps from the main army.
Seeing the danger, General Meade despatched
Getty's division, of Sedgwick's corps, to seize and
hold the important point until the arrival of Hancock. Shortly after Getty reached the ground, Hill,
having repulsed Warren, came in front of the cross-
roads. Uncertain of the strength of his enemy, he
took position across the plank-road and began to
develop it.

Very soon, by direction of Lee, communication
was opened with General Ewell. An examination
of the map will show that the Confederate line
extended from the woods on the right of the Orange plank-road to a point beyond the old turnpike, on the left. The distance was fully six
miles, and nearly all of it led through dense forest. Directly in front was the thicket occupied by
the Federal army.

Hancock secured the position on the Brock road,
and distributed his line along it. Late in the afternoon he received orders from General Grant to
attack Hill's corps and drive it back to Parker's
Store. Hill was drawn up in battle-line about fifty
rods distant, and received the impetuous assault of

Hancock with such a destructive fire that he was repulsed with severe loss. Again and again was the charge repeated, but in vain; the fighting ceased at nightfall, and nothing had been accomplished.

General Longstreet had set out from Gordonsville as soon as Lee's order reached him, and was but a few miles distant on the evening of the 5th; but, as no artillery was used, the density of the woods prevented his hearing the sounds of musketry. The first knowledge he received that a battle was in progress was the order from Lee to go to the assistance of Hill. The command was obeyed with such promptness that Longstreet reached Hill's position by daylight. As he was expected, Hill's men began retiring, but while doing so the Federals renewed their attack on his line. Both armies had arranged to open the fight that morning, but Lee anticipated Grant by advancing Ewell against Sedgwick's corps. His purpose was to turn Grant's left and compel him to retire to the Rapidan. Hill's soldiers were taken "on the hip" by the unexpected assault. The brigades of Heth and Wilcox were tumbled together and over upon Longstreet's column, which had not yet formed in battle-line. The furious rush of the Federals swept everything before it, until the disorganized masses were within a hundred yards of the spot where Lee had established his headquarters. Longstreet, however, proved himself the man for the emergency. Kershaw's division was thrown forward, and the Federals were held at bay until all of Longstreet's corps could be brought up, when they were launched against the Unionists, who were driven back, and the Confederate line was re-established.

Grant was now in the Wilderness, and Lee determined he should have no rest. It was not yet noon when Longstreet suddenly assailed Hancock's left with such fury that it was pushed toward the Brock road, which Longstreet determined to seize; could he succeed in doing so, Grant would be compelled to retreat to the Rapidan under the most disastrous circumstances. "Elated by his success, General Longstreet spurred forward to lead this movement in person, but on the way paused to receive the congratulations of General Jenkins, a young officer who by his rapid rise and extraordinary skill had become a favorite with the whole army; at this moment a heavy discharge of musketry was fired upon them by their own troops, who had mistaken them and their escorts for Federal cavalry, General Longstreet vainly shouted to his men to cease firing, but before he could make them understand their mistake he was shot in the throat, the ball passing out through his right shoulder. He fell from his horse by the side of his friend General Jenkins, who had been killed at the first fire, and at first his staff thought he too was dead. Discovering that he was only wounded, they procured a litter, and he was borne to the rear, the troops testifying their sympathy by loud cheers as the litter was carried along the line."* It was a strange coincidence that both Stonewall Jackson and Longstreet should have been shot through mistake by their own men.

The loss of Longstreet at this critical juncture was a severe one, and General Lee took personal charge of the serious business on the right. During the delay caused by the incident the Federals detected the intended demonstration, and made hasty preparations for it. The assaults of the Confederates were repelled, and after a time the line became so much shaken that it was ready to break. Realizing the desperate crisis, Lee galloped to the Texas brigade, determined to lead them in a charge that should be decisive. "Those who saw him at that moment describe his appearance as inexpressibly grand. He had removed his hat, and, bareheaded and with his hair floating in the wind and his features glowing with the fire of a true soldier, he pointed in silence toward the Federal line with a gesture far more eloquent than words could have been. For a moment the troops paused and gazed first at their commander and then at one another, as if hesitating whether to allow him to incur such danger. Then a ragged, scarred veteran, approaching the commander-in-chief, seized his bridle-rein and turned his horse's head, saying respectfully

* J. D. McCabe, Jr.

but firmly, 'You must not expose yourself, General Lee. You must go to the rear. We will obey your orders; we have never faltered yet, and will not do so now.—Will we, boys?' he added, turning to his comrades. Instantly the whole line took up the cry, 'No! no! General Lee to the rear!' and the men refused to move until General Lee had withdrawn to a safer position. Touched to the heart by this affecting proof of the devotion of his troops, General Lee bowed and rode back, while the line, with deafening cheers, moved forward to the charge."*

The troops redeemed their pledge. With their ear-splitting yells they charged once more, driving the Federals into the log breastworks they had thrown up on the Brock road. The assailants were almost against them, when they were seen to be on fire, caught from the woods, which had been aflame for several hours. The fighting then went on amid the blaze, smoke and heat, the Confederates finally planting their battle-flags on the captured works. Many of the Federals ran toward Chancellorsville, but others rallied and in a desperate charge drove out the captors. By this time it was dark, and hostilities ceased for the day.

General Gordon had done magnificently on the left. Ewell early in the forenoon repulsed the repeated efforts of Sedgwick and Burnside to carry his position. Toward night, Gordon, with several

* J. D. McCabe, Jr.

scanty brigades, leaped against Sedgwick's line with irrestrainable ferocity.   It was torn and rolled back for a distance of two miles, when darkness compelled the cessation of a charge which otherwise promised to overthrow that wing of the army. In this terrific assault Gordon captured Generals Seymour and Shaler and a large number of men.

Neither leader showed any wish to resume the offensive on the morrow.   The Federal position had been proven too strong to be carried, and Grant not only had suffered frightful losses, but had learned that Lee could not be driven from his position.   But, with that bull-dog tenacity so characteristic of the Federal commander, he spent the next day in hunting for some point where he could fasten his teeth in his watchful enemy.   He decided that Spottsylvania Court-House was the spot, and on the night of the 7th the Federal army marched thither by way of Todd's Tavern.   The lions were impatient that they had been hampered by the jungle; they now bounded into the open plain, where their rage would be without hindrance.

While making this movement, Grant sent General Sheridan with orders to make a dash toward Richmond and sever Lee's communications.   Moving to the right of the Confederate army, Sheridan cut the Central Railroad at Beaver Dam Station, and then, galloping to Ashland, tapped the Fredericksburg road.   Stuart and his cavalry were hard after the raiders, but their mount was scarcely equal to what was required of them. Sheridan, however, was overtaken while preparing to burn Ashland, and run out of town. Sheridan and his troopers then headed in the direction of Richmond, but Stuart, by a shorter route, reached the Yellow Tavern, where, within seven miles of the Capital, he again attacked the Federals as they came up. In the fight General Stuart was mortally wounded, and died in Richmond the next day. His loss was one of the severest encountered by the Confederacy during the war. The immediate effect of the fall of Stuart was a collapse of the energy usually shown by his command. The Federals withdrew to a stretch of woods near the turnpike, where they kept up a show of resistance while repairing the Meadow bridge, across the Chickahominy, over which they rode without molestation, and galloped down the Peninsula.

CHAPTER XXXV.

HAD the first commander of the Army of the Potomac been in charge after the battle of the Wilderness, he would have begun to fortify and entrench himself and awaited reinforcements; the second commander would have attempted several more utterly hopeless charges until his loss was greatly increased, and then would have fled; the third commander would have made all haste to Washington; but Grant, despite the shocking list of killed and wounded, did not stop or wait. Having determined to pass around Lee's right, he lost no time in making the movement. Hancock's corps held possession of the Brock road, leading straight to the objective-point, Spottsylvania Court-House, fifteen miles distant. The wagon-trains were sent off during the day, and the Fifth Corps were directed to start as soon as it was dark and occupy the village without delay. The rest of the troops were to move directly behind them, the expectation being that at daylight the entire Federal army would be concentrated between Lee and Richmond.

But the moving wagon-trains convinced Lee that something of the kind was intended. Uncertain, however, of the plan of his enemy, he ordered General R. H. Anderson, commanding Longstreet's corps, to hold himself in readiness to march to Spottsylvania early the next morning. Anderson, as directed, withdrew his men from their entrenchments and began hunting for a suitable place to bivouac. The burning woods rendered this difficult to find, and he finally decided that, inasmuch as his destination was Spottsylvania, he would make the march at night. It was this singular cause that took his corps to the battle-ground so much earlier than was originally intended. He reached Spottsylvania at daylight, and found Fitzhugh Lee's cavalry sharply engaged with Warren, who was just coming up. Lee had done his utmost to impede the Federal advance along the Brock road, barricading it and fighting continually wherever any opportunity presented itself. He was still contesting the advance, when Anderson came up and found Spottsylvania in the possession of a detachment of Federal cavalry. Anderson quickly sent a part of his command to the relief of Fitzhugh Lee, while he gathered the others together to drive out the cavalry from the village.

Believing he had only the advance-guard of the Confederate army in front of him, Warren continued to push on until he began ascending the ridge on which Anderson had posted his soldiers. Then such a destructive fire of musketry was delivered in the faces of the advancing Federals that

23

they broke and fled in disorder, Robinson, their leader, being severely wounded. Almost at the same moment the Union cavalry were driven from the village, and Anderson hurried forward his whole force with the intention of seizing and holding the valuable position. The remainder of Warren's corps were sent ahead on the double-quick and made a gallant and determined attack on Anderson, but were unable to carry the position. Falling back, the Federals began entrenching while they awaited reinforcements before renewing the attack. General Sedgwick came up during the afternoon with the Sixth Corps, but the day was drawing to a close when the preparations were completed. Crawford's division was advanced, but was repulsed. Ewell, however, while taking position, was suddenly assailed, and driven back with the loss of a hundred prisoners. The rest of Ewell's corps came up during the night, and Early took command for the time, on account of the sickness of A. P. Hill. Thus again Lee had anticipated Grant in securing possession of a coveted position, and there he held him at bay day after day, until the Federal leader had paid appalling toll in human life.

Monday morning, May 9, the Confederate army was in position at Spottsylvania, and confronted Grant with the same defiance it had shown for years. Anderson's corps formed the right, and reached from the river Po northward to the court-house; Ewell was in the centre and Hill held the left, his line curving backward toward the south. Thus Lee's line was in the form of a semicircle extending along a range of heights enclosing Spottsylvania Court-House. The Federal line was formed with Hancock on the right, Warren and Sedgwick in the centre and Burnside on the left. Most of the day was consumed by the Federals in assuming position, during which time the Confederate sharpshooters were busy. One of the results of their work early in the day was the killing of General Sedgwick, who was shot dead while standing in the breastworks along the lines. He was one of the bravest and most competent officers of the Federal army, and for a time his loss caused a grief almost akin to consternation.

The valley of the Po extended between Hancock's position and that held by Hill's corps, and one of the branches of that somewhat uniquely-named river flows through it. On the afternoon of the 9th, Hancock was sent across the stream to intercept a wagon-train moving toward Spottsylvania Court-House. The crossing was made, but before he could go far darkness stopped him. It is scarcely necessary, however, to say that it did not stop the wagon-train, which passed safely within Lee's lines. Hancock pushed on the next morning, and was not long in finding that A. P. Hill's corps was strongly entrenched along the east bank of the Po, so as to command the approaches to the stream. Early in the afternoon Hancock was ordered to return to his original position, and while doing so Barlow's division, covering his withdrawal, was fiercely assailed by Heth's division, of Hill's corps, and suffered considerable loss.

Bloody work was going on in other quarters. General Warren repeatedly assaulted Field's position, which was Hill's right. Again and again were the bluecoats rushed forward, and again and again were they driven back with scores and hundreds killed. When Hancock had safely returned, he was directed to unite with Warren's corps and make another assault on the same position. They succeeded in carrying the first line of breastworks, but were able to hold them only a few minutes, when they were driven out, leaving many dead behind them. On the left of Warren a part of the Sixth Corps assailed General Rodes, on the left of Ewell's position, pierced his line, and gained possession of the works, including nine hundred prisoners and six guns. The demonstration was unsupported, and Rodes, rallying his men, drove out the Federals and recaptured the guns.

The events of the day induced Lee to think Grant would concentrate all his efforts against his left; most of the night of the 10th and much of the 11th were occupied, therefore, in strengthening that wing. It was made so strong, indeed, that Grant declined to make the assault. He was convinced that the Confederate right centre was the weakest point; he resolved to attack his enemy there with Hancock's corps and to support it by his whole army.

The selection made by Grant was a wise one, being a salient which had been thrown out to cover a hill several hundred yards in front of the general line with the purpose of preventing the Federals from occupying it with their artillery. The blunder committed by the Confederates at that point was similar to the disastrous error made by General Sickles at Gettysburg. The salient was held by General Edward Johnson, of General Ewell's corps. As if to complete the first error, Johnson's artillery was withdrawn during the night, and he was left with nothing except his infantry to defend the position. Discovering the preparations for attack in his front, Johnson sent for the guns; but at daylight, while being placed in position, the Federal attack was made. It was an overwhelming rush gallantly but vainly resisted. More than three thousand prisoners were captured, among them being Generals Johnson and G. H. Stuart. Besides, twenty-five cannon were secured and the Federals held the works. Hancock's soldiers were so elated that they charged on toward the interior line of works, in the rear of Johnson's position. The Confederate line had been broken, and the wedge was driving the wings farther and farther apart. The fiery General Gordon, in charge of Early's division, threw forward his men, and Rodes and Wilcox hastened to his assistance. The strug-

gle was desperate and bloody, lasting for hours, but
it was repulsed. Grant believed that the tremendous resistance encountered at the right centre indicated that Lee had greatly weakened his lines
at other points. Generals Warren and Burnside,
therefore, were ordered to assail the Southern right
and left wings. They obeyed with great vigor, but
accomplished nothing.

Meanwhile, Lee was determined to retake the
line which Hancock had captured. During the
day he made five desperate charges against it, but
the Federal concentration there rendered it impregnable. The struggles in front of this fatal salient
displayed the ferocity of so many jungle-tigers.
The slaughter was horrible, the dead lying cross-
wise, mixed together and on top of one another, two,
three, four, and in some places more, deep. It was
the most dreadful massacre that had taken place
during the entire war.* At midnight it was seen
that the vantage-point could not be recovered, and
the Confederates, grimy, bleeding, sullen and baffled,
drew back, and Lee formed them on his interior
lines. Disappointed though the Southern leader
was, yet he had kept the Federals within the captured position, and had foiled every effort to penetrate farther or to pierce his lines anywhere else.
The losses had been very heavy, amounting to

---

* There has been preserved for years in Washington the trunk of
a tree eighteen inches in diameter which was cut in two by the bullets
at Spottsylvania.

eight thousand for the Federals, and they were nearly as great on the Confederate side.

Grant determined to pass around to Lee's right and shove back that wing. General Warren was sent to unite with Burnside on the left, and to take position on the extreme left. This was done after an arduous march, and early on the 14th the Fifth and Ninth Corps assailed Wilcox's division, but were repulsed. Some hours later Lane and Mahone made a sudden charge, which resulted in the capture of several hundred prisoners and a number of standards. General Meade himself narrowly avoided capture, barely succeeding in "readjusting" his position before Mahone could secure him, and thus escaped. The manœuvring of General Grant resulted in such a shifting of positions that he was compelled to change his base of supplies from Port Royal to Aquia Creek. On the 18th the corps of Hancock, Burnside and Wright were again hurled against the Confederate works in the rear of the salient Hancock had carried six days before, but the attempt was hopeless, and was soon abandoned.

General Grant had followed out his favorite plan of "hammering" his enemy. He had lost about forty thousand men, and the enemy in his front was still unsubdued. It looked, indeed, as though it was absolutely beyond the power of any force that could be brought into the field to dislodge the Army of Northern Virginia; indeed, there was but the one way—to move around between it and Richmond.

As before, Grant was prompt to resort to this method. His preparations were begun on the afternoon of the 19th. Detecting it almost immediately, Lee threw forward Ewell's corps, and delivered such a severe blow to the Federal left that General Grant was forced to delay his movement until the 21st. The Federal army reached Milford the next day. On the morning of the 23d, Grant arrived at the North Anna River. Rapid as had been his march, he found that Lee was there ahead of him, with his invincible army in position and perfectly willing to be attacked in the usual fashion. Here was another chance for pounding, and Grant got his hammers ready. General Hancock, with the Federal left, and General Warren, with the right, were ordered to force a passage of the river. Warren did so unmolested at Jericho Ford, and pushed on toward the Central Railroad. At Noel's Station he came in collision with Wilcox's division, of A. P. Hill's corps. The other divisions of this corps were hurried up, and gave Warren so much attention that he was held motionless the rest of the day. Hancock reached the river six miles above, driving off the three regiments guarding the telegraph-bridge. He held the bridge until daylight, repulsing several attempts to drive him away, and the next morning crossed to the south side of the river.

General Lee, previous to this, had established his centre at Oxford Mills, a mile above the telegraph-bridge. His right, extending southward to Hanover Junction, was protected by a series of almost impenetrable marshes, while his left, running west, rested on Little River. As the centre was strongly entrenched, it will be seen that his position was an admirable one. An examination of his line and the disposition of the Confederate forces was such that Grant could not attack, except with a part of his forces, without crossing the river twice, while the Confederates themselves could concentrate on any part of their line which might be menaced. Furthermore, Lee could assail the right or left and prevent either wing going to the assistance of the other. Lee's conception was such a masterly one that Grant found himself baffled before a gun was fired. With a view of gaining some advantage of position—or, rather, with a view of making his own less perilous—he sent Burnside to cross with the Ninth Corps at Oxford Mills; he was to push away Lee's centre from the river and open communication between Warren and Hancock. But when Burnside got one division over, it was shaken up so roughly that he was forced to withdraw it again. At the same time, Warren was assailed savagely by Hill's troops, and found it very difficult to extricate himself from his dangerous position.

Grant was now driven to the humiliating

conclusion that, in common parlance, he had undertaken a contract in which he was "unable to
deliver the goods." For him to "hammer" his
adversary would be like using an egg with which
to smite a stone. There was but the one thing to
do: that was to withdraw from his dangerous position while able to do so. Accordingly, on the night
of the 26th of May, he sullenly retreated across the
North Anna. Had Lee possessed an army anywhere equal in numbers to that of his adversary,
he would have fallen upon him while he was withdrawing and delivered a mortal blow, but the Southern leader could not afford·to lose any men; for when
one was gone, no one was left to fill his place.

Defeated though Grant had been in his effort to
cut the communications between Lee and Richmond, he decided to make one more attempt before
the Army of Northern Virginia could reach the
defences of its capital. He now hastened down
the north bank of the Pamunkey toward Hanovertown, preceded by the cavalry of General Sheridan.
Crossing at Hanovertown, after a hurried night-
march, he despatched a strong force to Hanover
Court-House to cut off Lee's retreat or to learn his
movements. But no discovery was made, for Lee
had not moved in that direction. He had marched,
instead, across the country on the direct road to
Cold Harbor. Reaching Tottapotomoi, he formed
his lines on the main highway between Hanovertown and Richmond.

And so again, and for the third time, when the Federal lion crept toward Richmond, he found the Confederate tiger crouching in the path and eager for him to approach within reach of his claws. Those claws were sharp, and the valor which controlled them knew no fear. The lion turned aside to hunt some path by which he could pass around the formidable adversary. It seemed to Grant that the wiser course was to move farther to the left, and to cross the Chickahominy in the vicinity of Cold Harbor. Accordingly, his cavalry was sent thither, and he followed rapidly with his infantry. As before, Lee was quick to detect his intention, and he sent Longstreet's corps to interpose itself between the Federal army and Richmond.

For the fourth time when the lion stepped stealthily along the forest-path he was arrested by a growl, and, raising his head, saw the tiger crouching before him, lashing his tail, showing his sharp teeth and inviting him to come a little closer. At last the lion forgot that the tiger is stronger than himself, and leaped upon him.

Considerable fighting took place while the armies were swinging into position, but the shock came on the morning of June 3, when Grant hurled his whole force against that of Lee. The attack was made all along the line, and the vast Army of the Potomac in the gray of the early-morning light rushed like demons at the throats of the Army of Northern Virginia. But the latter were not taken unawares. The struggle was one of the most bloody recorded in the history of war. Within the space of twenty minutes the Federal loss amounted to twelve thousand men. The assailants fought with all the courage that man possessed, but they had undertaken the impossible: every attack was repulsed in the same dreadful fashion. The slaughter is almost inconceivable, and no man who was engaged in that awful conflict can recall its memory to-day without a shudder. It is useless to give the movements in detail. General Lee had been reinforced by Breckenridge's command, of two thousand men, from the Valley of the Virginia, and also by Hoke's and Pickett's divisions, from Beauregard's army, south of the James. This brought his force up to forty-four thousand of all arms.

The second battle of Cold Harbor raged with more or less fierceness for four or five hours. At the end the Federals were defeated at every point; they had lost thirteen thousand men, while the loss of the Confederates amounted to scarcely twelve hundred. Every Federal soldier saw the utter folly and madness of the attack, in which there was no vestige of generalship.

As if enough poor fellows had not been slaughtered, General Meade, some hours after the failure of the first assault, sent orders to each corps commander to renew the attack without reference to the other troops. When the orders reached the men, not one of them stirred. It was not coward-ice which restrained them, unless that man be deemed a coward who refuses a plunge into a fiery furnace heated seven times hotter than before.

The loss of the Confederates from the opening of the overland campaign to its close, at the Chick-ahominy, was, as nearly as can be ascertained, about eighteen thousand men; that of General Grant almost reached the awful total of sixty thousand —greater than the entire army under Lee!*

The North began to ask whether this was to go on for ever. Humanity sickened at this eternal feast of blood, and the feeling showed itself in many quarters that the North was paying too dearly for the prize for which it had contended so long. " Now, so gloomy was the military outlook after the action on the Chickahominy, and to such a degree, by consequence, had the moral spring of the public mind become relaxed, that there was at this time great danger of a collapse of the war. The archives of the State Department, when one day made public, will show how deeply the govern-ment was affected by the want of military success, and to what resolutions the Executive had, in con-sequence, come."†

* Swinton.   † Ibid.

CHAPTER XXXVI.

HURLED back bleeding and stunned, the Army of the Potomac lay motionless for days, while its antagonist crouched fierce and defiant, awaiting another attack. But the lesson had not been thrown away on General Grant. The appalling losses of his campaign and the failure to accomplish anything substantial had taught him that it was useless to try to reach Richmond by the overland route. His "hammering" might be continued until the plain was strewn with the bodies of Union soldiers, and still the gate would be barred. He therefore gave up the attempt to capture the city from the north or east, and decided to move rapidly upon Petersburg, seize that place, and thus cut the Confederate communications with the South.

Petersburg lies twenty-two miles south of Richmond, and is connected with the South and West by the Weldon and Southside Railroads. The latter crosses the Danville line, the principal avenue of communication between the capital and the Gulf States. When these roads were seized, including those north of the city, Richmond would no longer

366

be tenable, and the authorities must surrender or retreat. With the fall of the capital the Southern Confederacy would pass out of existence.

General Grant held position in front of Lee until June 12, when, moving once more by his left flank, he passed over the Chickahominy and advanced to City Point, where the Appomattox and James unite. The latter was crossed on pontoons, and without delay the march was resumed toward Petersburg.

In point of fact, this city could have been taken weeks before by the Federals. General Butler, by direction of General Grant, had sailed from Fortress Monroe May 4 with a column of thirty thousand troops, and, landing at Bermuda Hundred, began throwing up entrenchments. Instead of seizing Petersburg, he continued entrenching, and the arrival of a force from the South under the direction of Beauregard caused him to devote all his energies to saving his command from destruction. As it was, he narrowly escaped. Finally, he retreated before the savage attack of Beauregard, and took shelter behind his works across the neck of the Peninsula. There his situation was such that General Grant wrote of him, "His army was as completely shut off as if it had been in a bottle strongly corked."

Although the Federal commander used the utmost celerity in marching against Petersburg, he failed to take it by surprise. He did not reach the vicinity until the 15th, but by the next day the entire Federal army was south of the James. Fully aware of his movements, General Lee offered no opposition, for the Army of Northern Virginia was too weak in numbers. He had just detached Early's corps from the army, and was left with only thirty thousand men. But, detecting the purpose of the Union leader, he hastened southward to confront him as he had done so many times before.

Petersburg offered such sturdy resistance to General Grant's attack, on the 15th, that the works were held until darkness ended the struggle. When the sun rose on the morrow and all eyes were turned toward the city, they saw long lines of soldiers defiling into the breastworks. Above the myriads of gleaming bayonets fluttered the torn battle-flags of the Army of Northern Virginia. Once more the exultant lion found the tiger crouching in the path before him.

General Lee lost no time in drawing a regular line of earthworks to the east and south of the city, but the first spade was scarcely taken up when Grant assailed him with such fierceness that the Confederates were forced from their advanced position and compelled to take shelter behind the second line of works, which were then in a fair state of completion. General Grant hurled his men against this second line with the same desperate valor as before. On the 17th, Hancock and Burnside renewed the attack, but it was not until near nightfall that they succeeded in carrying a part of the entrenchments, and these were retaken after dark.

The formidable line of works which General Lee had been constructing immediately around the city were sufficiently completed, and he withdrew within them on the morning of the 18th. A few hours later a general assault was made by General Grant, but it was repulsed. The attack was repeated twice, but in each instance the Federals were driven back with heavy loss. From the firing of the first gun until the close of the day above mentioned, the total Federal loss was slightly less than ten thousand men. This result proved that the whole Army of Northern Virginia was south of the James, and, overpowering as were the numbers of the Union host, it could not take Petersburg by direct assault. As General Grant had secured his grip, however, he did not loosen it, but set deliberately to work to besiege the city. Muskets were thrown aside and spades taken up. The thousands of men toiled like beavers, and it required but a few days for the Federal army to entrench itself from the river to the Norfolk Railroad. Then the left wing began slowly creeping around, so as to complete the investment of the city. The long arms of the octopus were gradually closing about the lusty victim, who, undismayed, fought fiercely to save himself from strangulation.

On the 21st a heavy Federal line was advanced

24

toward the Weldon Railroad, but General Mahone with his division plunged between the two Federal corps, doubled them up, repulsed the attack, and when he withdrew took with him sixteen hundred prisoners, four pieces of artillery, eight stands of colors and a large number of small-arms. Simultaneous with this demonstration, the Federals sent out a cavalry expedition under Generals Wilson and Kautz, with the purpose of operating against the railroads south of the Appomattox. Starting at night, the horsemen proceeded to Ream's Station, on the Weldon Railroad, where the dépôt was burned and considerable of the track destroyed. Then the cavalry struck across the country toward the Southside Railroad. Kautz galloped to Burkesville, the junction of the Southside and Richmond and Danville Railroads, where he did all the damage possible. Wilson went to Nottoway Station and destroyed several miles of track. General Lee sent Fitzhugh Lee's division of cavalry in pursuit of the raiders, and Mahone's infantry moved down the Weldon Railroad to cut off their retreat in case they sought to return by the route taken on the advance.

Fitzhugh Lee came up with Wilson near, Dinwiddie Court-House, but in his attack was repulsed. He annoyed the cavalry considerably, and the next day threw himself across Wilson's line of march. Wilson could not break through, and turned off to the Danville Railroad, where he effected a junction with Kautz. They then made for the railroad-bridge over Staunton River, but it was gallantly defended by a number of home-guards, and, Fitzhugh Lee arriving soon after, Wilson retreated, leaving his thirty dead on the field. Finding he was in hot quarters, Wilson galloped off with all haste, reaching Sappony Church toward the close of the 28th. There he ran against Hampton's cavalry, who were hunting for him. A sharp fight lasted through most of the night, but Wilson was defeated and hurried in the direction of Ream's Station; but when he reached the railroad, he was assailed by Mahone's infantry, while Hampton and Lee's cavalry closed in upon his rear. The situation for the Federals had become desperate, and they fled in panic, losing their trains, artillery and everything that could impede their flight. At last the terrified troopers managed to cross the Nottoway River, and rode breathlessly into the Union lines, having inflicted little substantial harm on their enemies.

The fervid days of summer wore on, and no collision of importance took place. General Lee steadily improved his defences, until on the 1st of July the Federal engineers pronounced them impregnable against assault. The line consisted of a chain of redans connected by infantry parapets of a powerful profile, while the approaches were completely obstructed by abatis, stakes and entanglements. Beginning at the south bank of the Appomattox, it enveloped Petersburg on the east and south, stretching westward beyond the farthest reach of the left flank of the Union army. A continuation of the same system to the north side of the Appomattox protected the city and the Petersburg and Richmond Railroad against attack from the direction of the front, held by Butler's force at Bermuda Hundred. The defence of Richmond was provided for by its own chain of fortifications.*

Despite the invulnerabilty of the Confederate lines, General Grant determined to make one more effort against them. This time he decided to avail himself of an extraordinary expedient proposed by Burnside, which was to explode a mine so near the works that a breach would be opened, through which the assailants could rush before the defenders would have time to recover from the terror into which they would be thrown. The entrenchments of Burnside's Ninth Corps were within one hundred and fifty yards of the Confederate line, which just opposite formed an angle covered by a fort. Under this fort was carefully stowed six tons of powder, the operation being completed without causing any suspicion on the part of the defenders. This enormous bulk of explosives was fired at forty-two minutes past four o'clock on the morning of July 30. A solid mass of earth, as if it were the vast lid of some volcano, rose slowly in

* Swinton.

the air until it had reached a height of two hundred feet, where it seemed to poise motionless for several minutes, when it shuddered itself apart and began raining to the ground again. As it started upward the exploding powder flashed through the dark pile in a hundred places, and a volume of black smoke rolled off in the sky. The thunderous shock was felt for miles around, and the report was heard distinctly in Richmond. But when General Grant described that which followed, he fitly called it " a miserable affair." In accordance with the prearranged plan, the Federal batteries immediately opened upon the Confederates, and soon silenced them. Then the assaulting column charged, but in a straggling and broken fashion. When they reached the site of the fort, it was gone; in its place was a yawning pit a hundred and fifty feet long, sixty feet wide and thirty feet deep. Instead of advancing, the column sought shelter in this crater. Other troops were pushed on, but they huddled like terrified sheep in the cavity or cowered behind the breastworks in the immediate vicinity, which the Confederates had deserted for the time.

The tremendous explosion astounded the defenders for a brief while, but, seeing the panic-stricken Federals in the pit, they ran back to their guns and opened on them. The horrible scene is thus described by one who looked upon it: "The 'white division' charged, reached the crater, stumbled over the *débris*, were suddenly met by a merciless fire of artillery, enfilading them right and left, and of infantry fusillading them in front; faltered, hesitated, were badly led, lost heart, gave up the plan of seizing the crest in the rear, huddled into the crater, man on top of man, company mingled with company; and upon this disordered, unstrung, quivering mass of human beings, white and black —for the black troops had followed—was poured a hurricane of shot, shell, canister and musketry which made the hideous crater a slaughter-pen horrible and frightful beyond the power of words. All order was lost; all idea of charging the crest was abandoned. Lee's infantry was seen concentrating for the carnival of death; his artillery was massing to destroy the remnants of the charging divisions. Those who deserted the crater to scramble over the *débris* and run back were shot down; then all that was left to the shuddering mass of blacks and whites in the pit was to shrink lower, evade the horrible mitraille, and wait for a charge of their friends to rescue them or surrender."

Finally, at nine o'clock Mahone rushed forth and drove out the wretched survivors. It is said he ordered the firing to cease, for the sight was so dreadful that he could not bear it. The Unionists lost four thousand men, of whom eight hundred were prisoners, including one general officer and twelve standards. The Confederate loss was a few hundred.

General Grant was still hammering away at Pe-

tersburg, when the startling news was telegraphed
him that a Confederate column had crossed into
Maryland, had scattered the force sent out to meet
it, and was then in front of the fortifications of
Washington. The news was alarming indeed; and
when it became known throughout the North, the
belief was general that at last the national capital
was doomed to fall.

A part of General Grant's plan of campaign
was an advance up the valley, with a second from
Western Virginia toward the Lynchburg and Tennessee Railroad, the object being to co-operate with
the main army in cutting the Confederate communications. Comparatively little was accomplished
by the force in Western Virginia, but that in the
valley, under General Hunter, easily forced its way
until Lynchburg itself was threatened. When the
news reached Lee, he was at Cold Harbor, shortly
after the battle there. General Early was promptly
detached with eight thousand men and orders to
attack Hunter or threaten Washington.

General Early quickly obeyed, and assailed
Hunter with great fury near Lynchburg. Hunter was defeated and driven in disorderly flight
toward the Ohio, and Early then galloped down
the valley and into Maryland, with a view of
threatening Washington, as Lee had directed.
When he reached the Monocacy, he was opposed
by a force under General Wallace, but, driving
him aside, he pushed on, and on the 11th of July

his column appeared before the capital. Two years before, when McClellan was almost similarly placed, a like diversion caused the withdrawal of a large number of his reinforcements to the defence of Washington; now Grant was left to do as he saw fit, and he sent only a comparatively small force to the defence of the city. Early was not long in learning that Washington was too strongly fortified for him to risk a direct attack. He skirmished several days before the city, and then withdrew in the direction of Winchester, taking several thousand cattle and horses with him.

As a matter of precaution, General Grant now sent the Sixth and Nineteenth Corps to Washington, from which point they went to Harper's Ferry. The old Departments of Washington, the Susquehanna, West Virginia and the Middle Department were combined in one command and assigned to General Hunter, who afterward gave way to General Sheridan. General Lee held Early's army in the valley, with the hope of inducing Grant to raise the siege of Petersburg in order to protect Washington against the real danger which threatened it; but the campaign was not well managed, and accomplished no good for the Confederate cause.

Meanwhile, General Grant retained his grip on Petersburg. Skirmishing and fighting continued, but General Lee was able to repel every assault.

Steadily advancing his line, he sent out a strong force in the latter part of August to seize the Weldon Railroad, a short distance from Petersburg. As General Lee anticipated, the effort was successful; for he had informed the authorities long before that it was impossible for him to hold it. An attempt, however, to inflict damage upon the road farther south was defeated by General Lee, who drove back the Federals with heavy loss.

But all these movements, fighting and forays were but by-plays which had no effect upon the general result. Like the line of demarcation which marks the creeping upward of death when the limb of a strong man is seized with gangrene, the Federal wing stole steadily westward until it had passed over the Vaughan, Squirrel Level, and other roads which extend southward from Petersburg, until in October it was firmly established on the left bank of Hatcher's Run. A little farther, and the Southside Railroad would be seized. The attempt was made October 27, but failed. The Federal column was assailed in front and flank by General Wade Hampton and his son, General Preston Hampton, who was killed, and by W. H. F. Lee with his dismounted sharpshooters. Infantry were hurried forward under General Mahone, who, to quote the words of General Lee, charged and broke three lines of battle. During the night the Federals retreated, leaving their wounded and more than two hundred and fifty dead on the field. On the Williamsburg Road seven stands of colors and over four hundred prisoners were taken.

No other movement of importance was undertaken during the year. The Presidential election in the North resulted in favor of President Lincoln, and what hopes the Confederates may have based on the growth of a peace sentiment in that section were dissipated. They saw that all that remained to them was to fight to the bitter end.

CHAPTER XXXVII.

CLOSING IN.

DURING the winter of 1864–65, General Lee established his headquarters a short distance west of Petersburg, on the Cox road, almost opposite his centre. Long before, his masterly genius must have foreseen the inevitable end, and doubtless he fixed, nearly to a certainty, the date and manner of the downfall of the Southern Confederacy.

Events in other portions of the country clearly foreshadowed the collapse that was at hand. In the Valley of Virginia matters had gone from bad to worse. General Sheridan had overwhelmed and dispersed Early and his cavalry, so that it may be said the valley was entirely cleared of all Confederate forces. Then, with his horsemen, Sheridan galloped into the lowlands to join General Grant in his last campaign against Richmond. General Sherman with his mighty host was sweeping through the heart of the South from Atlanta to the sea. General Johnston, with all his splendid generalship, could not with his fragment of an army stay the march. Savannah dropped like a mellow apple into Sherman's grasp, and, facing northward, he advanced to Goldsborough, North

Carolina, directly threatening Lee's line of retreat from Virginia.

The fate of the Southern Confederacy rested at this time upon the shoulders of one man. John Esten Cooke says, "It is doubtful if in any other struggle of history the hopes of a people were more entirely wrapped up in a single individual. All criticism of the eminent soldier had long since been silenced, and it may, indeed, be said that something like a superstitious confidence in his fortunes had become widely disseminated. It was the general sentiment, even when Lee himself saw the end surely approaching, that all was safe while he remained in command of the army. This hallucination must have greatly pained him, for no one ever saw more clearly or was less blinded by irrational confidence. Lee fully understood and represented to the civil authorities—with whom his relations were perfectly friendly and cordial—that if his lines were broken at any point the fate of the campaign was sealed. Feeling this truth, of which his military sagacity left him no doubt, he had to bear the further weight of that general confidence which he did not share. He did not complain, however, or in any manner indicate the desperate straits to which he had come. He called for fresh troops to supply his losses; when they did not arrive, he continued to oppose his powerful adversary with the remnant still at his command. These were now more like old comrades than mere

private soldiers under his orders. What was left of
the army was its best material. The fires of battle
had tested the metal, and that which emerged from
the furnace was gold free from alloy. . . . He was
now their ideal of a leader, and all that he did was
perfect in their eyes. All awe of him had long
since left them; they understood what treasures
of kindness and simplicity lay under the grave
exterior. The tattered privates approached the
commander-in-chief without embarrassment, and
his reception of them was such as to make them
love him more than ever. . . . He looked much
older than at the beginning of the war, but by no
means less hardy or robust. On the contrary, the
arduous campaigns through which he had passed
seemed to have hardened him, developing to the
highest degree the native strength of his physical
organization. His cheeks were ruddy, and his eye
had that clear light which indicates the presence of
the calm, self-poised will. But his hair had grown
gray, like his beard and moustache, which were worn
short and well trimmed. His dress, as always, was a
plain and serviceable gray uniform with no indica-
tions of rank save the stars on the collar. Cavalry-
boots reached nearly to his knees, and he seldom
wore any weapon. A broad-brimmed gray felt hat
rested low upon the forehead, and the movements
of this soldierly figure were as firm, measured and
imposing as ever. He was still almost an anchorite
in his personal habits, and lived so poorly that it is

said he was compelled to borrow a small piece of meat when unexpected visitors dined with him."

The Army of Northern Virginia suffered greatly for want of clothing and food, the commissariat being mismanaged beyond endurance. General Lee's appeals were unheeded, and many men were compelled to desert to save themselves from starving to death. At one time the army was on the eve of disbandment for lack of food. In the spring Confederate treasury-notes were worth scarcely a cent to a dollar, and thousands of soldiers had not received a penny for two years.* The Conscription Act brought forth no men, but diminished rather than increased the strength of the army. Gross

---

* In the last few weeks of the war a Confederate serving under Lee wrote home to his father that he was almost barefooted and completely discouraged. As soon as the old man received the letter he mounted his mule and set off at a gallop, but was soon halted by an acquaintance, who called out,

"Hello! Has there been another fight?"

"Not as I've heard of, but I've got a letter from Cyrus."

"What does Cyrus say?"

"He's out o' butes and clean discouraged."

"And where are you going?"

"Down to Abner Smith's to borrow seven hundred thousand dollars to send to Cyrus to get a cheap pair of shoes, and we're going to write him a long letter and send him a box o' pills, and tell him to hang on to the last; for if Cyrus gets low-spirited and begins to let go, the infernal Yanks will be riding over us afore we kin back a mule outer the barn."

"That's so! that's so!" nodded the other. "I kin let you have the money myself as well as not. I was saving up to buy three plugs o' tobacker and a box o' matches all at once, but the army mustn't go barefut when it only takes seven or eight hundred thousand dollars to buy a purty good pair o' shoes."—*Austin (Texas) Dispatch.*

favoritism was shown by the authorities, and the interference of the Executive threatened to destroy military discipline in the army. The proposition to arm the slaves was made in November, 1864, but the act did not pass until the succeeding March, when it was shorn of the wise recommendations of General Lee. As a consequence, the effort to raise colored troops failed, and possibly it was fortunate, under the circumstances, that such was the case.

January, 1865, was noteworthy as bringing forth an effort to secure peace. An interview took place between President Lincoln, Secretary Seward and others on the Federal side, and Vice-President Stephens, Senator Hunter and others for the Confederates, on board a steamer in Hampton Roads. The soldiers cheered the ambassadors—if they may be thus termed—and proved how such a blessed consummation would have been welcomed by them. Nothing came of it, however.

General Lee, by act of the Confederate Congress, February 5, 1865, was created commander-in-chief, and thus placed beyond all possibility of the interference of the Executive. But the advancement came too late to prove of any benefit; the Southern Confederacy was doomed beyond the power of mortal man to save it.

Operations were resumed in February, 1865, on the part of the Army of the Potomac, by an attempt to turn the Confederate right. Petersburg and the works were bombarded for several days, and on the 5th the Second and Fifth Corps and Gregg's cavalry division, after a few hours' march, reached Hatcher's Run. Part of the infantry crossed the Vaughan road and made their way to Cattail Creek, while the cavalry proceeded to Dinwiddie Court-House, where they were driven back by the Confederate cavalry. Later in the day portions of Hill's and Gordon's corps attacked the infantry, which was on the left bank of Hatcher's Run, near Armstrong's Mill, but the Federals were so strongly entrenched that the assailants withdrew. On the morning of the 6th, Pegram's division moved down the right bank of the stream to reconnoitre, and was attacked by the Fifth Corps. In the sharp engagement which followed, General Pegram was killed and his division driven back. Evan's division was sent to the support of Pegram's command, but that too was forced to withdraw. Mahone then charged, and the Federals were driven into their entrenchments. The Confederates then drew off, having lost a thousand men, while that of their enemies was nearly twice as great.

General Grant had failed to capture the Southside Railroad, but he extended his left to Hatcher's Run, which was connected by earthworks with the rest of his line.

In the month of March, General Lee's army numbered less than thirty-five thousand men. General Longstreet, who had returned to duty some time before, commanded the left wing, which was north and south of the James; General Gordon commanded the centre, at Petersburg; while General A. P. Hill commanded the right, extending from Petersburg to Hatcher's Run. The wretchedly-mounted cavalry, so far as possible, guarded the flanks. This line, spun out to the utmost extremity of attenuation, was forty miles in length.

Campaigning in the Army of Northern Virginia was no holiday parade during that terrible winter. The thirty-odd thousand soldiers had to do picket- and guard-duty and cover that entire stretch of ground, passing continually from one duty to the other. No reserves were available to relieve those who gave out, and the men were shifted again and again from one place to another to meet the menaces of the Federals. Let us recall the military situation. General Sherman with his vast army was at Goldsborough, only one hundred and fifty miles distant, and steadily pushing northward, directly upon Lee's line of retreat. The skeleton of an army under Johnston could do nothing but fall back before this overwhelming advance. When Sherman should unite with Grant, the latter would have an army of two hundred thousand under his immediate command; Johnston's force consolidated with Lee's would give about one-fourth that number, or fifty thousand men.

They were shoeless, gaunt, ragged and famishing while the embattled hosts were closing in around them, but they were as brave and defiant as ever:

25

so long as R. E. Lee was with them, they were content.

The plan decided upon by the Confederate commander-in-chief was to evacuate the line then held by his army, retreat hastily toward Danville, unite with Johnston and take a strong position in the interior. This decision was reached before Sherman had penetrated as far as North Carolina. Johnston was ordered to retire before Sherman, and to manœuvre with his left so as to bring it into communication with Lee's right. Ponton-trains were made ready and a large supply of provisions was ordered to be collected at Amelia Court-House, west of Petersburg, with which it is connected by the Cox road, and over which Lee intended to withdraw his army. But the extension of the Federal left had reached Hatcher's Run, which was dangerously close to the Cox road. Before the starving tiger could steal out from his lair it was necessary that the sleek lion on guard should be induced to turn his eyes away for a brief while.

With the purpose of compelling Grant to withdraw his left, which was so close to the Cox road, Lee prepared to attack his right. The Federal position was like adamantine. A cordon of redoubts of a powerful profile and armed with the heaviest metal studded this line; infantry parapets amply manned stretched from work to work. Covering the fronts of approach were labyrinthine acres of abatis, while all the appliances of ditches, entanglements and *chevaux-de-frise* lent their aid to make defence sure and assault folly.*

General Lee fixed upon Fort Steadman as the point of assault. This was close to the south bank of the Appomattox, and less than two hundred yards from the Federal breastworks. It was be- lieved that by a sudden rush the work could be surprised and captured. After the high ground in the rear was gained, the City Point Railroad, which was the chief line of communication of the Federal army, might be seized. The attack was to be made by two divisions of Gordon's corps, while the rest of the army were to be held ready to support the movement. If Grant assaulted immediately, so as to recover the ground lost, Lee would be ready to meet him; if he hastened toward City Point to regain his communications, then the Southern army would withdraw over the Cox road. It was quite certain, in any event, that the Federal left wing would be drawn in, and the Cox road thus opened. In the dim light of early morning, March 25, Gordon's two divisions emerged as silently as spectres from their works and in columns of attack ran across the open space, flung aside the abatis, bounded into Fort Steadman, and captured the work and garrison before the latter understood what was going on. Immediately the guns of the captured fort were turned on the nearest Federal works. Several batteries were abandoned by the defend-

* Swinton.

ers and one of their brigades put to flight. The impetuous charge had captured nine pieces of artillery, eight mortars and five hundred prisoners, among whom was a full-fledged brigadier-general.

Gordon had made a splendid opening, and there was every prospect of greater and more brilliant success; but his charge was not sustained as was promised. The troops which attacked Fort Haskell on his right did so in such a spiritless manner that they were immediately repulsed; many others refused to advance at the critical moment and huddled in the breastworks; seeing which, the Federals recovered their self-possession and concentrated a heavy fire on Fort Steadman. The situation became similar to that which followed the mine-explosion some months before. Gordon was caught in a frightful trap, from which his high courage and masterly leadership could not extricate his command. So completely were they encircled by the ring of consuming fire that two thousand Confederates surrendered on the spot, bringing up their total loss to fully three thousand, while that of the Unionists was five hundred less. The repulse was followed by the advance of the Federal Sixth Corps, which after a hard fight succeeded in capturing the picket-line in front. The Confederate army had suffered a loss which it could ill afford to bear, and General Grant still clung to his advanced position on Hatcher's Run, overlooking and commanding the Cox road, along which Lee meant to make his withdrawal.

Sheridan, having given a quietus to affairs in the valley, had rejoined Grant's army before Petersburg. Thus in the latter part of March the Federal leader had one hundred and seventy thousand men under his immediate direction, including the ten thousand sabres of Sheridan, which were of incalculable service in the last struggle.

On the 29th of March, General Lee discovered that a large portion of the Federal army was massing in the works beyond Bergen Mill; this proved that General Grant was making ready to assail the Confederate right. His first intention was to wait until General Sherman should cross the Roanoke River, but a fear that Lee would withdraw from Petersburg induced the Federal leader to move at once.

General Grant determined this time that his assault against the Confederate right should be resistless. Two days previous Sheridan's cavalry were moved to the left, and General Ord, the successor of General Butler in command of the Army of the James, crossed from Deep Bottom to the Southside with three divisions of infantry and one of cavalry. With these he relieved the Second and Fifth Corps in the trenches on the left of the Federal lines, so they were enabled to take part in the movement. The assault in column numbered twenty-five thousand, and was to be supported by the rest of the army. The Confederate right, against which this formidable demonstration was to be made, extended several miles south-west from Petersburg. The combined force was about fifteen thousand men, besides two thousand alleged cavalry under Fitzhugh Lee, if the few wretched, broken-down steeds can be viewed as of any account. With this force Lee took position behind the works extending along the White Oak road toward Five Forks. The force that remained north of James River and in front of Petersburg was barely twenty thousand.

The difficult character of the ground so delayed the Federal advance that it was not in position until the 31st. When it was gathered near the Boydton Road, beyond Hatcher's Run, and about ready to attack, Lee suddenly assailed it with such fierceness that the first lines were scattered like chaff. But a forest of bayonets seeming limitless in extent rose beyond, and there was no end to the legions of Federals which confronted the assailants. It was destruction to advance, and Lee fell back to his works. Five Forks had been seized by Sheridan, but he was driven out, and the Confederate infantry, after advancing toward Dinwiddie Court-House, were withdrawn. Fighting was over for the day.

Five Points was a valuable position, and Lee had stationed there the remnants of the divisions of Pickett and Johnston; they made a desperate resistance, but were overwhelmed and scattered. Thereupon, the whole right of the Confederate line and the Southside Railroad passed into the possession of the Federal army.

When Sunday, the 2d of April, dawned, Lee was in ill form to withstand the tremendous " hammering " to which he was to be subjected, but he was calm and undismayed. His right wing had been destroyed, and he was left with only the remnants of Gordon and A. P. Hill's divisions. General Longstreet still confronted his adversary, and no troops could be drawn from the north side.

At the earliest dawn the Unionists advanced upon the Confederate works, and in a short time the flame of battle outblazed along the whole line from the Appomattox to Hatcher's Run. General Gordon, who held the left on the Appomattox, was attacked by General Parke and the Ninth Corps, and after a furious resistance compelled to fall back on an inner cordon of works, which he held against other attacks.

The weakest part of the Confederate position was the left of A. P. Hill, on the right of Gordon, for the reason that the infantry for its defence had been withdrawn the day before, and it was now held only by the artillerists and a thin picket-line. When, therefore, the Sixth Corps bore down upon it, the pickets were driven in and the works were captured, including the batteries and artillerists. This success threatened the ruin of the whole Confed-

erate army, for Hill's works were scarcely carried
when the Second Corps drove the small Confederate force out of the redoubts of Hatcher's Run,
and then, connecting with the Sixth and Twenty-
Fourth Corps, completed the environment which
was slowly strangling Petersburg.

Two strong works were left, Forts Alexander
and Gregg, commanding the ground over which
the Federals must advance to reach the river.
Fort Alexander was closer to the assailants, and
was captured with a hurrah and a rush. This left
only Fort Gregg, on which for the time the fate of
the army depended. The garrison consisted of two
hundred and fifty men, made up of the Fourth
Maryland Battery with two three-inch rifles and
thirty men, a body of dismounted artillery-drivers,
Virginians and Louisianians, carrying muskets, a
part of Harris's Mississippi brigade and a few
North Carolinians, all being under the command
of Captain Chew of the Maryland battery. The
salvation of the army required that this fort should
be held until General Lee could take his new position; if it yielded before, the army was doomed.

Fort Alexander having fallen, General Ord
pushed forward Gibbon's division to storm and
carry Fort Gregg. It advanced in admirable order
until within fifty yards, when it received such a destructive fire that the troops reeled and fell back.
The attack and repulse were witnessed by both
armies. The Confederates broke into admiring

cheers, though unable to forward a single musket to the help of the little band of Spartans. A second and third charge was made with great daring, but they were repelled as splendidly as before; but a fourth assault prevailed. The assailants swarmed over and into the works, and found that, out of the two hundred and fifty men composing the garrison, only thirty were unhurt. All the rest were dead or wounded.

About ten o'clock General Longstreet, having discovered the weakness of the Federal line in his front, reached the battlefield with Benning's brigade, less than three hundred strong. It was just as the Federals were again moving forward to force an entrance into the city. Longstreet handled this "corporal's guard" with such great skill that he checked the advance until Lee could forward troops to his assistance.

The line now held by Lee was short but powerful, extending directly around Petersburg, with the right flank touching the river above and the left resting on the same stream below the city. This line was assaulted again and again by the Army of the Potomac, but without success. Finally, Heth's division, under General A. P. Hill, charged the Ninth Corps, on the Confederate left, near the river, with a view of recovering some commanding ground. The attack was made with the dash and courage of that officer, but the Federals, being reinforced, were able to hold the ground. In this fight

Lieutenant-General A. P. Hill was killed. Strange it was that after being exposed hundreds of times in battle he should be stricken down at the end of those lurid years, when it may be said the last gun of the war was aimed and about to be fired!

The day closed and the Confederates still held Petersburg, but it had become untenable. Lee saw that if he remained longer his whole army would be made prisoners; he determined, therefore, to abandon both Petersburg and Richmond, and, retreating into North Carolina, unite with Johnston. At eleven o'clock Sunday morning, April 2, he telegraphed to the authorities in the capital that it was his purpose to retire from Richmond and Petersburg that night at eight o'clock. He counselled them to make everything ready to leave the city that evening, unless he soon sent another telegram advising the contrary.

CHAPTER XXXVIII.

THE LAST CAMP-FIRE.

GENERAL LEE was anxiously waiting for night. His lines had been broken, the panic-stricken authorities and citizens were hurrying out of Richmond, and the circle of the Federal legions was narrowing around the gaunt skeleton of the Army of Northern Virginia. Every line of retreat, with a single exception, led to destruction : that was the route westward and up the Appomattox toward the Danville line. Even the shadow of the Army of the Potomac was already thrown across that path. The Fifth Union Corps was at Sutherland's Station, on the Southside Railroad, ten miles west of Petersburg, and on a line parallel with that of the intended retreat, while Sheridan with his cavalry and infantry kindled his camp-fires on the night of the 2d at Ford's, ten miles still farther west. It will thus be seen that Lee was compelled to withdraw along the northern bank of the Appomattox, thus throwing himself on the exterior line and adding much to the difficulty of his march.

But the great soldier was still undismayed and calmly nerved himself for the last struggle. When night at last slowly settled over Petersburg, the heavens were one immense glare and the boom of cannon and exploding magazines made the earth tremble. At midnight the cadaverous figures began withdrawing like shadows from their trenches, and in the glow of the blazing city hurried silently toward the river. They glided so stealthily along the hot streets crimsoned by the conflagration that the Union pickets saw not what was going on. At three o'clock the city was deserted, and the Petersburg force had reached the north bank of the Appomattox. Tramping northward to Chesterfield Court-House, they were joined by the division holding the front of Bermuda Hundred. The troops on the Richmond side were drawn in to Chesterfield, and the retreat westward was fairly begun.

The entire army that had defended so long and valiantly the line between Petersburg and Richmond and around the latter city numbered less than twenty-five thousand men. Nearly all were barefoot; they were in rags, were living on a few grains of corn apiece, were worn out, and in the dismal hours of early morning had turned their backs on their capital and the enemy which they had beaten times without number. Who of all the multitude could be cheerful and hopeful? And yet those who were near General Lee at that time tell us he was in good spirits. Petersburg was sixteen miles behind, and in view of the fact he said, " My army is safe out of the breastworks, and to follow me my enemy must abandon his lines, and he can derive no more benefit from his railroads or the James River." It is impossible that the Southern commander-in-chief dreamed of victory. It must have been he believed that by uniting with Johnston he could still offer such a bold front as to compel a peace on advantageous terms.

General Grant displayed prodigious vigor in pressing Lee to the wall. Confident that his antagonist would retreat, he completed his arrangements on the night of the 2d for prompt and unrelenting pursuit. The flight of the Confederate army was discovered on the morning of the 3d. General Grant left a garrison in the city and started on the run, determined that it should not escape him again. General Ord with the Army of the James was hurried along the line of the Southside Railroad to Burkesville, while Sheridan with the Fifth Corps and his cavalry made for the Danville road, just north of Burkesville. Lee was sixteen miles on the way, but the two Federal columns were hastening along a shorter line; and if they could reach the point before him, he would be headed off and compelled to adopt a long and more difficult route or take refuge in the mountains.

The Confederate leader had the most exasperating obstacles to overcome. First of all, the Richmond authorities had turned over to him a wagon-train thirty miles in length. It was loaded with valueless government rubbish, and, pausing just long enough to direct General Lee to take the best care of the same, the authorities resumed their flight toward the setting sun. Like a true soldier, General Lee did his utmost to obey orders; but the enormous train was a complete brake to his progress and delayed him greatly. Nevertheless, he pushed on, and, crossing the Appomattox again at Goode's Bridge, reached Amelia Court-House on the 4th. He was now thirty-eight miles west of Petersburg. It was there that he received the most agonizing blow of the campaign—made so by the fact that he was smitten by his own government and there was no palliation for the cruel thrust at his very heart.

When Lee decided to abandon Richmond and Petersburg, he telegraphed to Danville, as we have stated, ordering a large amount of commissary and quartermaster stores to be forwarded to Amelia Court-House and held there to await his arrival. When his troops withdrew from the entrenchments, two days before, they were without rations, and during the interval that had passed since had not secured a single meal apiece; they were actually undergoing the pangs of starvation. But they were cheered by the promise that when Amelia Court-House was reached they would find abundance. Such ought to have been the case, but a cruel disappointment awaited them. The train loaded with stores and provisions reached Amelia Court-House from Danville on Sunday afternoon, April 2. At that point the officer in charge was met by an order from the Confederate authorities to bring the train without delay to Richmond, as the cars were needed for transporting the public and private property. The officer interpreted the order to mean that the train and its contents were wanted there, and he proceeded with them to the capital without opening a car. It should be added that the train safely reached its destination; the stores were carefully unloaded, and shortly after were used to help make a bonfire of Richmond.

When General Lee learned the horrible blunder that had been committed and met the gaunt, starving eyes of the thousands of brave soldiers fixed despairingly upon him, his breast heaved with indignation and grief. Stupidity, selfishness and base ingratitude could inflict more poignant wounds than the Army of the Potomac. The stars in their courses were fighting against him and his suffering comrades; why struggle longer? But, with the inborn nobility of his nature, he controlled his tempestuous feelings and immediately sent out detachments to hunt for food and forage. That day and the next were consumed in this blind groping for that which did not exist. They were journeying through what may be called a desert waste.

This enforced delay gave General Grant the golden opportunity, which he improved with the same tremendous vigor displayed from the first. General Sheridan, who was straining every nerve, and was far in advance of the rest of the army, arrived at Jetersville on the afternoon of the morning General Lee reached Amelia Court-House. Thus the Federal cavalry and Fifth Corps struck the Confederate line of retreat seven miles to the south-west of the Army of Northern Virginia.

It was no longer possible for General Lee to reach Burkesville, for a force about equal to his own was entrenched before him in the road. It was impossible to give battle, and only a single course lay open to him: that was to push on due west in the attempt to reach the hilly region surrounding Farmville. That place was thirty-five miles off, but, once attained, he was hopeful of securing his retreat into the mountains. The famishing remnant of an army started for that point with their undismayed leader.

The whole Army of the Potomac was concentrated at Jetersville in the evening, and entrenched its line in the expectation of an assault by Lee. This was out of the question, and the next morning General Meade advanced upon Amelia Court-House to attack the Confederate army supposed to be there. Discovering that Lee was making for Farmville by way of Deatonsville, he turned in pursuit, sending the Second Corps direct to Deatonsville, while the Fifth and Sixth moved by parallel routes to the north and south. General Ord with the Army of the James had reached Burkesville, and he was now ordered to hurry to Farmville.

Meanwhile, General Sheridan was playing football with the wagon-train. He adopted the very effective plan of attacking it with one division, and when that was repulsed assaulting it farther on with a fresh division, and so on, delivering blow after blow until the vulnerable spot was found. This was the course followed at Sailor's Creek, where more than four hundred wagons were destroyed and sixteen pieces of artillery and a number of prisoners taken. Pickett, whose division was reduced to eight hundred men, found himself so hard pressed that he sent to General Ewell for reinforcements, in order to save the rest of the wagon-train. Ewell responded with his corps, forty-two hundred strong, but while taking position observed that Gordon's corps, forming the rear-guard of the army, were following the wagon-train by another road. As Ewell was at the rear of the wagon-train, it will be seen that he was now cut off from the rest of the army. Sheridan kept Ewell hotly engaged until the Sixth Corps came up. Ewell was immediately assailed by them, and he fell back slowly, contesting every foot with wonderful bravery. By and by the Federal soldiers could be seen on every side, but the Confederates fought on. A large number staggered from weakness, and were scarcely able to keep their feet; many were so worn out that they would drop the guns which they had just loaded or discharged, and, regardless of the firing, sink down upon the

26

ground and fall asleep.* Pickett's division had been broken up and scattered by the heavy column thrown against it, and Ewell was forced to fight the immense numbers without help; but his grim, starving veterans in the very depths of disaster proved the royal stuff of which they were made. They calmly awaited the advance of the Sixth Corps, and when it was at the right point delivered such a terrific volley that it broke and fell back. The Federals quickly rallied, however, and the cavalry closed in upon the rear and flank of the Confederates. Finding themselves surrounded by more than four times their number, the men threw down their arms and surrendered. This surrender included Lieutenant-General Ewell, General Custis Lee and three other general officers. Almost at the same time the energetic Second Corps captured, near Sailor's Creek, a number of prisoners, several pieces of artillery, thirteen battle-flags and several hundred prisoners.

Lee continued his retreat with what was left of his army, and on the night of the 6th crossed the Appomattox at High Bridge, near Farmville, and bivouacked on the opposite side of the river. That night the general officers gathered around a camp-fire to consult as to what should be done. "All present agreed that but three lines of conduct yet remained open to them—either to disband and allow the troops to make their way as best they

---

* McCabe states this on the authority of many witnesses.

could to some specified rallying-point, to abandon the trains and with the infantry cut their way through the Federal lines, or to surrender. The first course was equivalent to a desertion of the cause, for it was certain that the army, once disbanded, would not reassemble, and to turn such a throng of starving men upon the country would be to bring still greater misery upon the inhabitants. The second course was doubtful, for it was hardly possible to cut through such an army as that of General Grant with the little band of Confederates; and if it could be done, starvation was sure to follow. Nothing remained, in the opinion of the council, but to surrender. The army had done all in its power to uphold its cause. This decision was made reluctantly, and General Pendleton, the chief of artillery, was appointed to communicate it to General Lee." *

But the commander-in-chief did not think the crisis had come: the bell had not yet struck.

As soon as the Confederates were across the Appomattox the railroad- and stage-bridges were fired, but the brigade left by Gordon to see that they were destroyed was driven off by the Second Federal Corps, who saved the stage-bridge and part of the railroad-bridge. A dash was then made at the wagon-train and a number captured, but General Gordon returned, drove off the assailants and took two hundred prisoners. The next day was mainly

* McCabe.

enlivened by continual attacks on the wagon-train.
The Second Corps pushed on, but about noon found
itself brought to a stand by the main body of Lee's
army, strongly entrenched in a commanding position a few miles north of Farmville. The halt had
been made for the purpose of resting the army and
holding the enemy at bay until nightfall. The
works were too strong to be taken in front, and
Humphreys, the Federal leader, sent back for reinforcements. While awaiting them he concluded to
improve the time by attacking the Southern left.
The result may be summed up in the simple statement that General Humphreys was repulsed with the
loss of six hundred killed and wounded. When the
reinforcements arrived, the day was so far gone that
the attack was deferred until the next morning.

After occupying Farmville, General Grant sent a
messenger to General Lee with the following letter:

"April 7, 1865.

"GENERAL: The result of the last week must
convince you of the hopelessness of further resistance on the part of the Army of Northern Virginia
in this struggle. I feel that it is so, and regard it
as my duty to shift from myself the responsibility of
any further effusion of blood by asking of you the
surrender of that portion of the Confederate States
army known as the Army of Northern Virginia.

"U. S. GRANT, Lieutenant-General.

"GENERAL R. E. LEE."

This communication reached General Lee on the night of the day on which it was written. He sent off at once the following reply:

"April 7, 1865.

"GENERAL: I have received your note of this date. Though not entertaining the opinion you express of the hopelessness of further resistance on the part of the Army of Northern Virginia, I reciprocate your desire to avoid useless effusion of blood, and therefore, before considering your proposition, ask the terms you will offer on condition of its surrender.

"R. E. LEE, General.

"LIEUTENANT-GENERAL U. S. GRANT."

General Lee resumed his retreat during the night in the direction of Lynchburg, and had progressed a number of miles when his letter reached General Grant, who without delay forwarded the following:

"April 8, 1865.

"GENERAL: Your note of last evening, in reply to mine of same date, asking the conditions on which I will accept the surrender of the Army of Northern Virginia, is just received. In reply, I would say that, *peace* being my great desire, there is but one condition I would insist upon—namely, that the men and officers surrendered shall be disqualified for taking up arms against the government of the United States until properly exchanged. I will meet you, or will designate officers to meet any officers you may name for the same purpose, at any point agreeable to you, for the purpose of arranging definitely the terms upon which the surrender of the Army of Northern Virginia will be received.

"U. S. GRANT, Lieutenant-General.

"GENERAL R. E. LEE."

General Lee beyond all doubt was in desperate straits, but he was not quite ready to yield unquestioningly:

"April 8, 1865.

"GENERAL: I received at a late hour your note of to-day. In mine of yesterday I did not intend to propose the surrender of the Army of Northern Virginia, but to ask the terms of your proposition. To be frank, I do not think the emergency has arisen to call for the surrender of this army; but, as the restoration of peace should be the sole object of all, I desired to know whether your proposals would lead to that end. I cannot, therefore, meet you with a view to surrender the Army of Northern Virginia; but, as far as your proposal may affect the Confederate States forces under my command and tend to the restoration of peace, I should be pleased to meet you at 10 A. M., to-morrow, on the old stage-road to Richmond, between the picket-lines of the two armies.

"R. E. LEE, General.

"LIEUTENANT-GENERAL U. S. GRANT."

The foregoing letter reached General Grant late at night, and the next morning he replied:

"April 9, 1865.

"GENERAL: Your note of yesterday is received. I have no authority to treat on the subject of peace; the meeting proposed for 10 A. M. to-day could lead to no good. I will state, however, General, that I am equally anxious for peace with yourself, and the whole North entertains the same feeling. The terms upon which peace can be had are well understood. By the South laying down their arms they will hasten that most desirable event, save thousands of human lives and hundreds of millions of property not yet destroyed. Seriously hoping that all our difficulties may be settled without the loss of another life, I subscribe myself, etc.,

"U. S. GRANT, Lieutenant-General.

"GENERAL R. E. LEE."

The correspondence between the two leaders was written on the wing, Lee continually falling back and Grant remorselessly pressing him.

As we have stated, the Confederate army withdrew from its entrenchments on the night of the 7th, and the following night approached Appomattox Court-House. So little firing took place on the 8th that many began to hope they would reach Lynchburg, after all; but this hope, like all the others that had cheered them, was short-lived.

On the evening of the 8th, Sheridan reached Appomattox Station, five miles south of the court-house, and captured four trains of cars loaded with supplies sent from Lynchburg for Lee's army. Then, throwing his command across the Confederate line of retreat, he braced himself to hold the position, knowing as he did that the Army of the James would be up in the morning and the Army of the Potomac were treading on the heels of the Southern forces.

General Lee saw that all retreat was shut off, and he had to elect between surrender and cutting his way through Sheridan's lines. He chose the latter, and ordered General Gordon to carry out the desperate enterprise at all hazards at sunrise the next morning. It was a pitiful but impressive sight. The once proud and invincible Army of Northern Virginia under its matchless leader was reduced to eight thousand ragged, gaunt and exhausted men.

The impetuous Gordon formed his thin battle-line in front; the fragments of the iron-willed Long-street's corps composed the rear, and between the lines were the wrecks of the few wagons left of the immense train, while around and among them staggered several thousand stragglers like moving skeletons. They were too weak to carry their muskets. The three thousand cavalry looked as if riders and horses should be in the hospital. But the first beams of the morning sun were hardly seen in the horizon when Gordon moved forward to cut his way through the Federal lines. His assault was made with such fierceness that the cavalry, which had dismounted to resist the attack, was forced back upon Ord's infantry. At this juncture General Sheridan came up from Appomattox Station, whither he had been to hurry forward the Army of the James. By his direction the troopers slowly retreated until the infantry had time to form. This required but a few minutes, when Gordon saw the forest of bayonets advancing. He then began to give ground, and sent word to General Lee that the enemy were forcing him back.

Meanwhile, Sheridan was "pressing things," as ordered to do by Grant. The command to mount was sounded, and the cavalry dashed into position on the Confederate left flank. When about to charge on the doomed band, a white flag was seen advancing from the Confederate lines. The messenger bore a letter from General Lee asking for a suspension of hostilities looking to surrender. At the same time he forwarded the following note to General Grant:

"April 9, 1865.

"GENERAL: I received your note this morning on the picket-line, whither I had come to meet you and ascertain definitely what terms were embraced in your proposition of yesterday with reference to the surrender of this army.

"I now request an interview in accordance with

the offer contained in your letter of yesterday for that purpose.

"Very respectfully,
"Your obedient servant,
"R. E. LEE, General.

"To LIEUT.-GENERAL GRANT,
"Commanding Armies of the United States."

General Grant replied:

"April 9, 1865.

"GENERAL R. E. LEE, Commanding Confederate States Armies:

"Your note of this date is but this moment, 11.59 A. M., received.

"In consequence of my having passed from the Richmond and Lynchburg road to the Farmville and Lynchburg road, I am at this writing about four miles west of Walters Church, and will push forward to the front for the purpose of meeting you.

"Notice sent to me on this road where you wish the interview to take place will meet me.

"Very respectfully, your obedient servant,
U. S. GRANT, Lieutenant-General."

Generals Grant and Lee met at the house of Mr. Wilmer McLean, in the village of Appomattox Court-House.* The greeting was courteous, and

---

* Major Wilmer McLean, who died in Alexandria recently, was the man who literally saw the beginning and the end of the late war. It was on his farm that the battle of Bull Run was fought, and General Lee surrendered in his house at Appomattox, to which he had moved with his family in order to be free from the annoyances of the war.

everything was conducted in the best of taste. General Grant was delicate and considerate toward the vanquished chieftain, who appreciated the magnanimity of the one whom hard fate had designated to be his conqueror. General Lee did not proffer his sword, nor did General Grant demand it; but after a few of the exchanges common between gentlemen the two great men sat down at a wooden table, and in a few minutes wrote and signed the following two papers, which dissolved for ever the grand old army of Northern Virginia:

"APPOMATTOX COURT-HOUSE, VA.
April 9, 1865.

"GENERAL: In accordance with the substance of my letter to you of the 8th instant, I propose to receive the surrender of the Army of Northern Virginia on the following terms, to wit: Rolls of all the officers and men to be made in duplicate, one copy to be given to an officer to be designated by me, and the other to be retained by such officer or officers as you may designate. The officers to give their individual paroles not to take up arms against the United States until properly exchanged, and each company or regimental commander to sign a like parole for the men of their commands. The arms, artillery and public property to be parked and stacked and turned over by the officers appointed by me to receive them. This will not embrace the side-arms of the officers, nor their private horses or baggage. This done, each officer and man will be allowed to return to his home, not to be disturbed by United States authority so long as they observe their paroles and the laws in force where they may reside.

"U. S. GRANT, Lieutenant-General.

"GENERAL R. E. LEE."

"HEADQUARTERS ARMY OF NORTHERN VIRGINIA,
April 9, 1865.

"GENERAL: I have received your letter of this date containing the terms of the surrender of the Army of Northern Virginia, as proposed by you. As they are substantially the same as those expressed in your letter of the 8th instant, they are accepted. I will proceed to designate the proper officers to carry the stipulations into effect.

"R. E. LEE, General.

"LIEUTENANT-GENERAL U. S. GRANT."

The respective commissioners met the next day and drew up and signed the following agreement:

"APPOMATTOX COURT-HOUSE,
April 10, 1865.

"*Agreement entered into this day in regard to the surrender of the Army of Northern Virginia to the United States authorities:*

"1st. The troops shall march by brigades and

detachments to the designated point, stack their arms, deposit their flags, sabres, pistols, etc., and thence march to their homes under charge of their officers, superintended by their respective division and corps commanders, officers retaining their side-arms and the authorized number of private horses.

"2d. All public horses and public property of all kinds to be turned over to staff-officers, to be designated by the United States authorities.

"3d. Such transportation as may be agreed upon as necessary for the transportation of the private baggage of officers will be allowed to accompany the officers, to be turned over at the end of the trip to the nearest United States quartermaster, receipts being taken for the same.

"4th. Couriers and mounted men of the artillery and cavalry whose horses are their own private property will be allowed to retain them.

"5th. The surrender of the Army of Northern Virginia shall be construed to include all the forces operating with that army on the 8th instant, the date of the commencement of the negotiations for surrender, except such bodies of cavalry as actually made their escape previous to the surrender, and except, also, such pieces of artillery as were more than twenty miles from Appomattox Court-House at the time of surrender on the 9th instant.

"(Signed)

" JOHN GIBBON, Maj.-Gen. Vols.

" CHARLES GRIFFIN, Brevet Maj.-Gen. U. S.Vols.

" W. MERRITT, Brevet Maj.-Gen.

" J. LONGSTREET, Lieut.-Gen.

" J. B. GORDON, Maj.-Gen.

" W. N. PENDLETON, Brig.-Gen. and Chief of Artillery."

The last camp-fire of General Lee was extinguished.

THE END.

www.ingramcontent.com/pod-product-compliance
Lightning Source LLC
Chambersburg PA
CBHW021343110726
47900CB00005B/1585